AIMEE KNIGHTS

Second Chances

Contents

1

Prologue

Nine years ago...

"Well, well, well, look what we have here! Little Ava, fat and ugly as normal" I recognised the voice before I even looked at who it was. My tormentor. I had purposefully tucked myself away in the most out of the way corner of the schools' field as was possible. It was lunchtime and there were a few students milling around, giggling, joking, and gossiping amongst themselves. Clearly, my attempt at hiding from them wasn't successful. How did they always manage to find me?

"On your own again I see! Do you even have any friends?" He snickered. I turned my head to look at him, not saying a word.

My tormentor was gorgeous, to say the least. His eyes were the most delightful shade of hazel ever to exist. It was like looking into a pool of honey and, like every other girl in our school, I was captivated whenever I looked into them. His hair was a perfectly styled tousled mess of medium brown. That was just the start to this boys' gorgeousness. Even at fourteen, he was already starting to develop into a handsome, masculine man. But, as my tormentor, it was completely wrong of me to be attracted to him, let alone have a crush on him.

"Well? It's rude to ignore people when they're talking to you, you know" He had stopped just in front of me, his arms crossed in front of his chest, one eyebrow raised telling me he was waiting for a response. His cronies were scattered around him, preventing me from running away. There were a couple of laughs when he said this, and I just bowed my head down, to continue reading my book.

Suddenly, I felt a hard grip on my chin as he forced me to look up into his eyes. He had crouched down, balancing on the balls of his feet. I found myself looking into what once were an ocean of buttery meltiness, but now were replaced with a much darker shade that I had seen only a handful of times, filled with pure hatred. He was pissed at me. Big time.

"Cat got your tongue? Seriously Ava, you truly are such a sight for sore eyes. You should just leave, the world would look so much better and less ugly with you not in it" I could feel the tears sting in my eyes as I tried to stop them from making an appearance, but it was futile.

This was a daily occurrence and every day I was losing the will to live. Every day I was told how I didn't belong here, how the world would be better without me in it and truthfully, I was beginning to agree. I was constantly ridiculed and reminded of how ugly I am, that I was a lowlife and scum.

He pushed my head back as he let go of me with a sneer and took a step back, allowing for someone else to step forward. Through tear filled eyes, I looked up to see his second in command, Victoria striding towards me. This girl was a goddess. Beautiful in every way imaginable. All the boys wanted to get with her, and all the girls wanted to be her. She had hit puberty early and was blessed with a big chest and a tall, slim figure. Her hair had been styled into two French braids with a few strands of hair framing her angelic face. She was towering over me, hands on her hips, with her shadow casting over me.

"Who knew you could get uglier?! You look even more gross and hideous when you cry. I don't even know why you bother hiding from us, you know we will always find you" she laughed sharply. She snatched the book out of my hands and started ripping the pages out of it.

"Stop! That's my favourite book!" I screamed at her, reaching my hand forward in an attempt to grab it back. The book was a gift from my grandmother who had recently passed away. Not only was it my favourite book, but it had been hers too. I began to scramble and pick up the pages that had floated to the ground. All I could hear were the laughter of my tormentor and his cronies, and I just wanted the ground to swallow me up.

Victoria threw whatever was left of the book at me. It bounced off of my head, which only made everyone roar even harder with laughter.

"Oh, shit Vic, that was a good shot!"

"I hope the book's okay!"

"Maybe it knocked some sense into her?"

The snarky comments kept coming. I grabbed the book and my bag, throwing it over my shoulder and sprinted away like my life depended on it. I could still hear them laughing when I reached the other side of the field. At least they hadn't followed me. I couldn't be near them anymore. I couldn't be here anymore.

I made the quick decision that I was going to just bunk the rest of the day and go home. I left the school through the back gate of the school – I was not going to risk being caught going out of the front.

It only took me twenty minutes to get home. I couldn't stop the tears from streaming down my face as I walked home. I got a few strange looks from passers-by, but no one stopped me to see if I was okay. I mean, a young fourteen-year-old girl, walking the streets alone in tears during a school day should've seemed odd to anyone who saw me. The fact that I wasn't stopped made me feel even more insignificant and that truly no one cared for me.

Thankfully, mum wasn't home; she was probably out shopping at this time. I dumped my school bag by the door and dashed up the stairs, taking them three at a time – a great feat for me and my little legs. I went into the bathroom and began running a bath.

I stripped and made my way over to the sink and just stared at myself in the mirror, my thoughts and mind going a mile a minute. Was I really as ugly as people said I was? Mum and my grandparents had always said I was beautiful. They were forever showering me with compliments, but it seemed meaningless now. I had naturally blonde hair that flowed all the way down to my waist. My eyes were the lightest shade of blue I have ever seen, with a unique brown fleck in the right one. I wore wide rimmed glasses that had a leopard print design. My skin wasn't the clearest, but then again, what fourteen-year-old's was?

The longer I looked at myself in the mirror, the more faults I found. No. They were right. I am ugly. My phone beeped in my pocket and I pulled it out and looked.

"Run away like the scaredy-cat bitch you are, have you? Oh well, we've always got tomorrow to continue where we left off. I look forward to making your face look even uglier than it already is"

"Hey fatty! All that running you did won't make you lose the weight any faster you know"

4

"Hey Ava? I looked up "fugly" in the dictionary and your picture was next to it"

This wasn't the first time I had text messages from my tormentor and his friends. But this time, I had been pushed to the edge. I was at the end of my tether.

I turned the tap on the bath off and took out a brand new razor from the cabinet under the sink. I slid into the bath and submerged my head under the steaming water. The water was hot, burning almost, but I didn't care. I couldn't feel. I was numb at this point. I resurfaced and looked at the razor in my hand. I took the blade out and dropped the shell of plastic to the floor, before placing the blade along my wrist. I knew what I was doing. I knew how to do it properly. This wasn't my first rodeo and I had learned from my previous mistakes. This time, I won't wake to see another day.

I am ugly... I don't deserve to be here... The world would be better without me in it... Everyone would be happier without me... No-one would miss me; I don't even have any friends... I'm all alone...

These thoughts whirred through my mind as I carved vertically down my wrist. I closed my eyes and leaned my head back against the back of the bath, resting my arms palm-up on the edge of the bath. Feeling the blood trickle down my arm before quietly drip, drip, dripping into the bath water, I willed for the darkness to engulf me.

I awoke to distant sounds of beeps and someone crying.

2

Chapter 1

Present day...

I awoke to the sound of birds chirping merrily outside my window and the sunlight streaming in through the blinds. With a yawn, I kicked the duvet off my sweaty body and stretched out into a starfish, feeling the satisfying pops of my joints.

I was not a morning person. I hated waking up early and I loved my sleep, yet I always forced myself to. If I woke up any later than nine in the morning, I always felt like I'd lost precious time of my day. After my near death when I was fourteen, I decided to make the most of every minute of every day.

I laid there for a good ten minutes, enjoying the new cold spots in my bed I'd found.

I loved Sundays. They were my designated day of relaxing, just as God intended. I'd often spend my Sundays sprawled out on the sofa, drinking endless amounts of coffee whilst bingeing my latest favourite shows on Netflix. It was the best way to spend a Sunday in my eyes, especially if I had had a booze-filled night the night before.

I picked my phone up and decided to scroll quickly through my social media. I loved looking through social media. Even though I didn't have that many friends, I loved to keep up to date with what was going on in the world. I would occasionally search up for the people I went to school with, just to see what they were up to. I hoped that the demons from my past had changed, but I never really wanted to know, only observing through the private eyes of social media. I always had my profiles on private – no way did I want them to see me and what I've been up to. I never existed to them then, and I certainly didn't want to now. They had made my life a misery and I would be happy living the rest of my life never seeing them again.

I quickly typed in Victoria Summers into the Instagram search bar. The first account to pop up was hers. She still had that angelic face, but her personality had been anything but. I clicked on Victoria's latest post. She was posed in just her underwear in a rather provocative stance on a huge bed. She was positioned sat on her knees with them spread out as far as she could, one hand leaning behind her, keeping her upright. Her head was tipped back slightly with her eyes closed, and she had a couple of her fingers in her mouth while sticking her tongue out. She looked like she was mid moan. She still had a good body though – I'll give her that. She had grown her hair out so that it fell to her mid back, rather than stopping just above her breasts. She'd dyed it blonde and it looked trashy as hell. She really didn't suit being blonde and it just made her look even more like a prostitute.

I grew bored as I scrolled through all her other posts. They were mostly the same sort of content. In a way, I felt sorry for her. What had she experienced or gone through to have become the person that she is? To make her do the things she did for the attention that she so desperately craved? I hadn't forgiven her, not by a long shot, and I doubt I ever could, but I did pity her.

Next to be searched was my wonderful ex, Wyatt. His latest picture was of him in front of the Eiffel Tower with a stunning brunette clinging around his neck, both with a dazzling smile plastered on their faces. I stared at the picture and started feeling anger rise within me. I couldn't believe they were still together. I couldn't believe Wyatt and my ex-best friend and roommate Felicity had hooked up behind my back. Although, I can't say I'm surprised at what she did. She's always had a streak for stealing boyfriends, I just never thought she'd do it to me.

The caption under the photo read *"I'm so glad I tricked you into loving me. You light up my world".* I scoffed reading the cringey words. What utter shit. The only person who got tricked was me, being absolutely clueless and ignorant to their secret love affair that went on under my nose. Or, more precisely, in the room next to me whilst I slept.

I groaned as I forced myself up. No point moping about something I can't change. I was over him, completely, but it didn't stop the hurt. I dragged my sorry butt into the bathroom, played my favourite Spotify playlist and had a scorching hot shower. The drumming of the water on my head was enough to soothe me and take away my anger, almost hypnotising me into a state of relaxation.

After my one-woman performance in the shower, I secured a towel around me and wrapped my hair up in a towel. I still had long hair, and a hair turban simply wasn't big enough to wrap my hair in. After doing the usual routine of brushing my teeth and skin care, I made my way towards the wardrobe and threw on some work-out clothes. Sunday or not, I always went for a run in the morning.

I checked myself out in the mirror. If you can't love yourself, how can you expect someone else to? I didn't have the same body I did nine years ago. I'd grown into myself and developed into a reasonably good-looking woman. I had a decently sized chest that I was proud of. They weren't too small and they weren't too big – they were a perfect perky C cup.

I scanned the rest of my body in the mirror. These new leggings were doing wonders on my booty and toned legs. I hadn't grown in height much since my teens, I stood at a measly five foot three inches but that didn't bother me. What I lacked in height, I made up for in body parts. I had learned to love myself and I couldn't be prouder of myself.

With a final content smile, I turned away from the mirror and headed into the kitchen to make myself a hearty breakfast of porridge and fruit, washed down with an ice cold glass of orange juice.

By now, I was wide awake and more than ready to go for my run. I loved the feel of my feet pounding as I ran, the wind hitting my face. It was a good way to clear my head. I did a couple of stretches and a quick warm up before grabbing my earphones. With my work-out tunes on, I left my apartment.

As I jogged lightly down the steps, I noticed that the 'For Sale' sign had been taken down next door and had been replaced with a 'Sold' sign. Perfect. A new neighbour. Hopefully they aren't too noisy or problematic like the last one. The previous neighbour was a right psycho bitch. I'd lost count of the number of times the police were called because of her out of hand parties. She once threw a frying pan at me because I said she looked like shit after a long three day bender.

It didn't take long for the apartment to be sold – it had only been up for sale for about three months. But then, if you've got the money, it's no surprise that it was taken so quickly. The area was beautiful. It was perfectly situated between the city and the more rustic side of town.

These apartments were equally as beautiful. They all looked the same and the layout inside was the same. Modern both inside and out, they boasted huge, magnificent rooms, with ceiling-to-floor windows. Each apartment had a balcony that was more than decently sized. I often found myself on mine to do my workouts. The bedrooms were huge with walk-in wardrobes and en-suits, and the main space was all open plan, with the kitchen joining the living room, only being separated by the kitchen island and some stools.

There was a moving van outside, so I figured that whoever my new neighbour was must be moving in today. I made a quick mental note to introduce myself to the new neighbour once they'd settled in. Maybe take over a welcome cake or invite them over for dinner. As I began to jog down my street, I began to wonder what they're like. Were they a happy, loving family? Or perhaps an old couple wanting to spend their retirement living their final days in a grand apartment?

I was a little excited.

3

Chapter 2

I ran a good three miles, taking my usual route. The route I took was beautifully scenic and always put me at ease. I ran along the footpath from my apartment and made my way towards the massive park. I loved the park and not just to run through. It was a good place to come and sit to collect my thoughts. Huge trees with luscious green leaves blowing gently in the wind outlined the vast greenery. There were a handful of flowerbeds scattered throughout the park, all of different breeds and colours. The park burst with colour and life from all the flora and fauna that resided here, and it made me feel lucky to be alive.

There were a few families and couples having some quality time together, and I often found myself smiling as I watched them interact with each other. I really wanted to be a mum, it's one of the things I felt I had been destined to be and do with my life. Don't get me wrong, I was absolutely petrified of actually giving birth and some aspects of pregnancy, but I always justified that it would all be worth it to have a lifetime of happiness. With a warm feeling spreading through me, I continued my run and passed the huge pond that was a giant puddle of blue tranquility positioned in the middle of the park.

I was able to keep a steady, constant pace by running in time with the music that I had blaring through my ears. I had always used music as a way to keep my mind clear and as a way to stay focussed. I didn't have a favourite genre, as I used different types of music for different aspects of my life. For example, when I ran, I listened to a lot of remixed music, because the beat was easy to run in time to. Plus, I loved how alive it made me feel.

On my way home, I made a couple of stops to buy some groceries that I was running low on. By the time I was back on my street it was two in the afternoon and I was ready to flop on the sofa, in my comfies, and watch 'Gossip Girl'.

Upon reaching my apartment, I could see a man standing outside the recently sold apartment next to mine. He had his back to me, and since I was some distance away from him, I took this opportunity to approach slowly so I could take my time looking him up and down. He was dressed impeccably in formal clothes that hugged every inch of his delicious body, a laptop bag pressed between his thick thighs as he had one hand on the door handle, jiggling it up and down, the other twisting a key in the door.

He was tall, easily six foot, and built like a shit brick house, a sure sign that he spent a lot of time in the gym. As he fumbled with whatever was in his hands, his back muscles under his crisp white shirt rippled, and I felt my body tingle at the sight. I couldn't help but wonder what that body of his looked like naked. His suit trousers were slim fit, and hugged his backside snuggly. My eyes drifting further south, found muscular legs attached to his rounded bottom, the fabric starting to strain. I hadn't even seen his face yet and I found myself biting my lower lip as

I undressed him in my mind, doubting the legality of owning a body like that.

I shook my head to rid my brain of these intrusive thoughts and started to approach the steps leading up to my apartment, giving myself a stern talking to in order to get myself together. I didn't even know the guy or seen his face and yet here I was shamelessly eye-fucking him from the back. For all I knew, he could have a banging body but the face that only a mother could love. Although, I supposed in the unlucky event of being tangled in the sheets with him, I could always avert my eyes and focus on his delightful body.

I lightly jogged up the steps, taking them one at a time and upon reaching my door, started to unlock it. I'd just turned the handle down when I heard the mysterious hunk muttering to himself.

"Fuck!"

I turned to look at him and my eyes widened at what I saw. He. Was. Gorgeous. He was walking sex on legs. His hair was the colour of mocha with subtle hints of blonde highlighted here and there. It was shaved at the sides and back, and the top was longer and had been styled into a perfect mess. His jaw was expertly chiseled and his nose was perfectly sharpened with a faint roundness at the tip. This man was created by God himself.

I found myself chuckling at his murmurings to himself, only to almost choke on my own spit when he looked at me. Those eyes. They were a rich shade of hazel and I had found myself lost in them. The light from the sun was hitting his eyes at a perfect angle. It wasn't blinding him, but it allowed for the colour to be accentuated and I found myself drowning in a sea of butter. I'd seen eyes similar to these before, but who did they belong to? No. The eyes I'd seen before were nowhere near as gentle and soothing as these.

His cheeks had the cutest hint of pink to them. Not from a blush, but more from a fluster. I flickered my eyes to his mouth. It was set in an easy, natural smile and was a cushion of smooth, peachy plumpness. Again, I found my bottom lip securely tucked under my top teeth. A small voice in my mind reminded me: Get it together Ava.

I cleared my throat and offered him a genuine smile. "Hi! You must be my new neighbour. I'm Ava." I held my hand out and was surprised when I felt his big soft hand grip mine.

"Yes, that I am! It's nice to meet you Ava, my name's Leon. I hope we can become great neighbours and friends." He had a bright smile. His straight teeth perfectly white and blinding.

"I'm sure we will be. But, um, is everything OK? You seem like you're having a bit of an issue." His cheeks flared slightly redder, this time with slight embarrassment.

He laughed, a heavenly sound that made me feel a sensation ripple through me. He scratched the back of his neck, looking somewhat bashful. "Well... I, uh, have somehow managed to lock myself out of my apartment. Day one and it's already been a bit of a shit show."

I couldn't help but laugh back at him, a full-on belly laugh. What a way to start your first day in your new home.

"Oh dear, you really are having a bad day! Did you want to come into mine while you sort out what you need to do? It might be a good idea to maybe get a locksmith out." I wasn't usually this neighbourly. Not because I was a rude person, but I didn't really care for building any form of relationships with those who lived next to me. But Leon seemed different. An embodiment of perfection who didn't deserve to be making a complete arse of himself in the street.

"Really? Are you sure?" His eyes widened slightly with surprise, before flashing his beaming smile at me when I nodded in clarification. "Life saver, thank you." He handed me his laptop bag and hopped over the wall and followed me into my apartment.

"Oh my. Your place is beautiful." He gushed. I took great pride in my home. Once Felicity left, I had redecorated the apartment to make it my own. On entrance, the hallway had been painted a light grey. There was a huge mirror hung up on the wall, and underneath it was a shoe cabinet. I had decorated the top with a picture of me and my true best friend Ffion, with a candle and a dish for my keys situated beside it. On the floor next to the cabinet was a tall, magnificent white and grey vase; brimming with elegant fake lilies because killing real plants and flowers was a skill I had honed with pride. Throughout my home, the walls were dotted with fine line photos and one or two of me and my friends and family.

"Thank you. I try my hardest to make it look as presentable as possible." I spent a decent amount of time here and I wanted to live in ultimate comfort. I made my way into the kitchen and placed Leon's laptop bag on the kitchen island and put away my shopping before giving him a quick tour of my apartment. As I showed him around, he made comments about how he liked what I'd done with the place, soaking in any inspiration. His favourite room was one of the spare bedrooms that I had turned into a room showcasing my trophies and medals.

"Jesus Christ on a bike, these are all yours?" With a stunned expression, he made his way over to my trophy cabinet. I'd lost count of how many trophies and medals I owned, but I knew the total was in triple digits.

"Yeah. I used to be a baton twirler, competing nationally all

15

over the country, and once represented the country overseas. I don't compete anymore though, but I still twirl when I need to let off some steam. I even teach at my old team on occasion." I shrugged. It wasn't a big deal to me. I was proud of myself and what I had achieved during my twirling years, and I loved it when people took interest. But I liked to play it cool; I didn't want to seem egotistical and self-absorbed.

I had pictures of me in my costumes on the dance-floor in starting poses, mid performance and as I posed in photo shoots, placed in the cabinets or on the walls. Although I was part of a team, and had twirled as part of the team, I was more at home as a soloist. I didn't have anyone to rely on and didn't have to worry about anyone else messing up. I could make it up as I went along if I forgot part of my routine and really make the performance mine.

He turned towards me with his eyes full of amazement "That sounds amazing. I know a few people who used to do this, but I never thought much of it. Just seemed a bit pointless and boring waving a stick around. You'll have to show me what you can do one day." Ah yes, the 'stick' comment. People never realise just how much practice and skill it takes to 'wave a stick around'. Even now there's tricks I don't know how to do and haven't mastered yet. Without a doubt, the sport is arguably one of the most slept on.

"Maybe one day." I replied with a wink, before exiting the makeshift hall of fame. He followed me to the kitchen and stationed himself on one of the stools. He leaned on the kitchen island on his elbows, resting his chin in his left hand, whilst scrolling through his phone with his right.

I made us both a coffee after offering him something to drink and plonked myself on the stool opposite him. He really was some juicy eye candy. His long dark eyelashes almost touched his cheeks as he looked down at his phone. His perfectly carved eyebrows were furrowed together slightly in concentration. He must've been biting his teeth together hard because his jaw and cheekbones were even more prominent.

"Ah, found one! Do you mind if I quickly call this locksmith?" He questioned.

"Yeah sure, do what you need to. I'll just get out of these sweaty clothes. I won't be long." I pushed myself up off of the stool and placed my now empty cup in the sink before I headed towards my bedroom.

I had another quick shower, a nice cold one to relax my aching muscles, and threw on some shorts and a vest top. The shorts were slightly tight, just as they had intended to be, and they fit me in all the right places. They hugged me at the waist, and tightly kept my bum in place. I'd had them for years, but they were my fave and I wasn't planning on getting rid of them anytime soon. I scraped my hair up into a messy bun whilst making my way barefoot into the living room.

Leon was pacing whilst on the phone. His gaze fell on me when I entered the room. His eyes widened briefly, his mouth opening little by little as his eyes roved down my body, all the way down to my mint green painted toenails, before he quickly looked away and continued pacing. I made my way over to the sofa before sprawling out on it and draping my blanket over my shoulders. 'Gossip Girl' was prepped and ready to go.

"Shit." He quietly cursed. "The guy said because it's a Sunday he won't come to sort out the lock, but he will be here first thing tomorrow. How am I supposed to get into my apartment now?" His voice was full of frustration and irritation. I couldn't blame him though. I'd be annoyed if I couldn't get into my apartment

17

until the next day with nowhere else to go.

"I've got a spare bedroom you can stay in if you want to stay the night? Beats wasting money on a hotel or something, and it's much closer so you can be here when the locksmith turns up in the morning. Obviously, if that's a bit much for you, feel free to say no.' I didn't see anything wrong in offering a helping hand, I was just being neighbourly. Or so I kept telling myself.

"Are you sure? I wouldn't want to be in your way or intrude." Hesitation glazed his eyes. I mean, it's understandable. I don't doubt I wouldn't be cautious of someone I'd just met offering somewhere to stay the night.

"Honestly, it's no biggie. You won't be in my way or anything. Just relax and make yourself at home." I smiled back at him.

"Well, if you're sure. Thank you so much, I owe you big time." He had a huge smile on his face and his eyes glistened with relief. He slid his laptop out of its bag and got himself set up on my kitchen island. A contented smile played on my lips as I watched him make himself at home, a feeling embedding deep inside at a man being comfortable in my home, before turning away and settling down to be wholly enthralled in the drama of 'Gossip Girl'.

Chapter 3

It had been an entire month since mine and Leon's first encounter. We had bumped into each other a couple of times, and he'd knocked on my door to borrow something every now and then.

The night he had stayed over had been pretty chilled. I watched my show while he sat at the kitchen island typing away on his laptop. He would occasionally speak up about what I was watching. Even though he wasn't watching, he was listening, and for some reason that made me rather happy.

By the time evening had rolled around, it was time for my Sunday night ritual of takeout. Leon and I debated back and forth what we wanted and settled on pizza. He offered to pay, since I offered him a place to stay, proving his gentlemanly capabilities.

Monday lazily rolled around, dragging with it the depression that the weekend was now over, and at nine a.m. on the dot, the locksmith knocked on my door to unlock his door. Leon still had a few boxes to unpack from the moving van he'd had to hire for a further twenty-four hours. After he declined my help with the boxes, I made a point and suggested getting another key cut, just in case.

Today, I spent my day at a couple of my clients' houses. As an independent personal trainer whose services were only offered to women, I wasn't employed at a gym, but had an arrangement where I could have use of the local gym when needed; the benefits of being friends with the owner. To start, I would go to my clients' homes, taking basic items or using items in the home until they felt comfortable and ready to try the gym. It can be daunting for many women, especially those who are self-conscious about their appearance, to go to the gym, and so I slowly start to introduce them to the world of working out and the gym in the comfort of their own home – and occasionally mine as I had some specialist equipment that I am unable to take with me.

After what happened to me, I decided to live a life helping women to improve themselves and to see themselves in a better light. No one should have to feel less than what they are. Every life is precious, and I'd learned that the hard way. It made me feel good about myself that I was able to help those who feel low about themselves.

I had built really good relationships with many of my clients, and funnily enough, one of them was my best friend Ffion. I had just finished up at a clients' house when my phone started buzzing. I quickly looked and my face lit up when I saw Fi was FaceTiming me.

"Hey babes, everything okay?" I was always excited to speak to Fi. That girl was the bestest friend anyone could ask for. She knew me inside out and just seeing her bubbly face was enough to lift my mood. She was a ball of energy, a ray of sunshine, and I loved her like a sister.

"Hey sugar! Yeah, all good here, I was just wondering if you're finished at your clients? Fancy meeting for a coffee?" Her smile radiated through the phone. She was always happy, and I'd only seen her sad a handful of times, and that was usually when someone she cared about was hurting. She put everyone above herself, always.

"Oh, I'm so down, meet me at the usual place?" Coffee was my drug, one that I could happily have injected into my veins for a steady, constant flow.

"Sweet, I'll see you there in ten. Loves you, bye!"

"Loves you too, see you soon." With a blowed kiss through the phone, Fi hung up.

We always told each other we loved one another. It filled my heart. It was important to me that she knew how much I cared for her. Not just that, but if anything were to happen to either one of us, we'd regret not telling or showing the other how much we meant to one another.

I made my way to the small café on the corner, "The Coffee Hub", with a spring in my step. Fi had something up her sleeve. I could sense it. Her smile was just that little extra big today. Well. Either that or she'd finally got laid.

I found her in our usual chairs, tucked away by the window in the corner. Hearing the door shut behind me, Fi shot her head up and waved at me with the goofiest grin ever spread along her pretty face. I shook my head and giggled as I made my way over to her. She'd already got my order in. She's a good egg.

"So then, what's got you buzzing off your tits?" I wasted no time in getting straight to the point as I dropped into my seat, the cushion bouncing under my weight. There was no beating around the bush when it came to news as big as this.

She was visibly bouncing in her seat and I couldn't help but giggle at her. "OK, OK, so I met this guy and oh my god he's *so* FIT! He's got these big brown eyes like gooey chocolate, and he's got muscles like this." She wrapped a hand around the opposite arm with a gap between the body parts as she rambled on like a lovesick teenager. It was all I needed to know that she was infatuated with this guy.

"That's great Fi! So, what's his name? How'd you meet him?" Oh, I was going to get all the gossip. But then again, it was never hard to get juicy gossip from Ffion. She loved it just as much as I did.

"His name's Everett, he's twenty-five, so a few years older than us. I met him at work. He's the son of my boss of all things." She tucked a strand of hair behind her ear. As excited as she was about this, there was trepidation in her movements. She'd only had one boyfriend and he had turned out to be just as big a waste of space as Wyatt. He shattered her heart into a million pieces and left her high and dry. That's when I met her and became her personal trainer.

I placed my hands gently over hers and offered her a supportive smile.

"I'm so happy for you Fi, truly. I can't wait to meet him. But I tell you what, if he does anything to hurt you and I'll rip his balls off and shove 'em down his throat." It was threat and promise all rolled into one. She deserved all the happiness in the world. She had spent so much of her life making others happy, that she rarely put her own happiness first - it was kind of like looking in a mirror - and with her past... God knows she deserved all the happiness in the world.

She laughed out loud, tears brimming in her eyes. "Oh A, I really do love you. I can only imagine his reaction when you threaten him to his face." She was smiling and that made me ecstatic.

"Anyway, any news on Mr Sex on Legs?" I had known this was coming. I'd told her everything about him, and she was dying to meet him. Hell, I was dying to see him and talk to him properly again.

"Nah, nothing yet. I assume he's just busy with work and getting settled into his new place. I don't want to pester him and think I'm desperate." I grimaced at that. I was not the desperate type. Never had been, never will be. If I liked a guy, I only made it known if they told me first. I wasn't going to give my heart and spill my feelings to someone who didn't reciprocate them. That was a lesson I had well and truly learned the hard way.

Just then, my phone went off; an annoying buzz that vibrated the whole table. I was rather surprised when I saw who the caller was. His ears must've been burning.

"Hey, Leon. How's things? Not locked outside of your apartment again I hope." In an instant, Ffion was by my side. I had to stifle a laugh and I scooched across the seat to make room for her. I'd only said his name and she was by my side. I angled the phone between us so that we could both hear what he had to say.

We heard him laugh at the other end of the phone. "Hello to you too. No, No. It may come as a surprise, but I'm not locked out of my apartment. I was actually wondering if you would like to come to my housewarming party tonight? It's a bit late I know, but I figured I'd get settled and have a party when I had the time." It sure had been a while since I'd been to any kind of party, and with how hard I had worked recently, I damn well deserved to let loose a little. And bonus, it was a Friday so I would have the entire weekend to recuperate.

"Yeah sure, sounds like fun. Do you mind if I bring my friend with me?" Because, if I'm getting rat-arsed and going to make a tit of myself, then so is Ffion. She needed this just as much as I did.

"Sure, why not! Friend of yours is a friend of mine. It starts at seven p.m. so just come over whenever you're ready. I need to get everything prepped so I'll see you tonight." I swore I could hear him smile.

"No problem, I shall see you later then Leon." I hung up and turned to Ffion. If I thought she was buzzing about her news about her new crush, it was nothing compared to this as she took my hands in hers and held them tightly.

"You know what this means don't you... SHOPPING!"

5

Chapter 4

Fi and I were now in my bedroom, pre-drinking with our "getting ready to go out out" tunes on, as we got ready. It was eight p.m. and we could hear Leon's party through the walls. It sounded like it was in full swing already.

Ffion was wearing a pale gold halter-neck dress which exposed her back and stopped mid-thigh. It hugged her curves in all the right places. Her shoes were a matching colour and did up with lace wrapping around to above her ankle. She looked smokin', and to top it off, her makeup finished off the look. She had used eyeshadow to change the shape of her eyes into a sultry dark fox eye. Her hair was pulled back into a smooth low bun just above the nape of her neck. Honestly, the girl could turn me.

I, on the other hand, had opted for a silver satin lace up bodycon dress. Like Fi's, my dress exposed my back, but laced up at the back, and stopped just short of my mid-thigh. I had paired the dress with silver open toe heels, with a strap along my ankle. My makeup was a dark smokey eye that made my light blue eyes pop. My hair was scraped up high in a sleek, tight ponytail with a section of hair wrapped around the base. I was rather impressed with myself. I looked good and I knew it.

"Damn, A. If hunk-a-Lot doesn't make a pass on you tonight, then I sure as hell will.'' Ffion joked. She had a mischievous glint in her eyes. She was just as hyped for this party as I was. It had been a while since we had last had girls night.

I shook my head at her with a small smile on my lips. "Oh Fi. Don't get your hopes up. I'm not really looking for anything just this minute. I don't think I could handle another heartbreak yet." And I meant it. I had become a strong person in recent years. I knew my worth, I had confidence in myself to do whatever I set my mind to. But at the end of the day, I was still human. Wyatt had my heart in his hands and with one squeeze destroyed it. It had only been six months and my heart was still repairing.

"Ava babes, who said anything about being in a relationship? Just have a bit of fun." She wasn't wrong; it wouldn't be the first time I'd only had fun with someone, no strings attached and it could very easily become a possibility if we both wanted it. And I certainly wanted *something*. But situationships often get messy and complicated, and I really couldn't be bothered with that.

We left my apartment and made our way to Leon's door. Both of us were buzzed, on the cusp of being tipsy. We'd demolished an entire bottle of wine between us and was halfway through our second before we decided it was best to get going.

We'd barely knocked on the door and it swung open, revealing a smiling Leon. My slightly drunk mind was in a bid of a hazy overdrive. How had he got to the door that quick? Was he waiting for us? And then the rational side of my brain countered with the fact that he's the host, so obviously he'd be there instantly.

"Ava, hey! Wow, you look incredible." He was checking me out. His eyes ran slowly up and down my body, taking in every inch, every curve of me. His tongue poked out slightly and he pulled his bottom lip into his mouth before he let it bounce back from the grip of his teeth.

I felt my body shudder under his intense observation. But I was no angel as I returned the favour. He scrubbed up well himself. He had a teal silk shirt that was undone at the top, exposing the top half of his smooth, hairless chest and tucked in at the front. He wore tight black jeans and his hair was styled even more messily. He looked like every woman's wet dream.

He quickly snapped out of his trance and put on his most welcoming smile as he looked at Ffion.

"You must be Ava's plus one. I'm Leon, it's good to meet you." He hadn't checked her out the way he had me. He barely even did a double take, just kept his eyes focused on hers whilst he spoke to her. Respectful.

"I'm Ffion. I've heard a great deal about you Leon." She said with a wink. I stood there open-mouthed at her openly admitting that I had been talking about him with her. He looked at me from a side glance and smirked at me.

"Oh really? All good things I hope. Anyway, come in and enjoy the party! Help yourselves to whatever food and drink is out." He opened the door further and stepped aside to allow us to walk in.

The apartment was crowded. I had no idea who any of these people were, but it didn't matter. I was here to have a good time with Fi. Hand in hand so we didn't lose each other, me and Ffion made our way over to the kitchen. The surface of the kitchen island concealed in all kinds of booze.

"Here, this'll get your blood pumping." Ffion handed me a red cup of clear liquid. Just a sniff of it told me that it was strong and straight. I took a sip and felt the liquid burn down my throat.

It burned so good. We stood chatting and looking around whilst we finished our first drink. We had a couple more before we headed to the makeshift dance floor.

The music was intoxicating and mixed with the booze, I was feeling really good. Me and Fi danced like we were the only ones in the room. We were rubbing up against each other, just like we always did whenever we were out together. We could see and feel the eyes of most of the men around us. I would be lying if I said I minded it. I liked knowing that men found me attractive. I hadn't worked this hard to have this much confidence for it to be in vain. Before long, I grew tired and needed another drink.

"I need a drink, Fi, you OK for a minute on your own?" I hated leaving her on her own at parties full of strangers, but she knew how to hold her own if need be.

"Yeah babes, go hydrate and then go find your man." She winked naughtily at me. I laughed at her and then made my way, sliding through the gaps between people as I headed towards the crowded kitchen island.

I had chugged half of my drink when I felt someone standing directly behind me. He had placed his hands on my hips and held them tightly, almost in a pinch, and he was so close to my face that I could smell the rancid stench of alcohol on his breath.

"Hey there, darlin'. What's somebody with a body like that doing here?" Came the male slurred voice. I did not want to be dealing with this tonight. I just wanted to drink my drink and get back to dancing with Fi. I glanced over at her to make sure she was alright. I had already been replaced with some guy. She looked in her element, and there was no way I would be able to get her attention to come save me. Especially from this distance.

"What do you say we go somewhere more private?" He'd started to rub up and down one of my arms with his rough hand.

28

It made my skin crawl. I managed to turn to face him, taking a step back as I did so and banged my back into the hard edge of the table, annoyance that this toss-bag was trying to ruin my night settling in my face with my hands forming tight fists ready to swing for him.

"I'd start by telling you to get the *fuck* off me..." I didn't even get to finish my sentence. He grabbed my arm roughly, yanking me closer to him with a darkness infiltrating his eyes. But as quickly as he did that, he was pushed away from me, and in between us stood a tall, muscular man, who on second glance turned out to be Leon. The knight in shining armour that I didn't really need or ask for, but I appreciated the step-in.

"Not at my fucking party Clint. Keep your hands to yourself, or get out." He growled sternly at this Clint. I don't know if it was due to the alcohol consuming my brain, but I found this side of Leon to be very sexy, and I could feel my legs go to jelly as his voice rumbled through me. Clint hung his head down and mumbled a very quick "sorry" and hurried away from us.

"Thanks for stepping in, Leon, but I was getting ready to give him a left, right, goodnight." I chuckled, holding up my fist. He gently placed a hand on each of my shoulders and peered directly into my eyes. Those hazel puddles were a whirlpool of worry and concern, not a drop of amusement to be seen.

"Are you OK Ava? He didn't hurt you, did he? I swear to god I'll kick him out of here if he has." He barely knew me yet was protecting me and worrying about me. Having him show me genuine concern did something to me and I felt my heart swell.

"No, he just grabbed my arm a little too tightly but I'm fine. There's no need to worry." I hoped I sounded convincing. Because in reality, he had hurt me. I'd probably end up with a bruise on my arm in the morning, it was bad enough that I could feel his invisible hand there. Or maybe that was the drink playing mind games with me. Who knows.

I heard Leon sigh with relief. He took my cup of drink out of my hand, placed it on the kitchen top, and was surprised to find myself being embraced by him. He hugged me tightly and buried his head into my neck. One hand was on the small of my bare back, sending an electrifying shock through my body from the skin on skin contact, the other was cradling the back of my head.

"I'm so glad. The thought of someone of the likes of him touching you boils my piss in a way that I don't even understand." As he spoke, his hot breath brushed softly against my neck. I already had jelly legs, and this was not helping at all. I squeezed my legs together to keep from losing balance and composure.

He pulled away, and I found myself geld captive once again by those entrancing eyes of his. He dropped his gaze down to my lips, and I couldn't help but bite my lower lip. Him looking at me like this was stirring all kinds of things inside of me, and it had nothing to do with the amount of alcohol flowing through my veins. He flickered his eyes back to meet mine and leaned in closer, his lips parting slightly. A concoction of mint and whiskey floated towards my nose as he breathed out gently through his mouth.

Before I knew what I was doing, I moved towards him and found myself pressing my lips against his. They were as smooth and soft as they looked. He ran his tongue along my bottom lip, asking for permission to enter my mouth. With a moan, I allowed him entrance and my word did he taste wonderful. I pressed my hands against his chest, my hands grabbing fistfuls of his shirt as he pulled me flush against him, deepening the kiss.

And just as Leon's hands started to drift down to my backside, I felt someone stumble into me, pushing me further into Leon, which led to me biting my tongue.

"Ah, sorry sweetheart, didn't see you there." And no sooner had he appeared did he get swallowed up in the crowd. I looked back at Leon who was just staring at me wide eyed, fingers on his lips, like he couldn't believe what had just happened between us. I couldn't help but wonder if he was regretting the kiss, and it was enough of a thought to somewhat sober me up. Just a fraction, though.

"I'm sorry, Ava, if that was too much. It's just, you look so good and I've been wanting to do that ever since I laid eyes on you. When I saw Clint forcing and touching you with his grubby hands it angered me, and I guess I got a bit too protective of you. Which, I know I have no right to do." Well, I suppose he didn't fully regret it, he just felt bad for doing it without asking. Or without knowing if that was even what I wanted. But it was, in fact, very much what I wanted, but not close enough to what I fully desired.

"It's fine Leon, you don't need to apologise. I... I've been wanting to kiss you for a long time too." I blushed and found myself looking at the floor. Apparently I became a shy, bumbling idiot around guys that I like when I'm drunk. I felt Leon's fingers under my chin, gently tilting my head up, forcing me to look up at him. With his thumb he slowly grazed along my bottom lip, earning him a small gasp to escape from my lips. He smirked at the sound.

"Oh really? Well, I'm glad to hear that. I didn't think that you saw me in that way." He was speaking softly, a whisper among the music spreading through the building. Was he being serious? What did he see when he looked in the mirror? Because from where I stood, I would be very stupid to not want to kiss those plump, full lips of his. I was itching to feel those lips on mine again, but I was here with Fi. I didn't come here to actively engage with Leon. Maybe just make him notice me.

"I uh... I should get back to Fi, she's probably wondering where I got to." I definitely did not want to be out of this man's grasp, but I had to get away from him before I melted into a puddle.

He smiled and dropped his arms from me. "I understand. Enjoy the rest of your night. Don't let that kiss play on your mind too much." With a wink he sauntered off looking like he had won the lottery.

I downed the rest of my drink and hurried over to Fi. I grabbed her hand and hissed in her ear. "We need to go. Like now, before I cease to exist." She spun her head around to me. She looked at me and a playful smile slowly crept up onto her face. She looked like a damn Cheshire Cat.

"Ooh, did you get some lip action? Your lips are so swollen." She pointed a swaying finger at the evidence on my face. I touched my lips gingerly. They still tasted of him and his touch still lingered. I felt myself grow hot and tried to prevent a blush from once again appearing on my face. I was twenty-three, not a thirteen-year-old confused and horny teenager. Well, horny, absolutely, the rest definitely not.

"Yes Fi, I did, now can we go? We'll discuss this in the morning when we're both sober." I was starting to see double of people as the final half of my drink finally took hold of my bodily functions. With a chuckle, she nodded her head and arm in arm to prevent the other from going arse over tit, we made our way back to my apartment. As we weaved and shoved our way out of the party, I tried to look for Leon through the crowd so that we could say 'bye', but I couldn't see him anywhere.

Once in the quite of my apartment, Ffion headed to my spare bedroom after a goodnight kiss on the cheek, and I stumbled my way to my own. Taking my makeup off - a regimen I only rarely missed if I was passed out drunk -, I couldn't help but keep gazing into the mirror at my lips, still slightly swollen from my little make-out with Leon. As the image of his face floated to the front of my brain, I felt a tug in my gut. He was so familiar to me for some reason, like I'd known him for years. I was drawn to him like a moth to a flame and I couldn't stop myself. Yes, he was so incredibly attractive, so of course I would want to kiss him, and more. But there was more to this, and I really didn't know what it was. If I wanted anything more to happen, I had to pace myself and learn more about him.

Once I was in bed, I sent Leon a quick text:

A: Me and Fi are back at mine. Thank you for a great night, we really enjoyed ourselves

I was about to put my phone on my bedside table when it pinged, signaling a text.

L: No problem princess, thank you for coming, and thank you for my housewarming present. Sleep well

Not having a clue how to reply to that, I put my phone on my bedside table and laid on my back, spread out in a naked starfish underneath my cool sheet. I felt a smile plastered on my face just thinking about Leon, the kiss and his message.

I fell into a blissful sleep, the smile lingering on my face.

6

Chapter 5

Waking up the next morning proved to be a struggle. Even though I wasn't overly drunk last night, the mix of wine and whatever was at the party was the perfect concoction for a foggy brain the morning after. The sunlight burned my eyes as I tried to open them, and so I quickly dove under my sheets to relieve my eyes.

Whilst under the sheets, I took some time to gather my thoughts on what had happened last night. I'd had so much fun with Fi, dancing without a care in the world. I don't know why we don't go out more often. Everything was better with Fi there. She just makes everything so much more fun and we always have such a good time together.

But. That kiss was definitely the highlight of my night. I sighed to myself and folded my arms over my eyes, completely shutting out any light. It felt so good and so right, and I could only wonder how it would have felt if we were sober and our sense weren't compromised. It didn't bother me that I didn't really know him, I've had one night stands with absolute strangers without a second thought, and a kiss is just a kiss. But, I was growing concerned that if he did remember, would he regret it? It had been incredible for me, but how embarrassing would it be if he didn't feel the same? Ugh. I needed to talk to Ffion about this. Before I ended up engulfed in a wormhole of doubt and self-pity.

The smell of bacon and eggs wafted from the kitchen, flooding my senses and making my mouth water. Fi was a brilliant cook and she made the best breakfasts. I suddenly heard her yell "YOU ARSEHOLE!" and I let out a giggle at the multiple possibilities of what she was doing.

I grudgingly hauled myself out of bed and shuffled to the kitchen, my head instantly heavy and a hammer being whacked against the inside walls of my skull. Sure enough, Ffion was standing by the stove. Well. I say stood by the stove, she stood at arms-length away brandishing a spatula that she was somehow able to hold on to through oven mitts. To complete the ensemble, snorkel goggles encompassed her eyes. She'd raided my cupboard that was full of all kinds of random crap for her protective eyewear that I forgot I owned.

I couldn't contain my laughter. "Fi... Wha... What the fuck... are you wearing?" I couldn't even get my words out through laughing. I quickly found myself doubled over, one hand clutching my hurting stomach, the other holding me up by the wall, whilst struggling to breathe.

"This is no laughing matter Ava." She took on her serious tone, the tone I've heard her use when she was on the phone to her clients, whilst jabbing the spatula towards the sizzling pan. "The bacon won't stop spitting at me! I had to protect myself somehow."

I made my way to the stools, wiping away the tears from my eyes as I slowly controlled my laughter and sat down. With her back turned to me, I snuck a picture of her. This was definitely going to be posted on her Facebook wall on her next birthday.

"So then A," Here we go, I know where this is going, "spill the beans on that spicy kiss." She'd taken off her protective gear and had plated up our breakfast. There was a hint of mischief in her smile as she pushed my plate towards me, before digging into her own.

"I mean, it was something else, that's for sure. He tasted and felt so good. Even though it was fleeting, it was easily in the top ten of best kisses I'd ever had, and no it wasn't because I was drunk. There was this spark that I've never had with anyone else. It's just... as much as I enjoyed it, I can't help but wonder what it was like for him and if it meant anything. It was not how I envisioned our first kiss to go." I stabbed my fork into my sausage, "What if I was too sloppy because I was drunk and I was a bad kisses?" I sighed and shoved the now cut up sausage in my mouth and chewed thoughtfully. It sounded so stupid saying how I felt out loud. I didn't want to give him the wrong impression, that I was easy. Or bad, because I was many things but a bad kisser is not one of them.

"I get you. You didn't want your kiss to not be genuine on his part. You think it was the heat of the moment kind of thing. But A, it's just a kiss. You're thinking too much into it. It's not like he asked you to marry him." She shrugged her shoulders before guzzling half of her glass of orange juice. She had a point. I knew I was being silly, it was just a kiss and it's not like I couldn't ask for a re-kiss. But with how I was starting to feel about him, I wanted more. Of his lips, of his touch, but most importantly, more of him.

Ffion shoveled some more eggs in her mouth before carrying on. "I think the best thing to do is to speak to Leon about it. See where his mind's at." She swallowed her mouthful before continuing, pointing her fork at me, "And regarding your drunk kissing skills, I've kissed you drunk. You've nothing to worry about." I let out a choked laugh, appreciative that her experience can vouch for me and settle my worries on that front. But, as usual, she was right. I made a mental note to drop Leon a text before going for my run.

We nattered amongst ourselves as we ate, talking about the latest celebrity gossip until we had finished eating. Glancing at my watch, I raised my eyebrows at how late in the morning it was. It was time to get a move on. I got up and placed our plates in the sink.

"Right then Fi!" I clapped my hands together and turned back to face her. "Get your gear on, we're going for a run." Ffion rolled her eyes at me and let out a groan. She dragged herself back into the spare bedroom muttering to herself. I managed to hear what sounded like "she's the devil". With a giggle and a shake of my head, I headed into my bedroom and got ready.

We completed our run in almost record time. That was probably thanks to the dog that gave chase to Ffion. I'd never seen her sprint so fast, and I was laughing so much I got the worst cramp which earned me the snide comment of "Karma, bitch" from Ffion.

She didn't stick around once we got back to my apartment. She probably thought I was going to force her to work out with me. She would've been correct. The run had worked wonders on clearing my head, but it wasn't quite enough.

When Fi left, I put on my work-out playlist, took out the weights and a mat that were tucked away in the cupboard and stood in front of my full-length mirror and began to observe my form with every curl, lift and squat.

A good hour had passed, before I decided to call it a day. I glanced at myself in the mirror and found myself looking a right gross state. My cheeks were flushed. My top was drenched in sweat rather unflatteringly under my breasts and no doubt down the center of my back where I could feel the sticky liquid trailing down the crevice before collecting in the small of my back, turning the once light pink garment into a darker shade. My fly-away hairs that were too short to go into my ponytail clung for dear life to my forehead. I made my way back to the weight-stand and packed away my weights and the mat and headed to the bathroom and turned the shower on, leaving it to warm up. I still hadn't sent the text to Leon, saying that I wanted to speak with him. I was a bit hesitant. There was a chance that the kiss literally meant nothing to him, and he didn't see me in that way. But he had said to me last night that he didn't think I saw him in that way, but that didn't mean that he felt the same. I needed to stop being a pussy and just send him the damn text. Get it over and done with.

Standing by my en-suite door, I took a deep breath and began typing.

I let go of my breath when the text registered as delivered, tossed my phone onto the bed, peeled off my gym gear and hopped into the steaming shower.

* * *

Leon's POV

38

I stirred from my deep slumber around midday. Last night had been wild and I had ended up completely out of my face. I could barely remember what happened, and I could only imagine the mess that awaited me outside my bedroom door.

Despite my hazy memory, the one moment that stuck out in my brain was that spine-tingling kiss with Ava. What was I thinking inviting that creep Clint? He'd always been trouble, and he had a reputation of at least attempting to force himself on unwilling women. I should've known better. Even though I was sure Ava had the situation under control, and she definitely would've clocked him one if it came to it, I couldn't let it go unnoticed. Plus, there was the added benefit of satisfaction of rescuing her from such an uncomfortable situation.

It had taken me by surprise that she initiated the kiss. I mean, I was heading for it, but I half expected her to have pulled away. If that guy hadn't of shoved her, I would've taken her there and then. I wasn't done exploring every deliciously smooth surface of the inside of her mouth and I wanted to touch every curve of her body with my hands, and I was pissed the kiss was cut short.

The dress she wore clung to her in all the right places. Her backside was perfectly round, and the smooth skin of the side of her perky breasts teasingly peaked out from the side of her dress. I couldn't be sure, but I could've sworn I saw the outline of nipple piercings through the fabric of her dress.

Despite being short, she had a good body shape. She had an hourglass body figure and she was well proportioned. You could tell that she took care of her figure and that she worked out, as her legs and arms were beautifully toned. The heels that she wore last night only increased the attractiveness of her legs, making them seem longer and more defined.

Watching her dance seductively up against her friend really

did have me tugging at my jeans, and I had found myself wishing it was me who she was grinding up against. Just thinking about her and the feel of her lips on mine was making my dick twitch.

I didn't really know much about her, but from what I could tell, she was a confident and headstrong young woman; a characteristic I found incredibly attractive. I loved that she knows what she wants and how to get it. But most importantly, I loved that she knew how good she looked. She didn't come across as overly vain, just that she knew how to emphasise her body and her features. I had seen her with her natural face, in normal clothing, and even then, I thought that she was beautiful.

My phone buzzed from somewhere on the floor. Without getting off of the bed, I looked around to see where my phone was. I spotted my jeans that had been thrown into a heap onto the floor. I flipped onto my stomach and reached over, found my phone in one of the pockets before pushing myself back onto the bed. I adjusted my position, sitting up with a pillow propped under my head.

Upon seeing the name of the person who text me, I eagerly opened it.

A: Hey Leon! I hope you aren't feeling too delicate today. Anyway, we need to talk about last night... about the kiss...

The kiss that was engraved in my brain despite my drunken state. The kiss that I could still feel way over twelve hours later. I couldn't explain it, but I felt drawn to her. There was an undeniable attraction between us and I was sure she could feel it too. From the first moment I laid my eyes on her, I felt this pull to her.

Her eyes looked so familiar, like I'd seen them before on someone else. It sounded stupid, but like a bad case of deja vu, I really did think that I had met this girl before. Was she one of my patients? Had she been at one of my talks? No, no. I would've remembered surely. With a body like that, how could I not?

My mind wandered back to the first day I met her. She had been so kind and accommodating, allowing me to stay in her spare room to save me the hassle of getting a hotel room. Although we were doing our own things, it didn't feel awkward and I felt comfortable being in her presence. It had been a while since I had been around a woman in somewhat of a living with situation, but this felt easy. Calming. Natural.

Her lounging outfit that she had changed into had me drooling and I had to turn away before she noticed the raging boner I was growing. She had worn short shorts that showed every curve of her hips and bum and cinched her waist snuggly, and paired them with a vest top that fitted her tightly, exposing the soft smooth skin of the top of her breasts.

Since that day, we didn't really speak or see much of each other. we were more like two passing ships, but I made silly excuses to interact with her whenever I could; even if it was for five minutes. It would be something as little as asking if she had any milk to spare, and I had tried to bump into her as she left for her daily morning runs. I hadn't made enough effort. I wanted to know more about her. I wanted to hear more of her delicious voice. I wanted to see her more and more *of* her.

I hope I hadn't ruined any chance of getting to know her better.

L: I definitely woke up feeling worse than I do now – thanks for the concern. I'm free whenever this weekend so just let me know.

With my heart full of anticipation alongside a head full of questions and my nose started to stuff up with the scent of twelve-hour old booze coming from every pore on my body,

I jumped into the shower.

7

Chapter 6

I felt so relaxed after my shower, that I just collapsed onto my bed with my towel placed over-top of me. I closed my eyes and felt myself give in to the comfort of my bed. With my eyes closed, I was able to focus on the sounds around me. The gentle tick tock of the clock that had hypnotised me into a number of heavenly stupors, and the sound of the trees blowing in the wind outside. Before I could fall into a deep trance, I heard my phone ping somewhere above my head. I reached lazily above my head and moved my hand until I felt the cool surface of my phone. I had several messages from a handful of people.

The first was a picture message from one of my clients. She was in the gym and had posed in front of a mirror. She had one foot on one of the benches and her free arm positioned in a hero stance, flexing her bicep with the biggest smile on her face. I felt pride swell within me. I replied to her congratulating her and telling exactly how proud of her I was. She had come so far. When I first met her, she was so shy. Even though it was one-to-one sessions with it just being me and her, she was nervous to try anything and always thought she looked silly. But now, here she was bossing it in the gym on her own. This must be how parents feel when their kids say their first word or take their first step.

I had a missed call from my mum. She was probably just checking in on me. I hadn't spoken to her in a couple of days, so I could only assume that she was a little worried. Since the incident, I made sure to let my mum know how I was doing every day so that she knew I was fine and, more importantly, alive. I really had disappointed her that day. When I woke up in the hospital and saw her tear-stained face, my heart broke. I made a promise to myself and to her, that I would never do anything like that again. If I didn't call back soon, she'd probably be on her way here to check on me. I called her back and she picked up before the second ring. She must've been incredibly worried.

"Ava! My sweet girl, are you OK? Where have you been? I've been so worried about you." Her voice was heavy with anxiety and worry, and the sound of it made me immediately feel bad.

"Hey mama, I'm sorry I missed your call, I was in the shower. I'm fine, everything's good. I'm sorry for making you worry." And I really was. I hated knowing I was putting my mum through the wringer like this. It didn't matter how old I was, I was still her baby and she would not go a day without knowing how I was doing.

I heard her sigh with relief at the other end of the phone. "Thank goodness. I was about to jump in the car and come make sure you were still breathing!" I chuckled at her. I loved my mum dearly, and over the last nine years, we had grown incredibly close. She was my biggest supporter, my best friend and my confidante. Although, there were some things that I didn't tell her. Such as my recent activity with a certain male neighbour.

"Mama, you know you're more than welcome to come over

any time, and not just to make sure I'm still standing." I rarely saw my mum. She lived two and a half hours away and whilst I loved my independence, my heart yearned to be near my mum. She missed me as much as I did her, but she understood and respected my decision to be independent. She knew that I couldn't be near our hometown. It brought back too many bad memories. She loved the area however, and when I went to university, she had moved back.

"Well then, if that's the case, how about I come down for the weekend next month? I've got time off and I'd love to see my favourite daughter."

I let out a giggle. "I'm your only daughter."

"Exactly, and I want to spend as much time with you as and when I can."

We made arrangements for her to come see me in a months' time and ended the conversation. I was so excited to see my mum. I'd been living here a year and a half, and she had only been to see me a couple of times. I think that was mostly down to Felicity though. My mum hated the guts of the girl. She would always tell me that there was something about her. I should've trusted her instincts, because boy was she right.

I decided that it was time to get dressed. It was nearing one p.m. and I still had work to do. I had settled on some plain grey tapered joggers and had just pulled an over-sized hoody over my head when my phone went off again. When I saw that Leon had messaged me, my heart started pounding. I opened the message. It seems that he did in fact remember the kiss, which made me happy. He said that he was free all weekend. I mean, I wasn't exactly in any rush, but I suppose the sooner we clear everything up the better. I found my fingers flying over the screen.

A: Thanks, you free now?

I figured there was no point beating around the bush. Get it over and done with and save my brain from going into overdrive from overthinking. Not even a minute later and I had a reply.

L: Sure, I'll be over in five.

My heart was beating so hard I thought it was going to burst out of my chest. I was so nervous to speak to him about this. I was also nervous to see his handsome face. I always found myself lost, staring at his perfectly crafted face. I needed to be strong and not let that happen. This was a serious talk to me, even if it wasn't to him.

Five minutes later, on the dot, there was a knock at the door. I opened it and put on the most welcoming smile I could muster. I felt my breath catch in my throat. He was dressed in grey sweats and a white V-neck top. I don't know what it was about a man in grey joggers, but it really gets me going. Especially when it was this particular man. I scanned my eyes down his body. The outline of his chest and abs were visible, thanks to the tightness of his top. Further down, I could see the soft outline of his manhood. I quickly averted my eyes, bringing them back to his. He had a smirk on his face and had crossed his arms across his broad chest. He knew I was checking him out. Instantly, I felt my cheeks go hot.

"Hey Leon, thanks for coming. Please, come in." I stepped aside, allowing for him to walk past me into my home. We exchanged niceties as we made our way over to the couch.

"So then. You wanted to discuss the kiss from last night? I mean, I don't know what there is to discuss. I thoroughly enjoyed it, and frankly, I'm a little disappointed that it didn't last any longer." I was a little taken aback at how matter-of-fact and straight to the point he was.

"Uh... well... OK so I enjoyed it, I even told you so after it happened. But I want to make it clear that I don't want anything to happen between us right now. I don't know where your head's at, but I'm not ready to commit to anything right now." I could feel myself growing restless and found myself I was fiddling with my fingers as I forced myself to keep eye contact with him. I really wanted things to go well between us, even if that meant as friends. He had gone quiet for a few seconds, as if he was mulling something over in his mind.

"That's fair enough. I'm not particularly looking for anything right now either." He reached over and tucked a stray piece of my hair behind my ear, leaving his hand cupping my cheek.

"But, I don't know what it is about you, but I'm so attracted to you. It's like there's this invisible magnet pulling me towards you." *He felt it too?* He chuckled and took his hand away from my cheek. I felt his warm touch be replaced with cold air, and suddenly, I craved to be touched by him.

"But, that being said, I don't like how we know nothing about each other. So, lets get the basics out of the way. Is there anything you want to know about me?"

"How about starting with the little things, like your birthday and your favourite colour. I want to know about your childhood, your job, and your family." I couldn't help but notice he winced when I said about wanting to know about his childhood, so I can only assume that that will be a bit of a sore subject. I suppose we all have skeletons we want to keep hidden in our closets.

He nodded. "That seems good to me."

From that moment on, we spent a couple hours talking about each other. We went over basics and avoided talks of the past, which I was more than happy to do. I wasn't ready to delve into my messy past. I had worked hard to be a better person and to put what happened at the back of my mind, tucked away in the deepest crevice of my mind.

I was surprised to learn that he was a therapist for children and young people. "I wasn't the best person when I was a teenager. Something traumatic happened that threw me in turmoil and completely changed my perspective on myself and on life. From then on, I worked hard and dedicated my time to help those who needed it. I suppose you could say I wanted to right the wrong that I had caused in some way."

It was crazy to think that something bad had happened to the both of us that resulted in us wanting to help others. He hadn't completely disclosed to me about what happened, and I could respect that. I didn't want to open up fully about my past either. You'd need more than a crow bar to open that crate of devastation.

"Wow, that's incredible. I think it's inspiring that you decided to live a life making others happy." I went on to tell him about my job. "Something bad happened to me too when I was younger. I'm actually very lucky that I'm still here. Because I survived, I made it my mission to improve the confidence and self-esteem of women through fitness. That's actually how I met Ffion." His eyes were full of intrigue. He was interested in me and what I had to say, and that made me happy. It was nice to know that someone genuinely wanted to listen to me.

We chatted for a good couple of hours before Leon announced that he had to get going. Something to do with work. I was glad that he was gone, as I could get cracking on the fitness plans I was yet to complete, but I missed his presence. With a slap on my knees, I proceeded to stand up and make my way to my laptop.

These fitness plans wont manifest themselves.

8

Chapter 7

Leon's POV:

I leaned back on my office chair, kicked my feet up on my desk, crossing them at the ankles, and folded my hands behind my head. Today had been hard work.

The patient I had just finished up with was a sixteen-year-old girl whose arms were riddled with scars. She was having a tough time talking to me, but we managed to work through some of her thoughts slowly, yet thoroughly. She was a new patient, and new to therapy. It was only natural that she was nervous to talk to a stranger about her innermost thoughts.

She reminded me of the girl I used to bully when I was in school. The only drawback this job had was that I was forever reminded of that time of my life. Although, I suppose you could argue that because it was on my mind, it was the driving force and motivation I needed for me to continue being great at my job.

When I found out that she had tried to kill herself, I was filled with instant regret over what I did. I had never wanted to hurt

49

the girl, but it was a life I somehow managed to fall into through poor mistakes and my stupidity to uphold some silly reputation and it nearly cost someone their life. Someone, who behind closed doors, I had developed some feelings for, before all the madness happened. If she had succeeded, I don't know what I would've done. It's hard enough now that I live a life with the knowledge that I could've been the reason behind another ending their life. I couldn't even begin to comprehend what I would've felt had she died.

The headmaster of our school held an assembly the day after that had happened and informed us that one of the students had attempted suicide by slitting her wrists in a bathtub. He went on to inform us that if her mum hadn't found her when she did, she would've slipped into an eternal slumber.

I remember that there was a buzz around the hall as people gasped and whispered amongst themselves at who it could have been, a few heads turning as they checked the audience for anyone missing. He told us that the reason behind her attempted suicide was because she had been subjected to severe bullying, something that had gone unnoticed and unreported. Upon hearing that, I knew instantly who it was and I was filled with guilt and shame.

The school never investigated the bullying, so I guess you could say that I got away with it Scott free. Apparently, the girl just wanted it to be forgotten about and she wanted to move on with her life. For that, I was thankful.

Needless to say, the girl either dropped out of school completely, or she left town. I never saw her again. I never had the opportunity to apologise for my actions.

I wasn't fully to blame, the gang didn't help either, especially Vic. She sadistically fed off of that girl's fear and thrived from causing her pain. When she had found out what she had contributed to, Vic just laughed. After that, I dropped her like a sack of shit. She had felt no remorse for what she had done. Even though I was the ringleader, I couldn't let that go unnoticed. I distanced myself from most of the gang. I didn't want to be involved with people like that anymore.

From then on, I focused on my studies. I had gone from a below average student, to the top of my year. I achieved top grades in school, college and university. I was the perfect student.

As the years went on, the memory of what happened was tucked safely in the back of my mind, but I had forgotten the girl. Asides from the fact she had blonde hair and blue eyes, I forgot what she looked like and what her name was. I had forced myself to, because every night when I went to sleep, I was haunted by the vision of her face whenever I closed my eyes.

When Ava briefly told me why she became a fitness instructor and what the goal was, I was impressed. She had pulled herself out of a dark spot in her life, something that not many people have the strength and willpower to do, and turned it into this brilliant ray of light and shined that upon others to make them feel that they are good enough and loved. Ava had a heart of pure gold, and I didn't want to tarnish that with me and my past. I was not deserving of her attention, yet it was all that I craved.

I wanted to be honest and open about my past, but it wasn't time yet. It would only make her think of me as a horrible cunt and push her away, and I really didn't want that.

I was pulled out of my thoughts by a knock at the door.

"Yes? Come in."

The door creaked open and a woman walked in. She had vibrant red hair that had been pinned up skillfully in a bun by a couple of pens. She wore wide, clear rimmed glasses that sat elegantly on the bridge of her nose. She was dressed in a formal work dress that wasn't too tight but didn't stray far from her figure, giving her adequate room to move. She wore six-inch heels that were so thin they could easily be used as a weapon. It was a mystery how on earth she managed to walk and stay balanced on those pins.

"Yes Stacey, what's the problem?" I hoped she could hear the annoyance in my voice. Stacey was a fine enough receptionist. Sure, she spent a lot of her time on her phone or looking in a mirror but she was always professional towards my patients and their families and took whatever calls came in, even if it interrupted whatever she was doing. The biggest issue with her was that she was forever hitting on me and flirting. Any other time, I probably wouldn't have had a problem with it. However, I worked with her and therefore our relationship would and could only be professional. She was my colleague. Nothing more.

"Sorry to interrupt Mr. Myers, but you've got a patient ready waiting for you. He's a little early. Shall I send him in or wait until his time?" She batted her eyelashes, a small, coy smile a shadow on her lips. A perfect display of forced innocence.

"Tell him to wait please Stace. I'll give you a buzz when I'm ready for him." I could appreciate people coming to their appointments early, but I didn't appreciate it when they were twenty minutes early and I still had notes to write up of my previous patient.

With a nod of her head she walked back out of my office, closing the door gently behind her. I glanced at the clock. I only had one more patient after the one in the waiting room and then I'd be done for the day. I took out my phone and decided I'd send my best mate a text. I could do with a few beers after the day I've had.

L: Yo Ev! You wanna go to the bar tonight? Could do with a few after the day I've had.

Ev was like a brother to me. We had grown up together, gone to the same schools and were inseparable. The only difference being that he was two years older than I was. I had moved here for my job, but it was an extra added bonus that he also lived here.

Not many knew about my past, only those who were involved and Ev. When I told him what had happened, he was so disappointed and he made sure that I knew it. He was part of what pushed me to be who I am now. Yes, I wanted to make amends in some way for what I had done and become a better person, but I didn't want to disappoint my soul brother. He was so proud of me when I informed him of my chosen career and he has backed and supported me ever since.

My phone buzzed at his response.

E: Yeah man, I'm down! Mind if I bring that girl I told you about? Things are going really well with her and I want you to meet her. I'm sure she said she's got a single friend, maybe she can bring her for you?

I chuckled to myself. Ever since Ev told me about this girl, she was all he spoke about. I was happy for him. He had a long history of being a player and with that came an even longer list of girls he'd hooked up with, but he was done with that life and was ready to settle down. I was proud of him, and I hoped this girl brought him happiness and was everything he said she was.

L: Sure thing, but you know I've got my eye on someone else, so don't be surprised if I'm not interested.

Likewise, I had told Ev about Ava. How could I not? I didn't believe in love at first sight, but how I felt about Ava was close to it. I really did want to make a go of things with her, but she had made it clear that if things were to progress, then she wanted to know more about me. I liked that about her, that she doesn't blindly commit to people, that she wanted to know what she was getting involved with before she fell too far in.

Locking my phone in the drawer of my desk, I continued typing up the notes of the previous patient.

With a few minutes left to spare, I buzzed through to Stacey, telling her to let the next one in. Just a couple of hours to go and I'll be sinking pints with my brother.

9

Chapter 8

Ffion and I were enjoying our second cup of coffee, sitting in our usual seats by the windows in the far corner of The Coffee Hub. I think it was safe to say that I had an unhealthy addiction to coffee. I needed caffeine in my system the same way the local crackhead on the corner needed his daily fix.

The Hub was relatively busy today, most likely due to the poor weather. I loved sitting here whilst it rained. I enjoyed watching the rain droplets slide agonisingly slowly down the window whilst cradling my mug of piping hot coffee. It was a soothing sight, only to be made even more calming with the sensual bitter smell of coffee tickling my nostrils.

There was a low hum of voices as people spoke quietly amongst themselves. There was a wide variety of people who came here. There were the coffee addicts (like Fi and myself), there were couples, loners huddling in the booths reading books, people who needed the quiet to do work and there were even a couple of families that came here.

I could hear Fi giggle quietly to herself. She was sitting in the corner of her chair, with her feet tucked under her. She looked so

5

at home. All she needed was a blanket and she'd be set. She had her nose in her phone and her thumbs were moving at lightning speed. It didn't take a genius to work out who had made her giggle.

"Everett, I assume?" She didn't even take her eyes off of her phone, just nodded enthusiastically in response.

"Yeah, he's just invited me and you out! He's going to a bar with a friend and said we can come. You up for going?" She finally looked at me, but with pleading eyes. She'd been spending a lot of time with Everett lately and I was yet to meet him. However, despite seeing so much of him, she never forgot about me and I appreciated it. She spoke so much about him that it was easy to tell that she had already fallen hard for him. I just hoped the feeling was reciprocated.

A midweek drink didn't sound too bad in all honesty. I had an open day tomorrow so it wouldn't matter if I overdid it tonight. Plus, there was the bonus of finally meeting Everett. I couldn't care less about his mate, my friends' happiness was what was most important to me.

"Sure, why not? I've been itching to meet the man who's stolen your heart." I winked at her, watching a blush spread across her olive cheeks.

Ffion was a true natural beauty. She had gorgeous olive skin, which I absolutely envied. She's one of those lucky people that in the summer, she never burns, but instead gets this gorgeous glowing tan. Her eyes were a unique hue of green that reminded me of spring. Ffion spoke a lot with her eyes, and through them you could tell the kind of person she was. She was a strong determined individual who was incredibly kind. She had beautiful voluminous caramel hair that had long curtain bangs cut into the front, and natural soft waves cascading to her mid back. It always made me wonder how that prick ex of hers could hurt her the way he did.

Upon hearing my agreement, Ffion squealed in excitement. "YES! Ugh, we're going to have so much fun! I wonder what his friend's like."

"Yeah, no, I can guarantee you that I will not be interested in his crummy friend." I scoffed. I had eyes for one person after all and it would take a lot to turn my head.

"Hey, you never know, he might be an upgrade to Mr Sex on Legs." I highly doubted that. I just rolled my eyes and continued drinking my coffee. Fi just laughed at me and turned her attention back to her phone, probably telling Everett that we were up for going out tonight.

We spent the rest of the next hour discussing the outfits we were going to wear tonight.

* * *

For once, we had ended up in Ffion's flat to get ready. It was just easier since the bar was closer to hers than it was to mine. Ffion lived in a flat on her own. It was a comfortable size, perfect for her. If she wanted to, she could easily have a roommate, but I think she prefers to have her own space.

We were currently in her bedroom. I was on the floor with a mirror propped against the wall, curling my hair into loose beachy curls, and Fi was trying to suck her butt in to pull up her body suit. It was a funny sight. She started jumping around the room in an attempt to hoist the material over the last curve of her behind. I should remind her to thank me for all the hard

57

work I make her do to get her butt looking like that.

With one final grunt, she finally yanked the bodysuit up and slipped her slender arms through the straps. Ffion had an immaculate fashion sense. The body suit she was sporting was a tight fit, high-waisted short shorts that stopped just under the crease where her legs meet her bum, with the top half a shiny, sequined emerald strappy moment. Her choice of footwear was some black heels with a closed pointed toe.

She looked drop dead gorgeous.

With my hair finally curled, I sectioned a small area at the top of my head and proceeded to add three small French braids, before bringing them together into a ponytail at the top of my head, forming a half up half down style. I wrapped a small section of hair around the base and pulled out some baby hairs to frame my face.

The outfit I had opted for was some black leather jeans with a burgundy strappy crop top, with its neckline coming down into a V between my cleavage. I finished off the outfit with some plain black open-toe heels.

I heard a low sexy whistle come from Ffion.

"Ooh, look at you! You're going to have all the men drooling at your feet tonight!" I couldn't help but giggle at her. She didn't see how stunning she looked, if she did, she would realise I paled in comparison.

"Don't be daft Fi. Look at yourself! Everett's going to have a hard time keeping his hands off you." I reached over for my wine glass and downed the remaining contents.

I got up to place my empty glass on the desk when Fi let out a frustrated scream. She was trying to get her hair to wrap around itself into a perfect bun at the top of her head but it wasn't going the way she wanted it to.

"Stupid hair. Why was I given thick hair?" She was on the verge of literally ripping her hair out of her scalp.

"Sit still, let me see what I can do." I wiggled my fingers as if waking up magic within them as I assessed what I was working with. I instructed her to put her head in between her knees and proceeded to put in a backwards French plait going from the base of her neck up to her crown. Upon reaching that point, I secured the plait separately from the rest of her hair with a clear elastic, enabling me to gather the rest of her hair up without losing the braid. With all of her hair in my hands, I added the tail of the plait in and secured it into one ponytail. I skillfully folded her hair into itself, tucking it into the hair bobble and pinning it into a bun.

Finally, I pinned her long bangs up into a poofy quiff. With a final check and some squirt of hairspray, her hair was done. She looked in the mirror and a wide beaming smile flashed at me.

"You really are a magician when it comes to hair. Maybe you should think about a career in it." She half-joked. I had always loved playing with hair, and with locks as long as mine, I had to find hairstyles that kept it out of my way. But, as much as I loved playing with hair, I loved helping others more.

We quickly touched up our makeup, grabbed our small bags and headed to the bar.

The walk to the bar was a cold one. Even though we were coming into the middle of May, there was still a bit of a spring chill to the air. It was times like these that I envied men. When they go out, they always wear trousers and a jacket. Whereas us women never dress in such a way. When we go out, we dress purely to look good. Nothing more, nothing less. I felt even more sorry for Fi, she was practically naked and was shaking like a leaf. Luckily it was only a ten minute walk from Ffion's flat to the bar.

* * *

We walked into the modern bar and Fi was immediately perched up on her tippy-toes like a meerkat, on the lookout for Everett. She spotted him and jumped on the spot as she waved to him. She grabbed my hand and hurried over to him as fast as her heels allowed her to. She ran into his embrace and gave him a kiss on the lips that went on for what felt like ages.

I let out a subtle cough and Ffion jumped and looked at me with bright red cheeks. I rolled my eyes at her with a smile on my face.

"Oh right! Everett, I'd like you to meet my bestie, Ava. Ava, this is Everett." I reached over past Ffion and offered my hand out.

"It's nice to finally meet you Everett. She talks nonstop about you." He placed his hand in mine with a friendly smile.

"And you. Really? That surprises me. She's forever talking about you." I burst out laughing and we let go of each other's hand. In the corner of my eye, I saw movement just behind Everett.

"Ah there you are! Ffion, Ava, this is my best buddy Leon." Everett had pulled his friend to stand next to him with his arm wrapped around his shoulder. My jaw hit the floor, and Leon looked like a deer caught in the headlights. Of all the people it had to be him. What were the chances? I slowly turned to Ffion, who clearly also had no idea that the two men knew each other. Everett had a confused look on his face as he looked between us.

"Do you guys already know each other?" He asked curiously.

"Yeah, we do. Me and Ava are neighbours. They came to my housewarming party." Leon said, snapping back into reality.

"I see. Wow, what are the odds!" Everett said with a laugh. "What do you ladies want to drink? Me and Leon will go get the drinks in." Me and Fi reeled off our order and the men made their way to the bar. As soon as they were a safe distance away, I turned to Fi. She grabbed my elbows and started happy jumping and squealing.

"You know what this means Ava? We can go on double dates! And we'll be the best friend couple! Oh, this is perfect!" I really didn't know what to make of it all. But clearly Ffion was already envisioning and planning the benefits.

I was not expecting to see Leon here. He was looking panty wettingly good tonight too. But then again, when didn't he? He was wearing a black silk shirt that had these gold chain designs on it that was unbuttoned halfway down. His entire sculpted chest was on show, and it wasn't helping with my need of wanting to touch them.

By the end of the night, I was going to be a hot, wet mess, and I don't know how long I can hold out before I jump on him. It had already been nearly two weeks since that kiss, and I was itching to feel him again - one way or another.

10

Chapter 9

Leon's POV:

I couldn't believe it. Ev's girl was Ava's best friend. Well, you know what they say, small world and all that. But, knowing that it was Ffion who had Ev acting like a lovesick fool, I was sure that they would be in it for the long run. She seemed like such an honest and genuine girl, full of life and energy. I could see why Ava had her in her life and why Ev was head over heels with her.

She was a beautiful girl, both inside and out. But she had nothing on Ava. Though I could appreciate true beauty in any form, blondes held me in a choke-hold like no other. Especially when that blonde was Ava.

Ava and I weren't even a thing yet, we didn't have any sort of label. We just... were. But I was picturing the benefits this had. At heart, I was a soppy sod, and so I couldn't help imagining all the double dates, the get togethers and all the other things we could do, not only as couples, but as friends too.

I hadn't seen her or Ffion when they came in, so when me

and Ev had reached the bar to get our four drinks, I took the opportunity to glance back at her and really take her in. Ffion had a grip on her elbows and was jumping up and down, but Ava had stayed rooted on the spot, looking almost as dumbfounded as I felt.

Even from the back, I could see how stunning she looked. The leather jeans she wore worked wonders on highlighting the shapeliness of her legs. Her hair a blonde waterfall, flowing in loose curls down her back. I loved girls with long hair. To me, it made them seem even more feminine. And gave me something to pull on.

Ev's voice brought me back to my senses. "So that is the famous neighbour you've been telling me about. I can see what you mean, she's stunning, and very much your type. So, what's the deal? Pump and dump? Or do you actually want to pursue something with her?" An eyebrow frowned with the other raised, I shot Ev a look. Despite the crude way of putting it, he wasn't wrong to assume my motives. Just like Ev, I too had a colourful past with a long string of women. I had given up that life as soon as I graduated from Uni though, having decided that I wanted to start living as an adult, and not as a horny teenager who only thought with my cock.

"We've only had one kiss, but I do really want something with her. I don't know man, I really want to take things up a notch, but I don't want her to feel like she has to jump in feet first, you know?" I wanted her, and I wanted her bad. But I had enough respect for her to let her take whatever this was as far as she wanted, whenever she wanted. If being a therapist has taught me anything, it's that women base their actions mostly on emotion and I was clueless as to what emotion she was riding when it came to me.

"She wants you. I can see it in her eyes. Just go for it. You've been talking for what? Nearing two months? There's no way that she or you can hold out for much longer." He had a point. A very good point. I felt like I could explode any moment, and not in the way I wanted to with her. I needed to make my move. Tonight had provided me with the perfect opportunity.

I looked back at the girls while Ev ordered the drinks and saw that they were dancing with each other. They were doing that seductive dancing that they did at my party. A few eyes were on them, but they paid them no attention as they got lost in the music and each other, as if everyone and everything around them faded into a blur in the background and they were the only two in the room. Their movements were fluid and full of touching, hip swaying and grinding. If people didn't know them, they'd easily be mistaken as lesbians rather than two best friends who simply were comfortable with each other. At that thought, I felt a rise in my jeans. Not that I wanted Ava to be a lesbian, but I am first and foremost just a typical man who was impartial to some girl on girl action. I turned back to the bar and took mine and Ava's drink.

"So, what about you and Ffion then? Where do things stand with the two of you?" I questioned as we carefully made our way back to the girls, mindful of spilling the drinks or bumping into people, and desperate to calm my dick down.

"Oh, we've already had sex mate. And quite a number of times too. She's a right minx in bed, I've never jizzed so much in one night. I'm surprised I've got any juice left in all honesty." I burst out laughing. There was no sugar-coating when it came to Ev. Just hard, honest, and sometimes crude, truth.

"You are one lucky bastard Ev, don't let her escape you. Women like that are rare to find." Ev looked at me with a shit-eating grin on his face, before he looked over to Ffion, eyes completely transfixed on her, following her every movement. I'd never seen him look at anyone the way he looked at Ffion. Whether he already knew or not, he'd fallen hard for her.

His comment did have me thinking about what Ava would be like in bed, not like it was the first time I'd thought about her in this way. Was she a screamer? Did she like to be dominated? She worked out a lot so I could only imagine she must have incredible stamina, which led to me wondering how many rounds we could have in a day or night. And there was that damn twinge in my pants again. I needed to do something about this, and soon, because I cannot go on giving myself blue balls.

We reached the girls and they ripped their drinks from our hands. "Thank god. We were going to die from dehydration if you had been any longer!" Came Ffion's breathless voice.

They hurriedly put the glasses to their lips and downed the liquid in seconds in perfect sync with one another. Me and Ev looked at each other and then stared at the girls in awe. Two girls standing before us, who could drink and party just as hard as us. How interesting it would be to see who could drink who under the table. Both me and Ev had had our fair shares of partying throughout Uni, but it had been a very, very long time since we had come across girls able to keep up with us.

"Woah, woah, woah! Slow down, you'll be on your arses in the next hour if you drink like that." Ev laughed at them before taking a long swig of his own drink.

"Oh honey, you have got so much to learn about A and I. We would out-drink you to shame any day of the week." Ffion patted him smugly on the shoulder. Ava grabbed my pint from my hand, raised it to me in a 'cheers' and downed a couple of mouthfuls all whilst locking eyes with me, before handing me the drink back with a wink before she linked arms with Ffion, and danced their way to the bar to get themselves another drink.

I shook my head with an amused smile. "I think we may have met our matches. We're going to have our hands full tonight, brother." Taking a swig of what remained of my pint.

"You may be right there, but you know what? I can't wait. This is going to be a fun night."

* * *

Ava's POV:

I still couldn't believe that Leon was Everett's friend. It seemed like fate had drew us all together, and if that was the case, then it seemed like the universe was giving me the green light to take things to the next level with Leon. I couldn't deny my body what it craved for anymore, nor could I deny my feelings anymore, and I said as much to Fi as we waited at the bar for our drinks.

"Girl, it's about time you grew some balls and did something about it! Honestly, there's so much sexual tension between you two, I'm impressed you've held out this long." She pulled me into a side hug, and I wrapped my left arm around her back.

"You're the most feminist person I know, so pipe down with that misogynistic bullshit. It's always 'grow some balls', how about 'grow a vagina', they can withstand giving birth to an entire human, you don't see no cock and balls doing that." Fi just burst into laughter and it was so unhinged, it was beautiful.

"Fucking hell; that was funny." She pressed a middle finger to her lower lashes, careful not to smudge her makeup, before holding her hand up to the bartender and placing our orders.

"And anyway, as much as I'd like to out-drink those two, I can't get too drunk. If I'm finally going to get some action, I want to make sure I'm capable of not only remembering it, but also being decent." I was confident that I was going to up the ante tonight and there was no way I was going to have any doubts or qualms over whether or not I did a good job because I was too intoxicated. I knew I was good in bed, and I wanted to savour our firsts together. I wanted to enjoy all of him.

"Sounds like a plan." We picked up our drinks and clinked glasses.

We met back with the boys who'd found a table. They sat next to each other, leaving me and Fi to sit opposite them. I slid into the seat near the wall, facing opposite Leon. He swallowed his mouthful and flashed that heart stopping smile of his at me.

"Alright, sweetheart?" He purred as he winked at me, placing his pint glass onto the table. I wasn't used to being called sweetheart, but something about it coming from him had my stomach turning in knots that went straight down south, igniting a flutter.

I leaned onto my elbows, rested my chin in one of my hands and traced the rim of my glass with the middle finger of my other hand as I started rubbing my foot up his leg. I watched with a smirk on my face as the look on his face changed. His eyes looked like they were going to pop out of their sockets and there was a hint of pink on his cheeks. He started shuffling in seat, and after a split second, his confident smirk was back with a touch of the devil in his face before he leaned in towards me.

"Let the games begin." The floodgates had opened in my pants, and it was now my turn to shuffle in my seat. I took a side glance next to me to look at Fi and Everett to see if they'd heard or noticed us, only to find that they were lost gazing lovingly into one another's eyes and seemed completely oblivious to mine and Leon's game of who could turn who on the most.

I felt Leon's large hand on the side of my calf. He slowly started to stroke up my leg. The table prevented him from going any higher than my knee, and I was regretting wearing jeans. These two factors only added to my frustration and craving of wanting him to touch me. His hand then trailed at an agonisingly slow pace back down to my ankle before making its way back up again, except this time he was using a finger to touch me even more delicately, sending a shiver up my spine. His mouth was set with smugness, knowing just what he was doing to me. Challenge accepted.

I nudged Fi, snapping her out of hypnosis. "Let's dance." We downed our drinks and I took my hand in hers and stood up. We made our way to the dance-floor, Fi leading the way, swaying our hips seductively, knowing that the boys' eyes were very much glued to us.

I turned so my back was pressed up against Fi's front, her full breasts pressed against my back and started moving my hips in time with Fi's, the beat of the music our conductor. I took a peek over at the boys and found that they were literally drooling as they watched us. I lifted my hand up and held the back of Fi's neck, and I felt her hand snake around and held me gently at the waist.

I heard a chuckle come from Fi and she leaned into my neck to whisper in my ear, the bass of the music a rumble that made talking barely audible.

"I don't think either of us are getting much sleep tonight after our performance." I shook my shoulders as I laughed back at her.

"Is that not the whole point?" Fi spun me around and I wrapped my arms around her neck, and she placed her hands flat on my backside, her fingers splayed to cover as much surface area as possible. Both of us were as straight as an arrow, but more than once we have had people question which team we played for. Dancing like this had only started out as a way of getting out of unwanted one night stands. Eventually, we realised that we had more than a couple of interested eyes pinned on us one night after we danced together, and very soon it became something we did just for fun, enjoying the looks and attention.

We danced like this for a little while, singing the lyrics to one another until the boys decided to join us. I felt a hand on my stomach and was pulled away from Ffion's hold. I looked up and found Leon looking down at me, licking his lips.

"You can't be dancing like that and not expect me to come and have a turn at being your little dance pole." His breath tickled my ear. I looked at Fi but found that her lips were already busy eating Everett's face off. If he wants to be my dance pole, then I best give him the best damn dance of his life.

I took the stance I had when I was dancing with Ffion. I had one hand reaching up to hold the back of his neck while his right hand was placed gently on my hips. I pushed my back flush into him and was rewarded with the feel of his growing cock in my back. I heard him hiss and felt his free hand grip my wrist near his head. I rode my backside into him and interlocked my free fingers with his on the hand that was on my waist.

"Oh, shit." He breathed. I turned to look up at him again. He rolled his lips into his mouth and had his gaze fixed on my arse pushed into him. I pushed further back into him and I continued grooving my hips into him but this time, I brought his hand up

69

from my waist and put it to the front of my neck. He clenched my neck ever so slightly and I felt the walls of my cervix clench as I let out a small moan.

My hand by his neck had stretched up and reached to the bottom of his head. I started swirling my fingers over his freshly shaved hair. Its softness a relaxing sensation against my palm.

"I think you might very well be the death of me." His breath hot as it trailed along my neck, his words carrying themselves along my nervous system until they clamped down tightly on all my sensitive areas. With his head lowered to my own, I raised up, my lips lightly brushing the shell of his ear.

"Is that so? Well, let's make it worth it then." I turned to face him. I placed my hands on his chest and looked up at him. He looked directly back into my eyes with lust and desire. I snaked my way down until my face was level with his manhood. At this point, he had a full hard on. I connected my eyes with his again and licked my lips as I ever so gently traced my fingers over his bulge. He bit his lower lip and, on my way back up, I saw him mutter a dragged out "fuck," the music too loud for his words to be carried to my ears.

I continued to word tease him, tip-toeing up to gain some height, but not quite tall enough to match his height, Leon bowed his head slightly.

"This is only the beginning babes, I don't think you quite realise what you're up against." With that, he spun me around again, pulling me so I was flush against him with one hand on my waist and the other on my chest. He buried his head in my neck and started tickling it with his lips. I threw my head back against his shoulder and let out a whimper. He brought his hand to grip my chin, holding it up so I was unable move.

I suddenly felt his warm tongue lick my neck before he directed my head the other way to give himself access to the other side of my neck, matching the attention he gave the other side with this one.

Just when I thought my legs were going to give in, he stopped, and I opened my eyes. He had a huge smirk on his face, like he thought he had won in this game of who could out-tease who. But this was far from over. First, however, I needed more drink before I passed out from dehydration. The dancing, the heat and this room, the way Leon was making me feel, were all contributing factors to making my mouth feel drier than the Sahara. Fi and Everett were no longer playing tonsil tennis but were dancing at a much slower, less risky pace, with her resting her head on his chest. I took her by her elbow and gently tugged her to get her attention.

"Fi, I need a drink." I mouthed, whilst charading a drinking motion. She nodded her head in acknowledgment. She reached up on her tip-toes and planted a deep kiss on Everetts lips, promising she would be back soon, and together, we made our way back to the bar.

We'd barely made it off the dance-floor when she said with a knowing smile, "Things seem to be going well. *Very* well in fact."

They were indeed.

11

Chapter 10

I was rather drunk by the time the end of the night came around, but I wasn't in as big a drunken state as Fi – I at least could still see and walk straight. Everett had picked Ffion up and was carrying her bridal style. She snuggled closer into his chest with her arms tucked against her chest, and a big, satisfied grin on her face. She looked like a big baby and I couldn't help but giggle at the sight. Everett looked down at her with adoration in his eyes.

"I'm going to take Fi home. Make sure you both get home safely." Came Everett's voice. He was probably the most sober out of all of us. He stopped drinking after his fourth pint and had stuck to water from then on. I guess that was pretty responsible of him, and I was glad that he would be in a good state of mind to take care of Ffion.

Leon gave him a pat on the shoulder. "Sure thing man, take care of yourself and make sure Fi gets to bed alright. I've already called us a taxi, it should be here any minute." Leon and I lived a half an hour walk away from the bar, and neither of us cared to walk it. Not only was it unusually cold out for this time of year, but we were in no fit state to walk home. My heels dangled in my hand, my bare, throbbing feet grateful for the relief of the cool surface of the pavement outside of the club. The sooner we got home the better, and not just so I could rest my feet.

"Alright guys, I'll send you both a text when I've got Fi home." He nodded his head as a gesture of goodbye, and walked off with Fi still in his arms.

I looked back at Leon and found him looking at me. His eyes were glossed over, like he was deep in thought. Suddenly they snapped out of their daze and I found myself watching his golden halos shift to a dark syrup. He grabbed my hand and tugged me lightly towards him. He placed a hand in the small of my back whilst his other one tucked some of my baby hair behind my ear.

With his hand now cupping my face, he lovingly stroked my cheeks with his soft thumb. "I know you want to take this slow, but I really want you, *need* you, and I'm not sure how much longer I can control myself." My eyes widened at hearing his admission and I felt my heart rate pick up. His soft touch contradicting the desperation in his voice. I didn't say anything, I simply nodded. I wanted and needed him too.

We just stood there, staring at one another, not saying another word as we let our eyes do all the talking as they mirrored our feelings. I could see the hunger, the want, desire and need that raged within his body, a silent, internal battle as he continued to keep himself restrained. If I was being honest, I felt the exact same towards him. We were rudely pulled out of our staring contest by the honking of the taxi's horn.

We walked over and Leon held the door open for me as I got in. He gently closed the door and walked over to the other side and slid in next to me.

The atmosphere the entire ride home was intense. We barely

spoke a word to one another, but we didn't need words when our actions told each other enough about where our minds lay.

I turned my head to look at him. He was looking out of the window. The lights of oncoming cars as we drove passed them like a running conveyor belt in his eyes.

I inched my hand slowly towards his as I turned to look away out of my own window. My pinkie found his hand first and I felt his finger twitch at the sudden, unexpected touch. I delicately traced the back of his hand with my fingers, drawing little random patterns. I turned back to look at him and found him watching my fingers tickle the tanned skin of his hand. He gazed up and looked me square in the eyes. His beautiful orbs were overflowing with longing.

My fingers fell on the soft backseat of the taxi as he removed his hand from under mine and placed it on my thigh. I felt a fire ignite inside of me, as my entire body melted to his touch. He slowly trailed up my thigh until he reached the waistband of my jeans. Before I could even react, he'd slithered his hand underneath and cupped my sensitive area over-top my lace underwear.

I was incredibly wet for him at this point and I knew he had felt it when he sucked in a breath.

He started caressing me over the thin fabric of my underwear. I found myself subconsciously opening my legs wider for him in invitation and leaned my head back against the headrest. I had to bite on the insides of my cheeks to suppress my moans that were threatening to come out.

I looked to the interior mirror to make sure that the taxi driver hadn't seen what we were up to, and wasn't watching. His eyes were firmly focused on the road.

"You enjoying being teased, sweetheart?" Leon's voice was

low and husky as he whispered into my ear, blowing his light hot breath down my neck. I shivered at the sensation and pulled my bottom lip between my teeth with my tongue. He knew just how that term of endearment made me react and he was enjoying every minute of making me squirm.

Leon had just slipped his fingers underneath the thin fabric of my underwear, his skin brushing my folds, when the taxi driver slammed on the breaks, signaling that we had reached our destination. Leon pulled his hand out from my jeans and looked at me with a salacious look on his face.

After giving the taxi driver the fare, Leon took my hand and pulled me out of the taxi. Once out, I followed him up to his steps, my hand interlocked with his. We'd barely even got through the door and our lips were devouring each other.

We kicked our shoes off, and I lifted my leg up, hooking it around his waist. He gripped me by the underside of my thighs before hoisting me up, his hands sliding to grip my butt firmly. I wrapped my legs tightly around his waist and I could feel his hardness rub against me. I let out a moan, and my hips started rocking back and forth on their own, wanting to feel more of him. I could feel Leon smile against my lips, and he carried me into the bedroom, his lips never leaving mine.

He kicked the door shut behind us and threw me onto his bed. I took this moment to catch my breath. We were both panting as we looked at each other, catching our breaths like this was the only chance we'd get.

I felt the bed dent as he crawled on top of me, placing a hand either side of my head, caging me in. I couldn't stand the anticipation anymore. With one hand on the back of his head and the other scrunching his shirt, I pulled his lips to mine. The sudden impact of our lips merging once again sent goose bumps

75

all over my body. I was ravenous for him. I needed more of him.

I worked fast as I undid the buttons of his shirt. He leaned back up onto his knees and took his shirt off before tossing it to the floor. My eyes were all over him, not really knowing where to look first. His torso was incredibly defined, his chest smooth but just below his belly button, hair crept up from underneath his waistband, a teaser of what to expect further down. I found my hand reaching forward to graze my fingers along his soft, supple skin, outlining the shape of his muscles.

"You like what you see babe?" He had a confident smirk on his lips and his eyes were lit with an intensity that burned through my core.

"Oh I do, I really do." All thoughts of taking whatever this was slow left my brain. I didn't want to hold out anymore. I just wanted him.

I sat up on my knees to meet him. I lifted my top over my head and lassoed it to the floor. His eyes widened as he looked down at my bare chest, taking in the view before him. There was a deep hunger burning in his eyes as his lips dived for mine and started devouring me. His tongue darted into my mouth, tasting every inch of me. I bit his lower lip and tugged it slightly and was pleasantly rewarded with a groan from him.

I started unbuttoning Leon's jeans in a frenzy. He kicked them off along with his boxers and pushed me back down so I was laying on my back. The bed creaked slightly as he moved so that he was over me. He kissed me softly on the lips and began to kiss along my jaw, down my neck and onto my breasts, whilst his fingers tickled along my collarbone and down my arm.

"Fuck baby." He muttered. Gently, he started rubbing his thumb over one of my nipples, inciting a jolt to zip straight through me, whilst simultaneously his mouth had clamped over the other one, his tongue mimicking the motion of his thumb. I arched my back at his touch and let out a loud moan.

I was becoming increasingly impatient for him to satisfy me in the way I really wanted him to. I needed to feel him inside me.

He switched sides and gave the other nipple as much attention with his mouth as he had given the other, sucking, licking and gently biting. His big hand tenderly gave my breast a squeeze before he rolled my nipple between his index finger and thumb.

With a pop, he let go and began kissing down my stomach. His hands found the waistband of my jeans and he tugged them down. I lifted my hips so he could easily peel the jeans from my body. He flung them carelessly to the floor, returning his attention to my stomach.

He placed open mouthed kisses on my slightly curved abdomen and navigated his way down to the inside of my thighs. He hovered there for a few moments, sucking my delicate skin.

I gasped at the sensation. It was painful, but it was a good kind of pain. I looked down and found my lacy thong in between his teeth before pulling them off. He discarded them to the side and looked hungrily at me. He licked his lips and I felt his fingers stroke the entrance of my core.

"Shit, you're so fucking wet for me." A shudder rippled through my body as he slid a thick finger inside of me. After a few pumps, his thumb began massaging my clit and he added another finger. His lips found mine, suppressing my moans.

"Oh, Leon..." I breathed his name in between kisses.

He pulled his face away from me and smiled tenderly at me. "I love when you say my name like that. It's so sexy." He took his fingers out of me and sucked them clean of my juices.

"Just fuck me already... please." I pleaded with him. I couldn't hold out anymore, I needed him to quell this burning desire that was consuming me. He gave me a small smile and kissed me on the cheek. He leaned over to his bedside table and took out a silver foil from the drawer. He tore it open with his teeth and rolled the rubber over his throbbing manhood. I hadn't been able to get a look at it before now and I found my breath caught in my throat. He was huge. I had never had one that big before. I took a big gulp and looked up at him.

He chuckled at me. "It's OK baby, I'll be gentle." I nodded in response and prepared to have my insides split in half. He used his knees to push my legs wider apart. Holding my wrists together above my head with one hand, he guided himself to my entrance before slowly sliding into me with his other. I gasped as I felt him stretch me. He stilled for a few seconds, letting me adjust to his size.

"Alright?" He had a look of concern on his face. If I wanted to stop this, he would be happy to. He respected me enough not to go any further unless I was ready. And boy was I ready.

I bit my lip and nodded. He placed his spare hand on my waist and slowly started to thrust the rest of the way into me. It had been a while since I'd been intimate with a man, but I knew for a fact it had never felt this good before.

I tilted my hips up slightly and he held my legs up, spreading them even wider to allow him to go deeper into me. He picked up the pace, making the sound of our skin slapping together even louder.

"Ava... You feel so good... fuck!"

I could feel my brain begin to fog. All I could focus on was the feel of Leon gliding in and out of me. Holding my legs by the underneath of my thighs, he pinned my knees by my head, and I made a silent thanks to God for gifting me with flexibility. He pulled out of me so that just his tip was in, and with a grunt, rammed back into me all the way down to the hilt, this new angle allowing me to take every inch of him. It took the breath out of me and I let out a whimper. He continued like this, slow and tortuous, hitting the spot every time.

"Faster. Fuck me faster." I moaned breathlessly. I could feel my core tighten as I started to reach my climax. Leon pounded into me even harder and faster as my walls clenched around him. I screamed his name as I came, my legs shaking under his hands. He followed a second later and I felt him twinge inside of me. He rode out our highs as we both came crashing down.

He placed a kiss on the tip of my nose and pulled out.

"You're so beautiful when you come. I want to hear you scream my name like that more often." He discarded the condom before laying next to me and adjusted me so that I was cradled in the crook of his arm, my head on his shoulder.

I snuggled in closer to him, my fingers mindlessly drawing on his chest. I looked up into his face. He was propped up slightly on his pillows with his left arm behind his head. There were little droplets of sweat slowly dripping down his temple, and he had his eyes closed whilst focusing on getting his breathing back under control.

"Well, if you keep fucking me like that, you'll have me screaming it like a banshee like it's the only word I know." The alcohol had been pretty much fucked out of my system and I was feeling more sober by the minute, so I couldn't even blame the drink for my talking so crudely; the words simply fell out of my mouth before I even registered what I'd said. This man had me acting like a whole new person that I didn't know existed. I'd never acted or spoken this way with my past lovers. He had me acting like I was sex deprived.

Leon let out a low primal growl. "Is that a challenge? Because

I will have my way with you over and over until the sun comes up."

I cocked an eyebrow up at him and spoke in a sultry voice. "Oh? You think you can keep up with me?" A dark look flashed in his eyes and he licked his lips.

"Shall we put that to the test?" He was on top of me again, a cocky smirk playing on his lips. I glanced down and saw that Leon Junior was already standing to attention.

I flipped us over so that I was straddling him. I pinned his hands to either side of his head, interlocking my fingers with his. I leaned over and nibbled his ear. He hissed in response. Satisfied at his reaction, I pulled away and looked at him challengingly.

"Game on, big boy."

Chapter 11

Leon's POV:

As I woke up, I felt a heavy weight on my chest. I looked down and smiled at the sight I saw. Ava was laying on my chest, her arm laying protectively across my stomach. Her perfect mouth was open ever so slightly, letting a soft sleepy breath out as she exhaled. Laying here, with her in my arms, made me feel a level of content that I had never felt before.

I kissed the top of her head gently and slowly slipped out of bed, trying not to disturb her. She made a little sleepy groan and rolled onto her stomach with one arm under her head, the other stretched out slightly from her side. Her hair had fallen over her face, so I brushed it out of the way.

I made my way quietly to the bathroom, taking one last look at my sleeping beauty before closing the door.

Standing in front of the mirror above the sink, I looked at the light stubble that had grown on my face overnight. I lathered on some shaving foam and gracefully glided my razor along my skin. Once I was satisfied with my handiwork, I turned the shower on before jumping into it, not bothering to let the water get warm first. Whilst scrubbing my body, I couldn't help but let my mind wander to last night's activities.

I hadn't expected her to start the teasing back at the bar, but I was glad that she did. It let me know that she was ready to take things further. What surprised me even more, was how good she was in bed. She had incredible stamina and was able to keep up with me. We were at it until the early hours of the morning. If it wasn't for the fact that I had work this morning, we probably could have kept going until we saw the first light of day.

I thought back to the way she rode me so freely, my hands gripping her waist, but giving her full control. She had been a little apprehensive at first when she saw the size of me, but once she was comfortable, she took me balls deep. Not many women had been able to take the full length of me, and many had shied away from it, but Ava literally took the bull by the horns and gave herself up to me. And I found that to be such a massive turn on.

She was confident in what she was doing, and she wasn't afraid to use her voice. It didn't bother her that she could have potentially kept my neighbours on the other side of me awake.

I couldn't help but think about where this now left us. What sort of label do we put on it? Were we a couple now? Friends with benefits? Neighbours with benefits? I let out a frustrated sigh. This would have to be something to discuss with Ava later.

I stepped out of the shower and wrapped a towel around my midsection. I took another smaller towel and rubbed it over my hair to dry it. As I exited the bathroom, I was surprised to see Ava wide awake.

She had put on one of my t-shirts as well as last night's underwear. Seeing her in one of my t-shirts filled me with a warm wave of joy and happiness . She was laid with her head in the middle of the bed, her feet leaning up against the headboard, crossed at her ankles. She seemed engrossed in whatever she was looking at on her phone. She hadn't even heard me re-enter the room.

"Good morning beautiful, you're up early." I walked over and placed a kiss on her forehead.

She looked up at me with a smile that reached her eyes. God, she was gorgeous. "Hey you! Yeah, I figured I'd get an early run in before I go check in on Ffion. She's going to wake up with the worst hangover of her life." I loved how thoughtful and caring she was towards her friends. The entire time I'd known Ava, she hadn't ever been selfish. She rarely ever spoke about herself, and she only ever had nice things to say about others.

"That's a good idea. I've got to leave for work soon so you'll have to let yourself out, but you can stay as long as you want." I was in my wardrobe, putting on my work attire. I had settled on a lilac long sleeved shirt, a dark purple tie, and black tight-fitting trousers.

"That's fine with me." She responded, as she walked towards me. She wrapped her arms around my waist and pressed her face against my back. I turned to face her and gently lifted her chin up. I planted a soft kiss on her lips, lingering for a few seconds before pulling away. I tucked some of her hair behind her ear and stroked the back of her head.

She looked up at me adoringly. Her eyes were a mesmerising flood of blue that should've come across as cold, but instead managed to warm the hearts of those who looked into them.

Now that she was stood up, I could really see how big my t-shirt was on her. It stopped just under her butt. The neck was so big that it sat to one side, exposing the smooth delicate skin of her shoulder.

I traced my finger along her exposed collarbone. "I have something for you." She cocked her head to the side slightly and furrowed her brows at me as I let go of her and walked into the living room, heading towards the front door. I chuckled at the sound of Ava's bare feet pitter-pattering after me.

On the wall next to my door was a hook, and dangling from that was a key. I unhooked the key and spun around. Ava had made herself at home on my sofa. She'd sat herself in the corner and laid her shapely legs across the seats.

"Close your eyes and hold your hand out." With a curious expression, she did as I instructed. I placed the cool metal in her hand and when she opened her eyes, her head shot up at me. Her eyes were wide, and she was struggling to contain her smile.

"A key for your place? Are you sure? Don't you think it's a bit soon?"

I chortled at her. Ever the realist. "Well, when you said about getting another key cut, I got an extra one to give to you, in case I somehow managed to lock both keys in the apartment. I just haven't had the opportunity to give it to you."

She let the smile break onto her face, and she jumped off the sofa into my arms, kissing me all over my face. "You're so sweet! Thank you, I'll be sure to look after it." I kissed her on her lips as I placed her back down. She was so easy to please. It seemed to be the little gestures that made her the happiest. It was good to know.

"Good. Now, I need to leave for work. Like I said, take as long as you need in here. Help yourself to whatever you want." She tiptoed to give me a kiss on the lips before she started to walk back to the bedroom.

"OK, I'll see you later then. Have a good day at work." I

watched as her perfect round arse sashayed away from me. She stretched her arms up above her head, one hand holding the wrist of her other arm. This small movement caused the t-shirt to ride up, exposing the soft curves of the bottom of her backside. I felt my dick throb in my pants and let out a moan. She looked back at me over her shoulder, a cheeky smile on her lips, knowing just exactly what that motion would do to me.

I picked up my coat that I had lazily placed on the back of the sofa and picked up my briefcase that was by the door. With a final "see you later", I closed the door behind me and made my way to the office with an extra spring in my step.

* * *

Ava's POV:

I only stayed half an hour in Leon's place. Even though he had given me permission to help myself, I didn't want to invade his privacy too much. I spent the half hour mostly snuggled in his bed scrolling through my socials. His sheets smelt of him, and it relaxed and calmed me.

I couldn't be bothered to get dressed into last night's clothes, so I found a pair of his joggers and put them on. They were massive on me, so I had to roll them up a few times at the waistband. I took a selfie in the mirror of myself in his clothes and sent it to Leon. I had noticed his eyes had lit up when he saw that I was wearing his t-shirt, I saw how happy it made him.

Living next door came with many benefits, the first one being that I wouldn't have to do the classic walk of shame. I looked at the time on my phone and saw that it was eight a.m. I knew Fi would still be in a comatose state for at least another two hours, so I had enough time to shower, have a quick breakfast and then have my morning run take me to her house.

My shower was a quick one, I didn't have time to faff. I threw on some sportswear and made my way to the kitchen. I made myself some avocado on whole-grain toast, and poured some orange juice. I was surprised at how good I felt this morning, considering how much I'd had to drink last night and how little sleep I got. I suppose good sex (and lots of it) was a good way to sober up.

I'd just washed my plate and glass up when my phone pinged. My hands busy drying the plate, I glanced over at my phone on the counter, the notification lighting up the lock screen.

L: Fuck, you look so sexy in my clothes. I never asked, but how are you feeling after last night?

I couldn't help the smile that was on my face. Last night had been amazing. I didn't realise I was able to come as many times as I did in one night. I was also impressed with myself that I could keep up with Leon. Once I had gotten used to his size, I was able to take him fully and really enjoy myself. But that came with a slight downside.

A: Well then, I'll be sure to wear them more for you. I'm a bit sore so will have to rest up for a day or two, but aside from that, I feel incredibly refreshed.

It was true. Working out and going for runs helped me de-stress, but I had never felt as stress free and chilled than I do now. Wyatt had never been able to satisfy me the way Leon had. And in all honesty, I don't think anyone I'd ever been with had. Leon was on a whole other level.

I tucked my phone in my pocket and took off for my run to

Ffion's flat.

* * *

I had a spare key to Ffion's place, so I was able to let myself in. As expected, Fi was still in a deep sleep. I laughed to myself at the sight. Half of the duvet covered her body, and her head and the right side of her body was hanging off of the edge of the bed, still dressed in last night's attire, minus her shoes. I was impressed she hadn't slid onto the floor.

I snapped a picture of the scene before me and saved it before sending it to Everett, and then went into the kitchen and filled a glass with cold water. I had learned from previous experience that this was the only way to wake her from an alcohol induced coma.

I poured the water onto her face and Fi woke suddenly, spluttering and flapping her arms so fiercely that she slid the short distance out of her bed.

"Good morning sleeping beauty!" I laughed. She shot me a look that told me she would love nothing more than to put me six feet under.

"What the fuck A! It's too early for this bullshit." She crawled back into bed and pulled the sheets over her head.

"Uh, no, I don't think so! It's quarter past ten. You are getting up right now. Or I will make you do double the reps of everything during your workout."

That was enough to stir a reaction out of her. She slammed the sheets down under her chin, daring me with her eyes. "You wouldn't." Did she not know me at all?

87

I put my hands on my hips and gave her my most serious look. "Wanna bet? Because I will, and you know I will. So come on. Up. Now". She let out a groan and grudgingly dragged herself up. From behind, I placed my hands on her shoulders and directed her to the bathroom.

"Have a shower and get that god-awful smell of booze off you, and I'll make you a breakfast that'll soak up any left-over alcohol."

"You may be the devil incarnate, but you really do look after me. Thank you." She had a smile on her lips letting me know I was forgiven for almost drowning her.

"You're welcome, now go!" She blew me a kiss before disappearing and shutting the door behind her.

Twenty minutes later, Fi emerged from the bathroom looking like a new woman. She had got dressed into a matching gym set and seated herself down at her breakfast bar. I pushed her a bowl of porridge with a mix of fruits in it and placed a glass of ice-cold water in front of her.

A look of disappointment flashed across her face. "Not the breakfast I was expecting in all honesty. I was looking forward to a greasy fry up but thank you for making this for me."

I shook my head at her with an amused smile. "Fi, you know I would love to have made that for you, but it'll sit too heavy on your stomach when we start working out. That was a lesson we learned the hard way."

She pointed her spoon at me. "And that's why you're the personal trainer and I'm not." I chuckled to myself and sat down next to her.

"Do you remember much from last night?" She shook her head and swallowed her mouthful.

"I remember that I ended up dancing on top of the bar with you to that song from '*Coyote Ugly*', and some of the other women joined us. But after that, I haven't a clue. Oh, I remember being carried by Everett and then him tucking me in bed." I was relieved that she was able to remember who had brought her home, and I was glad Everett had taken great care of her.

Her porridge-full spoon hovered by her mouth as she asked, "What about you? What happened to you?" before shoveling the lot in her mouth.

"Me and Leon ended up back at his and pretty much fucked all night." Fi choked on her porridge and I laughed as I slapped her on the back.

"Jesus Christ, go on girl!" She patted my back, "I'm proud of you."

"You know what they say, go hard or go home, and we went *hard*." Fi rewarded me with a high-five before I continued on, "That's not all. He gave me a key to his apartment; said it was in case of an emergency." I couldn't help it but I felt a cheesy grin on my face.

"Bloody hell, the man moves fast, you'll be telling me you're getting married next. But I'm happy for you. I can see how much you both love each other." Now it was my time to choke, except I choked on air.

"Love? Oh no, it's way too soon to be throwing that '*L*' word around. We haven't even discussed what we are yet. We're just two grown adults getting our needs met." Fi let out an unconvinced "uh huh" and continued eating her breakfast.

13

Chapter 12

Ava's POV:

Ava's POV:

"Are you... trying to send me... to an early grave?" Ffion breathed in between her pants, hands on her knees as she leaned on them. I had worked Fi hard. I don't think I've ever seen her sweat this much. She wiped her forehead with the back of her hand.

"No, not at all. Why, did you want me to?" I was simply making her sweat out whatever booze was still settled in her system. She only had herself to blame. She had drunk so much last night. I had to hand it to her though, she knew how to handle her drink. As far as I was aware, she hadn't spewed at all last night.

She responded to me with a middle finger before asking, "Have you got any clients today after me? Fancy grabbing a coffee?" Such a silly question. She knows I will never turn down the offer of a coffee. We could be in the middle of an apocalypse and I'd still make a pitstop for coffee.

I shook my head. "No, just you today. I'll need to head back to mine and get changed, then I'll meet you there?"

"Sounds good to me. I'm going to give Everett a call anyway, let him know that I'm alive and well." She walked out of the room as I cleared away the equipment. Not five minutes later and I heard Fi yell at me "AVA YOU BITCH! You're so dead!" I laughed. Everett must've forwarded her the picture I took of her.

I decided to take that as my cue to hastily leave while I still had my legs. "Bye Fi, see you at the Hub, I love you!" The last word dragged out as I sprinted out of her flat. I closed the door on her just as I heard her trying to stop me,

"Oh no you don't! Hey, get back here!" I giggled at her empty words and began to jog home.

* * *

Ffion and I reconvened at the Hub. The café was a little on the quiet side today, with only three other tables being occupied. I lifted my chin in acknowledgment to Sam who was at the till and made my way over to make my order. Everyone who worked here knew who I was. I was in here too often for them not to. Sam smiled back at me and got to work on my order.

Sam was a good-looking lad with sandy floppy hair and deep blue eyes. He was a few years younger than me and was forever flirting with me. I didn't know if he had a crush on me, or if he was just trying to shoot his shot, but despite me turning his advantages down, he never let up. It was quite admirable, really.

"You're looking extra jovial today Ava, finally got some did you?" He shot me a cheeky wink and had a suggestive smirk on his face as I placed the money in his hand.

"I got more than some, that's for sure." I replied, equally as suggestive, returning his wink. All teasing had left his face and was replaced with a look of surprise. The thing with Sam was, bless his heart, he couldn't take when I was direct with him, he was never too sure how to take it. I could give as good as I could get.

His face changed as he shrugged his shoulders. He pouted his lip out slightly and faked looking sad. "Well, there goes my opportunity." With a chuckle, I thanked him for my drink and made my way to my seat.

Fi looked at me as I walked over to our usual spot, her face settled with feigned annoyance. "I'm so getting you back for that picture you know." I stuck my tongue out at her as I slid into my seat. I'd like to see her try.

I took a long sip of my coffee and closed my eyes, savouring the delightful taste that danced along my taste buds. There was a perfect blend of sweetness from the added sugar and the natural bitter of the coffee itself. With a relieved sigh, I sank into the comfort of my seat.

I opened my eyes once the burn from the warm liquid as it slid down my throat had dissipated and found Fi watching me with a glint in her eye, waiting to ask me whatever was on her mind. I rolled my eyes at her. "Go on then, let's hear it."

A smile broke out onto her face and she began asking me about my night with Leon. Obviously, I kept it as PG as possible. Despite the Hub being quiet today, I didn't want the whole cafe to know about my night of passion. Whenever I told her something juicy, she'd squeal in excitement and bounce in her seat. Back when I had been with Wyatt, I had told her some things about our sex life, but it had never been like this. Probably due to the fact that she didn't like him and our sex life was about as vanilla as it could get.

"So where does this leave you two then? Because there's no way you can just be friendly neighbours now." She was right, our relationship had changed but I wasn't sure myself what to. Did we really need to put a label on it just yet?

"I mean, I suppose there's no hurry, but I know if it was me, I'd want to know where I stood." She shrugged her shoulders and took a swig of her coffee. I knew I wanted to know where I stood with him, but at the same time, I was content with just having fun. After all, she was the one that had suggested it not too long ago.

"I'm happy just having fun for now. I don't want to commit only to end up hurt again." In this day and age, anything could happen. I mean, I never would have thought Wyatt would've gone behind my back with Felicity, my supposed best friend at the time, yet that's exactly what had happened.

Fi nodded with an understanding look on her face. She had been there for me when things blew up with Wyatt. I had worked myself so hard that I ended up in hospital. I would work out and run anytime I felt sad or stressed, and that had caused me to overexert. I lost a lot of weight from lack of eating and had become severely dehydrated. With Fi's support, I was able to put the weight back on and control my running and working out habits. That did prove to be difficult, considering the nature of my job. I had to cut down how many clients I took on a day and how often I worked with them in a week to give me time to rest. Thankfully, they were all understanding and were more than happy to lose a few hours with me a week until I had recovered.

"I get it, but you can't live you life walking on eggshells and scared of commitment because of that wank stain. You deserve to be find someone who respects you. You deserve to be happy,

93

Ava." I've said it to her before, and I'll say it again: Ffion should have her own Agony Aunts column. I knew I couldn't keep being scared of love and finding someone worthy, but I couldn't help it. And the irony wasn't lost on me that I had spent these last however many years teaching women how to appreciate and realise their self-worth when I wasn't doing it to myself.

"Anyway," I waved my hand as I changed the subject I wanted to get off of the topic of me and Leon. We hadn't spoken about her situation in a while, "how's things with Everett? I don't think I've ever seen you this happy." Her eyes lit up at the mention of Everett's name and we fell into a long conversation with her gushing over him.

* * *

Leon's POV:

Compared to the previous day, today was miles better. My mind was clear and free from doubts about what the day would bring. I arrived in my office ready to take on the day head on. The atmosphere in my office was of brightness and relaxation, one I had worked hard to create to help my patients to open up and talk to me.

Before I knew it, it was five in the afternoon. I was looking forward to going home and maybe seeing Ava again. As I was clearing my desk, there was a light tap on my door. Without looking up, I called for the mystery knocker to come in.

I heard heels click-clacking towards me before Stacey's light voice rang through my ears. "Just to let you know Mr. Myers that I'm now getting ready to leave."

"No worries." I liked to keep any conversation with Stacey to a bare minimum, otherwise I'm liable to giving her the wrong impression.

"You seem in a good mood today, a lot of the patients left looking so much lighter than usual." She stepped further into my office, clearly ignoring the hint. It's crazy the impact one person can have. Ava had affected me. I was on cloud nine today and it had caused a domino effect. She really was special, and she didn't even realise how incredible she was.

"That's good to hear Stacey. Thanks for today, I'll see you in the morning." I looked up and found she was standing next to me, her silhouette suffocating the light over the reports I was working on. I gave her a smile to let her know she was dismissed and carried on filing my reports. I wasn't going to tell her about why I was in a better mood. It was none of her business.

But she didn't move. Instead, she stepped closer and lightly trailed her fingers up my arm. I snapped my face down to look at her. Oh, hell no, this was not happening.

"You really are something you know. I admire how you want to help these kids." She pushed me away from the desk, the chair rolling me the distance and she perched herself on the edge of my desk before pulling my chair back to be as close to her as possible. She placed her heel clad feet on my chair, a foot either side on my thighs, trapping me between her fake-tanned legs.

I don't know where she got the impression that I had invited her over here. I had to try to put a stop to this. And quickly.

"Look, Stace-" She put a finger to my lips, preventing me from stopping whatever was going on.

She leaned back on her hands and pulled the pens out of her

hair, letting her hair tumble over her shoulders. "I'm not stupid. I can tell there's someone in your life that's influenced this change in you. But I can't help but feel a bit envious. You've never given me a second look. Why? What don't you like about me?" I was speechless. Yes, Stacey was incredible. She had big boobs, and a backside to match. She was pleasing to look at if you liked that sort of thing. She had a heart shaped face that had freckles splattered across her nose and cheeks. Her eyes were a delightful deep shade of dark chocolate.

When she first started working here, a few of the colleagues in my building had vocalised their fantasies about bending her over their desk, but there was something about her that just didn't do it for me. Probably the fact she was quite fake. Her lips were unnaturally big due to lip filler and her eyes were decorated with thick false eyelashes that tickled her eyebrows. It wouldn't surprise me if her boobs were fake too. Under all that, she probably had been a natural, beautiful young lady.

Suddenly, I felt her feet behind my head, and she jerked me towards her. The sharpness of the movement made me put my hands out, only for them to land on her thighs, the skin on skin causing a soft slap sound. I found myself face to face with her naked, glistening lady parts.

"Take me. Right here. Right now. There's no one to stop us." I gulped. It was tempting. Oh, so tempting. But even if I wanted to, Ava had emptied me of all my juice. There was no gas left in the tank.

"I can't Stacey. You're my secretary. It would be wrong of me to take advantage of my position like that." Plus, I could get into a lot of trouble if my higher ups found out. She put a hand on top of mine and slowly dragged it north along her thigh, heading to her dripping wet center. She was breathing heavily, and to be honest, I was starting to get hard.

I felt her dampness on my fingers. "Can't you feel how wet I am? Because of you? Just touch me. That'll be enough." She fluttered eyelashes at me and bit her lower lip. "I bet you I'll be better than whoever you've had in your bed recently."

Before I could say no, she thrust her hip forward and I felt the tip of my finger enter her. At this point, my mind wasn't even thinking straight. I slowly started pumping my index finger into her with her hand supervising the movement and watched as she threw her head back and let out a small gasp. Picking up my speed as her hand dropped to grip the edge of the wooden workspace underneath her, I added another finger as I used my spare hand to pull her dress up over her hips. I buried my head and started tickling her clit with my tongue. Her body shuddered under my touch as she cursed under her breath.

Soon enough, I felt her tighten around my fingers as she came to her climax, and she moaned my name as she came. It didn't sound right though. It didn't bring me as much pleasure as it did when Ava had said my name. And that's when I came to my senses.

I pulled my fingers sharply out of her and wiped them with a tissue from the box on my table. How could I be so stupid? I'd just spent the most amazing night of my life to date with Ava, only to let this siren compel me. Ava cannot find out. It would ruin us before we'd even begun.

Stacey had started to say some crap about how good I was with my fingers, but I cut her off.

"Get out of my office. Now. This will never happen again. You hear me?" My tone was cold and icy, just as I had intended it to be.

She looked at me like an abandoned puppy, tears brimming in

97

her eyes. "But-"

"No buts. Get out. Don't ever try to pull a stunt like that with me again, because I won't give in next time." She hopped off of my desk and pulled her dress down before turning away and walked out of my office, her tail between her legs.

And in the moment, I decided that I ought to look for a new secretary.

14

Chapter 13

<u>Leon's POV:</u>

It had been two weeks since that dumb mistake with Stacey and I hadn't breathed a word to anyone about it. I tried not to act indifferent towards Ava, but the guilt was eating away at me on the inside and couldn't help but be a little off with her. Naturally, she had asked me what was wrong, but I brushed it off with a comment about work. She didn't push me for an explanation, and I felt a little bad that I hadn't told her the full truth.

It was Thursday evening and me, Ava, Ffion and Ev were at Ava's place. The past couple of weeks had been like this. We'd all hang out together, eating, drinking and chatting. Today, we had the football on. Ffion didn't care for the match, but I was surprised at Ava. It was last Tuesday when I discovered her love of the sport and that she was a Manchester United supporter. We had been cuddling on my sofa flicking through the channels when she saw there was a match on and she had shouted at me to put it on, despite the fact that we had missed the first twenty minutes of the game. This little information about her felt like it was quite the bonus - I had found someone who enjoyed the sport as much as I did, someone who understood the game and its rules, so we could have an intelligent conversation about our mutual love of the sport. Plus, there wouldn't be much chance of her complaining if I wanted to watch a game in the future.

It was another Man United game, and tonight they were playing Chelsea. Since my team wasn't playing, I was supporting Man United with my girl, whilst Ev was supporting his team Chelsea. Ava was sporting her Manchester United nineteen/twenty home shirt and she looked good in it. I wanted to tell her exactly that, but I knew better than to interrupt her while the game was on. This was serious business.

"Come on, what are you doing?! PASS THE FUCKING BALL!" I turned my head to look at Ava and she was shaking her head at the TV. It was amusing to me seeing how into the games she gets. I chuckled at her outburst and put my hand on her thigh, only for it to slide off as she jumped up, pointing at the screen. One of Man United's players had received a dirty tackle from one of Chelsea's defenders, to which the referee had reacted with a yellow card, not even bothering to check the VAR.

"You can't be serious? That was a red! This ref's shit, doesn't know what the fuck he's doing." Ev was staring wide eyed and open mouthed at Ava, a perfect mix of amusement, shock and confusion. This was Ev's first time watching a game with Ava and experiencing football mad Ava. Ffion on the other hand, clearly used to this side of Ava, simply rolled her eyes and shook her head, returning her attention to whatever game she was playing on her phone.

Snapping out of his shocked daze, Ev spoke up.

"Nah, was nothing wrong with that tackle." I hadn't pre-warned Ev about what he may experience watching this game with Ava, and so he had no idea the dangerous line he was toeing. She was now slouched in her seat next to me with her arms crossed against her chest, with a serious case of resting bitch face settling into her features.

Ava looked over at Ev and shot him daggers. "You would say that. Your precious Rudiger should've been red carded." Ev just chuckled and muttered "If you say so," both of their attentions turned back to the TV. The game ended two-one to Manchester United, which meant that Ava was in a very good mood, and that usually meant I was in for a good time tonight, and I was very much looking forward to Ffion and Ev going home.

We were just chatting amongst ourselves when Ev decided to ask me about work. "So, Leon. Have you managed to find a new secretary yet?" After what had happened, I decided that it would be best if I let Stacey go. She was shocked when I told her, but she wasn't completely surprised. She must've known that there was no way on God's green Earth that I was letting her keep her job here with me. Just being around her made my skin crawl at the memory of what I so stupidly and blindly did, the shame and guilt a heavy burden that writhed inside me whenever I laid eyes on her. I had been kind enough to have another job set up for her at one of our other branches in the city, but she was to stay until we had found her replacement.

I sighed and ran my hand through my hair. "No, not yet. All the people who've applied either haven't had any experience or I just genuinely didn't like them. I'm not having a secretary who I can't relate to or rely on." I had been very picky and meticulous with what I was looking for in my next secretary. It was important to me that I had a secretary where I could have a relationship with them where they knew how I worked and could do jobs that needed doing without having to be asked. Also, one that understood boundaries and wouldn't dare to try it on with me, a skill-set that Stacey very clearly lacked. I had told Ava that the reason I had been off with her was because of the secretary at work. I had told her I was letting her go because of a conflict of interest and her response had been "So basically, she fancies you, but you aren't interested?" She didn't realise how close to the truth that was.

Ava looked up at me, her eyes bright with realisation. "Why didn't you say you were still looking for someone? We know the perfect person!" She had this bright smile on her face, whilst I had a confused frown on mine. She looked over to Ffion and Ev, who were looking at her with an expression that matched the one currently occupying my face.

Ev's face was the first to change. He suddenly broke out into an excited smile. "Oh yeah, of course! Why didn't I think of that?" I was still confused. All eyes were now on Ffion, looking to her to explain, who after a few seconds, had a crimson colour creep up her neck, spreading onto her face until she was completely covered in the brilliant colour in shyness from all of our attention focused on her. She looked down at her hands in her lap and started playing with a piece of thread that was hanging off her top. She scratched at her head before letting out a deep sigh.

"Well, basically, my job's in jeopardy because of mine and Everett's relationship. As you know, his dad is my boss and so a number of my colleagues have complained about me being his secretary, saying I get preferential treatment." I knew that Ffion and Ev met at his dad's workplace, and that she worked for his dad, but I didn't realise what a hard time she was having there. It was perfect, with the added benefit that there would absolutely be no way that she would try anything with me.

"Would you like to come and be my secretary instead then? You can start as soon as you've got things sorted with your current boss." Her eyes rose quickly to mine, the redness starting to dissolve, the olive tan of her skin resurfacing. Her eyes were excited, but there was a hint of uncertainty in them.

"Are you sure? You really think I'm capable of being your secretary?"

"Of course! You've got the experience, and you know me. Ev's told me how hard you work for his dad, so I know you'll be a perfect fit for me and the office." I wholeheartedly believed that too. Her and Ava were both similar with regards to the fact that they both were serious work demons.

She looked up into Ev's eyes, telepathically asking for his opinion and consent. He was smiling proudly at her, sending her an encouraging reply through his eyes. She nodded her head once and turned to look at me with the biggest smile on her face.

"I'll do it."

Ava jumped up and went to give Ffion a hug. "See, I told you everything would work out, babes!" There was my girl, being her wonderful, supportive self.

Ffion giggled "You did! And to think the answer was right under our noses the entire time." Ava came back over to me and gave me a kiss on the lips.

"Thank you, babe. Thank you for solving Fi's problem. It's been on her mind a lot lately and she's been worrying so much over it, she's been losing sleep." Now that she mentioned it, Fi has been a lot quieter lately, and she had faint dark circles shadowed under her eyes.

I looked over to Ffion who was now crying silently, the weight of her stress finally being lifted, as Ev stroked her hair, muttering encouraging words into her head, each sentence finished with a gentle kiss. Whilst I smiled at the loving interaction, the moment was somewhat bittersweet. Not only had I killed two birds with one stone, but I hadn't realised that Ffion had had things so bad at Evs dads office. Relief washed over her face, as her eyes found mine, a smile and a "thank you" mimed from her lips. I felt a blast of pride overwhelm me.

* * *

It was still relatively early, so we decided to put on a film. Ava picked the remote up from the table and handed it to Ev. "Everett, Leon, you choose the film. Me and Ffion will sort out snacks." I loved when she was bossy and authoritative. I watched her hips swagger away from my line of sight into the kitchen where she ducked under the kitchen isle and began hunting through the cupboards. Ffion followed her into the kitchen, leaving us two men to decide on a film. It was brave of them to leave such a huge decision to us – we were both useless at deciding films to watch. We heard the girls giggling and whispering in the kitchen.

We were still flicking through the options when the girls returned. They each had a bowl of popcorn and two bottles of beer. Ava placed herself in between the corner of the sofa and me and laid her smooth legs across my lap, balancing our bowl between us. She handed me my bottle and I kissed the top of her head. Ffion was in a similar position on the opposite end of the sofa, except her legs were tucked to the side, her head resting on Ev's shoulder. Seeing us all happy really was a wholesome feeling.

"So, what have you decided on watching?" Ava was looking up at me, a mischievous smirk fighting to appear on her face. She knew we wouldn't have come to a decision and no doubt was why she always made us choose. That way, there was no room for us to moan when they picked something. Clever. Our women were very clever.

"No, we haven't, there's just too much to choose from." Ev looked overwhelmed as his eyes flicked back and forth whilst he still looked through the films.

Ffion raised her hand and stroked his face lovingly. "It's OK baby, me and Ava will find something." The girls shared a knowing look, with a secret smile on their lips. This must've been what they were whispering about in the kitchen.

"Here, pass the remote, I'll put something good on." Ev reached over and placed the remote into Ava's waiting outstretched hand. With a grin she was attempting to hide behind with her lower lip tucked underneath her top teeth, she began typing in the search bar. Upon seeing what the girls had decided on, it was mine and Ev's turn to share a knowing look.

Jokes on them, little did they know High School Musical was our guilty pleasure.

Chapter 14

I stirred from my blissful sleep to find a peacefully sleeping Leon who had his head on my lower belly, hugging my waist. I smiled to myself and gently buried my hand in his hair and started to massage his head, feeling the soft movement of his hair as it tickled my palm.

My mind drifted back to last night. I was dumbstruck when I learned that both Leon and Everett loved High School Musical. Mine and Fi's plan to piss the boys off with our girlish behaviour had completely backfired. But it wasn't a complete disappointment. We had ended up watching all three of the films and sang and danced to our hearts content.

We'd barely got the door locked behind Everett and Fi when they left for the night, and me and Leon had been all over each other. I knew he had been itching to have his hands all over me the second I came out of my bedroom in my football shirt and shorts. He had come over to me with a dark look in his eyes, placed his hands on my waist, pulled me to him so that I could feel his growing hardness against my stomach and instructed lowly into my ear "You are not to take that off until we are alone.

Do you understand?" Sending a vibration of pleasure through me as I nodded my obedience.

I couldn't help but feel incredibly lucky to be surrounded by amazing people who brought so much love and joy to my life. I felt like everything was finally falling into place, and I was excited to see where things with Leon would go. I didn't stop the smile as a huge wave of contentment flooded my body.

I felt Leon move under my hand and I looked down to see he was gazing up at me, chin lightly leaning on my abdomen, a sleepy smile on his soft lips. He gave me a delicate peck on my stomach, making my insides feel funny. The light breaking in through the gaps of the blinds reflected in his beautiful yellow orbs, making them glisten with complacency.

"Good morning, my baby." He said, his voice thick with sleep, his eyes flinching against the brightness of the morning light.

"Hey, you." I smiled back at him. My hand hadn't stopped moving in his hair. The movement and feel of his fluffy hair under my hand was soothing and comforting, only adding to my feeling of fulfillment.

"You look very happy this morning. What's on your mind?" I removed my hand from his hair, noticing how hot he looked now I'd made his hair more of a mess than normal, and placed it on his face, stroking his cheek with my thumb.

"Just you. Us. Our little couple friendship group. The future." Leon moved so that he was positioned over top of me, as I shuffled down from my sitting-up position so that I was now laying underneath him, his hands either side of my head. I could see the love in his eyes as we looked into each other's gaze. Doing a semi press-up, he bent and gave me a lingering kiss on the lips.

"You want a future with me?" He had a big grin on his face.

We hadn't discussed our situation or put any labels on our relationship. I had thought long and hard the past month or so since being in my little bubble with Leon about what I wanted. I had come to the conclusion that I wanted him to be a permanent figure in my life, as more than just a friend, and certainly more than just a neighbour who I had the benefit of fucking every now and then.

I nodded at him. For some reason, I suddenly felt shy and I couldn't meet his eyes. Telling him how I felt suddenly felt like I was exposing myself a little too much. "I do. I don't want to just be someone you sleep with and spend time with anymore. I want to be permanent. I want to be the only one. I want to be yours. I... I think I'm ready for a label now."

His index finger was under my chin and he gently forced my head up to look at him. If I thought his grin couldn't get any bigger, I was sorely mistaken. His eyes were swimming with pure joy. "You have no idea how happy that makes me Ava. I would love nothing more than to give myself exclusively to you."

I wrapped an arm around his neck and brought his head down so that there was only a breath between us. With my spare hand, I trailed my fingers gracefully up his bare spine and was delighted when I felt Leon shudder from my touch.

"In that case, shall we seal the deal, boyfriend?" My voice came out quiet and husky. In response, Leon let out a growl and pounced hungrily on my lips. Our lips merged together like they were made for each other. Wanting to taste more of him, I took control and pushed my tongue into his mouth. He moaned in response and our tongues started fighting for dominance. I bit his lip and pulled it, asserting that I had won the lip battle.

I was rewarded with a deep throaty moan. "Fuck, you drive me crazy sweetheart."

I flipped us over so that I was straddling him. Last night had been all about me, but now it was about him. Leon placed his hands on my backside as I leaned forward and took his ear lobe into my mouth. I suckled it gently before giving it a tug with my teeth, to which Leon reacted by squeezing both my arse cheeks before slapping one. I gasped at the impact but the stinging sensation it left only turned me on more.

I left soft kisses on his neck, lingering in the crook between his column and shoulder to give it a little suck, before I continued my escapade of affection down his chest until I reached the deep ridges of his abs. I took my time licking down the center, the entire time, Leon was cursing under his breath at my gentle, tormenting touch, and a hand gripping my hair, the other gripping his cock as he slowly pumped himself.

When I reached the end, I was greeted by his rock-hard manhood against my cheek who was stood to attention, ready and waiting for me. I tapped Leon's hand in command to let himself go, positioning myself in between his legs and began to caress his thick shaft. Leon shifted so that he was sitting up on his elbows and looked down at me.

He groaned and rolled his head back as I began to tickle his tip with my tongue, his grip on my hair getting tighter. I dragged my tongue down his length before bringing it back to the tip. Without any warning, I covered his head with my mouth and pushed as deep as I could take him. He hissed a curse and grabbed a fistful of the bed sheet underneath us.

My mouth followed my hand that had a firm grip on his length as I bobbed my head up and down, sucking and slurping as I went, alternating my speed with Leon matching my pace as he thrust himself into my mouth, itching for me to take more of him. A few times I went a little too deep and gagged, and every time Leon would make a sound of approval. His moans were like music to my ears and it brought me great satisfaction that I could make him weak like this.

"If you carry on like this I will literally explode." His words were backed up by the pulsating I felt in my mouth. I pulled my head back and his dick bounced out, slapping him on his stomach.

Leon leaned forwards and kissed me quickly, eager to get back to our little rendezvous. "Wait here. I'm going to get a condom from my jeans. When I come back, I want you on all fours." I nodded as I wiped saliva from the sides of my mouth with my thumb.

He stood up and left my bedroom and headed towards the front room where yesterday's discarded clothes were. I couldn't help but let my eyes rake down his naked body, stopping at the toned cheeks as he walked away from me.

Being the good girl I am, I positioned myself so I was on my knees and had leaned forward onto my elbows. I angled my backside as high as I could get it and it aimed at the door so that Leon would get a welcoming sight as he came back. Shortly, I heard him come in and he sucked in a sharp breath. I looked over my shoulder and saw him gripping his throbbing cock. There was a burning need in eyes as he zeroed in on my ready-and-waiting core.

"Fuck me, that's a beautiful sight." He stroked his manhood a couple of times before he rolled the condom on whilst he made his way to my waiting pussy. He placed a warm hand on my waist, licked his fingers on his other hand before fucking me with them.

"Sweetheart, you're dripping for me." He bent down and bit my backside, enticing a moan to come from me before he removed his mouth and sucked his fingers clean. I couldn't take the suspense anymore. I was itching to feel him inside of me. I placed my hand underneath me in search of the body part I longed for. Having successfully attained it, I wiggled myself back a little further until I could feel him against. He chuckled having seen my impatience and replaced my hand with his own, making sure it was well aligned. With his tip almost in my entrance, he placed his hand on the other side of my waist and slid himself into me all the way to his base. I pushed myself further backwards into him as I silently commanded that he start fucking me properly.

After feeling his hand spank me, he began pounding into me, and as good as it felt, it somehow wasn't enough. Greedy for more of him, I spread my legs a little wider and slid down so that my chest was flat on the bed, arms stretched out above my head. Leon cursed under his breath as he rammed into me deeper, feeling him all the way up in my belly button, resulting in me screaming his name.

I let out a gasp as he wrapped my hair around his hand and pulled my head back.

"Holy shit!" I breathed. He was hitting the spot in a constant rhythm and I could feel my climax build.

"Just like that... Leon... Don't stop." His fingers found my clit and he started rolling it between his fingertips. I pushed myself back further into him, taking him as deep as was possible, elevating my state of euphoria.

"Fuck, I love my name on your tongue." Leon groaned breathlessly. He pulled me up by my hair and placed his spare hand around my middle and leaned forward to kiss me before he shoved me back down, my head now pressed into the mattress, all whilst keeping his rhythm. I felt my walls clench and tighten around Leon as we came in unison, and I once again found his name on my tongue.

It was at the same time I heard my front door slam and a shrill voice call out to me.

Chapter 15

"Ava, sweetheart!"

My first thought was that both of those words sounded so wrong after Leon had just called me both of those whilst he fucked the life out of me. My second thought was, what's she doing here so early? She wasn't supposed to be here until this afternoon. Leon pulled out of me sharply, causing me to suck in a sharp breath.

"Who the fuck's that?" Leon had ripped the condom off of his now growing soft manhood and was headed towards my bathroom. Meanwhile, I was hastily getting dressed.

"I'll be out in a sec!" I yelled, letting her know that I had heard her so that she wouldn't come in here looking for me.

"That would be my mother showing up fashionably early." I was hopping around in my underwear by now, with one leg in a pair of light blue skinny jeans. She was never early. She was one of those people who would tell you they were on their way but in reality, was butt-naked in front of a mirror while still deciding what to wear. The motto she religiously lived by was "Better Late Than Never".

"That's today? That came around quick." Leon emerged from the bathroom and was rummaging through his overnight bag. It was a good thing that he didn't leave it in the front room. Ah... bollocks.

"Leon..." I had stopped getting dressed, my jeans one final jump from being pulled all the way up, as the daunting thought came to my mind.

"Yes, babe?" He was now wearing some running shorts and was pulling a white t-shirt over his head, completely oblivious to what we had left trailing throughout my apartment. I pointed towards the door.

"Our clothes are out there and I haven't told her about you yet." I heard the kettle boil and rolled my eyes internally to myself as my mother had begun to make herself at home.

I pulled a baby pink off-the-shoulder top on and quickly ran my hairbrush through my ragged hair before hurriedly pulling it up into a ponytail. I could not have her see my post-sex hair. In her eyes, I was probably still an innocent virgin and I planned to keep it that way until I gave her grandchildren. Maybe. I looked over to Leon who was now fully dressed and making the bed. This was not how I expected my mum to meet my boyfriend, but here we are.

"You ready to meet the mother of your girlfriend?" He walked over to me and pulled me into a loving hug. He placed a kiss on the top of my head before looking down and meeting my eyes.

"Girlfriend... I like the sound of that." He bent down and gave me a quick kiss. "But I suppose I don't have much of a choice." He chuckled as he gently swept some of my baby hairs behind my ear before moving to pick up his overnight bag. Taking his spare hand in mine, we headed out to the snake pit to meet my mum.

"Ava, baby!" My mum came rushing up to me and pulled me into a tight, warm embrace that forced me to let go of Leon's hand. I took advantage of this opportunity and signaled to Leon to pick up our strewn clothes that were littered in the living room.

"Hey Mama, did you have a safe journey?" My voice came out slightly pained as she was squeezing the breath out of me. My mum was a great hugger and I always felt safe in her arms. But when I hadn't seen her in so long, the first hug always nearly crushed me.

She let go of me and held me by my shoulders. "I did baby, thank you. And for the record, I've already seen the clothes, there's no point trying to hide them." She winked at me before turning to give a cocked eyebrow and knowing smile to Leon, who had stopped mid-bend with my bra hanging off of his fingers. I laughed. I should've known that she would've seen them, that woman doesn't miss anything.

"Who is this handsome young man, and why am I only now finding out about him?" She walked over to Leon, who now had an armful of our clothes. He placed them on the sofa and offered his hand out to my mum.

"I'm Leon, it's lovely to meet you." I just about melted into a puddle on the spot. Having Leon act so polite and respectful towards my mum made me happy. When Wyatt had met my mum, he wasn't so polite. Instead, he had flicked his head up at her like she was one of his buddies and said "Sup Ms. B, name's Wyatt." Even thinking about it now made me cringe just as much as it did back then.

Mum took his hand and shook it gently. She had a warm smile

on her face, and I felt a weight lift off my shoulders. I knew she would appreciate being addressed in such a respectable manner. She was a stickler for old fashioned formalities despite being relatively young herself. My mum had me when she was only sixteen and had raised me on her own, since my deadbeat dad had run away when she told him they were expecting. Apparently being a dad was not an image he wanted to uphold, but the risk of being one hadn't been enough to not wrap it when my mum had asked him to. I've never met my dad and it truly wouldn't bother me in the slightest if I never did. Me and my mum have come so far together. She was my mum and dad rolled into one, and she was all that I needed.

I turned my attention to Leon and watched as he sighed ever so slightly, and I could see relief wash over his eyes. I hadn't realised he was this worried about meeting my mum.

My mum must have noticed his relief too, as she placed her other hand on top of his, gently cradling his hand in hers. She spoke in a soft motherly tone, "The pleasures all mine Leon. Please, call me Julia." They let go of each other's hands as Leon nodded in acceptance with a small smile on his lips.

"Well then, Julia. As much as I would love to stay and get to know my girlfriend's mum better, I don't want to intrude on your long-awaited mother-daughter time." He spoke kindly and respectfully towards my mum. I appreciated that he felt in the way and wanted to give me and my mum time to catch up. He stuffed his clothes into his overnight bag as I made my way over to him.

I walked him to the door to see him out. I really didn't want him to leave, I wanted to be back in bed with him. But at the same time, I needed to spend some time with my mum – we were long overdue a catch up.

"Thank you babe. I'll text you later." I gave his hand a squeeze and he dropped his head giving me a sweet peck on the lips. He shot me a wink before he gave a wave to my mum who copied the motion to him. He then turned and began walking down my stairs.

The door had barely even shut and mum was hitting me with a hundred-and-one questions. I picked up the clothes Leon had left on the chair and carried them to the washing machine in the kitchen. Mum followed me and sat herself on a stool up at the kitchen island, her chin rested in her hand.

"Boyfriend hey? Ava and Leon, sitting in tree..." I playfully tapped her on the hand that was resting on the surface next to the cups of coffee she had prepared for us, cutting off her teasing singing. My mum had been on her own for many years and I ached for her to find someone. She always put me first, but it was time for her to find her own happiness.

"He makes me very happy, mum. I don't think I've ever felt this way about anyone before." It was true. Despite the minimal amount of time that I had known him for, I could feel myself falling for him and I was falling fast. It scared me to think about a future with him and to think about my feelings. I was scared to give him my heart, soul, and body only to be hurt again. But the biggest fear was telling him about my past. I didn't want him to think I was damaged goods.

I needed to change the subject. Sliding into the stool opposite her, I took the coffee cup into my hands, the heat nearly seering my skin, the lip of the cup hovering just before my lips.

"Anyway, when are you going to find yourself a hunky man to look after you? It's about time you got back in the saddle." My mum was beautiful. Due to her young age, many people assumed that we were sisters. Thankfully, most of my genetics came from her. Like me, she had blonde hair, but it was much shorter than mine, finishing just past her shoulders. Her eyes were a darker shade of blue than mine, resembling a polished sapphire. She's had several men try to approach her, but she never showed any interest in any of them and always turned them away.

My mum let out a sigh and shook her head gently at me. "This again? When a deserving man comes into my life, only then will I consider it. But for now, as long as I have you, I don't need anyone else." My mum's last relationship was with a guy called Kelvin. I really liked him and so did my mum, and if I was being honest, I think her love for him stopped her from pursuing anyone else. He was a couple of years older than my mum and I remember just how handsome he was. He had jet black curly hair and these incredibly piercing green eyes that held so much kindness in them. He was rather muscular, but you wouldn't know how shredded he was unless you saw him naked. He was a modest man and he did everything he could to make me and my mum happy.

He treated me like I was one of his own but without acting all dad-like. He knew the boundaries and not to push them. Him and my mum had been together for two years when they split and although I knew my mum was desperately heartbroken, she never showed me. Because I was the reason for their breakup.

Because of me and my act of selfishness, mum broke up with Kelvin so that she could focus solely on me. We had moved to a different town and Kelvin had refused to leave with us. He had a valid reason; his job was too important, and he wasn't able to transfer to where we were moving to. I felt guilty for being the cause for their breakup, and I still do even to this day.

I leaned across the kitchen island and took my mum's hands

in mine. "You deserve to be happy mama. You've put me first for so many years, it's now time for you to be selfish and find someone." She gave me a sympathetic half smile and brought one of my hands up to her lips, planting a soft kiss on the back of my hand.

"I love you baby girl."

"I love you too mama."

* * *

Julia's POV:

All I had to do was look into his eyes and I knew exactly who he was. Even if she didn't remember, there was no way I could forget whose eyes they belonged to. I had paid good money for therapy to help her forget that monster, but that didn't mean that I couldn't remember him.

My baby girl deserved the world. She'd been through some hardships that no one should ever have to experience, but she had come out the other end better and stronger. I was so incredibly proud of the young woman she had become.

The image of her in the bath has never left my mind, and some nights it haunts me, holding me hostage like some sleep paralysis demon trapping me awake. I don't think I'll ever forget the panic and desperation I felt in that moment. I thought she was gone forever, and my heart felt like it was being ripped from my chest.

The doctors had said that she had lost so much blood that they were in disbelief that she was still breathing. She was "one lucky girl" they had told me. I thanked the gods that she was going to be OK and for allowing my only child to stay here with me. I don't think I would have been able to live if she was to be taken from me.

I had no idea the severity of the bullying she was subjected to. I knew it had been happening, but she was so good at hiding how she felt, that I never picked up on how bad things really were. She had begged me not to talk to the school about it but even to this day, despite seeing the incredible woman she had flourished into, I wished that I had. Maybe then she wouldn't have tried to kill herself. My mind was racked with guilt, and so as I sat next to my precious girl in the hospital bed, holding her hand as tears silently dripped onto the white sheets that covered her, the machines beeping around me, telling me that she was alive, I promised that I would do everything I could to protect my dear, baby girl.

She made the decision to become home schooled and I had suggested moving away. Away from the evil kids. Away from the bad memories. She had jumped at the chance and for the first time in a long while, I saw her genuine smile. The one that made the blue in her eyes sparkle like a body of water reflecting the light of the sun. The move had come at a cost to me, I had to give up my chance of happiness with Kelvin, but it didn't compare to the possibility of having to lose Ava.

She had thrived in our new town. She made some wonderful friends with the children in our neighbourhood who brought her out of her shell, and she became the bubbly, happy-go-lucky girl she used to be. Sure, she still had the occasional nightmare, but with me holding her hand every step of the way, we battled the demons the quelled in her mind and she finally became herself again. She eventually took up counseling after a particularly bad night terror and after a few weeks, the night terrors stopped entirely.

I remember when she had told me that she wanted to help others to feel better about themselves, that she wanted to use her harrowing experience to make other people realise how special and invaluable they were. She truly believed that every life was worth saving, and that every single person mattered. We had been sat on the swing set in our front garden one summer afternoon, the sun beating down on us as its heat hugged everything it touched, just watching the day go by. Some of the kids on our street were out playing and had tried to get Ava to go play with them, but she wanted to spend some time with me. I remember looking down at my not-so-little girl and just felt raw pride and admiration of her incredible strength and integrity.

Now, sitting opposite my daughter, I could see the happiness radiating off her, and it warmed my heart. I just didn't know how to feel about the individual who was making her happy. I wasn't blind, and I certainly wasn't stupid. I could see he adored Ava to no end, and I could see that she was falling hard for him.

He wasn't the same person he used to be, that much was obvious. Now, he was a polite, courteous and compassionate young man, who had made her smile bigger than ever before and stolen her heart. They both had used such a traumatic experience to do a complete one-eighty and become better people, and I could at least acknowledge his attempt at redemption.

I wasn't going to step in the way of my daughter's happiness. I knew she didn't remember him, and I doubt he even remembered her either, and quite frankly, I was happy to leave it at that. They didn't look how they did when they were teenagers. They had both developed into their bodies and features, blossoming into good looking young adults.

All I could do now was wait for the incoming shit-storm that would inevitably be rolling in and be there for her when she needed me. And lord only knows she's going to need her mama's love when that happens.

Chapter 16

The midday sun was beaming down on us, coupled with an intense heat. There was barely any wind, and so it was like we were wading through an invisible sea of humidity. It was only early June and already the summer heat was unbearable. It had been forecast that this would be the hottest June in well over a decade, courtesy of good old global warming.

After having a day of lounging around the day that mum had arrived, we had decided on a girly outing for the next day. With Fi in tow, we took to the shopping district, which was absolutely bustling with holiday makers and locals alike. Since it was a Saturday, the streets were abuzz more than usual. Usually, I loved seeing how busy it was, I loved the fast pace. But today, in this heat, I didn't have the patience.

All kinds of shops lined the streets like a maze as we walked through the crowded district. They were mostly clothing shops, offering a wide variety of brands and styles. None of us had expensive tastes so we didn't buy anything from the high-end brands, but that didn't stop us from looking. The was the odd food cart, the smells that usually had my stomach grumbling only turning foul as it mixed with the heat.

I was in dire need of a new summer wardrobe. I hadn't updated my clothing since I had finished Uni and I was getting bored of seeing and wearing the same clothes. We had already been into a number of stores and our arms were becoming heavy as they were laden with a number of bags; we had literally shopped till we dropped.

We came across a jewellery store and I stopped to look in the window. There were all types of jewellery on display, rings, necklaces, bracelets, and when the sunlight hit them, they shone and sparkled like tiny disco balls. I was a huge fan of jewellery, gold what my metal of choice, if I wasn't wearing anything, I felt naked. My ears were adorned in earrings, my middle fingers on each hand decorated with a ring, one of which and heirloom from my mums side. Only my neck laid bare. My eyes fell on an incredibly lavish necklace. It was a bit on the simplistic side, but that was my style. Hanging off the thin gold chain was a small, clear gem droplet that had a slight hint of blue to the colouring. It was beautiful. Fi and mum had spotted the necklace I was eyeing up and they both gasped at its dainty beauty.

"Oh wow, that is gorgeous A! I could definitely imagine that on you." Fi's voice, full of wonder, came from the left of me, whilst my mum's hum of approval came from my right, the three of us plastered to the window, gazing like magpies at the necklace.

I looked at the price and just about choked on air, pointing to the small label that was attached to its side. "It's truly beautiful and I really do love it. But I don't love it that much." I started to walk away with mum and Fi following behind whispering between themselves.

We were heading towards the park for a well-earned rest when we came across a lingerie store. The outside of the building was cladded in a sleek black material, and the name of the store was in big, red LED lettering. The windows of the store were huge and wide on either side of the double doors, allowing for four mannequins to be on display in each with a circular sticker on the window that had only the number eighteen and a plus sign. An adults only store.

Fi had spotted it first and she dragged us to one of the windows. The mannequins were dressed in incredibly sexy and lacy garments, all of different colours and styles. I was all for a good thong, but the ones these mannequins had on were literally a thin bit of fabric that would barely cover me, and would no doubt have my lips hanging out at the sides.

"Come on, let's have a look!" Fi shrieked excitedly. She had never been interested in clothing or accessories like this, but since being with Everett, she had become more adventurous and daring. I liked that she was becoming more confident in herself within the bedroom and how she dressed. In truth, it couldn't hurt to take a leaf out of her book.

I suddenly felt a warm hand grip mine and I was soon being pulled into the store. I looked at the back of the head of my captor and was surprised to find that it was my mum. In her other hand was Fi's hand. She turned her face towards me with a huge cheeky grin plastered on her face.

"We are going to get you two something that'll make those boyfriends of yours be at your complete and utter mercy." Me and Fi shot each other a look of utter amazement. I have never been lingerie shopping with my mum before like this and I was beyond speechless that she was so eager. It was only yesterday I was trying to hide that I was sexually active from my mum, and now here I was basically admitting to her about my lack of

125

innocence.

We scoured the rails for quite some time before any of us had found something that caught our eye. I made sure to avoid the back of the store where the toys were on display. Was I fuck about to shop for sex toys with my mum. But that didn't stop her from picking up a large, rainbow coloured, floppy tentacle dildo and windmilling it in front of her and singing "*You Spin Me Round.*"

"Oh. My. God. A, this'll look absolutely phenomenal on you!" I walked over to where Fi was, my mum having already joined her. When I saw what Fi had found, my eyes rounded like saucers. In her hand was a sexy lacy bra and thong set. It was red with black lace over top. The bra was slightly padded and had a dainty red bow in between the cleavage, and the thong had a matching red bow at the top in the middle. It looked like there was enough material to comfortably cover my lady area, and that was good enough for me.

I nodded to Fi in approval in unison with my mum. I took the set off her and held it in front of me as I stood in front of a mirror.

"I don't think Leon will be able to keep his hands off you when he sees you in that sweetheart." I looked through the mirror to my mum, who had an approving smile on her face. It was weird lingerie shopping with my mum. Sure, I'd bought everyday underwear with her, but this was different. It insinuated intimacy of which I didn't discuss with her, ever. I mean, I'm glad she has good taste in lingerie, and I was grateful for her honest opinion, but it was odd hearing encouraging words come out of my mum's mouth regarding things surrounding my sex life.

She laughed when she saw the face I had pulled, "Don't look so shocked. Your mama knows good lingerie when she sees it. Plus, I want grand-babies." I gave her a small smile before holding the garments in front of me so I could inspect the items. It wasn't very often that the subject of children and grandchildren came up; mum knew how I felt about it. I appreciated that she wanted grandchildren to spoil, especially as she struck lucky with me herself. Mum had spent her teens struggling with painful period pains before being diagnosed with endometriosis. It had been so bad that she wouldn't be able to get out of bed most days. Either luck or my dad having super sperm enabled her to fall pregnant with me, but after her luck ran out and it never happened for her again. She'd always wanted a big family, but her body had different plans for her. It seemed that the Brooks' girls were destined to be barren.

Before I could stop myself, I was launched into a time warp and spiraled into thinking about my past. I had suffered a miscarriage when I was only nineteen, back when I was in Uni, the apple not falling far from the tree. The baby daddy was someone who I didn't have anything serious with. We'd just hook up when either of us felt lonely or were just plain horny and looking for a quick and easy release.

I had been in absolute agony all day with a pain in my stomach that I thought was perhaps endometriosis that I may have unknowingly inherited from my mum. But as the pain spread down to my thighs and became even more intense, with an odd pain on the tip of my shoulder appearing, I called mum who took me to the hospital. After an ultrasound, I was told that not only was I pregnant, but I was experiencing an miscarriage. Understandably, I was shocked. My shock very quickly turned to heartbreak when the reality that I was losing my baby hit me like a train. I had been growing a life and despite having only just discovered its existence, it had been taken from me. To further rub salt to the wound, my doctor had told me that I would struggle to conceive in the future. The baby had been doomed from the get go due to the pregnancy being an ectopic one. The foetus that was beginning to form had damaged the lining of my right fallopian tube so severely that it had to be removed, and so I was told that if I decided to have any more children in the future, it would be a struggle to fall pregnant naturally. Though, not impossible.

My mum was, as ever, incredibly supportive during this time, and once I had grieved the loss of my unborn child, I eventually grew to accept the fact that I may not ever be able to have children of my own. However, my mum – ever the optimist – had never given up hope. She clung to the slither of chance that I could still conceive and is as sure I'll have children as she's sure that the sun will rise tomorrow.

That's just another secret I have to eventually tell Leon. Another reason for him to walk away from me. Unless he could work miracles or he too had super sperm, I couldn't help but think I would never be able to naturally give him a family of his own. I know there's the option of IVF, adoption and surrogacy, but all of these options were expensive and the last two just weren't the same. I ached to experience pregnancy for myself. To feel the life inside of me grow, to feel its little hiccups as it learned to breathe inside of me, to feel it kick out at me as it got comfortable inside of its warm cocoon. I wanted to experience it all.

I quickly flicked a tear away that I had unknowingly shed onto my cheek before anyone could see. This was not the time nor place to feel sorry for myself. Turning back to Fi and my mum, I put on a big smile.

"This is perfect! Now, we need to find something for you Fi," I turned and gave my mum a devilish smirk "and for you." Mum pulled a face at me and I laughed in amusement at her.

"Just because you don't have a man in your life... yet... doesn't mean that you can't dress up for yourself and remind yourself that you are a fine, smokin' mama." My mum was still young, she still had it and she needed to give herself a confidence boost. Maybe that would help with her finally finding someone.

"Ava's right you know Jules. It's about time you felt good about yourself." I knew I'd be able to trust that Fi would have my back on this. Despite only being in my life for two years, she had become an integral part of my family and my mum saw her as a second daughter. Fi knew how desperately I wanted my mum to find her own happiness and she knew that my mum secretly wanted it too. She was just too scared to take the leap. With a roll of her eyes and a small smile, mum surrendered and gave in. I threw her a crotchless thong and began to laugh as mum tried to figure out what body part went where.

* * *

We were sitting in the park on the grass under the shade of a huge oak tree, surrounded by our many shopping bags. The grass felt nice and cool under my bare, outstretched legs, and along with the vast shadow from the tree protecting us from the overbearing heat, I could feel the heat dissipate from my being.

Leaning back on my elbows, I let my head hang back and closed my eyes. With my eyes closed, I felt my other senses enhance.

I could smell the distant smell of food being cooked on a small disposable BBQ, making my mouth water slightly. The once faint sound of children giggling and laughing as they ran around now rang loud and clear in my ears. I felt a smile spread along my face as I sank deeper into my state of serenity.

To my right, I heard Fi let out a long gratifying sigh. I popped one eye open to look at her. She had laid onto her back with her hands tucked behind her head that was resting on top of one of her shopping bags she was using as a makeshift pillow. She was dressed in a gorgeous yellow strappy sundress that flowed gracefully to just above her knee. The yellow of the dress complemented her olive skin perfectly and brought out her bronze tones even more. She really was stunning without even needing to try.

I rolled my head over to the left and looked at my mum, switching my eyes. She sat up with her legs crossed, leaning back on her hands with her head tilted back, a small content smile on her lips. She looked beautiful in this position. Her medium length curtain of blonde hung away from her back, rippling ever so slightly in the faint breeze. Her black skirt with yellow flowers, delicately laid over her lap, was flapping gently at the edges. She looked so at peace; it was a calming sight. I hadn't seen her this relaxed in a long time. Returning my head to its central position, I closed my eyes again and enjoyed the calming atmosphere.

"I think it's time." My mum's voice piped up quietly, breaking the comfortable silence. I was confused at what she meant. Time for what? To leave?

I looked at her once again. "What are you on about?"

"It's time for me to find myself a man." I shot up and looked at her, my eyes bulging from their sockets. I turned to look at

Fi and saw that she was now sat up on her knees, excitement written on her face like she was hearing the most scandalous piece of gossip.

"You girls are right. It's been far too long and seeing how happy you both are with your men, makes me realise just how much I have deprived myself of it. It's high time I be selfish for once and find my happiness again." With a girlish, excitable squeal, me and Fi jumped on my mum, bundling her into a group hug. I was so glad that she was finally ready to start exploring the world of love and romance.

"I'm so proud of you mama, I just want you to be happy. God only knows you deserve it." I gave her a loving kiss on her cheek. I was starting to become overwhelmed with a feeling of pride, joy, and relief. She deserved this wholeheartedly.

"AH! I'm so excited for you Jules. I can't wait for all the juicy details." Fi winked at my mum.

"Ew, Fi. Gross." I faked a gag, which rewarded me with a laugh from my two favourite women. Whilst I too wanted to hear about the details as they come, I didn't want *all* of the juice. She was my parent after all, I didn't want to know about what she got up to like that, just as I'm sure she didn't want to know about me and what I get up to during sexy time.

My mum took one of our hands in each of hers. "Thank you girls, but I'm not jumping into the deep end straight off the bat. I'm not going to actively look, but I'll be more open-minded and less dismissive should someone approach me." That was all that I could have hoped for at this moment. It was better than nothing.

From then on, we spent the next few hours just discussing what kind of man my mum was looking for and what it was she looked for in a man. It had been so long since she'd been on the dating scene so she was asking us questions and advice. Even though there wasn't anyone in her sights yet, she was both excited and nervous about this new endeavour she was embarking on.

* * *

It had been the perfect day, and to round the day off, the three of us spent the night at mine drinking wine, eating take-out and watching '*Mamma Mia*'. We had pushed the sofas back slightly and moved the coffee table so that we had room to sing and dance.

We took a boat load of selfies and videos so that we would have these memories to look back on. I was on the sofa laughing and recording on my phone, whilst Fi and my mum were singing along to '*Angel Eyes*', with Fi singing Rosie's parts whilst my mum sang Tanya's. They both were brandishing hairbrushes as microphones, giving it their all. It was refreshing to see my mum so laid back, throwing caution to wind and letting her hair down so freely.

It truly had been a proper girls' day, the type that you would have as a teen with your girlfriends, just enjoying each other's company and messing around with no worries in the world. It was nice to see my mum relax and enjoy herself for once. She had a big genuine smile on her face, coupled with a twinkle of pure happiness in her eyes.

I was excited to see where my mum's future would head and to see who she would end up with. She deserved a lifetime of happiness and the biggest happily ever after.

Chapter 17

It had been two weeks since my mum had left and returned to her home. In that time, she had been on a date with a guy called Lucas who was the same age as herself. She said he was good looking and was well mannered, but "he was a self-absorbed wannabe model with the personality of a wet sock". She wasn't too downhearted about it though. She was proud of herself for taking the first step.

Presently, I was in Fi's flat with Everett and Leon helping her sort out her things for her new job working as Leon's secretary. I say help. I was helping, whilst the boys were dossing it, drinking beer and playing FIFA in her living room. She had worked her two weeks' notice and was due to start in Leon's office the next day.

Fi and I were in her bedroom and she was panicking in true Ffion form. At this moment in time, her room looked like a tornado had hit it. There were clothes everywhere. The boys had popped their heads round the door about twenty minutes ago. They took one look at the scene that laid before them and their eyes widened at the carnage, their mouths hanging open. Fi had screeched at them to get out and they very quickly disappeared without even speaking a word. It was a wise move.

Fi let out a muffled frustrated scream. She was laying on top of one of the many mountains of clothes that were on the floor, face down, in a starfish. "What am I going to wear, A? I've not got anything smart enough for Leon's place. This is a disaster." In reality, she did have clothes to wear, she was just over reacting and crazy nervous about her first day.

I rolled my eyes as I stood up from her bed and grabbed hold of Fi's limp arm by her wrist and attempted to gently lift her up. "Come on, let me have a look and I'll see what I can find." She grudgingly stood up and heavily trudged over to her bed, plopping herself down with an annoyed huff.

I sifted through her clothes, putting away items that I didn't want as I went. Half-way through, Fi decided to get out of her mood and came and helped me. She left me to pick the clothes that I thought would be good enough to wear whilst she put the clothes away that I handed to her.

An hour and a half later we had five outfits for the entire week and we could now see her bedroom floor once again. Tomorrow's outfit consisted of a beige high-waisted straight skirt that stopped just above the knee, paired with a crisp white shirt that had three-quarter length rolled up sleeves and a long, yet modest, v-neckline. To accessorise, there was a thick brown belt with a gold buckle, brown open toe heels and a matching brown bag.

I was pretty impressed with myself. Usually it was Fi helping me with what to wear. But the tables had turned and I had stepped up and out done myself. I think Fi was impressed with me too. She stood with her arms loosely folded underneath her chest, observing the outfits I had chosen for her with a very happy and approving look on her face.

"So, I may have been a little bit dramatic for a moment there." Ffion stated as she hung the last item up in her wardrobe.

"You think?" I was rewarded with a double middle finger. Sarcasm may be the lowest form of whit, but it was my absolute favourite thing in the world.

"Listen here, I am humble enough to admit that that was not my finest hour. But, you've pulled together some really nice outfits for me. Maybe now you won't need me to help you from now on." She had an amused tone to her voice as she winked at me.

"Oh no, you aren't getting out of that one. This was a one off fluke. You will always and forever be the fashionista out of us two. Therefore, I will always need your help." Fi never gave herself enough credit for her unspoken talent when it came to clothes. I'd suggested it to her before about the possibility of her pursuing a career in being a stylist, but she brushed it aside. She didn't think she was talented enough or that anyone would like the outfits she'd create, but I have witnessed her quite literally make a black bin bag look half-decent.

With a giggle, she pulled me into a warm hug. "Thank you for your help Ava, truly. I was on the verge of a meltdown." That was putting it incredibly mildly. She'd had a full-on tantrum that would put a four-year-old to shame. These outbursts of hers were super rare, but they were equally both scary and entertaining to watch when they happened. She would sit with her arms crossed tightly across her chest and furrowed her brows together into a deep scowl that gave her wrinkles on her forehead. With bright red cheeks and a pout to complete the look, she looked like a child who had been told to go on the naughty step.

We pulled out of our embrace and made our way out to the boys. They were no longer playing FIFA but were now watching a football news channel. Their reaction to seeing us had us in absolute hysterics. The pair of them had jumped up simultaneously, each grabbing their weapon of choice. Leon was holding the sofa cushion up behind his head, ready to launch it at us, and Everett was wielding the remote control, taking the stance of a fencer. Both of their faces had a look of faked fear on them.

"Don't come any closer. We're armed and we aren't afraid to use them." You would think that having been with Fi for nearing three months that he would be used to this, or at least have witnessed it a couple times. But as luck would have it, this was a first.

Leon gave Everett an encouraging pat on his shoulder, as if he was congratulating him on speaking up to Ffion. "Yeah, Ava you could've warned us you were friends with the devil's offspring." Leon had a serious face on, so I knew he was prepared to attack if Fi wasn't in her right frame of mind. It truly was an amusing sight.

Me and Ffion looked at each other and burst into fits of laughter. The boys shared a confused look, their stances faltering slightly.

"I'd be careful what you say," I pointed a finger, wiggling it between the pair of them, "You don't want to wake the beast. But, she's simmered down now. She's the Ffion we all know and love. No spawn of satan to be seen." I had managed to get my laughter under control now, but a smile still lingered on my lips. The boys sighed with relief and dropped their weapons.

"Well thank fuck for that. I do not want to ever cross paths with Ffion's alter ego ever again." Leon had now dropped back into his seat and leaned forward to pick his beer up from the glass coffee table.

"It's alright for you Leon, you're not the one who's potentially got a future with her. I can see it now: our children are going to come out red all over with two tiny horns on the foreheads." As soon as those words left his mouth, a look flashed across his face that would be similar to the expression "oh shit".

"Keep talking like that, *my love*, and my alter ego will come up from the deep dark depths of the underworld, and we wouldn't want that now, would we?" Her voice dropped, her face deadpan besides an eyebrow raised in challenge. Fi was now standing in front of a seated Everett, hands on her hips. I knew Fi wasn't being serious, but Everett didn't, and I had to stifle my giggle with a hand over my mouth. He took a large gulp and looked genuinely scared for his life as Fi loomed over him with a dark intimidating look on her face.

As he shifted uncomfortably in his seat he began to stutter. I had never seen Everett look like this. He usually had a natural air of confidence and never backed down from an argument. I mean, the nature of his job meant that he had to be this way, but when it came to Fi, he was completely wrapped around her finger and was a different person altogether.

In an instant, Fi's face changed back to its usual bubbly cheerful self and she patted Everett lightly on his head.

"Baby, I'm joking. But boy do I wish I had taken a picture of the look on your face. That was priceless." He let out a relieved sigh and rubbed his face to rid the tension.

* * *

Me and Fi had become domesticated housewives and had made a pasta dish for us all to enjoy together. Since Ffion's breakfast bar wasn't big enough for all four of us to sit up, we sat around the coffee table on the floor. It was pretty nice in all honesty, it felt homely.

The conversation had been flowing freely and the atmosphere was light and energetic. Suddenly, Everett's phone rang, startling us all. He took a look at the screen and his face fell. His usual full, beaming smile was replaced with an angry frown. Fi flicked her eyes to look at Everett and then she briefly lowered them to his phone, before she started to stare aimlessly into her plate.

"Excuse me." He got up and left the room. He'd closed the front door and me and Leon turned to look at Fi. She'd gone unusually quiet and was leaning her face on her fist, pushing her food around her plate. Noting the drastic change in her mood and behaviour as soon as Everett had his phone in his hand, I looked to Leon who was just as confused as I was. I nodded my head subtly towards Fi and Leon responded with a down-turned smile and a shrug before continuing shoveling his food into his mouth. Typical male.

"Fi? Is everything OK?" I was worried about her. I didn't know that there was something going on between Everett in Ffion. She hadn't said anything, and they didn't seem indifferent around us with one another.

"Yep. Why wouldn't it be?" She didn't look up from her plate. She was just spinning the pasta around and around with her fork. I didn't reply to her, I didn't know what to say and I didn't want to force the topic. It had nothing to do with me and I didn't want to make Fi feel any worse, so I didn't press the matter any further.

Everett walked back in a few minutes later, pulling his hand through his hair. Fi looked up at him and followed him with her eyes back to his place up the coffee table. He sat down with a sigh and rubbed his hand across his brows, covering his eyes. I caught a glimpse of red along his knuckles where there was some superficial breaking of the skin, indicating that he had taken whatever had got him so pent up out on an unsuspecting wall.

"Everything good, brother?" Leon looked perturbed as he placed a caring hand on Everett's arm.

"I appreciate your concern, but if it's all the same to you, I'd rather not talk about it." His voice was flat. There was no emotion behind it. There was no hint of anything that could tell us how he was thinking. Leon nodded his head once and removed his hand from Everett's arm.

All of a sudden, Fi stood up and stalked to her room, slamming the door behind her with such force I felt the room shake. There was definitely something going on, and I hated that I didn't know what it was. I felt helpless, I didn't know what to do. My friend was hurting for an unknown reason and I couldn't be there for her. I had never seen her like this and I was starting to worry about her. Leon looked just confused as I. He was looking between Everett and the back of Fi's bedroom door, itching the side of his head.

She reappeared soon after, but she was now wearing trainers and her handbag was on her shoulder. She wordlessly walked past us to the front door and I couldn't help but notice that she had a tear stained face. My heart ached for her and I just wanted to take her into my arms and take away all her bad feelings. She opened the front door and pulled it shut. It was a quieter slam than the slam of her bedroom door, highlighting that her emotions had altered from anger to upset.

I turned my head towards Everett. He had caused her to feel like this, to act out in this way. It didn't matter that I didn't know the reason. What mattered was that my friend was hurting over something *he* had done, and I wanted to rip his face off and feed it to him. I felt a wave of anger bubble up inside of me.

Before I could even open my mouth to give Everett a piece of my mind, he held his hand up at me, shutting me down.

"Don't start. I know. You're mad at me. I get it. But this is between me and Fi, and while I appreciate you wanting to protect her and look out for her, let me deal with it." His tone was level and cold and it matched the expression he wore on his face. He was right, this was between them. I shouldn't be trying to fight her battle for her when she was more than capable of doing it for herself. But at least he knew I was pissed at him for doing whatever it was he had done. Everett pushed himself up and walked to the door and slipped his shoes on. He didn't say anything more to us, just nodded his head as a farewell and left to go after Ffion.

I leaned forward and placed my head in my hands. "What the fuck just happened? How did we go from laughing and joking one minute to... well whatever that was?" I was truly dumbfounded. I couldn't make sense of it.

"I don't know babe. I'm just as mind-blown about all this as you are. But it's nothing to do with us. We'll just have to be patient and wait for them to be ready to tell us what happened." In the grand scheme of things, it was all that we could do. I'm sure they'll be able to work things out together. I mean, every couple has their ups and downs, it can't always be smooth sailing.

I picked up our plates and took them into the kitchen. May as well clear up so they don't have to if and when they come back. Leon followed me and scraped the plates that had the leftovers on them into the bin, whilst I got cracking with the washing up.

With the plates now placed on the side next to me with the rest of the dirty crockery, Leon stood behind me and wrapped his hands around my waist, leaning his chin on my shoulder.

"You know, I absolutely love how protective you get over your friends." He planted a kiss on my cheek and slowly worked his way down my neck whilst making complimentary comments to me. His hands had found their way under my top and were stroking my sides teasingly. "I love how strong you are..." Another kiss. "I love that you would give the world for those you care about..." And another. "I love your feistiness. It's such a fucking turn on." At this point, I had stopped scrubbing the plates that were in the warm soapy water. His kisses and sweet nothings a welcome distraction, slowly melting my insides and I was feeling giddy by the feel of his hand on my bare skin.

He nipped gently at the skin on my shoulder with his teeth and I let out a sensual moan.

"Baby... not here... not at Fi's place." As much as I wanted to give myself to him, it felt wrong to do it in Ffion's place. I knew she would probably high-five me for it, but it felt disrespectful - especially after tonight's events.

He spun me around so that I was now facing him. He kissed me deeply with our tongues interacting almost immediately. I now had a wet, bubble-coated hand in his hair and the other gripping his t-shirt at his chest. His kisses drove me wild and they always had me greedily wanting more. He had sneaked his hand up my top, leaving tingles of electricity as he trailed his hand along my bare skin up my sides, towards my breasts. Now under my bra, he was alternating between tugging and twisting my nipple bar and rolling my nipple between his fingers.

His spare hand deep in my hair, he roughly grabbed it and pulled my head back, causing my mouth to fly open as I gasped. My neck was exposed to him and he took it as an invitation for his lips.

Between the delicious feel of his lips on my neck and the jolts of pleasure from him playing with my nipple, I couldn't contain my moans of exhilaration. I was about to give in to him and let him take me right here on Fi's counter when I felt his lips vacate my skin. His warm hand was still caressing my breast under my bra, and he was looking into my eyes with his forehead against mine. I could see the burning fire of passion and need in his eyes, and it only added to my hunger to have him.

"So not here, but back at mine?" There was a sexy, mischievous tint to his voice and I felt the inside of my core flutter. I licked my lips before pulling my bottom lip under my teeth with my tongue as I nodded in agreement to him.

"Well then, we best hurry and get this cleaned up so I can spend my sweet time teasing you and showing you how you drive me crazy." With a final flick of my nipple, he spun me around and I felt a stinging sensation as his hand landed on my backside and I let out a little yelp. I loved it when he slapped my arse, it only turned me on more.

With a cocky smirk, he picked up a tea towel and began drying and putting away whilst I continued with the washing up. We worked quickly, both eager to get back so we could continue where we left off.

We were done in ten minutes and I quickly texted Fi.

A: Hey babes, hope you're alright? Just know I'm here for you and that I love you. Me and Leon tidied up for you and we're now heading back. Let me know when you're home.

And with that, me and Leon raced out of the Ffion's flat and headed back home, barely able to keep our hands off each other.

We had a very long night ahead of us.

19

Chapter 18

Ffion had taken to the office and her tasks like a duck to water. Once she knew where everything was and had become accustomed to the jobs and her desk, she was away. Her first day started off a bit shaky. I think that was due to her nerves, that coupled with the falling out she had with Ev the night before. Neither one of them had spoken to either me or Ava about what had happened but it seemed like it was water under the bridge now.

Thinking back to that night, it was an absolute roller-coaster. The atmosphere and mood had drastically changed with the snap of our fingers. Whoever had called Ev had really turned the night on its head and had severely affected him. I couldn't help but wonder what on earth Ev had gotten himself involved with; I'd never seen Ev like that before and he had never taken that tone with me before either.

He had outright refused to tell me what was going on whenever I had asked him, so it was clearly something serious. We told each other everything. But if he wasn't willing to talk to me about this, then I wouldn't force it. He'd tell me when he's good and ready.

Seeing how Ava reacted just made my feelings deepen for her more. She was fiercely loyal to her friends and as angry as she was towards Ev for whatever he had done to make Ffion feel and act the way that she did, you could see the pain and hurt in Ava's eyes as she watched her best friend walk out of the flat. I loved that she could empathise with Ffion's feelings, despite not knowing the reasons behind them. It was probably a weird time for my feelings to further develop for Ava, but I couldn't help but love all sides of her and her personality.

When Ffion had left, Ava's pain and hurt turned to anger and I watched as those beautiful crystal orbs of hers turned as dark as an oceanic storm. I could do nothing but watch as her wrath slowly begin to engulf her. I wanted to touch her to try to calm her down, but in all honesty, I was a little apprehensive to.

Ev had spoken to her in such an icy tone and I was shocked to hear it. The last time he spoke this way, was when he found out his dad had cheated on his mum with some whore in the neighbouring town. That was a dark time for Ev, and I hope that whatever was eating him up doesn't send him back to that. Once he had left to go after Ffion, Ava was able to gain control of her emotions again and her eyes shifted back to their light breezy colour.

It was absolutely not the right time to be turned on by Ava, but I couldn't help it. She looked delicious from the back in her body hugging bodycon dress. Her hourglass curves flowed in and out perfectly, and her arse... God, her curves had me drooling. It was perfectly perky, and whenever she moved, even the slightest movement, you could see it wobble ever so slightly under her dress.

Thinking about her body was getting me hard, and that wasn't helped when I remembered the activities that had occurred once we were home from Ffion's. The more sexual things me and Ava did together, the more confident and dominant she became. As much as I loved taking control and making her quiver and scream my name, I loved when she took the reins and made me at her mercy. Commanding and assertive Ava was the biggest turn on of them all.

I was reminiscing of when Ava had refused to let me touch her as she stripped sitting on top of me and all I could do was watch with the burning need to have her bouncing breasts in my mouth whilst I ran my hands all over her fantastic body, when there was a gentle rap at the door. Quickly adjusting my now raging erection in my pants, I called for my visitor to enter.

A middle-aged man with jet black, slicked back hair waltzed into my office with an air of power and authority about him. His posture was exquisite. At six foot four, he stood tall, his shoulders squared, showcasing his true broad stature. Despite his intimidating look, he had strong grey eyes and a brilliantly kind smile that made his eyes crinkle at the side.

"Leon, my boy! How are you?" I wasn't expecting to see him today at all. Usually when he was going to make an appearance at the office, he'd call in advance and let me know. The man that stood before me was called Toby, and he was the head of the therapist company I worked for. He very rarely came to our branch, as we were just outside of the city.

"I'm great thanks Toby, what brings you to this side of town?" I rose from my seat and walked around my desk to give him a welcoming handshake. He gave away nothing in his cool appearance. He seemed as laid back as ever.

"I see your new secretary has settled in wonderfully. She's a stunning little thing isn't she." He shot me a wink, ignoring my question. Now leaning against my desk, I motioned to Toby for him to take a seat. He sat down and placed the ankle of one leg on top of the other knee, resting his arms on either side of the armrests.

I chuckled at him and gave him a light shake of my head. "She would eat you for breakfast and she's off limits, she's my best mate's girl. But yes, she's doing really well. She's miles above Stacey if I'm being honest."

He nodded knowingly at me. I had told him the true reasoning for wanting to transfer Stacey from my office and he agreed unquestionably. He was the top dog in our company but he had also become a good friend of mine. It felt wrong to hide something as big as that from him, especially if it got back to him from a third party. He was the man who had dealt with Stacey's transfer so that none of the other employees would hear about the why, nor would anyone question the transfer. I was incredibly grateful to Toby for handling the whole thing with utter discretion.

"Well, she seems like a strong and competent secretary." He waved his hand to signal the dismissing of the topic of Ffion, moving swiftly on to his entire reason for his visit. "Anyway, the whole reason I'm here is because as you know, the Summer Ball will be here in a couple of weeks, and I'm here to deliver the news, personally, that you have been nominated for an award." I had completely forgotten about the ball. My mind had been so consumed with thoughts of Ava, that everything else seemed to have slipped my mind.

The Summer Ball was an annual extravagant and prestigious party held by the National Therapists Association. It was to celebrate the success of selected individuals who were nominated by colleagues and patients. Every year we had a different handful of ex-patients be invited and they would help give out the awards, and occasionally give a small speech. This would be my second time at the Ball, and my first nomination.

"I have? Wow, that's certainly unexpected. I'm honoured, thank you." I wondered what I had been nominated for. I was surprised that I had already. I'd only been here for two years, and it was uncommon for anyone to be nominated this early in their career.

"The award is for making a difference in the community. A few of the schools nominated you for your talks, and a handful of your patients did too." I didn't do talks very often, but when I did, they were always well received. I would reach out to local school and workplaces and would talk about confidence and self-esteem, the impacts of bullying and how to keep on top of their mental health.

"The same as last year, you'll be able to have a plus one. Your secretary doesn't count, though. She's automatically invited since she works for the company, and she too gets a plus one." Upon hearing that, I felt a rush of excitement run through me. I would invite Ava first in a heartbeat, without a second thought. I could picture her in a dress, her long gorgeous locks up in a magnificent up-do, a stunning smile plastered on her face as she stood next to me proudly.

"That's great. Thanks again, Toby." He stood up and patted me on the side of my arm by my shoulder with a friendly, gentle smile.

"No need to thank me, you've worked hard these past two years and have become on par with some of our senior therapists. I have to get going to the other offices and inform the other nominees of their nominations, so I shall see you at the Ball Leon." With a polite, yet curt nod, Toby left my office.

Since I had another twenty minutes until my next patient arrived, I decided to give Ava a call. The phone rang a little longer than normal, and just as I felt worry sit in my chest, she answered.

"Hey, baby." She was breathless. I had no doubt just interrupted her workout. The sound of her raspy, breathy voice was like music to my ears. It reminded me of the sounds she made the other night whilst she was on top of me. I could picture her with her head tilted back, eyes closed with her lashes fluttering ever so slightly, and her mouth cracked open to allow her sounds of pleasure to escape.

"Hey beautiful, have I just interrupted your workout?" I could hear her slurp and guzzle her drink down the phone. I was now picturing her with my dick in her small, delicate mouth, her head bobbing up and down as she took as much of me as possible. The hard on that I had only just managed to get down was now making a reappearance, and if I didn't know any better, I'd think that what she was doing down the phone was to tease me.

"No, no, it's OK. I was just finishing up anyway. Is everything alright?" She questioned. I never rang her during my working hours unless it was for something important, so no doubt that my unexpected call must have thrown her off.

"Yeah babe, I've just got something to ask you. In a couple of weeks there's an awards ceremony and party for my work. I've been nominated for an award and I'm allowed a plus one. I was wondering if you would like to be my date?" I could hear myself sound a little shy as I asked her to accompany me to the Ball. What was that about? I was Leon Myers, the legendary player and heartbreaker of high school, college and Uni. I had never been shy to ask anything of a girl. This could only mean that my feelings for Ava were genuine and were only growing.

She was quiet on the other end and I was beginning to wonder if I'd scared her away. Suddenly, she let out a small excited squeal and I felt a smile spread on my face.

"I'd love to! Oh my, you've been nominated for an award?! Wow, I'm so proud of you." I could hear the pride in her voice, and I felt a happy warmth spread through my center.

"That makes me happy, my love, so happy that you'll accompany me. I'll give you a text of the dress-code and any other information you'll need. I need to go as I've got a patient waiting. I'll speak to you soon."

"Speak soon, handsome." She blew me a kiss down the phone and hung up, just as Ffion knocked and popped her head round the door to see if I was ready for my next patient.

* * *

Ava's POV:

I was just finishing the last set of skipping rope when I heard my phone go off. I stopped the plastic rope a bit too soon and it whipped me in the shin. With a sting in my leg, I made my way over to my phone, trying to get some breath back before I answered and noticed that it was Leon calling. He never rang me when he was at work unless there was an emergency. A number of scenarios raced through my mind.

I was relieved when he said that there was nothing to worry about, but it took me a few moments to process what he had asked. Leon had asked me on a date. Not a normal one either. This was bigger and grander than any date I've ever been on. We will be making our debut as a couple to his colleagues. I was overwhelmed with a bundle of nerves and excitement. We were yet to even have a normal date together, and for our first to be this major was sort of nerve-racking. He had started the conversation off sounding his usual confident self, but when it got to asking me to go as his date, he had gone a bit sheepish, almost like he'd never asked anyone out on a date before. I was yet to experience this side of Leon and I had found it rather adorable.

As I thought about what the people he works with would be like, it occurred to me that Fi was now amongst those, and that would mean that Leon and I would be sharing our evening with Ffion and no doubt, Everett. That fact helped calm me down and my nerves morphed into pure excitement and joy.

My thoughts then took a brief detour to Fi and Everett. I hoped that they were both OK. Neither one of them had breathed a word to me or Leon about what happened last week, but they both seemed to have worked whatever it was out.

I was yet to receive a text from Leon about the dress-code and any other details, but I just assumed he was seeing his patient. So, I just spent the rest of the day searching online for evening gowns and had come up with a list of the ones that caught my eye, sending a few to Fi for her opinion. I made sure to get a range of dresses of different levels of formality. I'd narrow down my options once I knew exactly what the theme was.

* * *

Three hours later and I still hadn't heard from Leon, and I was beginning to get a little impatient and pissed off at him. I was sprawled out on my sofa with the fan on whilst the new show I had just started was on in the background. It was starting to get unbelievably hot during the days now, but even more so in the evenings. It was becoming unbearable and uncomfortable. I was literally dressed in just my underwear because it was just too hot for clothes.

I had just checked my phone for the millionth time since our call when I heard my letter box clink. I rose to my feet and lazily made my way to the door. On my welcome mat was a white envelope with my name written in beautiful calligraphy. I cautiously picked it up and headed back to the sofa, inspecting the envelope as I went. There was nothing else on the envelope except for my name. No hints at where this had come from, or who the sender was.

I carefully ripped the top of it open and tucked my hand inside to pull out the contents. A card fell into my lap as I opened the folded piece of paper. I ignored it while I read the letter. The handwriting was beautiful, almost feminine.

My Sweetheart Ava,

The dress code for the Summer Ball is black tie formal. I've given you my credit card. Use it to buy your dress, and feel free to buy your shoes and accessories with it too.

Don't show me what you've brought, I want to be surprised on the night.

I can't wait to have you proudly on my arm, my love.

Yours, Leon.

I picked the card up and turned it in my hands. On inspection, it had Leon's name on the bottom, indicating that this was indeed his card and he was serious about me using it to buy my entire outfit for the Ball.

I quickly grabbed my phone and pinged Fi a text, telling her what Leon had just posted through my door, before sending Leon a text thanking him.

I couldn't believe it. I felt like the luckiest girl in the world. I was truly looking forward to being by his side at the Ball, celebrating his success.

20

Chapter 19

It was a Friday morning and I awoke in Leon's bed on my own. He'd pulled the blinds up, allowing for the blinding sunlight to flood into the bedroom. The light was so bright that I had to hide under the sheets for my eyes to adjust to the brightness.

I could feel myself slowly slipping back to into the comforting embrace of sleep, when I heard Leon's deep voice call out to me. With my eyes closed, I peeled the sheets down from my head and slowly opened my eyes, one at a time. He stood in the doorway in nothing but his snug black boxers. His tanned, muscular body was a sight to behold. Despite having seen it a number of times, his physique always blew me away and I was forever looking at his body, taking in every muscle, the white and pink stretch marks that striped his body through years of hard work to get his body to look as incredible as it does now.

Starting from the top, I scanned my eyes down his body. He had a serious case of bed hair, but it looked so damn sexy and had me wishing that my hands were tangled in it. His perfectly sculpted face was set in an amused smirk with his eyes a glistening pool of buttery meltiness, holding me captive.

It took all I had in me to drag my eyes away from his and continue my expedition down to his torso. He had a triangular body shape, and all one-eighty degrees of that shape were packed with muscle. His shoulders were thick and broad with the arms attached to them being beautifully curved with muscles. One arm of which was currently leaning against the door-frame, the bulge of his bicep a smooth mound. He was strong, and he looked like he could easily squish me to death, but whenever I was in his arms, he held me like I was a delicate keepsake.

My mouth began to water when my eyes fell onto his softly carved abdominal muscles. He took pride in his body, more so because he was completely natural and had never used steroids to get the physique he honed now, something I respected deeply. It took not only good genetics, but also a lot of hard-work and commitment over many years to achieve a body as well sculpted as his.

Before I could continue my Tour de Leon, he let out a chuckle and his husky playful voice snapped me back to my senses.

"Are you quite done eye-fucking me babe? You haven't even noticed what I'm holding." Sure enough, in his big veiny hand was a lap tray holding a bowl of fruit with yoghurt and a cup of steaming coffee, the tendons in his wrist straining at holding all of the weight. I had been so entranced by his body that I hadn't noticed he had brought me breakfast in bed.

I licked my lips slowly and rubbed my hands together as he made his way towards me and Leon's face turned dark with lust. I flicked my eyes under the tray and, as I suspected, Mini Leon was starting to stir.

"Oh sorry, I wasn't licking my lips at you, I was licking them at the sight of the food you've very lovingly brought for me." I teased. Although, we both knew that wasn't entirely true. I took

155

the tray off him and placed it on my lap.

He gave me a soft kiss on my forehead before gently sitting on the edge of the bed next to me and adjusting himself. "You're a devil you know, teasing me like that." His tone was slightly serious, but his face was playful. I flashed him a wink and started digging into my breakfast.

"So then, what did I do to deserve this?" I was intrigued as to why he was being extra loving this morning. This was a first. I hadn't received breakfast in bed from him before. Or any male come to think of it. Whatever the motive, I was grateful that he looked after me and did little things like this to make me happy. Plying my mouth with a spoonful of yoghurt and fruit, I did a little happy dance before swallowing the lot.

"You mean, I can't do something nice for my girlfriend without there being an ulterior motive?" He gasped exaggeratingly, feigning denial and acting like he'd been shot in the heart. I laughed at his small performance. He never failed to make me laugh, it was one of the things I loved about him. He leaned over and tucked some stray hair behind my ear, before gently holding my chin up with his fingers so that I could look into his eyes.

"You look so beautiful when you laugh, you know." I found myself blushing. I wasn't used to being complimented on my laugh. I had always thought it was an ugly sound and it had been confirmed by Victoria in school, and ever since then, I hated my laugh.

He leaned over and left a soft kiss on my nose. "And you're very cute when you blush." His voice was soft, and his eyes twinkled with honesty.

Not knowing what to say, I let out a confused "Thanks?" to which Leon roared with laughter. Leon may like my laugh, but I loved his. His laugh was belly-deep and it filled the room, and filled my ears. It was such a sexy sound.

I continued scooping my breakfast into my mouth.

"This is some good shit." A mouthful of yoghurty, healthy goodness in my mouth, I pointed to the bowl with my spoon, indicating said 'good shit'.

A soft chuckle and then, "I'm glad to hear it. But once you've finished that, I need you to start getting ready."

"Why? Are we going somewhere?" Leon was now at the doorway. He'd stopped, looked at me over his shoulder with a sly smile on his face.

"We are. I'm taking you away for the weekend. We leave in two hours."

TWO HOURS? He clearly doesn't know me as well as I thought he did. How does he expect me to pack a bag and get ready in that short time frame?

As if reading my mind, Leon answered my question "I've got you a bag packed already. Ffion helped me last night when you were at the gym." I let out a relieved sigh. Knowing that Fi helped him brought me peace of mind. I wouldn't have to worry about looking awful.

"Don't you have work today?" I tapped on the screen of my phone and saw that it was eight-thirty a.m. He should've been at work an hour ago.

"I've taken today off. Now, stop panicking and do as you're told and get your arse into gear. And before you ask, I'm not telling you where we're going." He tapped me on my foot before leaning over and taking the tray. This side of Leon had me weak. Strong, demanding and self-assured, he knew what he wanted and how to get it.

I watched as his beefy, toned, boxer-clad backside swayed away from me. God he was just perfect.

Once Leon had disappeared from my sight, I threw the light bed sheets off me and began to get ready, my mind racing about where we could be going.

* * *

Four hours later, we were in the car, an hour away from wherever our destination was. I was still very much in the dark about where we were going, but I couldn't help the bubble of excitement and anticipation that was built up inside of me.

We spent the journey chatting and laughing. The atmosphere in the car with him was so light and natural. He was a good driver too, which I liked. I couldn't stand men who drove irresponsibly or to try to show off. Leon made me feel safe and comfortable.

I looked over to take him in. He was driving one handed, the other hand was interlocked underneath mine on his gearstick. It was such a small gesture, but it made my heart swell. His side profile was just as exquisite as his front. His jaw was so sharp you could use it to cut through butter. His chiseled nose was a perfect length and his naturally full and pouty lips stood out deliciously.

The radio station we were listening to was playing '*Forgotten Hits of the 2000's*' and I was having the time of my life. Every song so far had been an absolute bop, and I completely lost myself to the music. The windows were down, letting the cool breeze caress our faces as we drove in the heat. All we needed was a sunroof to lower and it'd be like our own two-thousands music video.

Suddenly, "*My Boo*" started playing and I let out an excited squeal, turning the volume up. Leon shot me an amused look from the side. He had gotten used to me reacting to my favourite songs and had found it to be rather entertaining.

Leon had sung a few songs with me, and I was taken-aback because he actually had a half decent voice. His voice was deep and beautiful, and I could honestly listen to him sing all day. But this song, he didn't sing. Instead, I noticed he was glancing at me every now and then. Looking at the road, or looking at me, his smile never faltered. It was a smile of joy and happiness. I felt so at ease with him, especially when he was wearing this expression.

"You know. You are full of surprises. I didn't know you could sing." He said once the song had finished. The commercials were now running before the next song would start to play.

"You're a fine one to talk. But if you think that's impressive, wait till you hear me rap." I gazed out of the window, taking in the scenic countryside that zoomed past us. I took a few mouthfuls from my bottle of water that I had been using as a microphone.

"I look forward to it." He said with a hint of a laugh in his voice. He started looking intently at the approaching sign, looking to see what exit we needed to take at the next roundabout.

The radio DJ introduced the next song and it made me freeze. Leon must've felt my hand squeeze his as my body tensed stiff. The song that floated through the radio waves into my ears was "*Stole*". I didn't sing at all. I couldn't bring myself too. As the song reached the chorus, the pain of nine years ago, that I had worked hard to keep down, was pushing its way to the surface. I couldn't move. I couldn't speak. I was just consumed by pain and anguish as snapshots of me in the bath flashed through my mind. I was so caught up in my memories and feelings that I hadn't noticed that Leon had turned the radio down and had pulled over.

"Ava... Ava baby... Speak to me." Leon had gotten out of the car and was on my side, door open, shaking my shoulders gently. I snapped out of my trance and looked to Leon. His beautiful eyes possessed with pain and worry. He pulled me into his arms and held me tight. His woody scent filled my nose and I could feel myself slip slowly back more to reality.

"What happened? You had me worried." He pulled away, holding me by my shoulders, his eyes flicking back and forth between mine, the concern still there.

I tried to talk, but nothing came out. I couldn't tell him about my past. Not like this anyway. I was scared he'd walk away. I wasn't ready to tell him.

"Baby? Talk to me, please?" He was desperate, I could hear the pain in his voice as it started to shake and wobble. He placed his warm hands either side of my face and used his thumbs to softly brush away my tears that were cool against my skin. I felt myself give into his warmth, instantly feeling soothed and calm.

I tried to speak again.

"That song... the lyrics... the music video... It's like a flashback of my past." My voice was irregular from the aftershock of crying.

"Oh sweetheart, it's OK. You're OK, I'm here." He pulled me back in for a hug, this time with a gentler hold. It was comforting being in his arms. He made me feel safe. Like everything really was going to be OK. I melted into his touch and hugged him back, breathing in his wonderful scent again. He had a hand stroking my hair soothingly, whilst the other was rhythmically rubbing my back.

Once Leon was sure that I had calmed down and my breathing was under control, he gave me a light kiss on the forehead before shutting my passenger door and getting settled back into the driver's seat.

Leon spent the last half an hour of our car journey making me laugh and bringing my smile back to my face. Soon enough, the panic attack was in the back of mind and I was back to enjoying myself.

* * *

Before I knew it, Leon was pulling into a driveway that led to a huge, gorgeous house. It wasn't until we had pulled up that I could smell and see the sea that laid to the back of the house. The house was a two-story building, with light grey stone and white paneling. The windows were big, taking up most of the wall space. The rooms on the top floor at the front of the building had a small balcony, only big enough to stand and lean on the railings.

Leon took our bags out of the car, refusing to let me help carry any of them, and we walked to the front door, the stones of the walkway crunching underneath our feet. The front door was light grey with a big silver knocker in the middle. I pushed the door open and stood open mouthed.

As soon as we entered the majestic hallway, we were greeted with a white marble staircase that was split into two before meeting in the middle at the top. In front of the stairs was a brown console table with curling feet, housing a vase of roses in the center. A light grey fluffy rug had been placed in front of the antique desk, with a crystal chandelier hanging directly above it. There were a couple of houseplants dotted around the foyer, bringing about the feel of life about the place.

"Leon... this place is beautiful." My voice was full of wonder, and I could only imagine how my face looked. I had never been anywhere so extravagant. I followed Leon as he gave me a quick tour of the place. There was an indoor swimming pool that extended outside and there was a game room with a pool table and a darts board.

The kitchen was huge. It looked similar to the one in my apartment, but just on a bigger, more expensive scale. I walked over to the massive American fridge and pulled the double doors open. The light from the appliance illuminated my face, and upon seeing the inside, my face lit up probably twice as brighter than the fridge had. The fridge was full of all kinds of food, and I felt inspiration well up in me at the prospects of all the different dishes I could cook.

Peeling me from the fridge, Leon took my hand and brought me into the main room. There was a giant fireplace with a TV hung on the wall above it. Two sofas were positioned, forming an 'L' in front of the fireplace with a long rectangular glass coffee table in the middle. The coffee table had a shelf underneath the top layer of glass, displaying a selection of magazines.

There were some canvases and pictures decorating the walls. I noticed one picture was a family one. I stood nearer to it so I could inspect it a little better. My eyes widened in shock when I saw Leon in it. He was kneeling on the floor with a man and woman in their mid to late twenties standing behind him, their arms wrapped around each other with beautiful smiles aimed at the camera. Leon had an arm around each child, identical in looks despite being different genders, who were standing either side of him. He looked so happy and carefree in this picture.

"That's my cousin and his wife. The two children are their twins Isaac and Isla. This is their summer home. They let me borrow it for the weekend." Leon suddenly appeared next to me. I could see the family resemblance. Leon and his cousin shared the same brilliant smile. Leon's cousin had beautiful blonde hair and sharp blue eyes, compared to Leon's luscious brown hair and hypnotising hazel eyes.

"I see. Their children look very sweet and incredibly fond of you." The children were both leaning their heads on Leon's shoulder as they beamed at the camera.

"They are, until they have one of their illustrious tantrums, then you need to hide and lock your doors. I spoil them a lot, that's why they love me so much." He chuckled. He was like the favourite uncle that everyone has. My mind wandered to the future, about what Leon would be like with our kids... if we were ever lucky enough to have them.

Continuing with the tour of the downstairs, he led me to the back garden and what lay before me took my breath away. Straight ahead, past the gates was the beach and then the sea. The midday sun was high in the sky like a glowing medallion, the crystal-clear water sparkling and rippling gently underneath its reflection. The beach was a beautiful golden colour and was completely stone and pebble free. It was a slightly darker shade near the shore where the waves of the sea were delicately rolling in and out.

"It's a magnificent sight isn't it? We can take a walk along the beach tonight if you're feeling up for it." Standing next to me, a hand on the small of my back, his voice was soft and level, and it matched how the scenery made me feel :at peace and relaxed.

"That sounds lovely Leon." My hand was in his and I gave it a squeeze in confirmation. He looked down at me and gave me a loving smile before placing a sweet peck on the top of my head.

"Come on, I want to show you the upstairs before we put our things away."

The stairs, as magnificent as they were, were a workout in itself. The steps were long and wide, but they weren't very high, and so there was a lot to climb. Once at the top, there was a U shaped corridor with six doors spaced out along it. Behind each was a bedroom, all decorated the same, aside from two that were the children's room. We didn't look in those rooms, or in Leon's cousin's bedroom, it felt too much like an invasion of privacy. Leon let me choose which of the other three rooms I wanted us to have.

The room I chose had a massive king size bed along the back wall. I say back wall, it was entirely made of glass. If we laid at the foot of the bed, we could look out and have a view of the beach at the back of the house. The bedroom also had an en-suite that put mine at home to shame. There was a big shower with glass panels and a sliding door. The bath was a big white claw-foot tub that was positioned in front of the one-way window, giving us a full view of the rear of the house and beyond.

I was in absolute awe of this house. It truly was the most exquisite house I had ever been in and I felt lucky to be able to have an experience like this. Leon led me back to the bedroom and we started unpacking our essentials from our bags.

"Thank you, Leon, for bringing me here." I looked at Leon and I could feel the sheer joy in my eyes as they zoned into his honeycomb-yellow eyes.

He walked over to me and wrapped his arms around my waist and pulled me flush against him. I could feel my heart rate pick up as I got lost in his eyes. His hands were dangerously close to my backside, and I couldn't help but will for him to give it a squeeze.

"Well, it is your birthday weekend, so I wanted to spoil you." I was shocked he had remembered when my birthday was, even more so that he wanted to spend the whole weekend with me in somewhere as lavish as this. I wasn't used to the princess treatment. It was something that I had always wanted, something I often begged Wyatt for, but it fell on deaf ears.

I stood on my tippy-toes and placed a hand on the back of his head and pulled him down to meet me for a kiss. His lips tasted delicious. He skillfully slipped his tongue into my mouth and tangled with mine. He tasted minty and fresh and I was very soon intoxicated by it. But we'd only just arrived, and I wanted to save this moment for tonight.

I pulled away and Leon let out a small whine in protest. I put my hand on his face and brushed his lower lip with my thumb.

"We will pick this up later tonight." That seemed to satisfy him enough as he put on his signature smile and nodded in agreement.

I was really looking forward to spending the entire weekend with Leon, not having to worry about anything or anyone. It would be like a small insight into our future together, and that had my heart pounding hard in my chest with excitement.

21

Chapter 20

Ava's POV:

Me and Leon were cuddled at the wrong end of the bed, watching out of the window as the sun began to rise. As promised, me and Leon had picked up from our make-out that night and we had yet to go to sleep. As worn out as I was, being here in his arms, looking out at the transfixing scene in front of us, I felt more alive than ever.

The sun was teasingly peeking above the sea, its red and orange hues perfectly blended together, slowly bleeding into the sky as it replaced the dark of the night with its blazing brilliance. Its rays stretched across the vast sea as it awoke, its arms reaching longer and longer for the shore as the sun gradually rose.

It was peaceful here by the sea. The only sounds were the odd birds chirping as they flapped freely across the endless sky, and the calming metronomic whispers of the waves of the sea, as they tumbled onto the golden beach.

Watching the start of a new day roll in made me feel at one

with the world and a great sense of peace washed over me. I took in a deep breath, breathing in the distant briny scent of sea, mixed with the fresh scent of cotton from the bedding, and let it out slowly through my lips. I felt Leon hug me tighter towards him. I looked up and found that he was looking down at me, a happy, sleepy side smile playing on his lips. The early morning sunlight reflected in his eyes like the flames of a fire dancing softly. His fingers were delicately running up and down my arm, making the hairs on my body stand to attention.

He bent his head down and placed a kiss on my lips. "I could spend the rest of my life here with you like this, you know." And just like that, my heart burst with love. There was that word again.

I snuggled closer into his chest and breathed in his heavenly scent. "I wouldn't be against that at all." I had never felt so peaceful, or so content. It felt right being here with Leon, cradled protectively in his arms. Whenever he held me, it felt like our bodies were perfectly moulded for the other, like two pieces of a jigsaw.

He was slowly drifting to sleep, his words becoming quieter and more slurred as he slipped further into unconsciousness.

"Good. Because... I couldn't imagine... my life without you in it..." I felt exactly the same towards him, and a warm feeling spread through my body. I couldn't stop my mind from repeating his words in my head. Once I'd finished hearing the end of the sentence, I'd press the rewind on my imaginary tape recorder and press play to hear it again.

We were three months into this relationship and even though it really was early days, I couldn't see my future without him in it. Despite being happy and surrounded by people who loved me, I had felt dormant for a long time, even when I was with Wyatt.

Up until now, I thought that I had loved Wyatt, but looking back and since being with Leon, I knew that what I felt wasn't love. He was just a temporary means to an end, filling the void in my heart for the time being until the right person walked into my life. And I couldn't shake the feeling that that person was Leon. He filled my life with excitement and colour. I had developed further into a different person since he had made an appearance in my life. He made me feel like I was the only girl in the world, and that I was special. I had spent the last nine years of my life making sure that people felt needed, wanted and important, so much so that I had forgotten to remind myself that I too was all of those things.

I knew that there was going to be some bumps in the road coming up, and I was scared to death to be vulnerable and expose myself fully to him. But if I wanted this to go the distance, I needed to bite the bullet and open up my old scars and show Leon the real me. I wanted him to love all of me, my past self and my present one. Yes, we were two completely different people, but if I hadn't of been the person I was before, I never would've become the woman I am today. I probably wouldn't have found Leon either. Or Ffion, for that matter. How different my life would have turned out if I hadn't of experienced what I did. Where would I be living now instead? Would I have followed my childhood dream of being a teacher? Would I have started finding my love for working out?

I wouldn't say I completely forgave my demons of the past, but I was somewhat thankful for them. I had become stronger, more confident and a much better person for going through that dark time, not to mention that I was surrounded by the best people; people who gave me purpose. As petrified as I was, I knew I would have to eventually tell him; let him in, but only when I was ready to. Exposing myself so nakedly, tearing my old emotional wounds open would take a lot of courage, something I didn't have much of, but I would do it. One day.

Seeing how worried he had been about me in the car yesterday after my panic attack just reassured me even more. It didn't feel fair for me to keep quiet about it to him when he was consoling me without really knowing what he was up against. I wanted him to understand, so that whenever anything like that happened again, he would know why and how to calm me down. It would be so much easier if he could just read minds so I wouldn't have to experience the pain of talking about it again.

I closed my eyes, and focused on Leon's heartbeat, allowing it to lull me sleep. Just as I was about to lose consciousness, Leon's sleepy words drifted into my ears.

"I love you."

* * *

Leon's POV:

I was trying to convince myself that my sleepy slip of the tongue had been a dream. But it was pointless. I knew that it hadn't been a dream. I had been hoping that perhaps she would be the first to have confessed her love and feelings to me, but as fate would have it, it just had to be me. I had felt so wrapped up in a cocoon of love and contentment with her in my arms this morning, I hadn't even given it a second thought about whether or not I should say it to her, it just fell from my thoughts and tumbled out of my mouth.

I don't regret telling her though, it feels like a big weight has been lifted off my shoulders. The words had been on the tip of my tongue for a while now, and I didn't have the balls to come out and say it; worried that she would freak out. But it would seem that I had nothing to worry about, because she either didn't hear me, or she did and is choosing to pretend that it never happened. I wasn't too sure how to feel about it.

We were taking a leisurely walk along the beach. Since the house led directly to the beach, we'd left our shoes there, and walked barefoot. The cool, wet sand beneath our feet providing relief from the heat. The compact grains slightly crunching as we walked, the colour disfiguring under our weight and our footprints being left behind under the pressure of our feet. Her small soft hand was intertwined loosely with my fingers and I had found myself subconsciously rubbing my thumb along the back of her hand. The breeze had picked up as we walked along the shoreline, making the water crinkle as it rolled onto the shore, before receding and dragging some sand back with it.

She was truly a picture of beauty and peace in this afternoon sun. Her hair was fanning out behind her, softly swirling and whirling in the gentle sea breeze. She had tilted her head back slightly with her eyes closed, and her full, luscious peach lips were set in a small, satisfied smile as she walked blind. I could feel my love for her spread through every ounce of my being. I wanted more than anything to tell her how I felt, but since she hadn't responded to the first time I told her, I didn't want to risk really freaking her out. Fuck it. There was only one way to silence my mind.

"Ava,"

"Mm hmm." She hadn't looked at me. She was still absorbing, savouring her surroundings.

"I'm sorry if I freaked you out this morning with my confession. I don't want you to feel like you have to say it back, because you don't. I want you to say it when you're ready to." I had prevented us from walking any further by standing in front of her. I held her hands in each of mine and looked into her eyes. I could get lost looking into her eyes. They were beautiful, and right now, they were full of gratitude. Her shoulders relaxed slightly. I hadn't even noticed that she'd tensed them up.

With a small smile on her face, she tip-toed up and placed a kiss on my cheek. "Thank you baby, I appreciate that you're willing to wait for me." I'd low-key wanted her to say it back to me just then, but I had to respect her feelings regardless of the disappointment that was now making itself at home in the chambers of my heart. At least I knew that she had heard me this morning. I knew what she was like. She was making sure that she was sure of her feelings and making sure that mine were genuine towards her. She didn't want to end up hurt, and that thought made me realise that she had been hurt by someone in the past.

Continuing our walk hand in hand, I tried to break down some of her walls. It couldn't hurt to try, I suppose. "I want to ask you something, but don't feel like you have to answer if you don't want to."

"Sure." She spoke indifferently, as if she was an open book and I was free to ask her anything, and yet, I got the impression that there were a few things that were strictly off-limits. We were all allowed to have secrets, it gave us all an edge; I had some of my own, but when was the right time to tell the people we care about?

"You're very cautious when you enter new relationships. You wanted to get to know me first before we even did anything, and you're very guarded about your feelings." She was looking up at me. Her expression was unreadable as she listened, trying to gauge where this conversation was heading. I didn't want to step on her toes or make her uncomfortable, so I had to tread carefully.

"That tells me that you've been hurt in the past before and... and don't feel like you have to tell me, because I don't want you to feel forced to... but I was wondering what happened?" It was out there, out in the open. She was quiet for a moment and I could see the battle in her mind take place as she argued with herself about whether or not to tell me. A number of hypotheticals flashed in my mind about what could have possibly happened in her life for her to be so restrained with letting others in; why her actions clearly demonstrated how she felt about someone, yet her words were kept on a tight leash.

With a deep sigh she spoke.

"There's a couple of reasons why my heart is guarded. I don't feel ready to tell you all of them all, but I will tell you one of the reasons. Two years ago, I got into a relationship with someone called Wyatt. We were together for a year and a half and we were very happy, for the most part anyway. He gave me all the attention I could've asked for, showering me in gifts, taking me out on dates, the lot. It was probably safe to say he spoiled me." She was confident as she spoke. Her voice was powerful and unfaltering. I felt a little privileged that she was prepared to tell me something about her past, and I could appreciate that she had disclosed that there was something else, but she wasn't ready to let me in on that secret.

"In the last six months of our relationship, he started acting differently towards me. I had no idea why, it was a gradual change; it took me weeks to notice. The gifts stopped, the attention stopped, and he only seemed focused on sleeping with me. One day, I came home from visiting my mum unexpectedly early and caught him deep inside my roommate and then best friend Felicity. It turned out for the last three months of our relationship, he was banging her in her bedroom in my apartment at any moment he could, including whilst I slept."

I could feel my therapist brain whirring. Not only had she been victim to penny dating, but she was also a victim of being at the hands of, for lack of a better word, a cunt. Not many people know what penny dating is, and it's hard to notice that the manipulative method is being used on you until you *really* analyse the relationship. One half of the relationship effectively love bombs you; investing all their time, effort and energy into you, before they then start to lower the bar inch by inch while occasionally giving little bouts of the person you fell in love with just so they can keep you interested and you get used to their new level of affection. Eventually they're only giving you the bare minimum but it's OK, because every once in a while they'll do something nice for you. Until one day you realise that you deserve more and better than what is being offered to you.

It was no surprise that she was cautious and protective of her feelings and heart. She couldn't give it to just anyone. She had to make sure that they were worthy of both it and her; she knew her worth.

"I'm sorry that happened to you. He sounds like a right fucking prick." There wasn't a word strong enough in the dictionary to describe the type of person he was.

"He is," She scoffed, "but it doesn't matter now, because I don't think I truly loved him. I mean, sure, I thought I did, but you never truly know what love is until you meet the right person. The person who only wants the best for you, embracing your flaws and all. The person who walks through life with you, helping you achieve your dreams and goals. The person who would go to the ends of the Earth to ensure your happiness. He was just a stand in while I waited for that person to enter my life." She looked up at me, meeting my eyes with hers. A soft pink blush had manifested itself onto her cheeks and her bottom lip was half tucked into her mouth. It didn't matter that she couldn't tell me she loved me back. What she had just said was enough to ease any doubt in my mind. She loved me. She was just a little apprehensive.

She shook her head dismissively, as if what she had said sounded stupid to her, telling me to forget what she'd just said.

"I'm sorry, that was forw-" I stopped her from speaking by clasping hold of either side of her face and planting a deep kiss on her lips. I felt her give into me, the tension in her body being exorcised by my lips. I opened my eyes briefly and saw that her eyes were closed, and any worry that had previously been etched on her beautiful face had been erased.

I pulled away and leaned my forehead against hers.

"Don't apologise. You have no idea how happy that made me. How happy *you* make me. You're an incredible woman Ava, and you shouldn't ever doubt yourself. You're stronger than you realise, and you deserve the world and more. I just hope I can be the man to live up to that expectation."

Her eyes started looking glassy as tears started to well up in her beautiful orbs. She wasn't sad, the big smile on her mouth verified that. She balled my t-shirt into her little fists and buried her head in my chest.

"I want you to be that man Leon. I don't want anyone else." She muffled into my chest before tilting her head up, resting her chin on my chest. Her eyes were glimmering with an intense tenderness as a tear slipped and trailed down the smooth curve of her cheek.

"My heart belongs to you Leon. I... I love you."

I don't think I have ever had a smile on my face as big as the one I had on now. I picked her up and spun her around, her legs swung round, her skirt blowing softly whilst her arms wrapped round my neck, clinging onto me tightly. Her giggle a heavenly song of the angels as it rang in my ears. I placed her back on her feet lightly before giving her a kiss that was gentle and passionate. She kissed me back with the equal amount of emotion, and I could feel her perfect lips smile against mine. I pulled back slightly with just a breath between us, looking her deep in the eyes.

"I love you too Ava. God, you have no idea how much I love you."

Chapter 21

"I win! Again!" I slapped down my red number two card, winning my third game of Uno in a row. Leon defeatedly tossed his cards on top of the pile that had steadily been growing in between us, sticking a middle finger up at me as they landed with a slap.

"You're a sore winner."

"And an even worse loser." A smug smile resided on my lips as I gathered the cards up. "Another?" We had spent the afternoon walking along the swash of the beach, revelling in the cool feel of the water rolling onto our feet, and I had finally told Leon how I felt about him; it felt liberating and now that the word was out there, I just wanted to scream it from the top of a building. But, those three little words held so much power that I didn't want to overuse them too much.

We had retired to the lounge in the evening, drinking wine, snacking and playing games that I apparently was far too good at.

"Fuck no." He scoffed as he took the cards from my hands, straightened them out and slid them back into their packaging.

He stood up, placing them on the table before turning to me, holding his hand out in invitation.

"I'd much rather play something I know I will definitely win at." Taking his hand, he pulled me up, his bicep contracting slightly with lifting my weight.

"Oh yeah? And what game would that be?" Curiosity filled me as I skipped beside him through the house, our bare feet quietly padding against the cold hardwood floors, and past the stairs to the opposite end of the building. The emotions of today mixed with the booze filtering through me had me on a happy buzz.

"Pool." Letting go of my hand, he pushed the dark, mahogany doors open, revealing the expansive, luxurious games room.

The walls were painted black, the colour spreading up onto the ceiling, recessed lights dotted about the area creating a star-filled sky right before our eyes, so close it felt like it was closing in on us. The cold floor beneath our naked feet was made from grey luxury vinyl tiling. In the center of the room, a large snooker table was situated, its red velvet plane with the balls set up already. Gold hanging lights hung down towards the table, creating better lighting for players. In line with the large playing table along the back of the wall was a golden bar with matching stools, a glass cabinet full of a variety of booze behind it, and a dartboard was hung on the wall in the far corner, away from anything fragile that could potentially be broken by amateur dart players.

I walked over to the bar, the tabletop made of clear glass, and ran my finger along it as I made my way round behind it.

"It's beautiful isn't it?" Leon followed behind me, taking up one of the stools.

"It truly is. It must've cost a fortune." The awe in my voice couldn't be faked. A place like this was only something that I could ever dream of owning, let alone being able to stand in it. I slid a glass of JD and coke on the rocks to Leon before getting to work on pouring myself a Southern Comfort and lemonade.

"Not nearly as much as what he'll get for it. Kian worked his balls off to build this from the ground up for Anna and the kids. The profit he'll make when the time comes to sell it will be astronomical and those twins of his will be set up for life." I didn't know any rich people, so being stood in this place simply blew my mind. It also ignited a life aspiration that I had never thought of before. I made my way around the bar and stood next to Leon, leaning against the counter as I pondered.

"I think that I'd like to build my own home one day. Create the layout, design the rooms completely from scratch." Leon let out a short but joyful laugh.

"Anyone who lets you loose on a digger would be both one brave and stupid individual." I playfully punched him in the arm as I faked offense.

"Rude. I'll have you know, I'm a good driver." Leon placed a hand around my waist, fitting perfectly in the curve, and led me over to the snooker table.

"Says the one without the drivers license."

"Don't need a license to know how to drive." I flashed Leon a wink as I set my drink down on the windowsill before making my way to the rack housing the pool cues.

"I'll have to find a quiet bit of road to let you drive my car on so you can prove this self-proclaimed title of 'good driver'." Leon had followed suit and picked the longest cue on the rack. I picked the green chalk up and got to work scraping it back and forth on the tip of my cue.

"Sounds good to me. But one thing I'm definitely not good at," I pointed to the table, "is breaking." A chuckle left Leon's mouth as he made his way over to me and wrapped an arm around my shoulders, pulling me closer to him.

"Then I suggest I teach you how to do it." He said quietly in my ear, his hot breath gliding down my neck before giving me a kiss on the temple. Not giving me a chance to respond, he pulled away and squeezed my arse before moving towards the head of the table. I followed after him and took position, sliding the tip of the cue onto the top of my thumb, gave a few strokes towards the white ball and bent down slightly.

I felt Leon behind me, a hand placed on the top center of my back as he gently bent me down further. "You need to lower yourself more, so you can look down the cue to the white ball. It'll help you aim."

My body close to a right angle, I could feel Leon getting hard against my backside that was now pushed out due to this new angle. Bringing himself closer over the top of me, he reached over and adjusted the position of my hand so it was standing up more on my fingertips, resembling 'Thing' from '*The Addams Family*', and with his other he held the back section of the cue.

"So, you want to level the tip of your cue to the white ball, right in the center. Pull back so the tip is almost touching your finger, like this. The power comes from your back arm, so then use some force and smack the white ball straight into the ball at the top of the triangle." He pushed the cue with me, sending the white ball bounding into the triangle of balls up the other end, which split across the table with a loud crack.

"Not bad, rookie. You'll be a pro at cracking balls in no time." With a parting smack on my behind, Leon made his way to position himself by the white ball. He had a clear, straight shot of potting the red ball in. A shot he couldn't fuck up. I walked around behind him, and softly spoke in his ear, "I'm already a

179

pro at that; you've got first-hand experience," as I cupped his semi in my hand. He hit the white ball off-center, sending the red ball bouncing off the cushion and into the opposite direction, instead of being potted straight into the pocket it had been stationed at.

"You're a fucking cheat." A smug smile played on my lips as he hung his head, still in his hitting position, his thin linen shirt taut against his muscular back. He sighed before straightening up.

"And do you know what happens to cheaters?" His voice deep. A dangerous calm that made my smirk vanish. I stayed silent, gripping my cue with both hands, wondering where this was going. He stood his cue up on the floor, leaning it up against the side of the table and then turned and faced me, a devilish look plaguing his face.

"They get punished." He took a singular long stride to reach me. Not quick enough to react, he ripped my cue from my grip and tossed it a little way besides us onto the floor and picked me up. He gently put me down on the edge of the pool table and swept the balls that were behind me out of the way with a single sweep of his arm. The balls now a safe distance from causing any injury or pain, Leon pulled my legs apart with a hand on either knee. The skirt of my dress rising further north towards my hips, the fabric no longer able to cover my thighs.

His fingers delicately traced up and down the top half of my legs, his touch sending sizzling tingles to my lower stomach that made me attempt to squeeze my legs shut and sharply intake air. Leon felt me tense, and held my legs open, his thumbs teasingly rubbing the inside of my thighs, inches away from the area I could feel was getting increasingly moist.

"Uh, uh." He moved his head towards my ear, his breath

a warm tickle that danced on the surface of the skin it made contact with. One hand still gently circling the top of my thigh, the other buried in my hair, tugging my head ever so slightly backwards, encouraging a soft moan to escape me.

"Leon, you're teasing me." He knew I had a love-hate relationship with being teased. Whilst for the first few seconds I loved it, I very quickly grow agonisingly achy for him to touch and fill me in the way I craved and needed him to, and all he'd done so far was play nervous with me.

"All give and no take." He tutted, his thumb was rubbing the front of my underwear now, the fabric a very thin and futile barrier between our skin.

"You can't grab my cock and then think you can get away with it." He took the thin bit of skin under my ear between his teeth and sucked lightly. I felt myself writhe from his touch, my hand reaching up to slide in his hair. He allowed me all of two seconds of gripping his hair before he pulled back and took my hand away from him, his rubbing also ceasing.

"That's enough of that. The more you touch me, the more I tease you. How this ends up completely depends on how much of a good girl you can be." My chin now being held by his thumb and forefinger as he gave me his instructions. "Do you understand?" I gave him a nod of obedience.

He returned his attention to under my skirt, to the little white lacy underwear that barely covered me. He bent down, and kissed his way up the bare skin of my leg, his hand caressing the other in tandem, my moans all I could do to show just how good his touch was making me feel; his skin on mine electric, zapping every nerve. He changed legs and gave the other the same treatment. I leaned back, giving him space to go further up, but was disappointed when he didn't go as far as I wanted, my protesting moan communicating this. He chuckled in response. He knew exactly what he was doing and how impatient I was getting. But he also knew that he can only tease me for so long before he too gets equally impatient and will undoubtedly bury his dick in me.

Without warning, he grabbed my ankles and placed them on top of his shoulders before giving me a single command, "Lay back." My head barely touched the table when he dragged me closer to him, and held my hips up to his mouth. He took a deep inhale, breathing in my arousal and letting out a satisfied moan. Keeping me lifted with one hand, he used the other to remove my underwear, switching hands when the other side was stuck by his arm before discarding them somewhere on the floor.

He resumed kissing and licking me everywhere but where I was longing for him to, further denying me the pleasure I was desperately reaching for, before he hovered mere millimetres from me, his hot breath sending vibrations from my clit, all the way up my spine.

"Baby, please." I pleaded. My only answer was the feel of his warm mouth on my pussy. His tongue took long strokes up my slit towards my bud, over and over, alternating between fast and slow, his moans oscillating against me. Every so often, he'd change tactic and dip his tongue in and out of me, the wet slurps of him feasting on me sending my hips driving up for him to get deeper. Soon enough, restless with desire, I once again found my hand on the back of his head, pushing him closer against me, wanting more and more of him and his magic tongue. He slapped me on the side of my arse before removing himself from me, my hand falling away. I looked down my body at him. His mouth glistening with my juices. Without licking or wiping the moisture away, he leaned towards me, my legs falling down his arms to his side.

"What did I tell you?" My insolence kept me quiet, wanting him to punish me more for not doing as I was told. He was so close that I could smell myself on his mouth. His hand found my throat and squeezed gently. Not tight enough to cut off my oxygen, but enough for me to feel my face start to go red.

"Don't make me ask twice. What did I tell you?" He repeated.

"The more I touch, the more you tease me." My voice a little hoarse from his grip. He let go of my neck and instantly I could feel the blood drain from my face.

"Indeed. So until I tell you otherwise, your hands are to remain here while I have my fun with you." He grabbed my wrists and pinned them under one hand above my head as he spoke. Giving me no time to respond, his mouth was on mine, my flavours being transferred from his lips to mine, the sweetness finding its way onto my tongue as Leon licked his way through my puckered lips.

Tasting myself was not something I thought I would ever enjoy. The thought of tasting myself with past partners made me internally cringe, but doing it with Leon, who gave me no choice but to taste it... It was intoxicating, hot and it turned me on in a way I had never thought possible.

Leaving my mouth, Leon navigated his way along my jawline and to my neck, where he spent his sweet time kissing, and sucking the thin, delicate skin.

Suddenly, I felt a cold breeze on my breasts. My dress had a deep neckline that tied up in the center, which meant wearing a bra was out of the question. Leon had pulled the strings on my dress loose, freeing them from the confines of the fabric. He pulled away and admired my bare mounds, giving me his approval with a whispered "fuck me" at seeing the girls free.

My nipples peaked at the sudden coldness that tickled them, swallowing the metal bar pierced through them as they became slightly engorged from arousal, a bodily function that Leon took as an invitation. His lips wrapped around my nipple and immediately got to work sucking them whilst one hand played with the opposite hand and the other cupped the breast his mouth was giving attention to.

His teeth and fingers worked in tandem on their respective nipples as he gently bit, sucked, flicked and rubbed them before swapping and giving the other the same attention. The sensitivity of the motions made me arch my back off the table, and pushing my breasts further into Leon's mouth and hands, my moans and his continued sucking sounds fueling our arousal.

Once both breasts were red from his manhandling, Leon pulled away, breathing heavily whilst observing his handiwork. His eyes roamed their way up to my own, stopping at the little love bites he'd left like patchwork tattoos up my neck before making another little pit stop to admire my plump lips which had faint remnants of my pussy juice on them before he stopped at my eyes. Without breaking eye contact, he licked his lips, rolling his lower lip under his top teeth before gradually letting it go.

"Turn around. Get on all fours." Being the good girl that I am, I did as I was told; leaning down on my elbows, elevating my backside in the air, and shuffling backwards as close to the cushion of the table as I could. Leon's hands didn't miss a beat in tenderly caressing the round expanse of the full moon I was giving him, muttering curses of approval. His hands finished their excursion, with one's final destination being underneath me. His thumb began massaging my bud in slow, circular motions, forcing me to jerk backwards at the sensitivity. Behind me, above the sounds of my gasps and moans, I heard Leon lick his fingers before sliding a couple inside of me, his thumb still working my clit.

"Holy shit, that feels good." The sound of my wet pussy increasing my level of horniness. I walked my elbows further back, lifting my backside up as far as it could go, which in turn made Leon's fingers hit just the spot that would have me squirting within minutes.

But me squirting all over Leon's hand wasn't in his plans just yet. He removed his hand from my clit, leaving it swollen and throbbing in his absence, unfurled the fingers that were inside of me and added another. I now had three of his thick fingers filling me. It was quite a tight fit; so tight that my eyes squeezed together and forced me to intake a sharp breath. I was so focused on adjusting to the extra finger, that I barely felt the saliva that had been spat on my arsehole.

And then there was a pressure I was yet to experience back there and a squeak came out of my mouth. Leon had done the unspoken. I now had a thumb pressed ever so slightly in my virgin arsehole.

We hadn't discussed anything regarding the back door entry; as far as I was concerned, that was an exit only. And yet, I was pleasantly surprised at how good it felt, especially with his fingers filling me simultaneously.

"Does this feel OK?" His domination faltered slightly, making sure that I was fine with this new sexual endeavour. My breath taken away from this new sensation, all I could do was answer with a nod.

There was no time to panic that he was now eye level with my starfish as his fingers started driving into me in a slow rhythm as my walls adjusted to him. His thumb and alien pressure remaining a silent and motionless partner, until he begins to pick up speed and his thumb starts to very slowly move within me, going no deeper than his first knuckle. The more he kept his thumb in me, the more surprised I grew at how much I was genuinely enjoying the feel of him filling my holes. I found myself grinding backwards into him, matching his pace, but also pushing all of his fingers deeper into me.

"Fuck, sweetheart. I can't wait for the day you let me stretch you out with my cock in your tight little hole." Emphasising the hole he was talking about, he swirled his thumb inside of me, my head and eyes rolling at the sensation that rippled through me with a moan slipping free.

But it was short lived as he pulled his instruments of manipulation and pleasure out of me. An abrupt gasp taking my breath away at the sudden removal and an instant feeling of emptiness and hunger held me captive. Just as I was about to protest, he used a singular hand to move and hold my own behind my back as I heard him rustle behind me. And then my wish was answered as he sunk himself down to the hilt in me.

Leon hissed as I met him halfway whilst he slid himself in. Still holding my hands behind me, his spare hand was in my hair - which was now a tangled mess - pushing my face into the table as he started pounding into me. My breath got heavier with each thrust, my moans came out quickfire and higher pitched, drowning out Leon's own sexual noises and praises, sounds I usually lost myself to. But I was too far gone, too horny to concentrate on anything but my orgasm that I was trying not to prematurely release. Neither of us lasted long in this position; it felt too good with him being so deep, I could feel him in my belly button.

Leon let go of my hands and placed both hands on my waist, holding me with a tight grip. His pace was slower now, more deliberate as he pulled himself out until his tip was barely inside of me, and drove hard back into me. He repeated this process, my screams getting louder until I could start to feel my walls clamping around his cock.

"No. You are not to cum just yet." With a final and deeper thrust, he then sharply drew himself out of me, the suction sound only just audible over my cry.

"Play with your clit."

"What?" He'd never asked me to touch myself for him. Not that I never had, I most certainly had in the safety and privacy of my bedroom, but it was something I had never done in his presence, it wasn't something I had ever thought of doing in his presence.

"Stay in this position and play with yourself. I want you to make yourself cum." Making myself orgasm was one thing when it was just me, my hand or vibrator, but doing it in front of Leon gave me a little performance anxiety. But I really, really wanted to cum and the need for that overrode any fear.

Leaning on my right elbow for balance, I trailed my left hand down to my bud that was tingling in anticipation of having some more attention being given to it. The instant I touched myself, it was like riding a bike. My thumb and fingers worked in harmony as they built and coaxed my high out of me, my hips jerking up with the sensitivity that shot through me like lightning with every stroke.

His hand loosely around his cock, Leon wanked as he watched me from behind. My touch became much rougher than what his had been as I violently rubbed back and forth on my clit. A warm substance spurted like raindrops on my sweat covered backside haphazardly; some landing on my back, some sliding down the curve of my cheeks, and some down the valley in between.

"I'm.. I'm coming..." I whispered with jagged breath. Leon ducked underneath me, his mouth open ready to catch every single last drop that spilled from me. It was all I could do as I looked under my arm and watched him. I reached the full height of my climax, my cunt gushing for him, spilling out of me and straight into his mouth.

Completely empty and fulfilled, I dropped and rolled onto my back, forgetting about the cum on my backside, and clenched my legs together as my pussy convulsed and twitched.

Leon brought over some serviettes from the bar, cleaning himself up as he walked back to me, his dick somehow still hard. Once my body had stopped acting like a shock-absorber, Leon helped me up and assisted with cleaning the areas I couldn't see or reach.

"Well then, I was not expecting a thumb in my arse tonight. Or any night for that matter." I joked to Leon who was now dabbing his cum off the snooker table. It was coming off rather easily, much to my surprise.

"Just preparing you for bigger and better things, sweetheart." He teased back, giving me a wink before scrunching up and launching the cum rags into the bin.

"In your dreams pal. You'll be waiting a while before anything bigger than your thumb is going in there." I took a sip of my drink that had now started to go warm, the ice cubes now melted. I curled my lips up slightly at the after taste. Despite still being drinkable, it didn't taste as good watered down. But that wasn't enough to deter me, so I had another mouthful, larger than previously, eager to finish the drink.

"So an anal plug is fair game then? Good to know." I barely managed to keep the liquid in my mouth. My hand flew up to prevent any stray liquid from spilling out and onto the floor.

Choking down the alcohol, Leon chuckled as he picked up our cues.

"Leon!" Was all I could reply with. I was still in shock.

"I'm just saying, you might want to experiment later down the line."He handed me my cue and gave me a tender kiss on my head before heading to the table.

"Anyway, let's restart this game. And this time, you're breaking without my assistance." He scooped the balls in his arm and rolled them back to the top end of the table and started putting them in order in the triangular frame.

"Fine. But don't cry when I win." Ignoring his experiment comment, - because secretly I knew he was right, I would get curious - I rubbed more green chalk on the tip of my cue despite it not really needing any more yet.

"Ha. Dream on sister."

I did, in fact, win. Twice.

Chapter 22

I awoke the next day in bed alone and confused, with the faint sound of water being run in the background. I stretched my limbs out, letting out a satisfying groan as I felt my muscles pull. Flopping back onto the bed, I wondered how I ended up in the bed. I was adamant I had fallen asleep on the sofa watching some stupid film Leon had suggested. I remember that I was laying along the sofa with my head in Leon's lap. He had been stroking my hair with his giant hand and it was enough to soothe me to sleep. It was like I'd been magically transported to the bed, but then common sense kicked in. Leon must've carried me in those strong, bulging arms of his to bed.

"Good morning birthday girl." Leon's voice was delightfully avid this morning. It had completely slipped my mind that it was my birthday today. But then, when I've had nothing but Leon on my mind recently, could I really be blamed?

"Hello you." I sat up on my elbows and looked at him. He had walked from the en-suite to the bed and was sat on the edge, his body turned to face me. He had his perfect smile on his face and his eyes were bright.

Thinking about yesterday's events made me smile. The big 'L' word was out in the open now, and I was scared because now it was absolute. Definite. No take backs. But I was relieved. I had been itching to say it to him for days, but I didn't know when the good time was to say it. Plus, I had to be sure that I loved him. I didn't want to say it and what I felt for him wasn't love.

I swung my legs out of my bed and moved to straddle Leon, wrapping my arms around his neck and my legs around his waist. His arms snaked around my back, resting at the bottom of my back. I looked into his face. His eyes glowing amber, full of passion and desire. His lips were set in a cheeky, sexy smirk. He was delicious up close. Unlike him, I was completely naked, and I felt his eyes burn through my body as they roamed me up and down, taking in every inch of my nakedness.

I teasingly began to tickle the back of his neck with my fingers, eliciting a shudder and a low moan to escape from his heavenly lips. His grip around my waist tightened and I was pulled closer towards him, his erection pressing on my core.

I reached down between us with one hand and started to agonisingly gently circle his tip through the fabric of his boxers. He sucked in a breath as his hands moved to my backside.

"Is someone happy to see me?" I taunted in as sexy a voice as I could muster. I was in the mood now. The feel of his manhood pressed against me had me craving for it and him.

"He's always happy to see you." His tone was husky and low. His eyes burning with need and desire. His deep voice vibrated through my ears, sending a shiver down my spine.

I leant forward towards his ear. "Well, perhaps you can show me just how happy he is." I whispered, before taking his ear lobe into my mouth and sucking it. I took it into my teeth and gently tugged at it. Dropping it my from the grip of my teeth,

I kissed down his jawline to his neck, letting out little teasing moans.

"Fuck, Ava." He growled. He stood up suddenly and next thing I knew, my naked body was pressed up against the giant glass window, still clinging onto Leon like a koala. It didn't bother me that anyone on the beach could look up and see my naked butt smushed against the cold glass, I was too wrapped up in Leon to care.

Without missing a beat, his lips crashed hungrily onto mine. My senses became overpowered by his scent, the taste of him as his tongue explored the inside of mine, the feel of his soft hair under my palms as I bury my hand in it. I was being driven wild.

His lips left mine and I instantly missed their presence. He trailed his open-mouthed kisses down my neck, suckling every now and then, down towards my chest. I tilted my head back against the glass with a moan, as I felt my insides melt at the softness of his lips against my smooth skin.

He had shifted ever so slightly, so I was now being supported by one of his powerful arms, his muscles bulging under my weight, whilst the fingers of his other had found my dripping wet center.

"My girl is so fucking wet for me." He licked his lips as his fingers worked their magic inside of me. He started off slow, but as my breathing became more hitched, he increased his pace. As he pumped his thick fingers in and out of me, his lips had found mine again, devouring me.

He was finger-fucking me so hard that the palm of his hand was clapping against my clit, sending a ferocious shock-wave of electric up my body, making me gasp in shock. It was still sensitive from our abuse of it last night. I was becoming breathless as my orgasm came closer and closer. He could feel my walls tighten around him as he slowed his pace and started stroking my sweet spot whilst his thumb caressed my bud.

"Leon..." And with his name a delicate whisper, I felt my legs shake and my stomach tighten as I came undone over his fingers. He pulled them out of me and held them up to me. He put his index finger inside his mouth, tasting my juices. He closed his eyes and I watched as he slowly pulled his finger out of his mouth.

"Mmm, baby, you taste so good".

He held his middle finger up in front of my mouth, wanting me to taste myself. Before last night, I had never known what I tasted like, and after realising it wasn't as bad as I though it would be, I wouldn't turn his offering away. I was prepared to do anything at this point for him. I opened my mouth a licked teasingly up one side of his finger whilst I looked directly into his eyes, before plunging it into my mouth. The taste of my sweet nectar lingered on my tongue, before gently trickling down my throat as I swallowed.

"That's it, baby girl." Leon had his lower lip in between his teeth as he watched me. The fire in his eyes were flickering more than ever and I knew he wasn't finished with me.

With his newly freed hand, he pulled his boxers down to his ankles, and positioned himself so his tip was just at my entrance. He placed his hand on my waist once he was in position. His lips found mine and as he gradually pushed himself in hands free, inch by inch, a soft moan escaped my mouth, mingling with his sounds of pleasure.

Once he knew I was well adjusted to his insanely thick manhood, he picked up his speed. With one hand in his hair, gripping for dear life, my other hand was working on scratching his back. I dug my nails in as he thrust harder, sending me to a new dizzying state of euphoria.

I needed more of him. I needed all of him. I squeezed my legs tighter around him, pulling him in closer so I could feel him deeper, until I could feel him all the way up in my stomach. I was rewarded with a deep sensual groan from Leon.

The sloppy sound of my wetness as he glided in and out of me was overshadowed by the sounds of our moans that vibrated through the bedroom as we both slowly climbed towards our climax. His name escaped my mouth. I loved calling his name as he brought me a world of pleasure. He had removed his hand from my waist and had now wrapped it firmly around my neck, forcing my head to be tilted up. This motion only increased my arousal and aided in bringing my orgasm closer.

I could feel Leon pulsate in me. He was as close to finishing as I was. His hand was no longer around my throat, but was clasping me under my chin, forcing me to look into his eyes, that were dark with lust and want. I was dangerously close to being liberated, and I scrunched my eyes shut as I felt the wave of my release wash over me.

"Look at me." Leon's demanding voice made my heart stop and forced me to look him dead in the eyes. I watched in awe as I saw his eyes shift in colour as we both came at the same time. They had changed from dark and lustrous, to his light honey-dew colour of satisfaction and love.

Even though my orgasm was explosive, I wasn't able to make a sound. My scream was stuck in my throat as the intense love, passion and need in Leon's eyes reflected into my own. As we came together, our eyes locked on one another, I felt like we had become one.

Once Leon had stopped twitching inside of me, he lovingly traced his fingers along my hairline and followed it down past my ears and along my jawline until my chin was between his thumb and index finger. He planted a tender kiss on my lips, lingering for a few seconds before pulling away.

"I love you, Ava."

"I love you too, Leon." I meant it with my whole heart.

He smiled adoringly at me and carried me into the bathroom, his dick still inside me, growing soft.

There was a sweet smell in the bathroom, and my eyes widened in surprise as I saw candles dotted around the room, their flames flickering steadily as they released their scent. I looked towards the ceiling-to-floor window and found the bath was steaming with a snowy mountain of bubbles.

He sat me down on the worktop next to the sink and pulled out of me. His eyes zoned into my now numb core, watching as his seed slowly spilled out of me.

"I'm sorry, I didn't wear a condom." He had a look of worry on his face, which worsened as it dawned on him. "Shit, I didn't last night either." His reaction justifiable though. It was too early in the relationship for us to even think about having a child, although the chances of that were slim on my part. We had just got too lost in the moment that extra precaution was forgotten about.

"Don't worry, I'm on contraception." Which I was. Despite my low fertility rate, it wasn't a risk I was willing to take just yet. Because there was still the incredibly thin possibility that I could fall pregnant. Christ, I was starting to sound like my mum.

With a relieved sigh and a smile, he reached for a cloth. He ran it under the hot tap until it was completely saturated, and then wrung it out so it wasn't dripping. He was careful in his touch as he cleaned me up, the warm fabric soothing on my abused core. This weekend had not only been a birthday weekend away, it had also turned out to be a weekend full of sex. Not that I was complaining, I couldn't get enough of Leon. He dumped the cloth in the sink and kissed the tip of my nose.

It was unusual for a guy to take care of their partner post sex, it wasn't something I'd ever experience. But then, for too long I hadn't been treated in the way I thought I had deserved, it was unfathomable to me that there was someone out there who could. I wanted to ask him what this was all about, when he seemingly read my mind by answering the question at the forefront of my brain.

"Today is the day I get to spoil you and there's nothing you can say or do to stop me. I want you to feel special, because you truly do deserve it." It was such a small gesture but setting the bathroom like this for me, taking care of me and his use of sweet words made my heart swell with love. Tears brimmed my eyes as a smile of gratitude and happiness spread on my face. A couple of droplets dropped to my rosy cheeks and Leon kissed them away, his lips soft on my skin. He gathered my hair up to the top of my head and tied it up into a messy bun with a hairband he had on his wrist.

"I didn't notice you were wearing one of my hairbands."

"I've been wearing it for a week. It makes me feel closer to you, like you're with me when you can't physically be by my side." He had a shy smile on his face and a hint of a blush creeping on his cheeks.

"Who knew you were such a softie." I teased. Secretly, I loved that he was wearing my hairband. What it meant to him and how it made him feel, was what it was like for me whenever I wore his clothing.

"I'm only a soft sap for you." Honestly, this man had my whole heart. I felt my heart expand with love.

He held his hand out for me. I placed my small hand in his giant one and slid off the counter. Leon led me to the bath, and with my hand still in his, I cautiously poked my toe into the froth, testing the temperature, before sinking into it.

The water wasn't burning, I suppose it had time to cool down whilst me and Leon were busy being intimate, but it was soothingly warm. I felt Leon slide into the tub behind me, his legs positioned either side of me.

Placing his hands on my waist he pulled me towards him, and I laid my head back against his rock-hard chest. Resting my arms palm down on either side of the baths edge, I closed my eyes and melted into Leon, letting the warmth of the water and the delicious smell of the candles hypnotise me into absolute bliss.

I wasn't tired, but I was in such a deep state of relaxation that I could have easily drifted off. I focused on my surroundings, taking in as much as my senses allowed me to. My head on Leon's chest was moving with the gentle rise and fall of his chest and there was a vibration niggling against my head as his low and pleasant hum melodically attacked my ears. I don't know what song he was humming, but it was beautiful. The foaming sound of the bubbles as they popped and moved with the swish of the water could be faintly heard underneath Leon's tune.

Leon had found a sponge and had dipped it into the water and was now letting the water pour slowly out of the sponge and along my collarbones. The trickling sound of the water, and the feel of it as it ran down my skin deepened my state relaxation.

I was so at peace, that if I died right now, I would die happy.

24

Chapter 23

We had spent the entire day lounging around, watching movies and just genuinely enjoying one anothers company. He hadn't let me lift a finger at all. If I wanted something to eat or drink, he would go get me whatever I wanted. If I wanted to change the channel on the TV, to save me from moving, he would get the remote and pass it to me. It was nice to be waited on. It was nice for someone to care for me for once, rather than me care for them. I'm always too busy worrying about other people's feelings and emotions, that I forget about my own.

Come the evening, Leon had instructed me to go get dressed up. Since I didn't pack my bags, I didn't even know if there was anything formal enough. I walked into our bedroom and was surprised to find a white dress bag laying across the bed with a folded card on top of it. My name was displayed on the front in the same beautiful calligraphy that the envelope with the Ball details had come in.

I picked the card up and opened it to see the familiar, elegant handwriting:

My Love Ava,
In the dress bag is something I would like you to wear for me
tonight. Don't worry about shoes, you won't need them.
Put it on and head on over to the beach when you're ready.
You have an hour.
I love you, Leon.

With a giggle I shook my head. I turned the card over in my hand, giving it a quick inspection. The expensive material was embossed on alternating corners with elegant swirls and thick enough that is was barely bendable.

He had only given me an hour, and since my outfit was already chosen for me, it was an achievable target time. I left the dress bag untouched and turned towards the bathroom. I had a super quick shower to freshen up, avoiding getting my hair wet. There wasn't enough time to wash and dry my hair, so dry shampoo would have to suffice.

I looked at my reflection in the LED lit mirror. I couldn't help but smile at myself. I was glowing with happiness. My eyes were bright and twinkling with joy. My skin was smooth and clear with only the odd small scar courtesy of teenage acne barely visible here and there, and I had a fantastic tan developing on my skin.

I started with my hair first. I kept it simple, with some loose beachy curls. Taking a section from one side, I split it into two and twisted the sections around themselves and pinned them in the center of my head at the back. I repeated this on the other side. Holding the two sections together, I removed the pins and secured them with a clear elastic into a ponytail. I then pulled some hair out around the front to frame my face.

Happy with my hair, I moved onto makeup. I wanted to keep

it light and almost natural. My skin was looking good, so I just applied a minimal amount of concealer, more so to brighten the center of my face slightly. I lightly bronzed my face, adding a light amount of depth the my features. Turning my attention to my eye area, I dusted a light brown shadow in my crease before applying a little black eyeliner on my top lash line, creating a thin cat eye, before coating my lashes with black mascara. Using a light hand, I filled in my brows, before moving onto my lips. I lined my lips with a brown liner then filled the rest with a slightly lighter nude.

I looked in the mirror and admired my handiwork. Pleased with the outcome, I turned back to the bedroom and headed to the bed.

I slowly pulled the zip on the dress bag down without revealing what was inside. Curiosity building with every inch of unzipping. Once the zipper was all the way at the bottom, I peeled the sides of the bag away and I gasped at the dress laid before me.

It was the dress that I had pointed out a few days ago when me and Leon had browsed the shopping district together. It was a silk blush pink coloured dress that had spaghetti straps over the shoulders. I slipped the dress on and looked in the mirror. Stopping to just above my knee, the dress was fitting, but it wasn't so tight that I couldn't move or breathe. Smoothing the fabric over my stomach, I admired how good my body looked in the dress.

With a confident smile, I stepped away from the mirror and checked my phone for the time. I had ten minutes. I quickly spritzed my favourite perfume to my neck and headed to where my presence was required.

I walked through the house bare foot to the back door and traipsed through the back garden to the gate separating the garden from the beach. A short distance away, I could see a small light and a silhouette. Unable to contain my excitement at what Leon had planned for me, I ran towards the light, using it as my guide.

As I approached the figure, he turned towards me, a smile plastered over his face. Leon held his strong, muscular arms out to me, and I ran into them. Holding me in his embrace, he kissed the top of my head. After a few seconds, he gently pushed me away from his body, holding me out at arms-length by my shoulders. His dazzling eyes scoured my body from top to bottom.

I used this opportunity to take him in as well. He had strayed from his usual hairstyle of a tousled mess, and had instead swept his hair up in a quiff, his blonde highlights striking throughout the mess here and there. He was wearing a thin white shirt that was rolled up to his elbows, exposing his burly, veiny forearms. He wore some light blue jeans that sat low on his hips. They were a skinny fit, but they weren't too tight, with the bottoms rolled up a couple of times until the cuff stopped at his ankles. Like me, he too was bare foot. In a word, he looked sexy.

"You look beautiful Ava." His voice was quiet and soft. I looked into his eyes and they were a glimmering ocean of butter.

"You don't look so bad yourself." I flashed him a wink and a cheeky smile. After this morning's steamy session, I didn't think I'd be able to handle anymore. It had been a weekend full of sex, and while I had enjoyed every single minute Leon satisfying me over and over again, I was starting to feel the repercussions of it. But looking at him now, I think I underestimated my thirst. It seemed, when it came to him, there was a bottomless well to my desire to have him. It didn't matter how many times we did it; it was never enough.

I looked around at my surroundings and I gasped at what was laid before me. There was a big tartan blanket spread out on the sand just behind Leon, with a big brown picnic basket placed to the side. The light that I had followed to get here was a plastic battery powered candle and I laughed when I saw it. While a candle would've been blown out by the small breeze from the sea, his chosen source of light was practical and still kept the romantic feel to our little date.

Because we were in summer, there was still a bit of light, although it was now increasingly dwindling as it was getting overwhelmed by darkness. The sun hadn't quite disappeared over the horizon, but where the light no longer reached, the black night was beginning to creep into its place. The breeze was light and airy, as it fluttered and tickled our skin as it swirled past us, keeping the temperature at a bearable level.

Leon took my hand in his and led me to the blanket and motioned for me to sit. I sat down and extended my legs in front of me, crossing my feet at the ankles and leaned back onto my hands. Leon put the basket in between us before lying next to me, leaning on his elbow, facing me. He opened the basket and pulled out two glass flutes and a bottle of champagne.

* * *

An hour later, the first bottle of champagne was gone, and we'd popped open another one. We were both on the tipping point of being tipsy. We had eaten most of the delicious food that Leon had brought for us and were now taking it in turns trying to throw grapes into one anothers mouth.

"Ava, stop cheating and open your mouth wider." Leon had a grape pressed carefully in his fingers, the soft surface bowing slightly under his grip as he aimed it into my mouth like he was about to toss a dart. He had one eye closed and his tongue was sticking out in concentration. I couldn't help but laugh. He threw the grape and completely missed my mouth, instead it hit me square in the forehead. I quickly stopped laughing and widened my eyes in shock.

It was Leon's turn to laugh now. His deep belly laugh rumbled through me. "That's what happens when you don't keep still." Quickly getting over my shock at being struck in the forehead by a grape, I joined Leon in his fit of laughter.

I always had fun with Leon. It wasn't always serious with him. I could let my hair down and be more carefree. I didn't have to worry about looking silly or stupid in front of him, because he was doing it with me. I loved that we could be ourselves with each other. Nothing was ever forced. Nothing was ever pretend. It was unadulterated, uncensored and real. How refreshing it was to be with someone who made me feel so alive.

Our laughter calmed down, and I looked at Leon. He was looking at me with such love in his eyes, it made me feel fuzzy inside.

"Close your eyes." The last time he asked me to close my eyes, he gave me a key to his apartment. I obeyed his instructions and closed my eyes. I heard him rummage in the basket. My curiosity got the better of me and I tried to sneakily lift my eye to try sneak a glance.

"No peeking missy, close them eyes."

Once he was done looking through the basket, he cleared his throat and instructed me to open my eyes. I fluttered them open and they clapped on a medium sized box in his hand. I flickered my eyes to his looking for an explanation of what was inside and was met with my own reflection staring back. He stretched his arms out, offering the box to me. I gingerly took it and stared down at it. Slowly, I pried the lid open and my mouth hung open as I gasped at what was inside.

"Happy birthday princess." I quickly shot my eyes up to his, tears threatening to spill from my eyes. Inside was a familiar necklace. It had a gold chain and a crystal droplet hanging in the middle. It was the same one I saw when I was out with mum and Fi. Those sneaky bitches, their whispering that I hadn't given a second thought about back then now made sense.

"I didn't know what to get you for your birthday and when I asked Ffion for advice, she told me about the necklace."

I didn't know what to say. I was speechless. This necklace was expensive, and I felt a little bad that he had spent so much on me. First the outfit for the Ball, our weekend away, the dress I'm wearing now, and now this necklace.

"I love it Leon, but you don't have to shower me with gifts, especially ones as expensive as this." I was easy to please, I didn't need luxurious things to be made or kept happy, he knew about my past with Wyatt and how he treated me. He knew all I needed was him.

He took the box out of my hand and placed it next to us before taking my hands in his. I looked into his eyes and they were over-spilling with sincerity.

"I know that Ava. I know that you aren't the type of person who expects the world. You take everything as it comes and you appreciate all of the little things in life. You don't need expensive things to fulfill you or to bring you joy. It's one of the things I love about you." I looked down at our hands. I couldn't meet his eye as he was complimenting me. I wasn't used to it. One of his hands let go of my hands and found its way onto my cheek. Leon tilted my head up so that I could look into his perfect face. His thumb grazed my cheek fondly.

"You're honest, genuine and down to earth. You put everyone above yourself and you have a heart of pure gold. Just because you don't need nice things to be made happy, it doesn't mean that you don't deserve them sometimes. You're allowed to be spoiled every once in a while." Speechless, I didn't know what to say, what to do with his kind words, besides absorb them and hold them close like I'd never get to hear them again. He understood me completely in a way no man ever has before. I was so ridiculously lucky to have him in my life. To call him mine. If I was unsure before, I knew now with my whole heart, with my whole being, that I loved this man to the very core. There was no doubt about it. I was head over heels.

I launched myself into his arms and gave him a kiss that I hoped conveyed to him just how much I loved him, and how much I appreciated him. He pulled away from me and tenderly brushed stray tears off my cheeks. Once my cheeks were dry, he reached to the side of me, picking up the box containing the necklace.

"Turn around, let me put it on you." I turned around for him and sat in front of him on my knees. I gathered my hair up with one hand so that Leon would be able to bring the necklace in front of me and clasp it shut without a hairy interference.

I felt the cold of the metal around my neck and the heavy gem sit just below the little indent at the bottom of my neck. I raised my hand to it and looked down. From this angle, it was a little awkward to get a good look at it, but with the sun was pretty much gone, I could see the shimmer from the stone as it bounced the moonlight off it.

Leon's fingers skimmed down my neck and along my collar-bone, sending an electric tremor through my body. He planted a kiss on my neck, following all the way down where his fingers had traced. I leaned my head back into his shoulder at his seductive touch.

He had a hand on my waist and the other had now found its way up my thigh, gradually making its way under my dress. I could feel myself give into his touch, getting wetter and wetter with every inch he got closer to my center. I couldn't wait, I needed his touch despite having already had more than my fill this weekend.

I grabbed his hand and he froze. He started retracting his hand, thinking that I was asking him to stop. I shook my head at him and placed his hand on my now dripping pussy. I heard him suck in his breath.

"No underwear." He stated, his voice thick with desire.

"Only for you, my love." He growled at that and in an instant, I was picked up and laid on my back. Wasting no time, my dress was up around my waist, one of my legs up on his shoulder, and the other so it was wide open and bent with my foot on the ground. I sat up on my elbows so I could watch him play with me.

He rubbed his fingers through my folds, teasing me until I was almost begging him to fill me with his fingers. He started with one, going slowly. So, so slowly. He knew I was itching for more; he had that cocky smirk on his lips. Giving me what I wanted, he inserted another finger, and I arched my back as I felt myself stretch to accommodate his thick fingers. He was now picking up the pace, strumming away in me like I was guitar, making me sing the tune he wanted to hear with absolute pleasure.

"Fuck, Leon..." I grabbed his hand that was buried inside of me and held his ring finger, adding it to the two that were already working me. Keeping hold of his hand, I controlled him. His surprised look appearing for a only a millisecond before being replaced with feral intensity as he began to enjoy watching me help him to satisfy me.

My moans were getting louder. I had forgotten where we were, and that members of the public could still wander on to the beach and catch us at any time. But at this moment in time, I couldn't care less.

As I began to reach my height of pleasure, I took my hand away from Leon's and grabbed a fistful of his hair. I directed his head down and taking the silent hint at what I was asking of him, he started to lick and suck at my throbbing bud. his fingers never ceasing their movement. Poor thing was feeling neglected. He moaned against me, attacking my clit with vibration after vibration, bringing me closer and closer to the light.

"Holy Shit... Keep going Leon... I'm close..." I couldn't contain myself any longer. Just as I was about to come, Leon's fingers slid out of me and his tongue took their place. I let out a loud scream as my powerful orgasm hit. He lapped up my juices with his tongue, gently bringing me back down to earth. My breathing was ragged, and my legs were shaking uncontrollably like a drug addict with withdrawal.

I felt fucking amazing.

"You taste so sweet baby." I looked down at him in between my legs, letting a naughty smirk play on my lips.

"Well don't be greedy, let me have a taste."

His eyes flashed dark and he came up my body, caging me in with his hands either side of my head. Leaning down, our lips touched, and I eagerly opened my mouth to welcome his tongue carrying my flavour.

He was right. I did taste sweet.

Chapter 24

Leon's POV:

Tonight was our last night away together, and honestly, I wished we could just stay here, in our loved up bubble forever. We'd had the most perfect weekend together and it had turned out so much better than I could have predicted.

Ava and I had finally told each other how we truly felt and because of that, I felt like we had grown closer. There were still some things that I didn't know about her, and that was OK because there were still some things that she didn't know about me. I'm sure she knew this too, and I was appreciative that we both had mutual respect for the other to not push to speak about something we weren't ready to discuss yet.

The entire time I've known her, she'd been confident, audacious and self-assured. She knew who she was, but recently, she'd flourished, and her personality had developed further. Last night on the beach, when she took control and directed me for how she wanted to be pleasured, was such a turn on. Recently, she had been more active during sex, and I while I felt proud that she had taken a steps out of her comfort zone, my ego had been inflated with the thought that I was the only one who had been able to bring this side out of her.

It was dark out and we were sat up in bed watching a film on low volume. With one arm around her, I was cuddling her into my shoulder, whilst gently stroking her arm that was hugging me across my stomach.

I looked down and my eyes followed my fingers as they delicately traced the thin white lines striping across her wrist that were only just visible from the light from the TV. There were several horizontal ones that were faint and barely visible. But cutting straight down the middle, across the older scars, was a slightly pinker, longer mark. I had found myself on a number of occasions stroking her war wounds. I had never asked her how or why they were there; I had a general idea, I wasn't stupid. I knew just how hard it was for someone to talk about harming themselves. I knew that once the gates of the past were open, it was a battle to close them again. But I couldn't help but wonder what pushed this incredible person, someone so amazing, flamboyant and genuine to such a devastating act.

I remember the first time I had seen them. It was the day that I met her. She was taking a break from watching that god-awful show 'Gossip Girl' and was scrolling through her phone, browsing her social media. I was sat at her kitchen island going through emails and writing up reports for work when I turned to look at her. From where I was, I could see from the layout on her screen that she was on Instagram, but I couldn't see who's pictures she was looking at. Her phone was in her right hand, scrolling with the thumb, whilst her left fingers were subconsciously stroking her scars. I wasn't able to see her scars from where I was, but the motion had me curious.

So, when I was seated next to her when we had ordered our pizza, I stole a glance at her skin when she leaned forward to pick up another slice. In the faint light, I could see the small white, transparent lines patterned on her skin. I was shocked, but I didn't ask. It was personal and not something you tell someone you've only just met.

Bringing my mind back the present, I was still swirling my fingers along her wrist. I always wondered if she realised what I was doing, if it was a subconscious comfort to her. If she did, she never said anything to me. I held her arm and lifted it to my lips, placing a soft kiss on her scars. She looked up at me, a mixture of confusion and bewilderment on her beautiful face.

"Will you tell me the story behind these?" She didn't have to; I wasn't going to push her. But I was curious, and we'd become so close that I hoped that by now, she trusted me enough to speak to me about it. I felt her stiffen in my arms and her eyes were frozen onto her wrists. She was quiet for a while, not moving, not blinking. I took her chin lightly in my hand and turned her head to look at me. Her eyes were swamped with fear and she had turned ghostly pale. Seeing her expression, I instantly felt bad for asking her.

"It's OK baby, you don't have to tell me. Not if you don't want to." The fear in her eyes dissolved slightly at my understanding, but it was still very present. She turned her head out of my grip and laid her head back onto my chest. I watched her as she started drawing along her scars with her slender fingers.

"I'm scared to; you'll walk away from me. You won't want me anymore... I'm just damaged goods." It was my turn to be shocked. This was the first time that I had heard her put herself down. I mean, I could understand why she would think that, but I doubt whatever her story was could compare to mine.

I shook my head and stroked her golden locks. "There is nothing that you could say or do that would scare me away. I love you. *All* of you. The good, the bad, the ugly and everything else in between." Her shoulders loosened slightly as she let out a shaky sigh.

"When I was in school, from age twelve to fourteen, I was a victim of bullying. It wasn't just with words. It would be receiving nasty texts, having food thrown at me, and sometimes one of the girls would get physical. It was constant. Every day. I couldn't catch a break. I had no friends, no one to stick up for me, so I was all alone. I started cutting to try ease the pain in my heart, but it didn't help."

She was physically shaking as she told me her story. I could hear the pain in her voice, and I knew she was crying as her usually bright and fluffy voice became wobbly and unstable. I tried to calm her by holding her tighter to my chest, stroking her thigh reassuringly.

"I tried to cut myself to end my life once, but I didn't hit the vein properly or something, and after that, I tried to stop harming myself. I was doing well; I hadn't cut for about four months when there was an incident at school that tipped me to the edge. I was almost successful, but I was found before I could slip away."

There was more to this story, she was holding back on some details. I couldn't help but notice she didn't tell me what the 'incident' was or how she was found, but I suppose she was protecting herself from hurting more than needed. It was more than she needed to tell me; I would've been OK with her not telling me at all, but the fact that she did made me feel like I knew her a little better. It explained a lot as to why she is the person she is today.

I had been the person on the flip side in her story, so it hurt me knowing some of what she went through because I had done that to someone else in my past. It angered and saddened me that people could hurt her in such a way that she tried to take her own life. She was like a sacred gem. She was so unbelievably precious. She was pure, genuine, and real. She didn't deserve to be treated the way that she was. But then, I was no better than those that had pushed Ava to do what she did, and I hated myself for that part of my life.

There was nothing I could say or do to change the past. I wanted to take her pain away, but pain like this stays with you for a lifetime, only making an appearance when you open the lid of the box its contained in. And I had just opened her lid.

"I'm sorry you had to go through that Ava, especially alone. No one should ever have to feel like their only way out, their only escape from their problems is to end their life. I wish I could take your pain away." She looked up at me, her face tear-stained, her eyes red and puffy, overflowing with shimmering droplets. I cupped her soft, wet cheek in my hand and brushed away the tears that were snail-trailing their way down her face with my thumb.

"You're so special to me, more than you know. I'm glad you were found, because otherwise, I wouldn't be lying here with you in my arms. I wouldn't have had the chance to meet and fall in love you." Her face contorted as she cried harder. I picked her up like she weighed nothing and placed her on my lap so that she was straddling me. She pulled her arms close into her chest, her fists balled tight as she buried her head into the crick of my neck and bawled her eyes out. I had a hand on her head and my other on her back, rubbing in rhythmic circles in an attempt to subdue her.

"What you went through was shit. But it's made you who you are today. Which is a strong, independent woman bursting with confidence. You should be proud of how far you've come. I know I'm proud of you." I glanced down at her and found that her sobs were becoming less violent. Her shoulders had stopped shaking but her breathing was still irregular.

Once she had calmed down enough, she spoke into my shoulder, her voice coming out quiet and muffled. "Y- You're not going to leave me... Are you?" Her voice, jaded and raspy, was slightly laced with fear.

"Look at me Ava, baby." She glanced up at me with watery sad eyes, her red swollen lips trembling as she fought to stop her tears. Her under eyes were slightly black from residue makeup that had run from the wetness. I tucked her hair behind her ear before continuing stroking it down her back.

"Listen to me. I'm not going anywhere. I'm going to stay here, right by your side. You don't have to go through anything alone ever again. I promise." Tears once again spilled over her dark lash-line, falling past her cheeks and plopping onto my chest, as she started silent crying as too took deep breaths to calm herself. My heart was breaking seeing her like this. I could literally feel it squeeze in my chest as my beautiful, perfect girl broke down in front of me. She aggressively wiped at her eyes, a little annoyed that she had shown weakness as she nodded her acceptance in reply.

"I love you, Leon." Her voice was a bit stronger as she said this, informing me that she meant it. But it was still hiccup-y from crying. I kissed her on the lips, tasting the salty flavour of her tears. I pulled away and guided her head back to my chest.

"I love you too, Ava. So, very much."

I began rocking her from side to side to soothe and calm

her. It didn't take long until her heavy, hitching breathing had transitioned to light, wispy breathing. I reached for the remote that was a little way next to me, whilst trying not to wake my sweet sleeping angel, and turned the TV off. Sliding down the bed with Ava still clinging to me with a slightly looser grip, I cuddled her and drifted off to sleep, dreaming of my own past.

* * *

Ava's POV:

"Ava! Come out, come out wherever you are!"

"You can't hide forever skank. We'll always find you."

Their taunting words carried across the empty corridor as they searched from classroom to classroom for me. I pulled my legs closer into my chest, hugging them for dear life. I was hidden under the teacher's desk in a dark and empty classroom. I could hear my tormentors getting closer, their footsteps echoing in the corridors.

I had spent most of my day avoiding them as much as I could, just like I do every day. But today, they had been unrelenting. They were lurking around every corner, waiting for me to walk past them so they could throw some harsh jeer my way. I had no option but to hide as best as I could, and hope that they didn't find me.

Changing tactics, they started to try coax me out by being 'nice'.

"We just want to talk Ava."

"Come play with us."

I squeezed my eyes shut as tight as I could and buried my head into my legs. Their voices were growing louder. They were getting closer. I could hear the sound of something being dragged along the wall.

The scraping sound was like fingernails on a chalk board, sending an icy shiver down my spine. What was that saying? Someone's walking over your grave?

Suddenly, I couldn't hear their voices or footsteps anymore. But my stomach turned, indicating that they were outside of the door. I heard the doorknob rattle as it turned, the rickety door creaking open slowly, followed by footsteps entering the classroom. I held my breath, trying my hardest not to make any noise, begging silently that they wouldn't find me.

"Ava..."

"We know you're in here."

Their slow words, the final words being dragged out made me quiver in fear. There was some chairs and tables being scraped, as they moved the furniture to look for me.

Without warning, a cold hand had grabbed me. Feminine, slender fingers wrapped around my ankle, and I was yanked out from under the desk. My eyes flew open and were instantly met with the evil black irises of Victoria's eyes. Her eyes were actually a beautiful chocolate brown, but when she was in this mood, they turned black, like she was possessed by the devil.

I felt my breathing increase as a panic attack began to set in motion. Victoria wasn't alone, but I was too focused on her face and trying to get my breathing under control that I didn't notice the others.

Grabbing my shirt at my chest with both fists, Victoria yanked me up so only my backside and legs were on the floor.

"I told you we would always find you. You really need to learn that you can't escape us." She threw me to the floor like I was trash. I closed my eyes as my head bounced off the floor. There was a high-pitched ringing in my ears, and my head had started to spin. black spots appearing in my vision. I felt a heavy weight on my stomach, causing me to gasp. Victoria had lumped herself on top of me and

was sat where my belly button was.

With an evil smirk, she leaned forward and clasped both of her hands around my neck.

"Please... Don't do this Victoria... Please..." I was begging her. I wouldn't put it past her that she would try to take my life. In all honesty, I'm surprised she hadn't tried to sooner.

My pleas fell on deaf ears as I heard laughing come from the few of the group that she'd brought with her. Her hands slowly started getting tighter around my throat until I was gasping for breath, the black spots getting wider, covering more of my sight.

Her laugh replaced the ringing in my ears, bouncing around in my head.

"WHAT THE FUCK VIC?! LET GO OF HER NOW!" A young male's voice thundered, breaking the pinball of Victoria's witchy cackle that was ricocheting off the walls of my skull.

That voice. It was different. But I recognised it...

"Ava! Ava baby... wake up... please wake up..." My eyes pinged open and landed on Leon's. They were full of panic and there was the hint of tears balancing precariously on his lower lash line. Leon's hands were on my shoulders, he'd tried to shake me to wake up. I was hot and sweaty from the nightmare that had attacked me. Trying to get my bearings, I looked out of the window briefly. It was still relatively dark outside, the sunlight threatening to break into the sky.

I felt tears that had slipped from my sockets during my nightmare. Suddenly, my chest felt like someone was sitting on it. My breathing was becoming restricted and short as my panic attack hit me.

Leon helped me up until I was sat on his crossed legs. He took my hand and placed it on his chest above his heart. I could feel the steady thump of his heartbeat pounding against my palm.

"Breathe, Ava. Focus on me."

I stared into his yellow orbs as I tried to regain control of my breathing, matching Leon's.

"In... and out... That's it baby, good."

Once my breathing had slowed right down, and the burden on my chest had been lifted, Leon touched my face, holding it in his warm hands.

"Do you want to talk about it?" Concern was in his voice. I must've really scared him. I didn't want to tell him what happened. All I needed was his touch. His loving, kind, touch to lull me back to sleep. I needed his arms wrapped around me, protecting me from the demons that lurk in the shadows of my subconscious.

I shook my head at him, the tears still silently slipping down my cheeks. "It was a nightmare; a memory from my past." I hadn't had a nightmare in years. The only reason I would've had one, was because I had opened the door to the past last night.

"I'm sorry baby, this is my fault. I never should've asked you to tell me about your past." It wasn't his fault; I didn't have to tell him. If I had kept my mouth shut, I probably wouldn't have had the nightmare. But, despite that, I was glad that I had finally told Leon some of my story, and I was even more relieved when he told me he wasn't going to leave me, that he still loved me despite being broken. Maybe I'll be able to disclose everything to him and come out better off.

Before I could protest to him blaming himself, he had laid down and patted his chest, inviting me to lay down on him. As I placed my head on his strong, smooth chest, Leon wrapped both of his arms around me. He had his right arm under my neck, his beefy hand holding me by my head, his thumb stroking the side of my face. His left arm was protectively holding my waist, keeping me as close to him as possible. I laid a leg and an arm over him so I could cuddle him with my entire being.

"It's OK baby, I'll protect you. I'll look after you." His voice was a delicate whisper that tickled my ear drums. I could feel my eyes grow heavy as his soothing touch and the beat of his heart lulled me to sleep. Just as the darkness took hold of me, I sleepily whispered out to Leon.

"Thank you, Leon... for everything..."

Chapter 25

"You're making great progress Kiera. You should be proud of how far you've come." I had fourteen year old Keira in front of me this hour. She'd been a patient of mine for a couple of months and truly had come a long way. We still had a ways to go with her mind, but we were breaking down her protective barriers, chipping away at them bit and bit. It had taken weeks for me to gain her trust. But we had got there eventually.

"Thank you, Dr. Myers. It feels good to finally be able to tell someone about what happened. I didn't understand how I felt or why I felt that way, but I think I'm starting to now."

I stood up and smiled kindly at her. She was a sweet kid who had been through a lot. She had spent the last five years jumping from foster home to foster home. She had become a problem child, and no one knew the reason behind it. Until now. Before being in foster care, she had been a bright, cheerful child, but when her parents died in a devastating plane accident, she had no choice but to go into foster care and her life took a drastic turn.

She missed her parents, that was a given. But she had ended up in a vicious cycle of being in foster homes where she was mistreated. She was placed with people who didn't care about her; they just cared about the money that they got through fostering. She had been abused in more than type of way and that had pushed her to be the troublesome, rebellious child she had become.

Her current foster family were the complete opposite of the families she'd previously been with. They were loving and amazing and did all that they could for Keira. You could tell that they genuinely cared for her well-being. They brought her to every appointment and had respected her wishes of not wanting them in the room with her, so they patiently waited in the waiting room outside my office.

One of the first things Keira had told me was that she didn't understand why they were so nice to her. She could see she was breaking them, but they kept fighting to help her. She had got it into her head that she deserved the abuse she received so she was thrown into turmoil when this family were so welcoming and kind to her.

I shook her tiny hand, my giant one swallowing hers completely. Following me to the door, I held it open for her. "I shall see you same time next week." She grinned at me and ran over to her family. Mr and Mrs Spencer looked up at me with a happy smile on their faces and we nodded our heads to each other in acknowledgment. It wasn't just Keira that had changed these past couple of months. Her foster parents had too. When I first met them, they looked completely worn out. They had dark circles shadowing their eyes and their skin was sickly pale. If they were real, anyone would have mistaken them for zombies.

Keira had been unruly, hard work and intolerable and dealing with her erratic behaviour was eating away at their sanity. But now, they both had healthy glows to their skins and their eyes shone with adoration and happiness. Keira had become better at home, and it was all due to her opening up and learning to deal with her emotions.

I returned back to my desk and started typing up my notes of Keira's visit. I had an hour before the next patient arrived, and that gave me plenty of time to get this done, and then do some reflection of my own. I turned my attention to the bright screen of my computer that was at my desk and after opening Keira's file to her records, my fingers moved at lightning speed across the keyboard.

Once I had meticulously re-read my report and was satisfied that I hadn't missed any details, I clicked off Keira's file and went and sat on my long sofa. Some of my patients found that laying down on here helped them to speak. I understood, I was exactly the same. I laid my head on the low curved arm, my arms tucked behind my head, and kicked my legs out in front of me. I was so tall that my legs hung off the end. I felt my body sink ever so slightly into the luxuriously plump cushions underneath me. Although the cushions appeared stiff, they were the complete opposite. It was like laying on a cloud.

Unsurprisingly, my mind wandered to thoughts of Ava. It had been a little over a week since our romantic weekend away together. I was still feeling guilty for causing her nightmare and panic attack, and I felt even worse because she had begged me to stay with her every night up until a couple of nights ago. She had had a couple more nightmares and they had been just as intense as the first one. She hadn't had one for three nights in a row, and so she had sent me home, assuring me that she would be fine and that if she needed me, she'd call me. I didn't want to leave her. Every fibre in my being ached at not being with her.

The first night I was back in my own apartment, I noticed everything. My apartment was eerily quiet, and I hated it. It was devoid of life. So empty of people and even objects, that every sound I made echoed hollowly. Her hearty laughter didn't fill the rooms and I missed the delightful sound of her voice. My bed was bigger than I remembered, and it was ice cold without her snuggling next to me, acting as my human hot water bottle.

She was becoming my drug and I could feel my addiction slowly taking a hold of me. I constantly craved her touch, even if it was fleeting or minimal; just grazing her soft fingers was enough to sustain me. The sweet taste of her had me dizzyingly drunk and her fruity scent was overwhelmingly intoxicating. Everything about her consumed me. It didn't matter that she lived next door to me. She wasn't far away. But the wall the separated us felt like it was putting a million miles between us.

Every nightmare she had, resulted in her screaming and crying in her sleep, and if her terrified screams didn't wake her up, then I would. The first nightmare she had when we were away, she had said someone's name, but I was so focused on trying to wake her up that I didn't catch or pay attention to it. But a couple of nights later she said it again. Victoria.

It was a name that upon just hearing it, made my blood boil. I hated that name and the only person I knew who owned it. Although I didn't speak to her anymore, I spoke to people who did. It turned out that she was the same egotistical, sadistic, self-centered piece of shit that she was nine years ago. I couldn't be sure if it was coincidental that we both knew a Victoria that had the same traits, but there was an annoying niggle at the back of my mind that refused to disappear.

Ava's story, although there were many holes yet for her to fill in for me, resonated with me more than I cared to admit. What she experienced; I had taken part in those same heinous acts. My mind was now deep in the land of the past, and I was walking down the dangerous winding path of memory lane.

Recordings played in my head of some of the harsh things that I did to that poor girl. Some were little things like throwing things at her from the back of the classroom, but some were the more horrible things I did. Like when she had tried to stand up for herself for the first time, but I grabbed a chunky handful of her sun-kissed blonde hair in my sinewy hands and I pulled her head back so forcefully I had unintentionally ripped some of her hair out.

Each incident that played in my head ended in me in fits of laughter; laughter that was fake and forced. It wasn't that I ever liked hurting her and causing her pain, that was what Victoria did. I knew why I had bullied her. It was some form of defense mechanism. I had always had the biggest crush on her but as I was popular, it was against the rules within the social hierarchy for me to have any such feelings towards her.

Before the bullying had started, I remember the day that I was leaned back against the wall, waiting for one of my friends to walk home from school with when she had walked up to me with such purpose and determination in every stride. Her gentle, innocent eyes were focused on me, but she was nervously playing with the hem of her skirt. She had stopped just in front of me and stuttered that she had a crush on me.

Naturally, I was mind blown. She liked me back. I was prepared to give up being popular just to experience being with her. But before I could tell her that I reciprocated her feelings, Victoria jumped over the wall whilst wickedly cackling. Vic had very soon put Ava in her place, explaining that "low-life scum doesn't get to date the king of our year" and that she "never stood a chance" with me. I watched as tears teetered before over-spilling down her pink cheeks. My heart broke as once released from Vic's vice-like grip, Ava ran blindly away. I had watched her run away from me until she turned the corner and disappeared from sight completely.

I then spent the next ten minutes being reminded by Vic about the hierarchy of the school, how stupid Ava was for even thinking she had the right to talk to me, to tell me how she felt. Finally, she decided that Ava needed to be taught a lesson. And so began the long two-year bullying. I was left with no choice but to hide my feelings and push them so far down that I almost forgot about them.

I didn't think twice when Ava had told me her name. It was a popular name, there were many Ava's in the world. But, as her young, radiant face came into the forefront of my mind for the first time in over half a decade, I felt someone shaking me.

"Leon! Wake up, you've got a patient waiting." Ffion's professional-like voice jolted me awake. Rubbing the sleep from my eyes, I stood up and straightened my clothing. As I quickly skimmed through my dream, it suddenly hit me.

Just before Ffion reached the door, I called out to her.

"Yes?"

"What's Ava's surname?"

Her eyes widened in shock at the fact I didn't know my girlfriend's surname. It wasn't like I didn't know, I'd seen her name everywhere; on social media, on the letters that were strewn across her doorway when she hadn't yet picked them up. I guess I hadn't put two and two together that she could be that Ava, until now. And despite now knowing, like a slap round the face to make sure of one being in reality, I needed to hear her name out loud.

"Brooks. Why?"

Well, shit.

* * *

I was in my apartment with no lights on. The darkness of my apartment really set the tone for what was to come. Doom and gloom. Emptiness. Loneliness. Pain.

I was pacing my living room floor with a hand buried in my ruffled hair. I was pretty sure I was going to wear a hole in the floorboards soon enough, but I didn't know what else to do with myself. My heart was pounding in my chest with anxiety and fear as adrenaline coursed through my veins. I jumped about ten foot in the air when I heard a loud three-rap knock at my door. I flung it open a sighed with relief when I saw Ev standing there with a hard look of wonder on his face, his coffee-coloured eyes full of concern. He followed me to my living room and seated himself on my sofa, whilst I continued furiously pacing, my hands stuffed deep in my trouser pockets.

Ev chuckled as he watched me.

"What's the great emergency then?"

Shit. *Shit, Shit, Shit, Shit, Shit.*

"It's her Ev. It's *fucking* her. How could I not remember her? I should've known those eyes the second I saw them." I was rambling, I was getting my thoughts out thick and fast without explaining anything, and still wearing my floorboards thin.

"Leon, chill. Her? Who's her?" He shifted in his seat, now turned to face me on the side with one knee bent, resting on the cushion, his arm draped along the back of the sofa.

"Remember that girl that tried to kill herself because of me and the others?" Ev nodded his head slowly, a look crossed his face.

I pointed in the direction of Ava's apartment. "It's her. It's *that* Ava."

Ev stared at me with eyes as big as plates. He looked like his soul had just left his body. "Leon... Are you sure that's the same Ava?"

"Am I sure that bears shit in the woods? Yes, I'm sure." I held up a finger, "Wait a sec." I walked into my bedroom and picked the book up that I had left on my bed: my year book. I made my way back to Ev and sat on the sofa next to him. His eyebrows twitched together slightly as his eyes fell on the book in my trembling hands. I opened the book and pointed to the blonde girl with wide rimmed glasses, sitting in the first row.

Her hands were placed neatly on her lap and she had a small, cute smile on her lips. This had been taken the day before... before *that* day. Her waist-length hair hung straight down. She had straightened it to show it's true length. It was beautiful. Her sparkling crystalline eyes shimmered in the sun that shone in all of our faces. Looking at this, you would never have thought that anything was happening amongst her and a select few of her classmates. That the next day, she would try to take her own life.

"Holy shit, Leon. This is serious. What are you going to do?"

I stared at the book, lingering on Ava's innocent smile. The innocence that I stole. Ruined. Tarnished. Was there any coming back from this? It didn't matter that I had mapped my life out to try and atone for what I'd done. What mattered was if Ava - by some miracle - forgave me.Eventually, I turned my gaze from

227

the book to Ev. I was scared about what was next. I didn't want to lose her. I couldn't. If I told her, or if she remembered me, it would be game over. I could wave my future, my happiness, my everything goodbye. This was beyond forgiveness.

"I don't know Ev. I honestly don't know."

27

Chapter 26

Ava's POV:

It was the day of the Summer Ball and I was a bundle of nerves and excitement. I hadn't ever been to anything as fancy as this so I had only thought it would be appropriate to go all out. Fi and I were sat in the salon. The stench of chemicals wafted throughout the parlor, invading our nostrils. It was strong, but as I got used to it, I grew to enjoy the smell. There was the sound of chattering between stylist and client being muffled by a hairdryer that was also drowning out the radio.

My entire head was currently covered in silver foils, half an hour into the colour developing. I was browsing through my pictures to help pass the time. There were some really cute ones of me and Leon from the other weekend and I smiled as I swiped through them. Fi was sat in the salon chair next to me, reading a trashy celebrity news magazine whilst her stylist was taking her hair out of foils.

I was experiencing a lot of firsts lately, and I loved it. Being out of my comfort zone and doing new things was good for me.

I had never dyed my hair. I had been scared to because my hair was naturally blonde and I didn't want to ruin it. Plus, I knew people would kill and spend a lot of money to have hair like mine. But I couldn't stop thinking that my hair was starting to look a little dull, so I thought some lighter highlights would liven it up a little. I knew Leon loved my hair; he was forever playing with it, so I didn't take much off the length, only a couple of inches.

He had been acting rather strange the past few days. He seemed so distant and I didn't know what to do. I had an unshakable feeling that I was tied to his change in mood and attitude. Whenever I asked him what was wrong, he would brush me off, saying that it was nothing, that he just had a lot going on. I didn't want to keep harassing him and make him feel any worse, so I had just dropped it.

He had been so brilliant with me and my nightmares and panic attacks and was there for all of them. He pulled me out of them, seemingly rescuing me from the abyss of my unconscious. He held me protectively in his arms until I was calm. He rubbed me soothingly until sleep took me over. After my second night of no nightmares, I knew I would be alright so as much as it pained me to, I told Leon to go home. I felt bad that he had spent a whole week with me. I could only imagine how tired he must've been from waking up with me every night and only going to sleep himself once he knew I was in a peaceful slumber.

I missed him being next to me in bed. I missed his presence, his reassuring touch, his calming scent. He had become my safety net; I had been falling into the darkness of my past, but he was there to catch me every single time.

My stylist came over to me with a big welcoming smile on her face. I smiled back at her through the tall rectangular mirror. She stood tall and confident. She was a beautiful thing. Not much taller than me, but she was a few years older. She had auburn hair that was naturally wavy and emerald green eyes that had sparkled with excitement when she had taken one look at my hair. She had complimented it endlessly, her hands running through my tresses like she was touching gold, and when I said I wanted it cut, she freaked.

"No! Your hair is beautiful, don't chop it all off!" I had laughed at her and assured her I only wanted a couple of inches taken off to neaten it up. She had sighed with relief and swiftly got to work.

The colour had developed perfectly, and I was thrilled with the outcome. It looked so fresh, so bright. I still looked like me, but a me who had made a little more effort than usual. She had offered to style my hair, but I already had an idea for how I want to do my hair for the Ball tonight, so I just asked for her to straighten it for me. Fi had finished before me and was patiently waiting in the waiting area for me. Her hair looked a little extra amazing than normal. She'd had her balayage touched up and her hair looked so much more vibrant and glossy.

After paying for our treatments, we made our way back to mine. We only had three and a half hours until we had to leave, and while Fi wouldn't take long to get ready, I had both my own and her hair to do.

* * *

Back at mine, both me and Fi were slipping into our dresses, our

231

hair and makeup looking flawless. Ffion was wearing a beautiful emerald green off the shoulder dress that complimented her skin tone perfectly. The dress had a lace overlay with flowers on the mesh, with a thin plain strip of green going around her midsection, all of which were the same colour. It fitted her voluptuous body down to her knee before it slightly flowed out and hid her feet, trailing a little at the back. She'd paired the dress with some simple silver heels that exposed her feet with criss-crossing straps by her toes. Her makeup was toned down at the eyes with brown and gold and a thick flicked liner. Her eyes appeared wider and more awake with the clever trick of white liner in the lower lash line. She finished off her look with a bold red lip. Her hair was in a half-up half-down style, with two chunky plaits, one either side, reaching around to the back. I had curled it and pinned it carefully to add volume.

"You look fucking amazing F!" She really did. She was beautiful without needing to dress up, but when she did, everything about her was accentuated.

"Thank you." She gave me a twirl. "Now get that dress on." She handed the heavy garment to me. Stepping into the shiny outfit, I pulled it up my body before putting my arms through the thin straps of my dress, before adjusting my breasts so they sat comfortably. The baby pink, fitted dress tapered in at the waist, falling to just past my ankles. It had lace over the top with fancy shiny patterns on it. The dress had a slit on one side, exposing my tanned, smooth leg from just above my mid-thigh. My shoes were rose gold with a clear, plastic band along the toes with leather straps wrapped around my ankles. I had created a smoky eye with pinks and browns before adding a rose gold glitter to my lids. The black liner made my icy orbs more strikingly fierce. I painted my lips in a shiny mauve colour that was just a couple of shades darker than my natural lip colour. The longest part of getting ready, surprisingly, was my hair. It was in an up-do at the lowest part of my head. I had a plait going from one side of my head over to the other. The bun was made of thick chunky plaits wrapped around themselves with a few short strands pulled out to frame the bun and my face.

I checked myself in the mirror and smiled a small, contemptuous smile. I turned to Fi and held my hands out, asking her what she thought.

"Well fuck me sideways and call me Barbara. If seeing you like that doesn't get Leon out of his foul mood, then I don't know what will." With a giggle I grabbed her hand and my clutch and we headed out to our awaiting taxi to take us to the venue.

* * *

Leon's POV:

Ev and I were stood at the foot of the stairs of the venue, waiting for our girls to show up. True to her word, Ava hadn't breathed a word to me about what she'd bought to wear, and I could feel the excitement and anticipation build up inside me.

The mid-June summer night air was surprisingly light. It was humid but there was a delightful breeze bringing the temperature down to a comfortable level. The sun was beginning to set and the dark vacuum sky was making itself known.

I was greeting a fellow co-worker as they walked past me when in the corner of my eye, I spotted Stacey. She had a mischievous look on her face, as she shot me a wink and a smirk. She was up to something and whatever it was, I just knew it spelt trouble. She turned away from me, flicking her bright hair behind her shoulder as she went.

Ev had picked up on it and watched as she sauntered up the steps, pushing her hips in a forced sway before disappearing into the building. I never told him about why Stacey was being transferred. I was disgusted and disappointed in myself as it was, I didn't need the beat down from him or anyone else.

"Seems someone's got their eye on you brother." He had a joking tone to his voice. He was teasing me, but it wasn't going to work. Stacey was one of the last people I needed to see right now, and if her and Ava met, it wouldn't be pretty. I was yet to see Ava angry. Like, really angry where it's being aimed at me. She was so laid back and chill, that I couldn't ever imagine her losing her shit. But then again, it's always the quiet ones that you need to watch out for.

"That's Stacey, the secretary I replaced with Ffion." I spoke seriously and Ev gave me a knowing look. He knew not to question it any further. He had the same opinion as Ava had about Stacey and me, and I was happy to leave it at that.

Changing the subject, Ev decided to ask me about what I was going to do about Ava. The day I told him who Ava really was, we had discussed in great length about what the best course of action was and had come to the conclusion that there wasn't one. There was only one outcome we could both see and that was the end to me and Ava. As much as it broke my heart to say or think it, there was no point denying the inevitable.

I had been a dick to her these past few days and I really hated myself for treating her the way I have. It was hard for me to be myself with her, knowing what I did to her. I was the reason behind her nightmares and panic attacks. I was part of the reason she tried to end her life on more than one occasion. I didn't deserve her and she was much better off without me in her life. But I needed her in mine. She had become the air that I breathe and if I was to lose her, I genuinely don't know what I would do. I tipped my head back and glanced up at the gradually blackening sky. There were a couple of stars winking down at the world, like they new a secret that we didn't. They probably knew how this situation was going to turn out. If only I could ask them what that was.

"I'll have to tell her eventually. It's not right for one of us to know and not the other. But for now, I just want to enjoy tonight with her." I wanted tonight to go smoothly. She was meeting my colleagues and that meant a lot to me. They were almost like my second family to me. But, this could very well be out last night together, so I wanted to make the most of and savour it.

Ev let out a cough and dug his elbow into my rib, causing me to snap my head at him. His face was frozen in a state of amazement. His cheeks were flushed, and his mouth dropped open slightly. I wasn't even sure if he was breathing. I followed his gaze to see what had him so tongue tied and ended up mimicking him. Standing a few feet away from us were our girls. No. Our *women.* They both looked sublime. Sure, Fi looked incredible, but my sweetheart took it to an entirely new level. I could feel the drool pooling in my mouth as my eyes ran over her glorious body, taking in every detail of her. Even from this distance, I could see she'd had her hair done. It looked lighter and I liked it.

It was going to be hard to keep my hands off her tonight. I already knew that other men would try their luck with her; I could see their predatory gazes fixated on her and Fi as they made their way towards us.

I had to make sure every man in that building knew who she belonged to. She was mine, even if it is short-lived.

Chapter 27

The taxi deposited us outside the ground walls of the venue and Fi and I were in awe. Before entering the grounds, there were high walls surrounding the building, and a giant iron gate that had been swung open. Hoards of people poured through the gates in a swarm of black and white, with the odd splash of colour thrown in the somewhere. Merging with the newest group heading in, we followed the crowd and made our way toward the building. As we walked the short distance to the white stoned mansion, we were able to get a better look at the venue. The outside of the building was majestic. Recently trimmed trees lined the walkway, standing tall in uniform. Wide, steep, white stairs led up to the giant golden double doors that served as the main entrance, with pillars decorated either side of the door. Numerous arched windows expanded along the width of the two-story building. Beneath our feet laid beige loose stones, loudly crunching under the feet of well over a hundred people in unison.

The boys were waiting for us at the bottom of the steps with a rounded streetlight spotlighting down on them. They seemed to be in a deep conversation, and Leon had his head tilted up to the sky, taking in the vast eternal heavens. Everett was the first of the pair to spot us, nudging Leon to get his attention, his eyes glued to us as we approached. Leon tore himself away from the stars above and clamped his eyes on me, surveying me from top to toe.

A massive grin on my face as I enjoyed Leon's obvious checking me out, I reached the boys and snaked my arms around his waist. He looked just as delicious as always. He was wearing a dark navy suit with a white shirt and a black bowtie. His blazer had black lapels, contrasting with the navy colour of the rest of his attire. His hair was freshly cut, but the top was slightly longer than he usually had it cut. It was a styled in it's usual disheveled mess.

He wasn't smiling, but his eyes had turned a shade darker, ablaze intensely with thirst and lust. His hands gripped my waist and he roughly pulled me flush against him. He bent down and spoke deep and lowly into my ear.

"If another man lays a single hand on you or even so much as looks at you in a way I don't like, I won't be held responsible for my actions." He took my earlobe in his teeth, tugging it slightly before he stood back. I looked at him, taken aback at his new, public, possessive behaviour. I must admit, it was turning me on.

I rose up to him on my tiptoes, my hands flat on his chest, biting my lip in the way I knew would get him hot and bothered instantly. "Well then baby, you better make sure they know who I belong to." I challenged, knowing Leon couldn't resist a challenge. I shot him a wink before turning around and started making my way up the stairs, when I felt a big hand crack down on my backside, followed swiftly by a hot stinging sensation. I turned back and saw that Leon had a cocky smirk on his face as he rubbed his hands together like the slap hurt him as much as it did me. Serves him right. He placed a hand low on my hip, almost touching the side of my butt, whilst his other gracefully held my hand closest to him.

"Oh, don't worry sweetheart. I plan to." His voice matched mine and I felt a flush creep up my cheeks.

Upon reaching the top of the seemingly endless stairs, we pushed the grand entrance doors open and took a step into a large reception area. There was a sign dead in front of us with gold fancy writing and an arrow directing us which room our function was in.

I fought to prevent my mouth from hitting the floor as we walked in. The room was dark, only being dimly lit by the sparkling crystal chandeliers that hung high on the tall ceilings. There were six thick pillars, three on each side of the room, that stretched from floor to ceiling with dainty lights twisting up their length. A stage had been set up and there was a podium positioned front and center. To the left of the room was a super long table covered from end to end with finger foods, and to the right was a bar. The room was already bustling with people, many of whom finding their seats at the tables the littered the vast space. Softly in the background played some music that anyone could barely hear over the babble of the guests.

The four of us made a fast beeline for the bar and ordered our beverages. We were taking the first sip of our drinks when a tall man strolled towards us. His torso was proudly broad, and I was surprised that the suit wasn't bursting at the seams. His eyes came across stern and strong, but his smile told a different story. With a kind and inviting grin, he reached our group.

"Leon, Fi, it's lovely to see you both." He shook both of their hands and then made the effort to introduce himself to Everett and I.

"Toby. I'm the big boss man if you like, of the company Leon and Fi work for." That would explain his omnipotent and domineering aura. He was courteous and respectful to us and after a short easy chat, he made his leave.

* * *

The next hour, the conversation was light and jovial, and the alcohol was flowing. So far, Leon had given sharp warning looks to three men who were ogling me from some distance, one of whom was the young bartender. Leon hadn't left my side once and it was nice to see him enjoy himself. It seemed that he had gotten over whatever had him pent up, as he was back to his usual cheeky, playful self.

A few colleagues had come up to greet Leon and to congratulate him on his nomination. It seemed that everyone thought he had it in the bag. He introduced me to everyone he spoke to with the biggest, loving smile I'd ever seen, and it made me feel warm and mushy inside. All of his colleagues were friendly and polite towards me and that made me tingle with acceptance.

There was a fuzzy sound through the speakers before a very deep male voice resounded through them. "Welcome everyone, to the Annual National Therapists Association Summer Ball."

With that, the awards ceremony was underway.

* * *

All too soon, the next award to be announced was the Community award, the one Leon was nominated for. Before it was introduced, a woman strutted up to us. She walked one foot in front of the other, like a model on a runway. Except this was forced and it looked completely unnatural. She had vivid, red-dyed hair that was curled tightly and draped over her shoulders. On the bridge of her thin, pinched nose sat skinny, tortoise patterned glasses. Her eyes were focused solely on Leon the entire time she walked towards us, and she had a look that only she must have thought was sexy on her face with her eyes downcast and a stupid smile haunting her face.

When she was close enough, I could see that she was an almost walking Barbie doll. Fake boobs spilled out the neckline of her dress; her nipples only just covered. Her eyes were so heavy with lashes that I couldn't make out her eye colour, and her lips were abnormally symmetrical and big. She was trying too hard to become something she wasn't, and I almost pitied her. What a sad little life it must be to not be able to be comfortable in your own, authentic skin.

She reached Leon and placed her hands on his chest whilst looking up at him, fluttering her lashes. I had to stifle a giggle as I thought about how they were probably coming in handy for Leon; it was hot in this room. I felt him tense still under her touch. She flicked her eyes briefly to mine and a malicious look flashed on her face.

"Hi, Leon." Her voice, light and sugary, was irritatingly girly. She was trying to flirt with my man. I squeezed hold of Leon's hand, letting him know that I was absolutely seething. I hadn't ever thought of myself as a jealous person, but this woman had managed to bring that trait out of me.

"Stacey." Leon was blunt with his reply. There was no

emotion in his voice, he didn't care for her and that brought me some peace of mind.

She started walking her fingers up his chest with a fake sweet smile on her face. Her eyes gave her away though. She was looking for trouble.

"I've missed you. You haven't called to check in on me at the new office." She spoke in a whiny baby voice that made me roll my eyes as I cringed internally. So, this was the secretary Leon had replaced with Fi. The one where there was a "conflict of interest".

She had kept casually glancing at me, making sure that I was watching their interaction. My anger was bubbling at this point, threatening to erupt. She was holding the metaphorical blood-red cloth at me, shaking it to tease and taunt me, trying to incite a reaction from me. I wasn't going to give her the satisfaction.

"Firstly, don't touch me." Leon let go of my hand and grabbed Stacey's elegantly slender hands, squeezing them tightly. Her face winced either in pain or at his harsh words, showing just how tight his grip on her was. He threw them to her side.

"Secondly, I don't miss you, and I don't give two shits about you and what you're doing. Now, if you don't mind." He turned his back to her, dismissing her, and leaned up against the bar. He turned his face towards me with a questioning look, telepathically asking if I was OK. I nodded slightly and turned my attention back to Stacey who was now stood with her weight on one hip, hands folded under her breasts, not appreciating his rude dismissal. She had a perfectly arched eyebrow raised and a cocky smirk.

She stalked towards me so that we were just shy of being toe to toe. She was taller than me and she towered over me intimidatingly, but I wasn't going to show this bitch any sort of weakness. I held a steely glare at her, and I could feel Leon's eyes burning into me.

She looked me up and down slowly, scrutinising my appearance before her eyes bore into mine. "So, this is your new bit?" Bit? Who did this bitch think she was? She had an evil smirk on her face and my palm was itching to slap it off her plastic face.

"Excuse me? Just who do you think you are?" My voice was laced with venom. I hated this woman with every atom in my being. I didn't hate many people, but it was instinctual at this point to despise her. Her face eyebrow twitched and I knew I had just fallen into her trap. Whatever she was going to say next, I wasn't going to like. I could feel it in the pit of my stomach.

She took a step closer and I could feel the edge of her shoes against mine. I had to crane my neck slightly so I could look her in her amusement filled eyes.

"Me? Oh, I was just his bit of fun before I left. Seems that it was easy enough to make him forget about you whilst he was playing with me." Leon's head shot to look at Stacey so fast, that I was surprised he didn't give himself whiplash. His face looked stunned but his eyes were heavy with guilt. He'd been caught out.

I was fucking livid. It made sense that that was why she was transferred and why Leon had been so on edge at that time. I'll be dealing with him later. But right now, this bitch needed to be put in her place.

I closed my eyes and focused on steadying my breathing and contained myself enough to put on a calm, yet murderous tone. Leon tried to interrupt, attempted to smooth over the truth when I flung my hand out, finger pointing to the ceiling as I silenced him. I didn't care to hear what he had to say. And if I even heard a single word come out of his mouth trying to save himself, then these white walls would soon be painted red.

"Oh? Is that so? Then if you were that good and that much fun, why did he send you away? Why is it me fucking him rather than you?" She clearly wasn't used to be spoken back to, and it was satisfying to put this tramp in her place. Her mouth was swinging, gaping like a fish. She tried to say something, but a pathetic little bit of air came out instead. Behind me I heard Everett choke on his drink and Fi had said a very quiet "Oh shit" whilst chuckling at my come back.

I could feel eyes on us. It wasn't just Leon, Fi and Everett's. We had attracted a bit of an audience. That just fueled me even more to shut her down.

"I thought as much. Now, I suggest you get your wannabe Barbie self the fuck away from me before I beat the silicone out of you." She flicked her eyes to Leon in the hope he would intervene, but he was too busy staring at me. I couldn't place the emotions I saw swimming in his eyes but there was a mix of pride and shame.

With a huff of defeat, she scuttled away with her tail between her legs.

If I was pissed at Stacey, it was nothing compared with how I felt towards Leon. Anger was coursing wildly through my veins and I was ready to explode. I pivoted towards him, Fi's hand slipped its way into mine, but I didn't hold it back. There was nothing that could simmer me down. I was past rational.

Leon was visibly petrified. The colour had drained from his face and his eyes were black with fear. I had never been this angry before and I was on the precipice of losing my shit. Maintaining my cold and dangerous tone I spoke to Leon.

"Care to explain?" His eyes flicked to the ground in remorse as he began to find his words. But, before a coherent sentence could come out of his mouth his name was announced through the mic.

"The Winner of the Community Awards goes to none other than Leon Myers!"

Myers... Leon Myers...

Like a switch, my anger vanished and instead fear, shock and disbelief flooded my body. I stepped away from Leon shaking my head at him.

"No... No... It can't be..." I was on the brink of crying. My voice was starting to wobble and shake. His eyes were full of sorrow.

"Ava, baby... please..." He tried to reach for my hand, but I yanked it back, away from his grip. I held an uncontrollable trembling hand up at him and I took another step back.

"Stay the fuck away from me." The tears were streaming down my face at this point and I couldn't stop them. I turned on my heel and legged it as fast as my heels allowed me to. Leon must've tried to come after me, because behind me, I heard Ffion's stern voice. "Don't. Let her go."

And just like in the fairy tale, Cinderella left the Ball, leaving her Prince Charming behind. But unlike said fairy tale, there probably wasn't going to be a happily ever after in my story.

Chapter 28

Leon's POV:

Fuck. She wasn't supposed to find out like this. About either bombshell. I was supposed to have told her myself. Her rage had consumed her wholly; her anger burned like a wildfire – bewitching to watch but dangerous to be near. She had held her own against Stacey and won and I was proud of her, in spite of my fear at what was in store for me. Considering fourteen-year-old Ava would've cowered in a corner, she truly had come such a long way from being that shadow of herself.

But, when her fury turned on me, I didn't know what to do. I could barely look her in the eye from dread of seeing the furious storm of fire and hatred that I knew would be residing in her features. Acidic bile rose up from my stomach, burning the back of my throat as I anticipated what was to come;

I couldn't blame her for how she felt, I absolutely deserved whatever hell she would rain down on me. She appeared calm and collected, but her tone was deadly, and her eyes held a violent thunderstorm of pure, unfiltered rage. When she had asked for an explanation about Stacey, I was rendered speechless through guilt. No amount of explaining was going to make what happened go away, and there was nothing I could say that could justify my actions. She held me captive with her thunderous eyes, her aura intimidating as it suffocated me in a serpent's grip that sucked the air out of me.

Just as she was about to tear me a new one, my name had been called out and I thanked the gods that I had been temporarily saved from her clutches. That was until I saw the recognition register on Ava's face. As if one slap round the face wasn't enough, I had been rewarded with a whopping backhand on the other cheek.

I'd barely blinked and her whole persona had changed. Her faced drained of all colour, despite the layers of makeup and her eyes glazed over as the face from her past morphed into mine. The storm in her eyes subsided; the thunder had stopped striking, but now all that remained was the rain. And it had started to rain hard. Ignoring the heads turning as everyone in the hall hunted for me, waiting for me to go up and claim my award, I tried to get to her, taking a step towards her with my shaking hand outstretched to stop her from leaving so I could explain. But she flinched away from me, refusing to let my evil, filthy hands near her, unable to bear my touch. Her tears trickled down her face in black streaks as the water washed away her makeup. I wanted to go after her so bad, to hold her close and tell her it would all be OK. To tell her I was sorry. To tell her the words that had been dormant for the past nine years, waiting for the day when I would finally get to confront the girl from my past; to try and make things somewhat right. The glass trophy that had my name on it was meaningless, it could have waited. The reminder of what I was a haunting voice telling me I didn't deserve it anyway. However, Ffion had stopped me from going after her.

I tried to keep my cool when I was up on stage, and after a short speech thanking everyone for all of their support and for nominating me, I hurried back to Ffion and Ev, impatient to just get the fuck out of here and go to Ava; to the woman I love and whose trust I had just destroyed undoubtedly beyond repair.

Ffion was furiously tapping on her phone, her nails rapidly clicking against the glass screen, with a worried look smothering her face, and Ev just looked at me with sympathy, not really knowing what to do or suggest. We both knew this was coming, but not here and most certainly not like this. It felt like the room had somehow gotten much quieter, the energized buzz of the room a mellow murmur. Few people in our immediate vicinity had noticed the commotion and had tried – and failed – to hide the fact that they were eavesdropping, to find out what was going on; turning their heads or having their friends look over their shoulders to try and spy on what drama had unfolded.

Once her phone was tucked in the safety of her gold clutch bag, Ffion snapped her head up and looked at me with a mix of anger and disappointment radiating from her eyes.

"I can't believe you Leon. What even possessed you to go for that tart?" She spoke with a sharp tongue. I had it coming though and there was absolutely no way I was getting out of this unscathed.

"I... I don't know. I wasn't thinking at all." I hung my head in shame. I had royally fucked up with Ava and I wouldn't be surprised if this was the end to us. She may be able to forgive me about Stacey, but the past had caught up with her and she had been staring her tormentor of the past in the face for months without knowing; had laid with one of her demons without

248

knowing, and I don't think that there was any coming back from this.

"That's the problem Leon. You didn't think and now you've broken Ava's heart. I swear to God, if she ends up the same as she did after Wyatt, I'll shove that trophy so far up your fucking arse, it'll be shining out of your fucking eyes." Her finger had been pushed into my chest so hard, it felt like her pointy acrylics were stabbing my already aching heart. As certain as I am that the Pope is Catholic, I was sure that Ffion wouldn't hesitate to turn me into a walking display case, but that wasn't the part of that sentence I cared about. My brows twitched together in confusion. Ava and I had discussed her history with Wyatt, but she never told me the aftermath of it. Just that it had broken her.

"What happened after Wyatt?" Ffion cocked her head; all anger replaced with surprise and bewilderment. Misplaced assumption that Ava had told me everything beheld in her piercing eyes. The fact that Ava hadn't disclosed all of the facts meant that the consequence of their break up must have been serious.

"You don't know," a lowly spoken statement that amplified my worry at the seriousness of what happened to Ava, "she ended up in hospital from malnutrition and exertion." The sharpness died like water leaving the rapids and entering a smooth-flowing pool, from Ffion's tongue, an urgency replacing it.

Ev, who had been quietly sipping his drink, smartly staying out of the way to avoid receiving the tail end of Ffion's wrath, shot me a look from over his glass as he lazily sipped, pausing mid flow. We both knew this was bad.

With my mind was racing, my stomach became a tangled mess

of worry. I'd already put her in hospital in the past, I didn't want to be the reason for it again. Overwhelmed with relief that she hadn't been in hospital with something as dire as nine years ago, and secondhand pain that she had still suffered and neglected herself, I could feel the therapist in me kick in as I ignored my nervous system going into overdrive. Her past habit was that abused herself when things went south, and if she hasn't broken that cycle, then she's going to spiral again, and the third time might just be her charm.

"I need to go to her. Before she does something stupid again." I started downing my pint, not letting it go to waste; not with how extortionately priced drinks were in here. I wasn't about to let history repeat itself. Gulping down my last mouthful, I clocked Ffion's face shift from confusion, to shock, before finally landing back on her original emotion: anger. Whatever she had worked out in her head had clicked and I could see the light bulb ping in her eyes.

"That's why she left shitting bricks... you're *the* Leon." She didn't shout, but her voice was slightly raised, causing some of our already attentive audience to look over to our direction, before turning away with raised eyebrows. Nosey fuckers. From my peripheral, I could see Ev's head turn from me to Ffion as if deep in watching a tennis match. The knowledge that Ffion knew so much about Ava's past was only a temporary surprise. The pair were inseparable; they spent any spare time they had together, they told each other everything, and if they weren't together physically, they were on FaceTime. It was a given that they knew each others' life stories.

"Good luck with getting her back Leon. Don't be surprised if you've lost her for good." And with that, she turned and walked away from me and Ev and headed out of the building.

Ffion's parting words were the final twist of the knife in my gut for me and I felt my body cripple in pain. I leaned up against the bar on my elbows and buried my head in my hands. She wasn't the same person she used to be, so I was holding onto that with the hope she wouldn't do something drastic. I could just about live with not having her in my life, as long as she was happy and well. But, if she wasn't here full stop, then I don't know how I'd ever live with myself.

I felt Ev to the right of me, his hand placed comfortingly on my left shoulder.

"You OK, brother?" His voice was soft and full of concern. I was glad that he already knew about my past, I wouldn't have to explain this whole blow-up and that made it a little easier. He wouldn't be judging me or giving me a hard time for it. But the thing with Stacey... I'll probably get an earful about it at a more convenient time.

I shook my head slightly, still in my hands. I wasn't OK. Not by a long shot. But it was my own doing, and I'll spend forever beating myself up for what I have done. I was hurting her. Again. And whilst the the fire-seed of my anger started to flourish into a wildness, it became drowned out but heartbreak and sorrow. With fresh, hot tears in my eyes, I looked over to Ev, my voice breaking as I tried to fight back the sob that was tearing its way through my chest.

"I've fucking lost her Ev. I'm never going to get her back. Am I?"

* * *

Ava's POV:

My apartment was dark when I arrived home, but it wasn't quite dark enough for me. Blinded by my tears, I stormed through the apartment closing all of the curtains, blacking out the entire space. The dark had become a comforter to me in my times of need and despair. It was easier to cry and hurt when you couldn't see anything or anyone.

Submerged in complete darkness, I entered my bedroom and stripped off, before pulling an over-sized t-shirt over my head that I had tossed on the bed. My phone had been going off non-stop with messages from Fi making sure I was alright. I had replied saying that I was fine but just to make sure Leon doesn't try come see me. That was the last thing I needed. I switched my phone off and tossed it on the bed.

The entire way home, the tears hadn't stopped flowing from my sockets, and they weren't making any move to stop now. I headed to the kitchen and pulled out the wine from the fridge. No point bothering with a glass when I was the only person drinking it. I placed it on the counter and hunted for the corkscrew, with the light from the fridge providing me with adequate vision.

The cork had barely popped out of the bottle before I sank down to the floor with my back against the cupboards. The floor was cold on the exposed skin of my rear and legs, but it was soothing. All I could hear were the sound of my sobs and the deafening echo of my thoughts that ping-ponged in my head.

I took a long chug from the bottle and felt tears trail to the side of my face, dripping into my ears. The sweet liquid was cold and crisp, with the slight mix of salt from my tears that had slipped into my mouth. It fizzed therapeutically on my tongue before tickling my throat as it slid down to my stomach.

I skipped past the thoughts of Stacey. That bitch meant nothing to me, and she wasn't as important as the connection me and Leon had. The thought of Leon's name made my cries come even harder. Why did it have to be him? Of all the Leon's in the world, it just *had* to be him. Was I just not destined to be happy? Did I not deserve it? Every time I find true happiness, something bad always happens and it gets taken away from me. Why can everyone else be happy but me? Maybe mum had it right the entire time. Focus on yourself. Don't give yourself to anyone, because it'll only end in tears. Literally. At the thought of my mum, my heart began to yearn for her presence, her comfort, the safety of her embrace. But I didn't want her to worry about me while I was in this mess. I couldn't bare facing her with another failure that could be added to my life tally.

I took another deep sip from the wine bottle, and I could feel my head start to buzz as the alcohol started to spread through my system. Drinking was never the answer, but right now, I just wanted to stop feeling. I wanted to be numb. Just for a little bit.

I had literally been in bed with the devil himself. I had fallen in love with him, and that was what was making this all the more harder. If we were just platonically friends I could easily have walked away. But he owned my heart. I had given myself to him fully. As I thought about how deeply I felt for him, I felt my chest contract with pain, and I let out a blood-curdling scream.

With one hand, I scrunched my t-shirt into my fist over where my heart was, the organ of life trying to punch its way out of my chest. My tears were rolling down my cheeks harder now and I was getting a headache from all of the crying I'd done.

How had I not recognised him? His perfect, melty eyes had always seemed familiar, so why couldn't I pinpoint who he was? I never paid any second thoughts to his name, it never triggered any alarm bells, and I supposed I had therapy to thank for that. Now I knew who he was, I could see the resemblance to his fourteen-year-old self. The difference was, he was a man now. He was a major contradiction from the person he used to be. He wasn't malicious, harsh or derogatory anymore. He didn't get enjoyment at seeing or causing me pain and suffering. Instead, it had hurt him seeing me suffer. Whenever I needed him, he was there without fail. He was my comfort blanket, calming and soothing me when I was inconsolable. He was the anchor keeping me grounded.

I had just poured the last drop of wine into my mouth when my front door opened and Fi walked in. Her face was washed with concern and worry as in the faint light from the door, I could see her looking for me. In my now drunken state, I couldn't help but find it a little funny and I let out a giggle. She looked like a kid standing in her parents' bedroom doorway, ready to tell them she weren't well. Using that as a guide, Fi found me, now slumped against the counter, my feet almost touching the kitchen island.

"Hey, bestie! Look, my bottle's empty." I greeted her with sadness that I was out of this miracle numbing liquid, tipping the bottle upside down, only to get a little splash of the sticky substance on my leg.

"Ava, why are sat in the dark?" Her voice soft as she gently removed the bottle from my grasp and placed it somewhere nearby. I loved that about her. She looked after me. I didn't need my mum when Fi was here. I must've done something right to have someone like her in my life. For a moment, for a little flicker of a millisecond, I felt the longing for Leon to be the one who was here to comfort and look after me.

"No-one can see me cry or hurt if it's dark." I hiccupped at the end of my sentence and blurrily looked towards Fi, who was now crouched next to me. She placed a warm hand on the top of my head, and I closed my eyes at her touch, before remembering there was more of the magic stuff in the fridge.

"If you're staying, get the other two bottles of wine from the fridge, we'll have one each." Fi chuckled and did as I asked. She returned after popping the corks and I shifted my bum across so she could sit next to me. She passed me my bottle and I leaned my head on her shoulder, taking a swig from the bottle but with the angle, having a little dribble out the corner of my mouth, drying on my neck.

We sat in quiet for a little while and I appreciated it. She helped my take my hair out of my bun so now my hair was sticking out wildly at all angles. She then wrapped an arm around me, snuggling me into her shoulder whilst I let my tears out slowly and quietly.

"What..." *hiccup* "What do you..." *hiccup* "What do you think I should do?" I was the first talk and my speech was slightly slurred and my hiccups were growing uncontrollable. Fi started stroking the side of my head in a rhythmic motion. She took a big gulp from her bottle before she spoke.

"I think you should do whatever you think is best for you. You don't need to make a decision now or anytime soon. He hurt you and he hurt you bad. If you decided you want nothing more to do with him, no one could blame you. But, if you somehow found it in your heart to forgive him, then I'll be by your side, awfully proud that you could overcome that." I felt fresh tears in my eyes. Fi supported me through everything. She knew this was a big decision for me and all she wanted was for me to be happy. God, I loved her.

I drained the last of my wine and snuggled deeper into Ffion

255

with my eyes closed.

"Thanks, Fi. You're the best sister ever." I could faintly hear her lightly chuckle before feeling her place soft kiss on the top of my head as total blackness took control of my body, sending me into a drunken stupor.

Chapter 29

"Ava... Ava wake up." A faint voice that sounded like Fi's fluttered through my ears, gently pulling me out of my sleep. I ignored it and felt around for my duvet to pull it back up to my chin. But instead, my fingers stroked a cold hard surface. My brows pulled together in a confused frown and I attempted to open my eyes. I was greeted with the blazing sunlight, causing me to suck in a breath, as a dagger pierced my brain and I closed my eyes again. Sunglasses. I needed sunglasses.

After a few seconds, I carefully lifted my eyes open one at a time, shading them with a hand in front of my face. My head was beating like a drum as I looked about my surroundings. I found that I was collapsed on the kitchen floor with my head uncomfortably propped up against the cupboards. I pushed myself up so that I was sat up completely, my back now level with the cupboard behind me. My neck was stiff from being in such an awkward position and there was a shooting pain going up my spine from being on a hard surface all night.

There were three empty bottles of wine littering the floor around me. I reached out with heavy arms and picked them up, before dragging myself upright, holding one hand to my head to try ease the pain, my eyes still burning from the brightness of the day. I'd just put them in the recycling bin when Fi's voice sounded again.

"Well, you look like shit." She was leaning against the doorway that separated my bedroom from the main room, with her arms loosely folded across her chest and a smirk on her face. I could tell that she had helped herself to my shower and my wardrobe, but I didn't mind; mi casa es su casa and all that jazz. My over-sized t-shirt she wore looked like a normal, perfectly fitted one for her and my shorts fit her a little too snuggly over her wide hips.

I laughed at how blasé she was. "Yeah, I feel it too." The thudding in my head had been increasingly getting worse the longer I'd been awake. I rummaged through the first aid box for some aspirin to expel the elephants that were parading about in my skull. Turning on the cold tap, I dipped my head and drank straight from the flowing water. Popping in the pill, I washed it down with some more water.

Fi walked over cautiously. She had an uneasy look on her face as she approached the kitchen island before settling into a seat, and tucking a loose strand of hair behind her ear.

"How are you feeling... about last night?" She was hesitant in her question, but I didn't know what she was on about. My brain was too foggy to think. I sat myself down opposite her and wracked my brain, trying to jog my memory.

Last night we had gone to Leon's Ball. We were laughing and having a good time together, and Leon had been making sure no one tried it on with me. I remember feeling extremely loved that he was protecting me from others, that he just wanted me to himself. The awards ceremony had started, and we were anxiously waiting for Leon's award to come up when some woman with bright red hair strutted over to us.

Stacey.

I clenched my hands into tight fists, my nails digging into my palms, as I felt last nights anger reawaken and flood through my body like a tidal wave. I was mad at the audacity of her. As if she thought that she could just prance her way up to us like she owned the world, cause a scene, and get away with it unscathed. My anger towards Stacey was one thing, but my anger directed at Leon was on a whole other level.

I looked up to Fi who was watching me slowly remember last nights events when it hit me. Leon had acted weird with me because of Stacey, and although he didn't tell me what it was, I knew without a doubt why he had replaced her. But that wasn't what clicked in my head. This happened a day or two after we had first slept together. How could he have done that to me?

If it was possible, I'm sure I would've had steam billowing out of my ears by now. I was livid. Fi must've sensed something else had triggered me, because she reached across the table and placed her hands on top of mine.

"Ava? What is it?" She had confusion in her voice. She knew I was angry about Stacey and Leon, but she didn't know what had just tipped me over the edge.

"That prick... how could he? I'm going to feed his dick to him when I see him, I swear." Fi stifled a laugh, it was no time to laugh. This was serious. She could see there was more to the story, so she silently sat, waiting for me to tell her the knowledge I now knew.

"He did it around the time after we first slept together. That was why he was acting strange, and why he was so desperate to replace her as his secretary." I watched as Fi tried to work out the timeline for herself. Her face set into a stony expression. That was all I needed to know that I wasn't crazy, that I wasn't overthinking.

I needed to confront Leon about this. I needed to know everything.

As I was thinking about the situation, I felt an annoying niggle in the back of my mind that there was something important I needed to remember. My fury slowly sizzled down so I could try to think clearly. But my hangover was too strong, and it thickly clouded my memories.

"Fi, what else happened last night?"

Her beautiful mossy eyes softened with sympathy but there was a hint of sadness and disappointment in them. She stood up and walked round to me and sat next to me. We were face to face, our knees barely touching. She cocooned my hands in both of hers and let out a deep sigh, preparing herself to speak only one word that would completely shatter the fog in my brain.

"Myers."

And just like that, the dam bust open and the events of last night flooded my mind. It had been him all along. I'd been sleeping with my tormentor and I had been completely clueless. I felt tears well up in my eyes and my heart became heavy. Where do I go from here? I couldn't be with him, could I?

Fi stood up and pulled me into a hug. I wrapped my arms tightly around her waist, buried my head into her stomach and sobbed my heart out. The pain was unbearable. It ripped through my heart like a lion mercilessly ripping into its prey. Fi was making soothing noises and stroked my hair to try comfort me, but it was futile.

"Why him Fi? Why did it have to be him?" My voice was muffled as I let out my thoughts to Ffion's midsection. Of all the people in the world for me to fall hopelessly in love with, it had to be him, like the universe was playing some sick joke on me. I sent a big, fuck-off middle finger telepathically up to God or whoever was pulling the strings. Actually, make that a double middle finger for extra measure of how pissed I was at Them.

"Everything happens for a reason A. You just need to decide if this reason is something worth forgiving and fighting for." I didn't know if it was. I didn't know if I could be with someone who had caused me so much grief and pain that the only way out I thought was available to me was to top myself. But what I did know was that I loved him more than I have ever loved anything or anyone, and the thought of him not being in my life crushed me.

After fighting with myself and for other people, I finally found someone who fought not only for me, but beside me. But now that had been taken away from me, along with any ounce of happiness and joy I had acquired over the last three and a half months. It felt like it had all been a lie, that I had been living in some sort of fantasy world where I finally had someone who truly loved and cared for me. It wasn't my reality. With that thought hanging in my mind, I let the anguish engulf me and I gripped onto Fi even tighter with this double contradiction only making my screaming headache worse.

After what felt like a lifetime of crying, my tears ran dry and Fi dragged me into my bathroom, instructing me to take a shower. With the door shut, I turned the shower on without stepping in, letting it get hot. I shuffled to the mirror and looked at the sorry sight that stared straight back at me. I still had last night's make up on. Well, whatever was left after I had cried more than half of it away. My eyes were red and puffy from the excessive crying with a ring of black from my mascara and eyeliner circling them.

It was only then that I noticed I was wearing one of Leon's tops. I must've accidentally put it on when I was getting dressed in total darkness. I brought it up to my nose and inhaled deeply. His scent still lingered and while it calmed my mind, it made my heart scream.

The last time I looked in the mirror like this, was nine years ago. My mind flashed back to that dark time. I had been overwhelmed with self-hatred, pain and hopelessness. It had taken me mere seconds to decide what I was going to do. I hadn't thought about the repercussions my action would bring, I had only thought of the blissful freedom that awaited me on the other side.

These thoughts of mine continued to rattle in my mind as I stepped under the steady stream of burning hot water. Since then, there had been a couple of times where I thought about injuring myself, and this was one of those very few times. My eyes flicked to the razor that laid on the clear shelf in the corner of the shower booth. I picked it up and ran my finger along the shiny blade, hard enough to feel the sharpness, but soft enough not to draw blood. It would be easy; I already had a guide mapped for me. I turned my wrist over and stared at the white tiger stripes that decorated my skin like medals. Medals that commemorated my strength, survival and stoicism. I looked back and forth at the razor in one hand, and the scars on the other.

No.

I'm not the person I was all those years ago. I'm so much stronger now and I'm not about to let him be the cause of my downfall again. I had to deal with this in a much better, healthier way. I placed the razor back and turned my back to it. Never was I going to steep that low ever again. I had made a promise to myself, to mum and Fi that I would continue to walk the Earth when times were hard and find healthier ways of dealing with the hardships that came my way. I couldn't leave the people I loved behind – and that included Leon.

I stepped out of the shower feeling a little better. I looked back in the mirror, my face now makeup free and looking more refreshed. I gave myself a stern telling off for my moment of selfishness and reminded myself that it was OK for me to feel hurt and sad; I just had to go through the motions of it.

With a white fluffy towel wrapped around me, falling to just above my mid-thigh, I stepped out of the bathroom and left my damp hair to hang in scraggly strands down my shoulders and the back of the towel. I heard Fi's raised voice as she spoke to someone.

"She doesn't want to see you... Haven't you done enough damage?" I followed her voice and froze on the spot when I saw who she was talking to. Leon stood at my door with Ffion stood in front of him, preventing him from stepping a foot inside. He jerked his head sharply to my direction with sad, pleading eyes. Fi sighed and turned to me, still blocking Leon from coming in.

"I'm sorry A, he wont leave." I took a deep breath and calmed myself down. As terrified as I was, I had to hear him out. It was better for me to have all my emotions together rather than get over them, just to be hit with them again later.

I smiled to Ffion. "It's alright Fi. I'll deal with it, you can go. I'll be fine." Ffion looked at me with surprise. She hadn't expected me to be willing to see Leon this soon after the Hiroshima sized bomb that dropped yesterday, and if I was being honest, neither had I. Once I'd nodded to her in reassurance, she opened the door for Leon who took slow steps until he was stood next to Fi. I turned my attention to Leon, my smile wiped off my face and replaced with a cold, blank expression.

"Sit down." Keeping my interaction with him short and blunt, so he knew he was in for a rough interrogation, I turned and went into my bedroom and started getting dressed. I lazily threw on some leggings and a random top and walked into the living room with my head held high. He was not going to see me weak.

I sat down as far away from Leon as possible. Being near him made me feel funny and I didn't want anything to weaken me. None of us spoke for a few minutes. I had no intention of starting the conversation. He had come here to talk to me of his own volition; therefore, he could start. But it seemed he didn't know where to begin.

He was looking into his hands that he was wringing in his lap. He was still in last nights attire and he had dark shadows under his eyes. His hair was sticking up every which way from constantly running his hands through it. Even from a distance I could hear how jagged his breathing was, and I watched as I saw a shiny crystal drop from his face. My heart ached for him, my hands longed to be wrapped around him to soothe him, but my mind was stronger. He had done this to himself, not me.

He slowly looked up at me and I saw the tears trickling down his cheeks. His beautiful hazel eyes were now dark with regret and torment. Seemingly able to find his voice, he began to speak.

"Ava... I... I'm so sorry. I-" To stop him from stuttering like a complete fool, I held my hand up to him. I didn't want his apology. Not yet anyway. I needed to know the details before I could even think of the possibility of forgiving him.

"Start with Stacey."

31

Chapter 30

Leon's POV:

Ev and I hadn't hung around at the Ball much longer after Ffion had left us. The ride back home was a blur as my thoughts were solely focused on Ava and any and all possibilities of our future. I had royally fucked this up. And though what happened in our past couldn't be changed, it didn't mean that Ava had ever forgiven me for my role in almost stealing her life. The thing with Stacey she may be able to forgive, may be able to see how stupid and sorry I was for it, but either way, there was no certainty of there ever again being an 'us'. Hatred for myself pummeled its way through me; hatred for both past and present me.

Ffion had sent Ev a text telling us that she was with Ava and that I was to stay away. She hadn't told us how she was or anything, she just left us on read. Once I reached the apartment, I had to fight with everything in me not to knock on her door, and instead entered my home with Ev following behind me.

We still hadn't discussed the Stacey situation and although I knew he wanted to talk to me about it, I told him that I needed to try clear the air with Ava first. Making things right with her was my first priority. I was desperate to know she was OK, so much so that I pressed my ear up against the wall a couple of times, only to be disappointed and filled with more worry when I couldn't hear anything coming from the other side.

I had been up all night thinking about her and what to say to her. I needed to explain myself. I needed to try fight for her and for us, no matter how against the odds it was. My mind had been crowded with what she was doing and how she was feeling. I prayed that she wasn't hurting herself, that she hadn't fallen into the vicious cycle of despair that she'd been in so many times before. But somewhere in the depths of my mind, I knew and had hope that all was well. She was stronger than she was then, and I clung to that little bit of faith in her like my life depended on it.

Ev had stayed with me but he had crashed after two hours of watching me pace aimlessly around the apartment. There was nothing he could do, nothing he could say to ease the battle in my mind with myself, not when I was too lost in it, entrapped in my own despair. I was imagining the conversation I would have with her when I was finally able to speak to her. I didn't want to make this any worse than it already was, but I was having a hard time picturing how else it could go.

I ended up seeing the new day in sat on a chair on my balcony. As I gazed up into the night sky, I became entranced by the twinkling of the stars as they stood out against the blank black canvas. Like grains of spilt sugar, the white specs haphazardly dotted across the sky, creating all kinds of pictures and constellations. The longer I stared, the more connected I felt with the blanket of black stillness. Slowly but surely, the sun crept up like it was trying to get the jump on the moon. The black started to fade out as the rich, rosy tones of the sun's rays invaded the sky.

Once Ev woke, I informed him that I was going to attempt to speak to Ava today. His response was a scoff, followed by a curt "good luck with that mate." Knowing Ffion, I'd have a tough time getting past the door, but it was worth a try.

Ev had been texting Ffion all morning, and so far, Ava hadn't woken up. Apparently, she had gotten black out drunk and passed out on Ffion's shoulder. That was better than I could have hoped for. I'd rather her try to drink her pain away than the alternative. She had sent a photo to Ev of the state she was in. She was slumped on the kitchen floor with her head propped up against the cupboard behind her, chin dipped so low that it rested on the delicate skin that the neckline of her t-shirt was too big to cover. Her arms were limp at her sides, whilst one leg was bent with the foot resting against the knee of her other, straightened out leg. Her makeup had melted off her face from her tears, and she had three empty bottles of wine laying around her, one of which still in her hand. Whilst it would've normally made me laugh, the circumstances that had caused her to look like that broke my heart. I had done that to her. A small smile appeared on my face when I realised that she was wearing one of my tops. To me, it signaled that there might just be hope after all.

* * *

Two hours later, I found myself at Ava's door, with a pissed off

Ffion refusing me entrance. No surprise there.

"You're not coming in Leon. End of." She held the door open but blocked me with her entire body. I tried to look through the gaps for a glimpse of Ava, but she was nowhere to be seen.

"Please Ffion, I need to explain, I need to try make this right." I could feel the tears well up in my eyes, I was becoming impatient to see her.

"What part of 'no' do you not understand? Do I need to say it in a different language? She doesn't want to see you." Her voice was gradually raising, getting louder as she became more annoyed at my persistence.

"Ffion, please. I need to see her." I clasped my hands together as I begged her to let me in.

"Haven't you done enough damage?" I let out a defeated sigh. She was right, I had caused a lot of damage. But because it was my mess, I needed to clear it up. I needed to take responsibility.

I was about to give in when a white movement in the corner of my eye caught my attention. I turned my head sharply towards it and found my beautiful, perfect girl stood there, alive and well. She had a short white towel wrapped tightly around her, and her damp, long hair hung raggedly around her.

She looked petrified. She was frozen on the spot, her once crystalline eyes were now a deep ocean blue of fear and anger pinned on me. The temporary paralysis only lasted a few seconds before she turned to Ffion and instructed her to let me in. Her sweet smile came onto her face as she spoke to Ffion and I felt my heart swell, how I envied Ffion for being able to have that smile directed at her, and how my hatred for myself grew that it was my fault I wouldn't get a smile that like. Nevertheless, at least she wanted to talk and listen to me. That was as much as I could have wished for. Her face dropped instantaneously when she turned her attention back on me. It was cold and empty, showing me not a hint of emotion as to what she was feeling. I could feel my heart cramp as it received another stab at her sudden change in expression towards me.

I stepped in, my legs a little wobbly from anticipation. I had no idea what was in store for me, but I knew it wasn't going to be good.

"Sit down." Her tone was blunt and to the point, and like a dog, I did as I was told. There was no expression to it, and I instantly knew that I was in for a rough ride. I watched her walk away from me and fought with myself as the thought of what she looked like under that short, teasing towel crept its way into the forefront of my brain. She had a sensational body, and I would give anything to see it again. But now was not the time.

She walked back in not a minute later, now dressed in some black leggings and a top that had the motto '*Be Loyal To The Nightmare Of Your Choice*'. I smiled internally at the irony. I hoped I was the nightmare she chose. She walked in looking full of confidence, but as usual, her eyes told a different story. She was a mixture of negative emotions. She perched herself on one of the stools in the kitchen, staying as far away from me as possible. I felt a little hurt, but I could understand why she didn't want to be near me. I knew how hard it would be to refrain from touching me – because I was finding it difficult myself not to pull her into an embrace.

We sat in silence for a few minutes, neither of us talking. I didn't know where to begin. My staying up all night had clearly done nothing for me, and all my planning of what I wanted to say to her went out of the window. The longer we stayed quiet, the more uncomfortable I got, and I started to look down into my hands, and began pulling at my fingers.

269

I could feel the tears prickle in my eyes as I began to think that this could very well be my only chance to try to redeem myself. The last nine years didn't mean anything if Ava couldn't forgive me. I didn't want to lose her, and although I knew we wouldn't be back to how we were anytime soon, I wanted her to at least give me a chance. A single tear dropped from my eye, landing on my knee as I thought about how I may never see her again after this.

Deciding it was better to say something than nothing, I looked up at her and my eyes fell to her luscious orbs. They were the gateway to her soul. I could see that she was hurting, I could see she was fighting to come be near me. But she was stronger than anyone gave her credit for and she held her ground. I started to speak but it came out as a stutter as my tears started pouring out of my sockets. "Ava... I... I'm so sorry. I-" She cut me off by holding up one of her petite, delicate hands.

"Start with Stacey." Her tone was direct and sharp. I was a bit more relieved to talk about Stacey, it seemed a bit more easier than talking about the past and everything that entailed. I sighed, but it came out shaky and irregular. I looked back at my hands that were now trembling like a leaf. I knew this was going to be hard, but I felt ill-prepared.

"Where do I start?"

"From the beginning." Still blunt and to the point, her voice held a tone of annoyance. She wanted to get this over and done with. It stung a little, I wanted to be around her for as long as possible, but she didn't care for it. She wanted me out as soon as possible, like my presence was too much for her to bare.

Taking a could of deep breaths to get my voice under control, I looked up into her awaiting face. I began telling her how I was packing my things away in the office, preparing to leave for the day when Stacey sauntered in to tell me she was taking her leave. I told her how she had complimented me on how much happier my patients were after their sessions, and that she thought that it was due to the introduction of a woman in my life. I saw pride swirl in Ava's eyes when I spoke of that part. She knew it was about her, that she had made me better in my work.

From there, I explained how Stacey had made the move on me and that I had tried to stop her, but she forced me to touch her. I spoke deeply, because this was where the problem was to start. I didn't miss the pain flash through her eyes before she closed them, forbidding me from reading her emotions. She blindly listened, knowing what part was coming next as I continued.

"Before I knew what was going on, Stacey had guided my hand inside her. My mind went blank, and it was over in only a couple of minutes. I swear Ava, she made it out worse than it was to you. I never slept with her." Her eyes snapped open and rage filled them. Not quite the emotion I was expecting to see; I was hoping my explanation would've calmed the situation down a little and that she would understand. Apparently not.

"Oh, and I suppose that makes it better does it?" She snapped sarcastically; her voice was hard but there was a tint of hurt behind it. Though, she did have a point; it didn't make the situation any better. I had just assumed it wouldn't hurt her as much.

"Well, no–"

"You're fucking unbelievable Leon. There's no such thing as "try". There's only 'do' and 'don't' and you chose 'do'. You didn't "try" to stop her Leon, or else it never would have gone as far as it did. How many times did you tell her to stop? How many times did you tell her 'no'? Did it stop when you "blacked out", or was you enjoying yourself too much to stop it?" She cut me off again, her voice raising with every question fired my way. With every rhetorical question she asked, raised a new thought alongside the knowledge of what the answer was and she was *pissed*. I couldn't deny her inquisitiveness though, because she was absolutely right. I could've done more to stop anything going any further with Stacey. I *should've* done more. But I didn't and now the guilt was weighing even more heavily on my heart. But I was in no position to complain about it. This was my own doing. and Ava wasn't done handing me my arse.

"And in all of this," her hand waved in an invisible circle for emphasis, "not once did you think about how it would affect me when I found out. Not once did I cross your mind until it was too late, not even when you were knuckle deep in that cunt of hers. And yet, you want my forgiveness?" I was speechless. There was nothing for me to reply to that because that would be signing my own death note. It hadn't occurred to me just how much of a prick I was; not until Ava had put everything into blinding perspective. Her thoughts hadn't dwindled as she continued on.

"This was after we slept together wasn't it? It was why you wanted to get rid of her. Why you had been so... weird with me those couple of weeks." She had thought long and hard about this situation, and her conclusion was once again accurate. She already knew all of this, but she wanted to hear the confirmation come from me. She knew it would be hard for me to say it, knowing I was going to bring her more hurt. But she didn't care. She wanted to see me suffer, just like she was, and boy was I experiencing a whole new world of suffering.

I nodded, flicking my eyes down to the ground. I couldn't look at her, not when I knew that what I was going to say next would be the final nail in the coffin for her with regards to the Stacey drama. Death note signed: Yours Sincerely, Leon Myers, the arsehole.

"It was the day after. The day I gave you a key to my place." My voice was low, full of sorrow. I heard her choked up sobs escape from her mouth and I hesitantly looked up. She had her head in her shaking hands to hide her face. Her shoulders shook as she began to break down in front of me. The refusal to yield giving way.

"Do you know how that makes me feel Leon? Was I not good enough for you? Did I not satisfy you enough?" She was doubting her ability at pleasing me. It broke my heart, because that was not the case at all. I had just been a stereotypical, fucking male who thought with my cock and not my brain, without even giving a seconds thought to what I was doing and the repercussions that would follow.

My body moved on its own before my brain could stop it. In only a few long strides and I was sat on the chair next to her. I swiveled her around by her seat so that she was facing me and I took her hands in mine, gently prying them from her face. She reluctantly let me, and once I placed her wet hands in one of mine, I used my other to tip her head up by her chin to look at me. Her beautiful face was shining with tears that streamed slowly over the curves of her rosy cheeks. Lips that once were light pink were now a deep red and trembling, as she quietly let her pain out. Eyes the colour of ice look sadly into mine. Her tears sparkled in the light as they hovered precariously on her lashes. The anger had gone from her eyes but had been replaced with agony and heartache.

"Ava. Listen to me. You are it for me. You are more than enough for me. Everyone else pales in comparison to you; there is no one in the universe who brings me as much light, love and laughter into my life as you do. I don't want anyone else; I just want you." Tears were rolling down my own face now. My life had become technicolour since having her in it, when I had been living in a life of monochromatic black and white. I couldn't let her slip from me now.

"I'm so sorry, Ava. I'm so fucking sorry. And the hard truth is that no matter how I try to explain myself and my actions, it doesn't detract from the fact that it happened. All I can do is apologise to you, and promise you that this will never, ever happen again."

Her face scrunched together as a wave of emotion hit her and she let out a gut-wrenching cry. I stood up and pulled her head into my stomach. She clung to me for dear life, soaking my shirt with her salty tears. I cradled her head with one hand and placed my other hand on her back. I rubbed her soothingly, as I had done many times before. Seeing her like this was breaking me and I didn't know what else to do. The damage was already done and I didn't know how else to minimise it without making matters worse.

I bent down and planted a soft kiss on the top of her head. Although the fear of losing her was running feral in my veins, a small wave of warmth mingled in with the fear. My girl was in my arms again, where she belonged, allowing me to give her some sort of comfort. I knew this wasn't me being forgiven though, we were nowhere near forgiveness yet. But she needed this, just as much as I did, and so I cherished this moment with her, since I didn't know if or when the next time I'd be able to hold her would be.

After a while, her shuddering stopped and her sobs quietened down. With her head still buried in my stomach, her voice was barely audible as she spoke into my abdomen.

"How did I not clock who you were?" She was done discussing

274

Stacey, and onto the much harder topic. Her question was a valid one, and I owed it to her to answer whatever questions she threw at me.

"I use my mothers maiden name most of the time. I'm not allowed to use my real surname on my social media accounts." A silly rule if you ask me, but it is what it is.

"But I know your real surname."

"Trauma will do that to you. You forgot about me as your way of coping. You've been remembering more of your past recently and I suppose hearing the announcement of my name made everything fall into place." It was the only explanation I could give her. The only one that made sense to me. She nodded once against me, her only acknowledgment of my answer before she reeled off the next one, head still buried in my stomach.

"How long have you known who I was?" I sighed resignedly.

"Since Wednesday. I was at work thinking about how you mentioned Victoria's name in your sleep. The more I thought about our time together, the more I started to remember details, and then I started thinking about the past, and put things together until it clicked who exactly you were. I asked Ffion and I about had a heart attack when she told me." She stayed motionless, listening intently. She wasn't crying no more and the only sounds I could hear were her occasional sniffs and the clock in the distance tick-tocking melodically. I pulled away from her and looked down to her tear stained face. Her eyes were now puffy and red and her nose resembled Rudolph's. I tucked a strand of her now dry hair behind her ear and cupped my hands on her damp cheeks.

"You know, I never meant to hurt you back then. The day you told me you liked me, I was about to tell you I liked you back. I was prepared to give up my popularity for you, but Victoria got in the way. If she hadn't of interrupted, things might have been different." Her breath got caught in her throat and eyes softened as fresh tears shimmered in her eyes. But hearing the childishness of my reasoning out loud made me cringe internally. As an adult, I didn't give a shit about popularity, it wasn't a trait or a concept that bothered me. But back then, up until Ava left, it was the be all and end all; status meant everything.

"I love you Ava, and I'm so incredibly sorry for all the hurt I've caused you in the past and present. Please, just give me a chance." My eyes held hers as I pleaded with her. She glanced down at her hands still wrapped around my shirt. She let go of me and shook her head.

"I love you too Leon, but I don't know if I can forgive you. At least not yet anyway. I need time to think, to figure out what I want to do." She didn't look at me, and her voice was starting to wobble again. I felt my heart skip a beat at her words. She still loved me, but she didn't know if she could forgive me. Which meant there was a chance I wouldn't get her back. This was completely out of my hands now. The ball was in her court and I had no choice but to leave her to decide how she wanted to play.

"I... I think you should leave now.... please." I nodded to her and gave her a lingering kiss on the forehead. Wiping a stray tear from her cheek, I smiled lovingly to her. I turned around and walked towards the door and opened it reluctantly. I looked over my shoulder to her to find her silently crying as she watched me leave.

"I'm sorry Ava. I truly am." She simply nodded in reply and I took that as my cue to leave her be.

Once back in my own apartment, I leaned my head against my door and closed my eyes, letting out a deep hoarse sigh. All I could do now was wait for as long as it took for Ava to make her mind up about me and about us, and that could take weeks or even months. But that was OK. I was prepared to wait for her. No matter how long it took.

Chapter 31

It had been a week since Leon and I had spoken, and I hadn't seen him since. I'd spent most of the time crying. I wasn't too sure how I was feeling at this point, my brain was like a washing machine, swirling all kinds of emotions around. I was sort of happy that Leon hadn't slept with Stacey, but I was still hurt that he'd even touched her at all. He had told me that I was it for him, he didn't want anyone else. Those words, the sincerity in his voice, the honesty that gleamed in his eyes, only made my heart almost jump out of my chest as relief swept through my body. But asides from betrayal, my biggest feeling at this moment in time was pride towards myself. Giving myself over to the rage that had started to consume me, I had spoken up and put Leon in his place, and I'd be lying if I said that didn't feel damn good.

With that out of my system, I had to address the worst of our issues. I had to ask him how long he'd known who I was. The question had been burning in the back of my mind. Because if he had known for a while, it would have made forgiving him even harder than it already was. So, I was weirdly relieved that it had only been for a few days, and it explained why he had been a bit flaky those couple of days.

I'd surprised myself when I let him comfort me, but I was glad that I did. I really did need it. It felt nice being held by him again. The entire time he had been sat at the other side of the room from me, my body had been vibrating with an ache to touch him, and the second he took my hands in his, the ache dulled. As soon as he had closed the door my cries came hard and loud. I had taken myself to my bed and buried myself under the covers, where I remained for days, only getting up for food and the bathroom.

Fi came and checked up on me later that day, a coffee and a slice of lemon drizzle cake from 'The Hub' in each hand. After placing the goodies on my bedside table, she took her place in the middle of the bed, sitting cross-legged and therefore forcing me to come out from the security and warmth of my hibernation station. I told her everything that happened with Leon, from start to finish. I told her about the almost falling off the wagon in the shower. There was no interrupting. No opinions. Just non-judgmental listening. That was one of the things I loved about Ffion, there was never any shame or fear in telling her anything. She knew all the right things to say and when to say them, and she knew when to just simply say nothing at all. She just listened and fetched me tissues when the ugly crying started. She knew comfort sometimes made me worse, made me weaken and lose my footing with words. Once I'd finished, she got off the bed, threw the duvet back and laid next to me, gently pulling me down next to her and resting my head on her chest. The arm behind me held me tight as the other stoked my hair whilst she told me how proud she was of me, and I just hugged her back even tighter. She had insisted on spending the night, just to keep an eye on me but I just needed space and time to rot in my bed. Finally, after watching me eat the cake in three mouthfuls, she left with a warning to make sure that I ate and drank plenty or else she'd be back to force feed me. Aeroplane noises and all.

From then on, I felt like I was drowning in a depthless ocean of pain and sadness, but the last couple of days, I felt like I was slowly learning how to swim and tread the water. Fi had still checked in on me every day, making sure that I was making good of my word. She was concerned that I was going to end up the way I did with Wyatt, a worry that wasn't completely entirely far-fetched, but I was determined not to let myself slip to that again.

Today, I was in a better frame of mind to give my mum a call and let her know what had happened. I'd already text her to let her know that something had happened, but that I was OK and would tell her everything when I was ready. She was understanding and didn't try force me to tell her what was going on.

I was sat on the sofa, the first day out of my bed in a week, with my feet up on the coffee table, crossed at the ankles. The afternoon sun was warm on my bare feet as it gently shone through my blinds, spotlighting my narrow lower extremities . I found myself somehow entertained as I watched the small specks of dust dance freely in the tinted yellow light. Quickly getting bored of staring into space, I found my mums name on FaceTime and gave her a call. She picked up after a few rings and she had a beaming grin on her face. She always greeted me with a smile, but this was different. *She* was different. I thought I saw someone move just off the screen, and I felt my brows twitch slightly; my spidey-senses tingling.

"Hey, mama." I kept my voice indifferent. I was interested to see if she would give anything away. If she was normal, then it was most likely just my imagination playing tricks with me.

"Hey, baby!" She was happy, happier than usual. Her voice was slightly higher-pitched, and there was excitement literally emanating from every surface of her being. She had some news to tell me. I crossed the fingers of my free hand, hoping it was the news I had long been waiting for.

"Mama, is there someone with you?" Somehow, her grin widened and her head shook wildly up and down like a bobble-head before her eyes diverted to the side, looking at someone behind the phone. She knew that she couldn't hide anything from me, especially when she looked like she was literally going to burst from keeping whatever it was from me.

"There's someone I want you to meet... well, re-meet I suppose." Just as confusion set on my face a familiar male came into view on the camera as he stood behind my mum. He had changed a little in the nine years since I last saw him. He had grown a light, thin beard that made him look slightly older. But his eyes were still that beautiful piercing emerald green, and they crinkled a little more at the sides when he smiled.

"Kelvin!" Kelvin wrapped his arms around my mum, and she brought her free hand up to hold onto his tattooed forearm. All three of us were now wearing matching facial features. He was the last person I expected to be seeing, but if there was anyone that could make mum happy and give her the world, it was him.

"Hey there little legs! Look at you all grown up." Happy tears came to my eyes as I heard him use the nickname he had given me all those years ago. It was so good to see him again, and it was even better seeing them reunited after so many years. Him and my mum truly were destined to be together, and sometimes it took for two people to be apart for them to find their way back to another, a sentiment that I hoped could be the same for myself and Leon.

"You don't look like you've aged a day! It's so good to see you again Kelvin, I'll have to come home soon so I can see you in person. You guys have no idea how happy I am that you've found each other again." I wiped the tears from my eyes before they fell, and I smiled brightly at them. My mum was finally happy and that truly meant the world to me.

Kelvin had always treated her with the utmost respect. He doted on her and he had done all that he could to look after the pair of us. I remember he once said that she was the butter to his bread, and the memory made me giggle. Looking at them through the screen, they looked like smitten teenagers. I was overjoyed for them both, and over the moon that they had found their way back to one another.

"I'm glad too Ava. I missed your mother so much, that I haven't dated anyone since her. She's the only one for me. I love her like it's nobody's business, flaws and all." He winked at my mum and we both laughed when she swatted him playfully on the arm and then she rolled her eyes with a shy smile on her face.

Flaws and all hey? My mind briefly floated to thoughts of me and Leon. Before we knew who the other was, he had loved me despite knowing I had secrets. He had continued to love me as I told him little bits of my past, accepting me for what and who I was. My heart ached as I thought about him; I was missing him so much. I missed his gentle touch that showed his love and reassurance when I was feeling insecure. I missed waking up next to him in the safety of his arms. I missed his calming, stimulating scent that flooded my body. But I still hadn't forgiven him. That was a long way off; there was still so much to think about. I couldn't be with him without forgiving him, and at this very moment, I wasn't sure if I would be able to.

Shaking my head to rid my mind of these intrusive thoughts, I asked mum how her and Kelvin had found each other again. Mum had been in a bar on a date, not knowing that Kelvin was working there, helping his brother out as he was short staffed. The date was going awfully, and mum was desperate to get away from it. Apparently, this guy was an arrogant pig who had it in his head that he would be going home with my mum that night and take her for the "ride of her life."

Mum had excused herself to the bar when she came face to face with Kelvin. They had got to chatting and after a few minutes, she looked back at her date and found him with his tongue down some younger girls' throat. She didn't care though; she had used that as an easy way out of the date. They exchanged numbers there and then and the rest is history.

The entire time they were telling me their story, they had been sharing loving looks. I felt like I was watching a soppy chic flick. Their love for each other was so abundantly clear, that even a blind person could see it. These two truly were made for each other.

"Well, as much as I'd love to hear more, would it be possible to speak to you alone mum, please?" It was time to tell her my news. I hated to break the good-natured, light atmosphere that had been created, but this couldn't wait any longer. Mum nodded with a puzzled look on her face.

"Speak to you later, Ava!" Kelvin's distant voice rang through the phone as he walked out of the room, giving me and mum some privacy.

"What's going on Ava? Is it Leon?" I dropped my gaze and nodded slightly. I could feel the tears brewing already.

I explained the Stacey situation and I could see the fury burning in her eyes. She didn't speak a word whilst I told her the story, but her eyes and facial expression spoke a thousand words. She was seething. Nostril flaring seething. He had hurt her baby, her only baby. She was under the same impression as I was. It didn't matter that he didn't sleep with her, his action was still an act of betrayal. He could've stopped it if he really wanted to. Yes, she put his hand there, but he didn't pull it away.

"I can't believe him. After all these years, he still finds a way to hurt you."

I didn't reply to her for a few seconds as I processed what she said. What did she mean, 'after all these years'? Did she know who Leon was? If so, why didn't she tell me sooner? She must've realised why I'd gone quiet, as she held her hand to her mouth and let out a barely audible "shit." Her eyes were as round as saucers as she anticipated my reaction.

"You knew who he was..." Realisation hit me full force like a truck. "You've known the entire time, since you met him, haven't you?" My tone was accusing and hard. Mum still didn't say anything. She just looked down at the floor like a child who had just been scolded, her hand sliding up from her mouth to her forehead. It was all I needed to know that I was right.

"Why the *hell* didn't you tell me when you were here? Do you know how much heartache you could've saved me?" I was getting angry now. Something as big as that and she couldn't tell me. Instead, she'd left it until two and a half months later to tell me. Until I had fallen hard for him. I couldn't wait to hear her bullshit excuse.

"I just... I wanted you to find out on your own. You went through so much to forget about him, I didn't think it was my place to tell you." She was getting upset, her voice was starting to shake as she held back her tears. She looked up at the camera at me. I felt bad that I had to get angry at her, but this was a big thing for her to have kept from me and right now, I couldn't give a toss that she was upset. She had given me an extra two and a half months to fall more and more in love with Leon.

"As my mother, you thought it was in my best interest to *not* tell me something as life changing as this? Something that you knew would break me if I found out when I was in too deep with Leon?" A sob escaped her mouth as she realised just how misplaced her judgement had been. Her heart was in the right place, I knew that, and I appreciated she maybe wanted to protect me, but it was wrong of her to just assume. It wasn't her place to decide if me knowing was damaging or not. But what's worse, if not just as bad, is that she led me to believe she liked Leon. There was never a hint of any doubt or dislike on her face or in her tone whenever we spoke about him. Had I of noticed, I would have doubted Leon myself - my mother's judgement of people was never wrong.

"That's four people now. Four people who were supposed to love me and bring me joy and happiness that have hurt me in an unimaginable way." Mums head turned to the side in shame, trying to recompose herself, and I though felt awful for having a go at her, a fresh wave of outrage rolled through me. She should have told me about Leon. Maybe then, I wouldn't be hurting so bad now. Maybe, I wouldn't have gone any further with Leon. Maybe, I wouldn't have found out about Stacey. I would have been able to move on and leave Leon in the dust. But instead, here I am, madly in love with my ex tormentor, in two minds about whether I should forgive him and take him back or call it a day on us.

"I'm sorry Ava sweetheart, I didn't intend to hurt you." Her sobs were stronger now, as guilt and sadness overwhelmed her body. I spotted Kelvin hovering to the side of the doorway behind her, no doubt having overheard the drama unfold.

"You aren't the first person to have said that to me this week, or this year. It seems that everyone who has hurt me never 'intended' to. First it was Wyatt and Felicity, then Leon, and now you. You know what? I'm done talking about this with you mum."

"Ava baby, wait-"

"I'll speak later." I hung up on her, refusing to give her the courtesy of hearing her plead for me to stay on the call or her anymore of her apology. I was too angry to cry. I was sick to death of everyone treating me like a doormat and tip-toeing around me so as not to upset and trigger me. I stood up and stomped over to the shoe cupboard in the hallway. I slipped on some flip-flops and grabbed my handbag. I needed some air and good coffee.

I opened my door, taking the key out of the lock as I did so, only to freeze on the spot when I saw a stunning brunette with sapphire eyes on my doorstep, her fist was raised as she was about to knock on my door.

You have got to be fucking kidding me, I seriously cannot catch a break.

33

Chapter 32

If I thought my week couldn't get any worse, then I was being incredibly delusional. She stood in front of me, her slim figure silhouetted against the bright daylight. I didn't speak a word to her; she wasn't worth my breath. But what I did do, was scrutinise her. She looked rough, but for once, it made her look like a normal human being. Her hair was up in a messy bun and she had purple rings under her eyes from lack of sleep. She wasn't standing tall like she normally would, like she owned the air we all breathed. Her shoulders were slumped, as if she was carrying the weight of the world on her shoulders. She had lost a bit of weight. Her once full face was starting to look gaunt. Her collarbones protruded more prominently than they used to. Scanning my eyes down her body, my eyes widened slightly when I saw her stomach gently rounded, her top stretching against the growth. I wanted to pity her, but after what she had done and the foul mood that I was in, I wasn't feeling empathetic.

"Hey Ava, long time no see." She smiled weakly at me. I stepped outside the door, locking it behind me. I had no intention of inviting her in or giving her the time of day. I folded my arms across my chest and sat on one side of my hip. I felt my eyebrow raise in a questioning arch and put on my most bored expression that I could. I really did not want to be dealing with her and her shit.

Ignoring her greeting I flicked my eyes down to her bump before meeting her gaze again. "Come to rub it in my face have you Felicity?" I spoke coldly, showing her no emotion. Neither one of us were who we were ten months ago, and she was in for a rude awakening if she thought I would roll over for her again.

She knew about my infertility. She had been at the hospital with me when the doctor gave me the news. She was well aware that it was a topic me and Wyatt had discussed to great lengths. He was the only man that had made me believe that my dream of being a mother was possible. That was until Leon came into my life, and when things weren't in such a fucking mess, I had found myself daydreaming every so often about what our babies would look like.

Her face dropped into what could only be described as shame and embarrassment, and her quiet voice matched. "It... it's not Wyatt's..." I laughed scornfully at her. Once again, this girl never failed to live up to the low expectations I had of her. She couldn't even have the courtesy to keep hold of him after stealing him from me.

"What a shocker!" Sarcasm dripped viscously from my mouth. "And whose poor soul's boyfriend have you trapped this time?" I had never spoke to her with such hatred before. I had been too nice back then; I let her walk out with Wyatt without voicing my emotions. She thought she had got away easy then, but I've had time to process everything since then. The time had come, and she will finally feel my wrath.

"It's not like that Ava. Not this time. I really care for this one." She placed a bony hand on her curved stomach and rubbed it lovingly. Her voice was still low, but her eyes held mine. They were sad, but were tinged with hope that I'd believe her, that I'd hear her out. But I had heard enough, I couldn't care less about what she had to say anymore. And I most certainly didn't give two bollocks about her poor, unlucky child.

She had taken Wyatt away from me, and whilst I now knew Wyatt was not the one for me, the pair of them had betrayed me both behind my back and in front of it. When I caught them, all I did was stare wordlessly with tears streaming down my face. They hadn't noticed me until I managed to find my voice and shakily screamed at them both to get out. Felicity had come back a couple of days later to explain, but her excuses were half-hearted. I could hear that she wasn't really sorry for doing what she did. She was just sorry that she had been caught. My feelings meant nothing to her then, and hers meant nothing to me now.

"I've heard that one before. If I recall correctly, you said that about Wyatt not too long ago, not to mention every other guy you've snatched from some unfortunate girl. People's hearts are just your little plaything, you don't give a shit about anyone else apart from yourself. As long as Felicity's happy and getting whatever she wants, no one else matters." I spat. There was no holding me back now. My emotions were running high with everything that had hit me this week, and she was a perfect outlet.

She didn't say anything. She just hung her head, staring at the pavement. When she didn't speak for a few more seconds, I let out a sharp, short snort and started making my way down the steps. I didn't want to waste any more time on her. I had more important places to be.

I had stepped down a couple of the steep steps when I saw Leon ascend his. He flicked his eyes to Felicity behind me before looking back at me. His brows were knitted together in worry, and he looked at me, asking me if I was alright with his eyes. When we were a couple of steps apart, he opened his mouth to say something, but I could feel my face was set in a thunderous glare and he thought better of it. Instead, he gave me a small, slightly sad smile, before he continued making his way up to his door.

Felicity's squeaky voice blurted my name out behind me, and I spun around so fast to face her, I could feel my eyes spin in my head.

"What Felicity? Why are you still here?" I snapped, my tone thick with annoyance. She was really becoming a thorn in my side right now. Her eyes were heavy with tears and her lip was trembling uncontrollably. Once upon a time, I would've been by her side in an instant, pulling her into a warm, reassuring embrace. But not anymore. I'm not a weak person, far from it. But my weakness has always been my heart. I'm too trusting, too giving and far too kind. It was time to be more strict with who receives my care and sympathy.

"I don't have anywhere to go Ava. I don't have anyone else. You're the only person I could think of or trust to help me..." She was breaking down in front of me. Her words were high-pitched and wobbled as she spoke them. I did feel a little sorry for her, but not enough to care or do anything about it. This was her problem, her mess. I wasn't going to be the mug who was going to clear it up again. Those days were long gone.

I took the few steps up to her and stood besides her and pointed my finger in the air. "You see that?" Felicity's head tilted up with squinting eyes to see what I was pointing to. "That's the fuck I don't give flying away."

I fixed my stony gaze onto her as her head snapped back down and looked her dead in the eye and kept my tone level and emotionless. "I don't know if you've noticed, but we aren't friends anymore Felicity. You lost that privilege when you took Wyatt from me, something you maybe should've thought about before you let him shove his pencil dick in you." And with that, I turned my back on her and walked off, leaving her not only satisfyingly speechless, but crying whatever heart she had out on my doorstep.

* * *

Twenty minutes later I launched the door of 'The Hub' open, causing it to bounce back on its hinges when it reached its limit, and stormed over to Sam behind the counter. He had watched me enter and followed me as I made my way over to him. He looked a little scared and yet concerned at my outburst. I wasn't one to publicly show my anger, but my rage was coursing strongly through my veins right now and I was struggling to control it.

"The usual please Sam." Without replying, he nodded his head and I placed the exact change on the counter, before I made my way over to my usual seat in the corner by the window. I sunk deeply into the soft cushion and laid my head back, closing my eyes.

I tried using the flower and candle technique I had learned years ago when I was learning to control my panic attacks. I breathed in slowly and deeply through my nose, imagining I was inhaling the spicy bubblegum scent of a lily, before pouting my lips to slowly blow out a candle. I repeated this a few times until I felt my head lighten and become clearer. I hadn't realised just how blinded by my fury I had been.

The sound of Sam putting my coffee on the table and a quiet clink of metal on glass brought me back to my senses and I opened my eyes. Sam was sat in front of me, slouched slightly with his thick arms resting on the arm rests. I reached forwards to pick up my coffee, when I spotted my change neatly piled next to the saucer.

"It's on the house today." Sam's deep voice was kind and soft. He wasn't pitying me and my state, he was just being a friend. I smiled appreciatively at him and picked my mug up. I left the change where it was, I would no doubt use it to buy a second round.

I leaned back into my seat and took a long sip of my coffee. Feeling the caffeine zap through my body, I let out a moan of pleasure. I could already feel myself calm down. Sam was looking at me with an amused smile on his face.

He really was good looking. His floppy hair had been trimmed and his fringe was swept to the side from a deep parting. The rest of his hair fell to just around his ears. It made him look boyish, but his features were far from it. His baby blues were the colour of the sky. They had the power to calm anyone just by looking into them. His facial features weren't as sharp as Leon's, but they weren't exactly blunt either. His full lips were a light shade of pink and were always set in a friendly, welcoming smile. He put anyone he met at ease just by them looking at him.

He placed his hands in his lap and loosely clasped them together. "Boy trouble?" He asked, his masculine voice was relaxed and light. It wasn't inquisitive or intrusive, and I instantly felt at ease and comfortable to tell him my woes.

I rolled my eyes and shook my head at him. "That obvious huh?"

Sam shrugged his shoulders slightly, raising his brows and down turning his lips as he did so. "What can I say, I'm a guy. I know when one of my kind has broken a girl's heart." A boyish smirk played on his lips and I felt my mood lighten slightly. I giggled at his describing human males as if they were a species unto their own. I mean, he wasn't wrong to do so. Men were confusing.

"Well, there's more to it than just boy trouble. How long have you got?" I said the last part with a laugh. My life had become a roller-coaster of trials and tribulation, and the list was seemingly growing. Sam looked at me with gentle eyes. He didn't pity me, and I appreciated it - the last thing I needed right know was a pity party.

"Well, I finish in ten minutes. Hang around and you can tell me all about it if you want?" I had only been joking about asking how long he had to listen. But he was serious about hearing me out, and maybe an outside perspective wouldn't be so bad. I nodded my head at him, giving him a grateful smile. He pushed himself up from the chair and straightened his apron that was folded in half and tied around his waist.

"Hey, Sam." I called after him. He spun back around to face me with eyebrows raised in question.

"I'm sorry if I was rude to you when I came in."

"It's cool, don't worry about it Ava." He waved his hand downwards like it was no big deal before turning to head back behind the counter. I watched as he walked the short distance away from me and pulled a face of appreciation as he walked towards the counter. His posture was immaculate. He stood tall like a pole was shoved through his skull and down to his tailbone.

With flat shoulder blades, his chest was naturally pushed out and his broad shoulders sat squarely. His firm butt stood out in his tight black jeans, and his hips wiggled slightly when he walked.

Once back behind the counter, I turned back to my coffee, feeling a little guilty for ogling another man when I was still trying to decide on Leon. But then again, we weren't together anymore, and I was free to do whatever I liked... right?

True to his word, ten minutes later Sam walked over to me. I had just drained the last dregs of my coffee and had stood with my change in my hand, ready to get my second serving, when Sam held out a takeaway cup to me. The transparent mist wafted the delicious bitter scent of coffee into my nose, making my mouth water.

"I thought it might be better if we sat in the park and talk. Gives you a little more privacy." I picked my handbag up, placing it on my shoulder before taking the cup from him. Wrapping both of my hands around the blue decorated cardboard, I offered him a grateful "thanks."

We walked side by side through the park and he listened to me whilst I spoke. He would look down to me occasionally, so I knew that he was listening. I didn't tell him my full history. As easy to talk to and trust as he was, I hadn't even openly told Leon the full story, so I wasn't prepared or comfortable to tell him. Instead, I just told him that Leon was a ghost of my past, that he had hurt me in an unexplainable way. Over the years I had forced myself to forget about him, his name and his face, just so I could move on with my life.

I went on to say how I felt about Leon. How everything came naturally with him. It was easy, it was fun, and it was wholesome. His love was genuine, and it consumed my soul and body. It made me feel alive and filled the void that was in my heart. I spoke about the first time we said we loved each other, how he had been there for my nightmares and panic attacks, and how he never questioned my hesitation in talking about the past. Rather, he was patient, respectful and understanding with me and never pressed me to talk about anything that made me uncomfortable.

This was followed by his betrayal. I described how I had found out, how I lashed out at Stacey, how the memory of Leon hit me full force like a train, and how I had got blind drunk at home to numb the pain. Reliving this as I told Sam brought tears to my eyes again and I was hit with a fresh wave of pain. It had taken me a week to dull the pain enough for me to function, but it was back with a vengeance.

We had long since ditched our takeaway cups, and we were now sat on a bench. Sam had an arm around me, and I was laying in the comfortable crook of his arm. He was smoothly grazing his hand up and down my arm, soothing and reassuring me. My voice was strained as I fought the sob that was stuck in my throat. Letting my tears trickle slowly down my cheeks, I continued on with my story.

Soon enough, we had been sat in the park for an hour and half. Sam had listened to me the entire time, and my voice was now hoarse from speaking so much. I had told him of my telling Leon I needed time to think about what I wanted, of my mum already knowing who he was to me and not telling me, and then I rounded the whole tirade off with Felicity showing up pregnant and unannounced on my doorstep. Now my anger had subsided from that debacle, I was feeling a little regretful at how I treated her, but only a little bit. I wasn't usually such a bitch, but it felt good to be one towards someone worthy of my bitchiness.

I had been quiet for a few minutes, and Sam was waiting to see if there was anymore of my story to come. Once he concluded I was done, he let out a deep sigh and lifted me up placing me on his lap. He wrapped his arms around me, pulling me into a full-bodied embrace. He had a hand on head, holding it to his chest whilst stroking my hair. His other hand firmly held me respectfully at my waist. With my head pressed against his chest, I could hear the rhythmic, constant pounding of his heart. His affection caught me unawares and I realised that I had been missing this; someone to hold me whilst I let my emotions out. Yes, Ffion had been there, and I had told her everything, but I needed someone to hold me and just listen.

Sam's kind voice floated into my ears. "You've really had it rough, haven't you? I'm sorry that you've had all of that happen to you." I let out a pathetic little whimper as my sob threatened to make an appearance. I snuggled deeper into his chest and focused on the vibration in his chest that reverberated through me as he spoke.

"If you want my two cents on the matter, I think you need time away from Leon. Live a little and have some fun. Take your mind off him and, in a few months maybe, revisit him and see how things stand. With regards to this Felicity bird, I don't think you was out of order to her at all. She abused your trust and took someone who at the time meant the world to you. She doesn't deserve you and it was ignorant of her to think you would just open your door to her willingly."

I had planned to take time away from Leon already, but I hadn't thought about it being long term. I hadn't even considered what I would do with myself in the time whilst I worked through my emotions and thoughts about him and us. It felt nice Sam not telling me that I should or shouldn't take him back. He knew that this decision was mine and mine alone, and he held no judgement about the fact I might take him back, even if he had hurt me. It was also comforting to know that I hadn't over-reacted with Felicity. It was like a weight had been lifted from my shoulders and I felt better about the situation. Leon would be an ongoing thing, I don't know when I'll ever feel OK about that, but what I could do, was put it to the side and come back to it when my head was clearer, when I could look at things from a different angle.

"Thank you, Sam, for listening to me ramble for hours. It felt good having someone just listen to me, rather than having to discuss the ins and outs of everything. It's not so confusing when I don't have to explain or think too much about it all." I pulled away from his chest and he looked down at me with caring eyes. He had a sweet smile on his face as his eyes skimmed my face.

Wiping the wetness from my face, he spoke tenderly to me. "You look better for it. The tensions gone from your face." Thinking about it, my face didn't feel so tight now and my head didn't feel so heavy with a headache I had felt all week. Whilst I had obviously spoken to Fi and she had made me feel better, she was the only person that I had spoken to about this. It was nice to speak to someone else and someone new.

"Come on, it's getting late. Let's get you home." I hopped off his lap and I looked up at the sky. Sure enough, the sky was now painted in a mixture of orange and pink and the sun gradually began to go to sleep for the day. The breeze had picked up slightly, and the hem of my dress waved dangerously, almost exposing my intimate areas. I heard Sam chuckle as I became flustered and grabbed at my dress, holding it down so the wind didn't blow it up again.

* * *

He walked me to my door and I was about to walk in when I realised that I didn't have his number. I turned back to him and he looked at me in bewilderment.

"Sam, can I have your phone number please?" His face lit up with a beaming smile.

"Yeah of course you can, pass me your phone and I'll put it in." I unlocked my phone and handed it to him. As he was sending a text to himself, Leon came out of his house and he paused, looking between Sam and me. Hurt flashed in his eyes and his shoulders sagged slightly. Not saying anything, he locked his door and walked away with his hands in his pockets, kicking a couple of stones in frustration as he went.

Sam had seen it and had watched on as my gaze followed Leon.

"That must be the illustrious Leon." I pulled one corner of my mouth up into a half smile and flexed my eyes. I took my phone out of his hand as he handed it back to me. I laughed internally when I noticed he had saved his number under the name "Agony Aunt Sam."

"That would be the very one." Sam turned back to look at Leon, but by then, Leon had disappeared from our vision. I was grateful he was gone; it was hard seeing him. He had seen me with another male and I knew that would've hurt him like a dagger to the heart. Like he had any right to be jealous of me being with another man that wasn't him. But there was nothing going on between me and Sam, and we weren't together anymore so what I did and who with was none of his business.

"Anyway, thanks again Sam, I'll hit you up if I need someone to listen to me ramble again." He placed a warm hand tenderly on my exposed arm whilst a friendly smile played on his lips. I was shocked at how it felt having him touch me. With Leon, it was like a spark of electric that violently rippled through my entire body. But when Sam touched me, I felt a soft warm tingle tickle down my spine to my core.

"You had better! I expect a goodnight text tonight." He winked at me as he joked. Turning away, he raised his hand into the air and waved without looking at me. Once he was out of my gate, I entered my apartment. I kicked my flip flops off, not bothering to put them back where I got them from, and jumped onto my back on the sofa and stared up at the white, shell patterned ceiling. I felt a smile spread on my face. Sam was like medication to me. I had been feeling down but with his magic touch, and his words, though were they were few, had helped me feel a little better about myself and my situation.

I sent him a quick text, my heart thumping in my chest.

A: Fancy coming out with me next weekend so I can "live a little and have fun"?

Not even a minute later he had replied.

S: I thought you'd never ask. Prepare yourself for a night of non-stop dancing, singing and drinking

With butterflies excitedly fluttering in my stomach I lurched myself up and skipped to the kitchen. For the first time in a week, I felt energised. I was determined this next week would to be a good one. I had so much to look forward to.

34

Chapter 33

Leon's POV:

The building that housed my office was unusually quiet as I strolled through it, the only sound that could be heard was the echo of my strident footsteps that whispered my loneliness into my ears. There was no one in the vicinity due to it being Sunday and we were closed on the weekends. I did this regularly when I needed space and time to think. Sometimes it was nice to be away from the problems, the noise and all distractions so that I can reflect on my thoughts and feelings clearly and straight.

As I walked down the long, wide corridors, making my way towards my office, I tried my best to keep my mind quiet. I wanted to save my thinking for when I laid down on my long sofa. My mind had been consumed by thoughts of Ava all week, and after yesterday, it was on overdrive. And so, I decided that I needed to give myself some independent counseling.

I pushed the door to my office open and I was greeted with the sweet citric smell of orange. I had found that myself and my patients were a lot calmer if there was a scent in the air. It helped relax our minds, relieving any feelings of stress and anxiety. I inhaled the zesty scent deeply, instantly feeling lighter, and made my way to the sofa.

Once I had settled myself into my usual position of laying down along the entire length, my arms behind my head and my eyes closed, I finally allowed my thoughts to wander to Ava. I had stayed away from her all week. It had been relatively easy to do, since Ffion had told me that she hadn't left her bed at all, so there was no way I'd have bumped into her. But on the flip side, knowing that she was bed bound because of me pulled on my heartstrings and I felt the guilt sit heavily in the pit of my stomach.

When I wasn't working, I was thinking of Ava. I'd think about how she was, if she was taking care of herself, and more importantly, if she was still fighting to stay on the wagon. In her, there was a relentless determination and resilience that I had a great amount of faith in her that she would go about dealing with her emotions in a more healthy way. I hadn't failed to notice how much she had changed over the years, and I often found myself comparing her to her old self.

Before the torment me and my group had caused her, she was a bubbly, free-spirited girl who believed that the world was her oyster. It was one of the reasons I had found her so attractive, not to mention her prettiness. Long hair was something that for as long as I can remember, have loved and had a soft spot for and I always used to imagine running my hand through her hair. It was a golden waterfall of light that put the suns rays to shame. In school, she wore glasses that were wide rimmed with a black outline. It made her look as smart as she already was and took up most of her small, perfect face. Behind those crystal-clear glasses, were glacier eyes. Her eyes were blue, but they were the faintest shade of blue I had ever seen, and I was captivated by them, just as I am now. Whenever I looked into them, I was always able to read her, and she had become my favourite book. They gave away every emotion and every thought that flooded her being.

Then the torment began. Between me and the group, we had stripped her of all the good that made her who she was, and she became a shadow of herself. No-one wanted to be around her because of us – they didn't want to be associated with her through fear that they would also become our targets. She became self-conscious and isolated. We'd completely destroyed her strong personality and replaced it with a closed off, sheltered one. She stopped laughing and smiling and instead began crying more. She stopped contributing in class and retreated to the back, so she couldn't be seen by the teacher.

I grew to miss watching her run around the school field with her friends without a care in the world. Her hair used to fly behind her chasing after her wherever she went, before catching up to her and tangling itself on her face. I missed how carefree she was, and it wasn't until the worst had happened that I realised just what I had done to her.

I had told everyone in the group that what I did was for my own enjoyment, my own entertainment. But that was never the case. I hated myself for letting Victoria invade my conscience the way that she did. I wished I was as strong as Ava was, it was a trait that even to this day I envied of her. Had I been stronger, Ava wouldn't have been subjected to that pain and suffering, at least not alone. If I had stepped away from the title of "King of our Year", I would have no doubt received a lot of stick at the hands of those in the top tier of the Hierarchy. But I was naïve to think I would be better off carrying on how I was, that it was better to push her away in the harshest way possible. Looking back, I know I made the wrong choice. I've known for years, ever since I found out what the outcome of my actions were. Even though throughout the last few months of Ava's bullying I had pulled myself away from it as much as I could, letting Victoria take the lead and staying in the background and observing, it didn't make a lick of difference. None of the group followed my gradual retreat, and if I was being honest, I think that they all preferred Victoria running the group. She was more ruthless, domineering and malicious than I ever was or ever could be. She made bullying people more fun.

I was grateful that I had been given the opportunity to apologise for the past though. It was all I'd ever wanted to do. I never had the chance to back then. I remember I had waited a few months before I found the courage to go to her house and apologise for what I had caused, for what I had done. But when I arrived, the property was deserted. I had knocked on the door, but when there was no answer, I peeped through the muggy windows, barely able to see through the grime beginning to build on the glass. The house was completely barren and stripped of all furniture. She'd moved away and my heart had collapsed to my feet. I had resigned myself to the belief that I would never see her again, and she would never see that changes that I had made to my life both for, and because of her.

I knew there was really nothing I could say or do to make her change her mind about me with regards to her past. I had spent years changing my ways, not knowing that I would ever see her again. Now that I had, all I wanted was to make her proud that I wasn't who I was anymore. I wanted her to truly believe I was sorry for what I did and was trying my hardest to be redeemed to some extent.

She had blossomed into this beautiful, confident and amazing young woman, and it was such a contrast to her past self. This personality of hers wasn't the same as pre-bullied Ava. It was an enhanced version. She was tenacious and wasn't easily swayed by temptations. She knew how to stand up for herself; she wasn't scared to speak her mind and she gave as good as she got. She had always put others before herself, but her dedication to that now was something else. She wasn't satisfied with someone telling her they were just OK. She wanted them to feel great about themselves and to feel seen. She knew the value of life and used her knowledge and experience to make others feel that they deserved their place in the world. She truly was an inspiration to many, myself included.

I saw her for the first time in a week yesterday and it couldn't have been at a worse time. I was coming back from a shopping trip when I saw her stood on her doorstep in a bored pose, with a face like thunder. She was standing in front of a tall woman who had her head hung down, looking at the bland pavement. Ava hadn't seen me as she started down her steps, just as I was walking up mine. When she had, I had looked at the woman, who's tears were slowly dripping down her sharp, emaciated cheeks, and back to Ava and was going to ask if she was alright. I took one look at her face and decided against it. She had a murderous look on her face that was almost as fearsome as the one she had on at the ball. Instead, I gave her a small smile and carried on to my door. Whatever mess that was, she had it under control.

Once at my door, I sneakily glanced to the corner of my eye to look at the woman and noticed that she was with-child. I couldn't help thinking that it was strange behaviour of Ava to leave a pregnant woman crying on her doorstep. Ava had a heart of gold and would do whatever she could to help others in their time of need. I was stepping into my apartment when the woman called out for Ava in a weak squeak. Everything clicked into place when I heard Ava say the woman's name. It made sense why she was being so callous towards her. She was her ex-roommate and best friend who had betrayed her by sleeping with Ava's boyfriend behind her back. She was in for quite the shock if she thought Ava was going to help her, and by the looks of it, Ava had no intention of offering her caring heart out to her. I was proud that she was able to face someone else from her past and finally be able to get out how she felt and get some form of closure.

I wasn't expecting to see her anymore that day, or for a while at that. But I was leaving to meet Ev and she was stood at her door with another man who had her phone in his hands. I wasn't an idiot; I knew he was putting his number into her phone, I'd been in that position myself many a time. I had frozen on the spot as jealousy powerfully surged through my body. I felt a primal instinct to pull her to me, to ascertain and assert that she was mine. But she wasn't mine, and if I acted out, I wouldn't have a chance of ever being hers again. I knew I had no right to be jealous, but I couldn't help it.

Ava's beautiful, crystalised orbs met mine and instantly I saw the difference. She looked happy and completely stress-free, which was not how she had been looking this morning. Her eyes were no longer drooped or haunted by sadness and anger. The tension that she was carried had diffused from her body and her stature was much more relaxed. Her head was tilted high and her shoulders sat naturally low. She looked like she had before the Ball, and it didn't take a scientist to know that it was to do with the guy stood in front of her.

I had turned away from them and continued down the steps

and headed in the direction of Ev's house. I could feel Ava's eyes burning into my back, as she watched me walk away from her as fast as I could. I didn't want to ruin her good mood at seeing me. I was relieved that she was slowly getting back to herself, but I was pissed that it was because of another man. I took out my annoyance on a few small stones that were strewn along the bumpy pavement, kicking them out of my way.

When I arrived at Ev's, unsurprisingly, Fi was there. I rolled my eyes as I turned away from them to close the door. As much as loved them both, it was hard to have a man to man conversation with Ev now, as he spent a lot of time with Ffion. Ever since the night of the call, he hadn't left her side. Both Ava and I were still waiting on an explanation of that night, but they had assured us that we would be in the know soon. It was weird Ev keeping things from me, we didn't have secrets. But I trusted and respected him enough to know that when the time was right, he would disclose all. Though, I couldn't blame him from keeping it from me when I had kept what happened with Stacey from him.

Ffion had been cold to me all week. I mean, it was to be expected. I'd hurt her best friend, who was essentially her sister, in such a deplorable way that it dangerously bordered unforgivable. She was able to remain professional with me at work though, and I was appreciative of that. It meant that work wasn't too awkward or weird. But despite being aloof with me, she still gave me daily updates on Ava. She knew that me not knowing how she was would eat me alive inside-out. I didn't want to know what they spoke about, or if Ava had told Ffion where her mind was at with the situation because that would go against my promise of giving her space. I just wanted to know how she was doing in herself, that she was looking after herself.

I had sat down heavily on the one-seater chair with an irritated groan, leaning my head back and staring at the blank cream ceiling. The annoying ringtone of Ffion's phone chimed through the room, but it was cut off quickly as Ffion answered the FaceTime call. I snapped my head in Ffion's direction as I heard Ava's light voice float from the device into my eardrums and it calmed me. That was until Ava began to tell Ffion that she had been with Sam from the coffee shop today. Her voice was full of excitement, and she sounded like she was going to burst. I hadn't heard her sound like that in a while, and even though it was a delightful sound that would normally warm my insides, I couldn't help but feel the return of the jealousy as it swirled around inside of me. Ffion shot me a look to see if I had heard the brief conversation, and quickly hurried into Ev's bedroom so they could carry on their conversation in private.

"Talk about a slap round the face." Ev had been sympathetic. I was yet to tell him that I had seen her with this 'Sam'.

"I saw her with Sam on my way here. So that was more like the after sting of a slap to the face." I leaned forward, resting my elbows into my knees and holding my head in my hands. I then began telling Ev about the part of Ava's interaction with Felicity and then what I had seen with her and Sam. He listened intently, not interrupting me as I went off on my long spiel. When I was done, he let out a deep sigh and ran his hand through his already ruffled hair, preparing himself for what he was going to say.

"Firstly, I don't blame her for giving Felicity the metaphorical middle finger. From what we know, she's a selfish bitch of the highest order, and it was only a matter of time before she reaped what she sowed." I nodded my head in agreement. As hypocritical as it was, I hated Felicity for hurting her in such a treacherous way.

307

"And with regards to Sam. I get why you'd feel how you did, but you've got to let her get on with it man. She needs time and space to clear her head, and if being with someone else helps her, then so be it. Sometimes it takes two people to be apart for them to realise how much they love and want the other person. Be patient and give it time. Things will work out the way they're supposed to." I looked at Ev with a touch of surprise. He was good at giving advice, so much so that he gave me a run for my money. But that was deep, even for him.

"Plus, you pretty much chose two girls over Ava, so really, who are you to talk?" Those words stung. After I had told him about Stacey, I got the ear bashing of my life. He took Ava's side without question, and I didn't blame him; if the shoe was on the other foot, I'd be the same. I was in the wrong, there was no doubt about it. Despite being a bit hurt by Ev's to-the-point words, the more I thought about them, the more I realised just how right he was. I wasn't going to question or judge Ava's choices whilst she figured out what she wanted, when I had chosen someone else over her on more than one occasion.

After that, we fell into a chat about the football and the like. The atmosphere was chill and relaxed, and I welcomed the change. It was getting depressing being at home on my own, left alone with my wandering thoughts.

Eventually, Ffion had re-emerged from Ev's bedroom with an indifferent expression on her face. Whenever she had a conversation with Ava around us, she never gave away anything. Not in her words, tone or expression; she disclosed nothing. She was fiercely loyal to her best-friend and I knew that meant the world to Ava. She trusted her wholeheartedly, and I knew that if Ffion ever broke that trust, that would most likely hurt her more than the pain that anyone else had ever caused her.

I was glad that she had someone like Ffion in her life. Someone who kept her on the right path. Someone who encouraged her to pick herself up and keep going. Ava worked so hard on doing those exact things for others and making them happy and to realise their self-worth, that she forgot about herself. Whenever I was with her, I would always compliment her, and offer little gestures so that she knew how much she meant to me and how special she was. I had noticed her confidence in all aspects of her life build over the months, and it brought me a great sense of achievement that I had helped her in that way. I just hoped my recent actions didn't tarnish that side to her.

And that brings us to now. I had been lying here for so long, that the bright white light that shone through the thick gaps of the blinds when I arrived here were now tinted orange. I wasn't ready to go home yet, so I made no move to leave. Instead, I turned onto my front, and circled my arms around my head, plunging me into total darkness.

With my mind still on Ava, I decided that I needed to make some changes to myself, so that on the off chance she came back to me, I would be a better version of myself. If she saw me making the effort to change, perhaps it would improve my odds of her coming back to me. I was going to be someone she was proud of. Someone she didn't have to be in fear of being hurt by, and someone she could trust with her life and heart once again.

I began thinking of ways in which I could change, and the biggest, most important way was making a promise to myself that I wasn't ever going to touch another female. The only person my body belonged to was Ava. She was the only one I wanted to touch me intimately. She was the only one who's touch, taste and sense I craved. She was the only one who could control me and bring me to new heights of euphoria. She was the only person who was capable of bringing out my animalistic instincts as she drove me wild. When I had told her she was it for me, I wasn't lying. I could be the only man left on Earth with endless women to populate it, and I still wouldn't touch any of them. I'd let the human species die out. Why would I want to be on this planet if Ava wasn't?

I didn't want her to come back to me only to find I had slept around casually and mindlessly. I had to take her into consideration with everything I did. It was something I should have been doing right from the start, and I was appalled at myself that it had taken me this long to figure that out. I had promised her and myself that I would wait for her. And wait for her I will.

The mistakes of my past were going to be my lessons, and I will learn from them.

Chapter 34

Almost a week since I had confided in Sam and I was feeling a little bit lighter. I had spoken to Sam pretty much every day. I woke up every morning to a little text from him and it always put a smile on my face. I had started every day with a smile on my face, and that seemed to make all the difference to how the rest of my day would go. He would text during the day to check in and if there were any times when I had a little relapse, he would send me a stupid joke or picture to make me laugh.

When I told Ffion about him, she was a little excited about it. We both knew Sam had had a little crush on me ever since he started working at 'The Hub' just short of a year ago. I wasn't interested in him then, and although I was attracted to him, I didn't want to use him as a means to block out thoughts of Leon. It wouldn't be fair to him to lead him on. He was good company at the moment, and he helped keep my mind from straying too far to thoughts of Leon. I only worried that I was giving him the wrong impression.

I had invited Fi out with us, but she said she was busy with Everett. She'd been a little weird lately and I couldn't put my finger on what it was. I thought that perhaps it was something to do with her and Everett again, since it had gone radio silent on that front, but she said she was fine. She seemed like she genuinely didn't think there was anything wrong with her, but my sixth sense was tingling like crazy.

I was just on the last few hundred yards of my run when the music that was booming through my ears paused and was replaced with a tinkling shrill. I stopped running, bringing myself to a light walk and pressed the button on the side of my wire that connected the earpiece to my phone and answered to call.

"Ava, where are you?" Ffion's voice was full of urgency and desperation, and I instantly felt worry pile on my chest.

"I'm nearly home from my run. Are you alright?" I spoke slowly as I tried to catch my breath, but there was still panic in my voice. All kinds of thoughts raced through my mind as I began worrying about what had her so riled up.

"I'm fine, but I've got some news that you most definitely will not like." I let out an annoyed groan. For fuck's sake. There was only so much bad news that I could take right now. Anything else and my brain will probably explode.

"Brilliant!" I exclaimed sarcastically before I let out a sigh. "Can you not just tell me over the phone?"

"No, not really."

"Fuck me sideways. Alright, I'll be there in a few. Loves ya." This was all that I needed; more shit on my doorstep.

"Alright A, loves ya too."

I hung up and jogged the rest of the way back to my place, with my head full of wonder with what Fi had to tell me. It wasn't about her because she said that she was fine, and she didn't sound upset or anything. She just seemed desperate to talk to me. Which meant it was something to do with me, Everett or Leon, and if it was the latter, then there was a possibility I would come face to face with him and would actually have a conversation for the first time in over a week with him. With that thought weighing heavily on my mind, I prayed that he wouldn't be at Fi's and made my way into the apartment. But knowing how my prayers went to the Big Guy above, I wouldn't be surprised if he pissed me off just to spite me.

* * *

Half an hour later, freshly showered and now wearing a floaty red and white polka dot sundress, I let myself in to Fi's. I shouted out a cheery hello, making her aware of my presence, and was relieved when only Fi replied. That she was the only one who greeted me, I felt a bit more at ease that the others weren't here. I removed my shoes as I normally do, leaving them neatly on the floor near the door. With my fingers crossed on both hands, I headed into her living room. The entire way here I had prayed to the creator of this ambiguously mystifying universe that Leon wouldn't be there. I even promised I'd worship him every day if my prayers were answered.

If I needed proof that God doesn't exist, it was here. Lo and behold, sat opposite Fi and Everett was Leon, looking as handsome as ever. He tensed when he saw that I had entered the room, and I quickly took him in. He was wearing white chino shorts that were decorated with navy vertical stripes with a folded cuff that stopped just above his knee. His polo shirt was the colour of sage, and it hugged his torso deliciously. Thick arms bulged as he changed his position so that he was sat with his arms leaning against his sturdy thighs and was looking at me intently. My body shuddered slightly as I drank him in. I couldn't help the way my body reacted to him. It was almost instinctual for me to, and I cursed myself for it.

I returned his gaze and found that his honeysuckle eyes held anticipation and concern and his mauve lips were set in a half smile. He wasn't too sure how to react at seeing me, and if I was honest, I didn't know either. I gave him a small smile that I tried to pass off as friendly, but instead it felt awkward, and sat down on the stool at Fi's breakfast bar, leaving them still sat on the sofa. I had asked Leon for space, and whilst this perhaps couldn't be helped, I'd like that wish to be upheld.

I looked towards Fi and I was struggling to read her expression. It was a mix of annoyance and anger. With my brows furrowed, I looked around the room. There was a sombre atmosphere, and it was seriously putting me on edge. Leon remained in his leant forward stance, Everett was looking as casual as ever with his arm along the back of the sofa behind Fi, and his ankle resting on his knee. Fi scooted a short distance away from Everett. If she wasn't being lovey-dovey with him, then that meant that this was serious stuff.

I cleared my throat. "Would someone care to tell me what's going on?" I questioned. Ffion shifted uncomfortably in her seated slightly and gave Leon a pointed look. He looked exasperated and flicked his eyes to the ground. What could he, of all people, possibly have to tell me? I hadn't seen or spoken to him in over a week.

"Tell her." Ffion pushed with a stern, level voice. He looked uncomfortable as he shifted his gaze from the floor, to Fi and then to me. He rubbed his burly hands up and down his thighs slowly, preparing himself to speak, and cleared his throat.

"You had a visitor at your door earlier." I looked at him in confusion. A visitor? It wasn't very often I got visitors unannounced. Maybe the odd Jehovah Witness, but that was about it. Who on God's green Earth could possibly have shown up to cause this much of a to-do?

His voice was steady as he continued on with his explanation. "I heard someone banging on your door and calling your name, so I went to investigate. I asked what business they had with you and they said that they needed to speak to you, but when I said you weren't in, I was given a piece of paper with a number on it. He was very insistent that I made sure you got the number." I didn't like where this was going. Not one bit. I could feel that things were about to go south very quickly. Again.

"Who was it?" My voice was starting shake as I thought about who could possibly need to speak to me so urgently. Only a handful of men knew where I lived, and I didn't like the chances of one of them. Two were in the same room as me and knew each other. The other was currently at work. But the last one... I felt my heart rate increase as I waited for Leon to tell me who it was, hoping against hope that it wasn't who I thought it was.

There was a short deliberative pause, and Leon looked me square in the eye, all hesitation gone from his eyes. "Wyatt." I felt the blood drain from my face as it pooled to my feet, and I froze as still as a statue as my suspicion was confirmed. God had struck again. Seriously, what have I ever done to end up on His shit-list? The oh so omnibenevolent one clearly had favourites, and I was most definitely not one of them.

Dealing with Felicity had been a piece of cake. I was already in a foul mood that day and that had helped majorly. But Wyatt was different. He too had broken my trust in one of the worst ways possible. But unlike Felicity, I'd had my future mapped out with Wyatt, and that made everything hurt even more.

I stayed quiet, not knowing what to say. I no longer loved Wyatt, but that didn't mean that what he did pained me any less. He had knocked me for six and had sent me back to a dark place that I hadn't been in for so long, more so because he continued on with Felicity. If he hadn't then I would've thought that there was nothing there between them, that it was just a meaningless fling. But that hadn't been the case and so I was thrown into a pit of despair.

I could feel all their eyes on me as they waited to see my reaction. I had no idea how to or should react. I wasn't sure if I would be able to face him. It had been ten months and I hadn't seen him since. I had only recently stopped looking through his social media, which if you ask me, showed that I really had moved on from him. I had discovered that I no longer cared about what he was up to, or who with.

This last week had been insanely wild. Almost everyone from my past had come back into my life one way or another. The more I thought about this, the more I thought that I was being given the chance to confront them, to give them a piece of my mind and then to either leave them in the dust or forgive them. I was uncertain with what I would decide with Wyatt. It was a difficult decision to make without hearing him out.

Maybe Our Saviour was actually trying to help me out. I'll have to ask Him when the curtains close on my life and I see Him in the Angel City, because he for sure had a lot of explaining to do.

I let out a long sigh and looked at Leon with a determined look on my face and spoke with a tone to match.

"Give me his number." All three of them looked at me incredulously. None of them had expected me to be this willing to contact him, and honestly, I hadn't either. But I could do this.

Growing impatient that Leon still hadn't given me Wyatt's number, I turned my hand up and wiggled my fingers in a wave, before holding my hand out flat again and raised my brows. It seemed to wake Leon up from his dumbfounded daze and he dug inside his pocket and pulled out a neatly folded piece of paper. He passed it to Everett as he was closest to me, trying his best to maintain his distance. I was glad that he was still respecting my wish to have space from him, despite being in the same, enclosed room. He knew touching me would confuse me even more, and right now, I needed a clear mind.

I looked down at the paper now in my hands and felt my heart skip a beat at the familiar, cursive handwriting. A stray tear caught me off guard as it dropped from my eye as realised that this would be the opportunity for me to get some proper closure from Wyatt, and I could really move on with my life. I would get the chance to tell Wyatt exactly what he did to me, and I hoped that he hated himself for it.

I pulled my phone from my bag and with shaky hands, I punched in his number. My thumb hovered over the green button as I hesitated to call him. I'd been so focused on whether or not to do it, that I hadn't noticed someone had placed a hand on top of my wrist as I clutched the phone.

I didn't need to look up to see who the hand belonged to. I was instantly filled with a warm feeling that flooded my body and my breathing - that I didn't know had started to get short and heavy - started to slow down. His touch was magic and always made me feel at ease. This contact broke our agreement at staying away, but I needed his touch right now to calm me down and bring me out of my panic attack.

"You don't have to do this Ava. Not if you don't want to or feel

ready to." His voice was calm and measured. He wasn't talking
to me as my boyfriend but as my friend. His words took me back
to how whenever he'd ask me a question about my history and I
would be hesitant to tell him, he would always reassure me that
I didn't need to disclose anything. He had never forced me to
say or do anything I was uncomfortable with. My feelings were
always taken into consideration and even though he had no duty
to anymore, he was still here when I needed him.

"Yeah, I'll happily meet him instead and shove his dick up his
own arse, Lord knows the fucker deserves it." Fi chirped, trying
to lighten to mood. Although, I wouldn't put it past her that she
was genuinely serious.

With a grateful, small smile, I placed my spare hand over his
and gave it a light squeeze in appreciation and the corner of
his lips lifted slightly. He thought he'd overstepped the mark,
which he sort of had but I was glad for it. He was the only person
who could calm me like that.

"It's OK. I need to do this. I need the closure." He nodded and
removed his hand from mine and returned to his seat. As usual,
my body whined at the loss of his contact, but I ignored it as I
pressed the call button and put it onto speaker. It rang for a few
seconds before it was picked up.

The other end was quiet, with only the faint sound of someone
breathing, and I had found that I'd lost my voice.

"A... Ava? Is that you?" Wyatt's normally booming voice was
quiet and restrained. He sounded defeated and it surprisingly
pained me a little hearing it. I wasn't used to this Wyatt. He was
normally so loud and boisterous. I took a deep breath to steady
my voice. I needed to be strong. I needed to show him that I
wasn't weak.

"Yeah, it's me." I heard him let out a shaky sigh that made

the sound crackle on my end.

"I'm so glad to hear your voice. I didn't think you'd call me." His voice was sad and strained. My heart went out to him, but then I quickly reeled it in when I remembered that he deserved whatever had happened.

"Trust me, I very nearly didn't." Fi snorted in her seat and I shot her look, telling her to be quiet and she shrunk back into her seat, with Everett slapping a hand over her mouth.

"Look, is there any chance I can meet you? I need to talk to you." He had managed to regain some control over his voice as he spoke to me earnestly.

"Now, why the fuck would I want to do that? We haven't got anything to talk about, Wyatt." I spoke to him coldly and abruptly. I wasn't going to make this easy for him. As much as I wanted to find out what it was he wanted to talk to me about, I wanted him to grovel for it.

"Please, Ava. Just meet me once and you'll never have to see me again if you don't want to." That was a very tempting offer, but I wanted him to realise he wasn't dealing with old Ava anymore.

"That's the thing Wyatt. I don't want to see you again, so why should I give in to you just because you asked me oh so nicely?" I looked around the room to see where everyone was at. Fi held her thumbs up to me, Everett had an amused smirk on his face, hand still over his gobshite girlfriends mouth, and Leon gave me a singular, reassuring nod of his head.

"What the fuck Ava? What crawled up your arse?" Sadness was gone from his voice and was instantly replaced with anger. He had no reason to be angry with me. If he hadn't of been a prick, slept with my best friend for months under my nose, this would be going a completely different way.

"Firstly, I don't know who the fuck you think you're talking to, but don't take that tone with me. You have absolutely no right to. And secondly, I just learned not to let arseholes like yourself walk all over me. I'm sick to death of asking how high I should jump whenever someone tells me to. I'm done being walked over Wyatt. So suck it up buttercup, because I do not have the time, nor the patience to be dealing with the likes of shitty people like you." I snapped. I could feel my anger slowly rile up inside of me. My audience was looking at me in utter surprise. Last time they heard me snap like that was at Leon back at the Ball.

Wyatt had gone quiet on the other end, I could only hear his angry puffs against the fuzzy static of the phone. I had shocked him just as much as I had the others. I was a force to be reckoned with right now. I don't know what was happening to me lately, but I'm loving the power and strength I've been feeling. I have been too nice to people who didn't deserve it for far too long. It felt good to finally take a stand for myself and find my inner bitch.

Apparently, Wyatt had found his voice and he spoke in a low, quiet tone, trying to retain his anger and annoyance that he wasn't getting his own way. I'd forgotten that he didn't like the word 'no'.

"I'm begging you, Ava. Please, just meet me and hear me out. I know Felicity turned up on your doorstep the other day. Don't you want an explanation as to why?" Not particularly, no. But that doesn't mean that I hadn't been wondering ever since she turned up why she had come to me instead of going to her baby daddy. After a quick deliberation with myself in my head, I let out a sharp sigh.

"Fine. Meet me at The Coffee Hub in an hour. If you aren't

there, I'm walking away."

"Thank you, Ava. I'll see y-" I hung up on him mid-sentence, growing sick of his voice and slammed my phone in annoyance on the breakfast bar. I'd given him too much of my time as it was. I looked down into my hands and watched as they shook uncontrollably. I didn't know how I managed to hold it together and keep my cool for so long. But it felt good to let out just a little bit of my anger towards him. Now that he knew what he was dealing with, whatever it was that he needed to see me about had better be good.

I looked up the group. They all looked proud of me, that I had stood my ground. Whereas I was feeling completely confused, angry and bewildered. I leaned my forehead down on the cool hard surface of the breakfast bar and took a deep breath, trying to unscramble the thoughts that crowded my head. "What the actual *fuck* is going on with my life right now?"

Fi let out a chuckle as she came over to my side and pulled me into a side hug. "I don't know babe, but you're handling it like a boss. I'm proud of you." I looked over to Leon and there was guilt hazing his eyes. He was one of the problems in my life and I felt a little bad that I had said that in front of him. But I couldn't help feeling like someone was out to get me. While I was grateful that I was being given the chance to get closure one way or another, it was really starting to get on my tits that I was being hit with it all at once.

Everett and Leon were sharing glances at one another, talking telepathically. With a joint nod, they both stood up and made their way over to us, Leon hanging back slightly. He met my gaze and smiled sadly to me. He didn't like that I was going to see Wyatt. He didn't like I was going to be in such a close proximity with someone who had hurt me so mindlessly. I could see it in his eyes. They had always been expressive, and they told me all I needed to know about him and what he was thinking. His beautiful buttery orbs were a window into his mind. His thoughts right now were rather hypocritical, but for some reason, it made my heart swell that he wanted to protect me.

The boys made their excuses to leave and wished me luck. They thought that Fi and I needed to prepare me for my meeting with Wyatt. It had been a long time since I'd seen him, and I was wondering what he looked like now. I mean, I knew what he looked like thanks to Instagram, but I hadn't checked his profile in months, and a lot can change in that time.

Soon enough it was time for me to leave. I left Fi's with a strong mindset, but my heart was crying on the inside. I took a deep breath as I made my way to 'The Hub', preparing myself for Round Three of fighting the demons of my past.

Chapter 35

I arrived at 'The Hub' ten minutes early so that I could try to compose myself for when I came face to face with Wyatt. The entire walk here was a bit of a shaky one. I was nervous about seeing him again after so long. I was plagued with thoughts of the past; how I had caught him with Felicity, but more importantly, the dilapidating aftermath he left behind. The one question that had burned in my mind and was yet to be asked, was why. I'd never had the opportunity to ask either one of them why they did what they did, and I was going to make sure I heard his reasoning today.

With a heavy sigh, I walked into 'The Hub' and headed towards the counter. Sam was working today, and he greeted me with one of his bright smiles. But on seeing my depleted facial expression, his smile turned into a concerned scowl. He'd already got to work on my order as soon as he saw me walk through the door and I was grateful for that. The sooner I have caffeine running through my veins, the more calm I'll feel. With all the drama going on at the moment in my life, maybe I ought to think about streamlining the coffee into my system via an IV.

為開

"What's up, kitten?" He had decided to give me a nickname, and after a week of hearing it, I had grown accustomed to it. I kind of liked it. Apparently, it was fitting for me because I'm "small, cute and feisty like a kitten." He had spoken softly so as not to let the whole café hear. I let out a long sigh, blowing my cheeks out as I did so.

"Blast from the past part three is on their way here." I placed the money for my beverage in Sam's hand as his eyes widened in disbelief. I hadn't given him much insight into my past, but he already knew Wyatt as we used to come here when we were together. Not wanting to go into any more detail, I took my mug from the counter and after giving Sam a quick "thanks", I went to sit in my normal spot.

After taking a mouthful of coffee and savouring the hot, bitter taste, I gazed around at my surroundings. 'The Hub' was busier than usual today. It was mostly couples or friends, there weren't many families about. As crazy as it sounds, I was glad that there weren't any families in my line of vision. Wyatt and I had spoken about starting our own family and he had seemed genuinely excited and serious about it. He was prepared to go through the trouble I may have to take in order to conceive myself. But I guess that was short-lived as he decided that Felicity was worth more of his time. Either that or he just said all the right things to keep me sweet and happy. Seeing a family when Wyatt was here would hurt me to no end, at the reminder of what could have been. But then, thinking about it, things working out the way that they did I suppose was a blessing; there was nothing and no-one tying me to Wyatt.

Every time the door swung opened, I kept looking towards the door, to see if it was Wyatt. And every time it wasn't him, I felt relieved but a little disappointed too. I glanced up at the giant art-deco styled clock that was on the wall behind the coffee machines. He had a minute before the hour. I had been serious about walking away if he wasn't here on time. I deliberately gave him a short time frame to get here, because he could never be on time for anything when we were together. If he really wanted to speak to and see me, then he would be here on time.

The clock struck the hour and on cue, Wyatt walked into 'The Hub', making my heart flutter with nerves. In the corner of my eye, I saw Sam glance over and then his head shot into my direction with his eyes almost hanging on his cheeks, as he realised that this was who I had meant.

I watched Wyatt as he walked towards me, his hands deep in the pockets of his jeans. He was still good looking, but seeing him again settled something in me. He most definitely was no longer my type and there was no residual feelings for him. He had let his mousey brown hair grow out and it was tied neatly into a little loop at the base of his neck, with the smallest strands of hair framing his face. He wasn't as broad as Leon, but he was still very well built. Like me, he looked after his body like it was a temple. Or at least, he used to. He's lost a lot of muscle weight, noticeably more around the top half of his body. His still had some definition, but it was nothing compared to what it had been when he left me. His neck had thinned out, his traps almost non-existent and his arms and chest were smaller than he had been for a good few years. His deep-set, dark blue eyes were focused on me as he made his way over. But the closer he got to me, the more worse for wear he looked. He had a bit of stubble growing on his squared jaw and his eyes tiredly drooped slightly.

Now standing in front of me, I didn't say anything to him, and I didn't stand to greet him. I simply pointed to the seat opposite me, silently instructing him to take a seat. I was holding my ground, showing him that he wasn't dealing with the Ava he once knew. I had never been cold to him, so this was most likely coming as a shock to him.

He dutifully sat down and slouched slightly in his chair. He had an easy going smile on his face as he looked at me, but his eyes were glazed over with anxiety. "You're looking well Ava." His usually confident tone was anything but. He wasn't too sure how to approach me or the situation. I shuffled all the way back into my seat, keeping my back straight and crossed one slender, exposed leg over the other, interlocking my fingers together in my lap.

"What did you want to talk to me about?" I didn't have time for niceties. As much as I wanted to hear whatever it was he had to say, I didn't want to be here any longer than need be. It was awkward enough as it was and it was starting to make me uncomfortable. He placed his elbows on his knees and rubbed his face. With his face buried in his hands, he contemplated what to say. Finally, he removed his face from his coarse hands and stared at the ground.

"Felicity... me and her are done. For good. I threw her out after she told me she was pregnant. I thought it was mine, but the dates didn't add up. Once I confronted her about it, she confirmed my suspicions." I leaned forward and picked up my mug and brought it to my lips. I didn't say anything and waited for him to carry on.

"I wasn't going to raise some other guys kid that she'd conceived behind my back, so I told her to go to him. But she couldn't because his girlfriend didn't know about Felicity. He didn't want Felicity and the baby and so when she turned up on his doorstep, he turned her away. Which then led to her going to you." He looked me in the eyes when he said the last part. That made sense as to why she said that I was apparently her only hope. I didn't regret turning her away though. She'd made her bed. They both had.

"With Felicity gone, I've been able to do some soul searching. I... I miss you Ava. You were the best thing to happen to me and I threw it all away." He spoke quietly and was now looking at the floor. I was stumped. This had quickly taken a turn. However, he was right, I was the best thing to enter his life and he wasted it. He chose someone who he knew would do him the way she does everyone else in the future. That was on him.

"That sounds like a you problem, Wyatt. You knew what you was literally getting into bed with, so you've only yourself to blame. Maybe now you understand a little about how you made me feel." I spoke indifferently to him. I didn't miss him. Not anymore. It had taken me far too long to realise what a piece of shit he is. Looking back, him and Felicity were perfectly suited; they were two of the same. Both had their heads so far up their arses that they didn't know whether to fart or shit. They were arrogant, self-centered and self-absorbed and cared only for themselves.

When me and Wyatt had been together, he would give me endless amounts of attention and spoiled me with gifts. But looking back, I now realised it was all a façade. He thought that by putting on his "kind boyfriend who did everything for his girlfriend" exterior, he could hide his true self. That by giving me attention in drips and drabs, it would be enough to keep me. Which it would have for some time, until I'd inevitably wake up and realise I deserved more than the bare minimum.

He didn't like it when I said no to anything, from sex to even trivial things like getting him a drink. Yes, we had planned our future, but I had been so stupidly blindsided by the nice and good things that he done that showed he "loved" me. It was only now, as I sat here and really analysed our relationship, that I realised just how controlling he had been. Though it took a good while for Wyatt to show his true self, it begged the question of what he would've have been like if he hadn't of been caught or I had stayed. But never again would I let that happen to me. The best thing about being with someone like this was learning what to look out for next time. The first sign, the first red flag of any form of narcissistic and controlling behaviour and that would be the end of it.

"I'm sorry Ava... I'm sorry that I hurt you." He couldn't meet my eye as he attempted an apology. But his words were empty and meant nothing to me, and I made sure to tell him as much.

I let out a little scornful laugh. "You're sorry?" I spoke indignantly. "Wyatt, while you were off on your little honeymoon period with Felicity and taking her to fancy places, I was working myself into the ground. I was barely eating one meal a day and I worked out from sunrise until sunset every day, never taking a break. I neglected myself because I was so heartbroken over you and your treachery and I ended up in the hospital. But I suppose that doesn't matter anymore because you're *sorry*." The last of my tyranny of words were thick with sarcasm. I watched as his face changed from shock to complete and utter shame. His ocean-deep blue eyes were almost black with regret as the tsunami of his tears spilled over his lash line and rolled steadily down his cheeks.

"You ended up in the hospital? I had no idea." His voice was unstable, and his lower lip was trembling as he tried to keep his crying quiet.

"That would be because you never once gave me a second

thought. Not *once* did you apologise or ask how I was. You hurt me Wyatt, and you expect me to be OK with you turning up out of the blue and saying you miss me? You expect me to think your apology means anything?" I hissed. I was doing my best to keep my voice down. 'The Hub' was starting to empty out so there wasn't as much background noise to block out my voice. People didn't need to know my business or feel uncomfortable whilst they relaxed with their friends and family in what was a safe space for all, and I could see that a couple of eyes were on us.

I went to take a sip from my mug, I needed the caffeine to calm me down. But I was only disappointed when no warm liquid poured into my mouth. I looked over the where Sam was to find that he was already looking at me with worry in his eyes. I nodded to let him know that everything was fine and held my mug up to him, tapping the ceramic with a freshly scultpted crimson nail, signaling a refill. Wyatt still hadn't said anything when Sam brought me a fresh mug of coffee. I went to give Sam my money, but he held his hand up and shook his head before walking away with my empty mug. I took a sip of the coffee, ignoring the burn as it dripped down my throat and relishing in the satisfaction of the coffee as it curbed my craving.

He still had nothing to say to me. Still couldn't look at me as the world outside seemed more interesting. I'd hit the nail on the head and he knew it. He hadn't given my feelings a second thought when he was with Felicity. Just like her, as long as he was getting what he wanted, no-one else mattered. Realising we'd be here all day if I waited for him to find his response, I asked him the question I had waited just shy of a year to ask.

"Why did you cheat on me?" My voice was strong and stern as I asked him the one, most important question that had been left unanswered. Back then, I wouldn't have liked the answer

329

and it probably wouldn't help with my spiraling out of control. But now, I don't think I'd bat an eye to it. Nothing he said or did surprised me anymore. Nor could it hurt me. My feelings for him were long dead.

He looked blankly at me as he tried to think of his answer. The fact that he had to think about it, only proved to me that there wasn't really any reason behind it. He had done it simply because he could.

"I... I don't really know to be honest." After all that I had done for him in the relationship, he had gone behind my back for no reason. He couldn't even justify why he did it. I did everything for him when we were together, and this was how he repaid me. I forced out some air out of my nose as I shook my head with an unsurprised smirk on my face. At least he had been honest, I suppose.

"Classic. Too busy thinking with your cock, hey?" Hurt flashed on his face.

"Look, Ava, I really am sorry. I know it's too little too late but knowing what I did to you... it was unforgivable, and I really do despise myself for putting you in that position. I didn't deserve you and you certainly didn't deserve what I did to you and put you through." He looked at me with sad eyes as he leaned forwards, sitting on the edge of his seat. I could tell that he meant what he was saying. But it was all too little, too late.

"Please, can we just start again? I'll change, I'll do anything." He held his hands together under his chin and looked at me with pleading eyes. I wish that I could have forgiven him, and I think I would have if he actually had a reason for cheating on me. I had spent months in despair, blaming myself, thinking I had done something wrong to drive him to Felicity. But the reality was, I had been the perfect girlfriend. He was just a greedy, thoughtless arsehole.

I didn't answer him straight away, instead, my thoughts wandered to someone else. Wyatt's words had made me think about Leon. The difference between Leon and Wyatt was that Wyatt would only change himself for me if it meant I took him back, whereas Leon had been changing ever since he found out about what his actions had driven me to. He had dedicated the past nearly ten years now to making himself a better person and focusing on a career that helped those who were in a position similar to my own. He didn't want anyone to go through what I had. His whole entire personality was the complete polar opposite to what he used to be like. Whether or not he thought he would ever see me again, he had changed for me and was continuing to do so, and that struck a chord with me.

I shook my head, bringing my mind back to Wyatt. I took a deep, noiseless breath and looked at Wyatt dead in the eyes. His own were reflecting hope and anticipation. His face was slowly drying from the tears he had shed a few minutes ago, leaving a thin trail of matte residue.

"Now, why would I do that? After what you put me through, you now have the audacity to come crawling back because things with your little tart didn't work out the way you thought they would. I won't ever take you back; I'd rather shit in my hands and clap that ever get back with you, and it's a little conceited of you to think that I ever would." Wyatt, the man who always had an answer for everything now had nothing to say. It was rather gratifying knowing that I had put him in his place.

It wasn't just because he had hurt me that I could never take him back. It was the type of person he was. He would never change his ways, no matter what his crocodile tears said. People like that don't just change overnight. They prey on the easy

331

women, and because he thought I was still the Ava he had cheated on, he wrongly assumed he would be able to crawl and worm his way back into my life. I had been blinded by what I thought at the time was love, and I think my loneliness before I was with him made me oblivious to any of his flaws. I had stuck by him, grateful for any love and attention that he gave me, but it had been misplaced. I sincerely hoped that he could be a better man for someone else, because I was not the one for him.

His breathing became ragged as he pushed himself back in to his chair and stared up at the ceiling. A few tears escaped from his eyes and slid slowly down his freckled cheeks. He made no effort to wipe them away. Instead, he left them to trail under his chin and down his neck, before they disappeared under his t-shirt. It was an odd experience, watching a man cry and show his vulnerabilities. When it was someone you love, there's a tender intimacy about it, where you just want to pull them close and cry with them. But this was just pathetic, laughable even. I'd never seen Wyatt cry before. He'd always said it was a sign of weakness for a man to cry. And while I thought it was important for men to cry, I could care less for these theatrical tears that sought out pity. I just sat here and watched on indifferently.

Neither one of us spoke and I was feeling better. I had told him the damage he caused, and it had made him feel guilty, which was exactly how he should have felt. I wondered if he genuinely did feel remorseful for his actions, and if so, at least I knew he was somewhat human.

I didn't think there was anything else to say, and so I stood up, preparing to leave. He still had his head leaned back against the chair, but his eyes were focused on me. I took my mug to the counter and then returned to seat to pick up my bag. He was wiping his tears away roughly with his big hands.

"Thank you for hearing me out Ava. It really was good to see you... even if it didn't go the way I perhaps wanted it to." His voice was steady and controlled despite the silent crying I had just bared witness to, and he gave me a small appreciative smile.

"I like this new headstrong, takes-no-shit Ava. I'm sure the next guy who steals your heart will have his work cut out for him." He chuckled. He wanted to leave on good terms, and I could understand that. He wasn't forgiven, I couldn't forgive someone who didn't know why they had done what they had, but I didn't want things to be left anymore awkward than they needed be.

"Well, when you've been through as much as I have, there's no choice but to grow a backbone. I just wished I had done so sooner." He looked a little offended, but it was soon replaced with an understanding look. Taking a deep breath, Wyatt rose from the chair, the cushion slowing rising with him as it regained it shape that had been distorted under his weight. As I walked past the counter with Wyatt following at a distance behind me, I said goodbye to Sam who gave me a wink and a cheeky smile. Once outside, we stood facing each other.

"Take care of yourself Wyatt." I spoke with finality. He nodded back to me with a small smile and offered a sincere "and you" before he turned and walked in the opposite direction to me.

As I made my way back home, I lifted my head up to the warmth of the sun's rays and smiled to myself. I was slowly being freed from the monsters that hid in the shadows who had been holding me back. I held my arms out to the side of me as I felt the weight lift from my shoulders. I had successfully closed the book on another section of my life and gotten the closure I had long cried out for.

Chapter 36

It was the night after my confrontation with Wyatt, and I was in just my underwear, elbows deep in my wardrobe rummaging for an outfit to wear for my night out with Sam tonight. He hadn't given me any hints as to where he was taking me, just that the dress code was casual. It was hard to decide on an outfit when I had no clue where I was going. Knowing my luck, I'd rock up either over-dressed or under-dressed. I had spent an embarrassing amount of time in here and I was running out of time. I sped up my search and once I had found an outfit I was happy with, I laid them out on my bed and inspected the items. With a pleased smile, I turned and headed to the bathroom.

As soon as I saw the steam begin to fog up the glass doors, I hopped into the shower and stood underneath the everlasting waterfall. The water was soothing as it drummed on the top of my head, trickling down in streams down my body. It didn't matter to me that it was the summer. The water had to resemble the temperature of the fiery pits of hell, or else I was unable to enjoy it. If it didn't feel like my skin was melting off my body, then it wasn't hot enough.

I found that being in the shower was a good place for me to think and collect my thoughts, and so as I scrubbed and washed the days impurities from my body, my mind wandered to what tonight would bring. I was so excited to be letting my hair down and briefly forgetting about the events of the last couple of weeks.

I hadn't forgotten my dilemma with Leon, and while we had spoken the day after all was revealed and he had given the space I asked for, I was still confused. I knew beyond all reasonable doubt that I loved him. But what I was on the fence about was if I could let sleeping dogs lie and forgive him for the past, because there was no way I would be able to just forget about it. It didn't help that I was seeing him a lot more, now that I was going out of the house again. We were always bumping into each other and although we would only exchange greetings, just hearing his melodic voice and seeing his gorgeous face pulled at my heart. We had an unmistakable connection and as much as I tried to fight it, it was hard to when I was so close to him physically.

I shook my head and returned my thoughts to tonight. I was a little sad that Fi wasn't joining us tonight. We hadn't been out together since the Ball and it felt like she really needed an outlet to let whatever was going on with her out. She had promised me she would make it up to me though, so I suppose I can't be too sad about it. I'll just make sure to send her pictures and videos of me having a good time.

I was increasingly growing worried about Fi. It wasn't that she was miserable and moody all the time, it was just that she seemed down more times than not. She hadn't been training with me much, saying she just wasn't feeling up to it or had the energy to. I wondered if maybe she was working too hard at Leon's office. She was known to over work herself, which was

SECOND CHANCES

ironic since she was the one beating it into me how important it was to take it easy. I didn't like to keep asking her how she was or if there was anything going on, because it would only piss her off, and a pissed off Fi was not a beast I was willing to tame. She appreciated that I was worried about her and that I was looking out for her, but she had told me a number of times there was nothing to worry about, so I just had to take her word for it.

My skin was starting to feel numb, and I was starting to look like a lobster. I turned the shower off, already missing the stimulating sensation of water beating down on me and stepped out. With a towel wrapped around me, I walked to the sink and began brushing my teeth.

With the basics done, I got to work on myself. I sat down at my dressing table and looked in the mirror. I had found myself looking in the mirror at myself a lot lately. Normally I only looked in the mirror to do my makeup or to make sure I looked decent. But these days, I'd get lost in my own eyes and my thoughts whirled freely in my head. These last few weeks had been a blessing in disguise for me. I had become stronger than I ever thought possible. I'd had the courage and bravery to stand up for myself to three people who had hurt me the most, and even told my mum off for the first time. While I was feeling bad about the way I'd left things with my mum, I was feeling proud of the outspoken person I had become. If Wyatt had been right about one thing, it was that takes-no-shit Ava was a brilliant upgrade to basic-bitch Ava. I was liking the person I was growing into.

Re-focusing my eyes, I made a start on my hair. Once it was dry, I tied it into my signature night out high ponytail and wrapped a thick piece of hair around the hairband. I spritzed hairspray on my locks to hold it in place and used a fine-toothed

336

comb to brush back any stray hairs that might have slipped from the hold of the hairspray. I kept my makeup simple, with brown tones on my lids with a semi-thick cat eye liner, finishing off the look with a bold, red lip.

With ten minutes to go until Sam would be here to pick me up, I shimmied into my black, square-cut bodysuit and high-waisted jeans with holes in the knees, that were a combination of light and dark blue. I looped a belt with a big, gold circular buckle through the belt loops, before putting on some black open-toe heels that had a chunky heel. I took in my figure in the full-length mirror and gave myself a satisfied smile.

There was a light rap at the door, so I grabbed my phone, keys and bag as I made my way to it. I flung the door open to a smiling Sam. He looked gorgeous. He was wearing a long-sleeved chequered flannel shirt on top of a pristine white t-shirt. My eyes traveled down his body as I took him in. His jeans were black and had several slits going up and down the leg. He finished his outfit off with some blindingly white trainers. Finding his eyes, I discovered that he too was checking me out. It was undeniable that he was good looking and that there was a bit of attraction between us, but we were strictly friends. His eyes were making their way up my body when they lingered on my chest.

With a chuckle I clicked my fingers at him. "Hey, eyes up here buddy." He snapped his beautiful baby blue eyes that shined with amusement back to my face as I laughed at him. He offered me his arm and escorted me to the waiting taxi. Once settled in the hard chairs in the back of the vehicle, I decided to try my luck.

"So, where are we going?" I raised a brow questioningly at him and let a smirk play on my lips. He looked towards me and tapped his nose twice with a wink.

"That's for me to know, and for you to find out when we get there." I rolled my eyes at him, slightly annoyed that I hadn't been able to get any information out of him. I looked out of the window and tried to work out where he was taking me by the area we was in. I had been near here before with Fi and a couple of my other clients for a hen do about a year ago, but I hadn't been back to this end of town since.

* * *

Soon enough, the taxi came to a screeching halt outside of our venue. We paid the driver and stepped out. I was stood outside what looked like a bar. The exterior was marvellous. Big windows were lined on the inside with fairy lights and allowed for outsiders to look in, and there was a neon sign with the name of the bar above the door. I still had no idea what kind of bar Sam had brought me to. That was, until we stepped in and there was a stage at the back of the building with a selection of microphones and acoustic guitars.

I turned to Sam with my eyes ablaze with excitement. He'd brought me to a karaoke bar. I went to find us a table in the middle, not too far from the stage whilst Sam went to the bar and got us our drinks. It was eight p.m. and there were already people up on the brightly lit up platform singing. I was already itching to go up, but I needed some alcohol infused courage first. I was dancing in my seat when Sam came over clutching a tray with an assortment of drinks. He hadn't lied when he said to be prepared for non-stop drinking. He had bought two lots of our drinks, alongside four shots each.

My eyes bulged when he placed the tray on our table and he sat down next to me with a proud smile. "It's my mission to make sure you have fun tonight. And to get us pissed." I laughed at him and we picked up our first shot. We clicked the minuscule glasses together and threw the liquid back. It burned as it went down my throat and once swallowed, I stuck my tongue out at the strength of it.

"Don't wimp out now, we've got three more to go." He teased. He had no idea who he was up against when it came to drinking – I had a liver of steel. I chased my shot with the other three and by the time they had sat in my stomach, my oesophagus was on fire and my stomach was nice and toastie warm. I wasn't confident enough yet to go up and sing, so I sipped through my straw at my drink whilst I sang and danced in my seat, with Sam joining in next to me.

* * *

Two hours later, and the bar had filled up. There was no spare seats and so some people were forced to stand. The buzz of the alcohol coupled with the atmosphere vibrated through my being as I made my way to the stage after having my name called out. I took my position on the stage and readied the microphone at my chest. I looked at Sam and he gave me a big toothy grin and two thumbs up. The song I had chosen hit me in the feels and it was a hard enough song to sing as it was. The instrumental started and the gentle melodic tempo of a piano began to play. With a deep breath, I began singing.

There were nights when the wind was so cold,
That my body froze in bed if I listened to it right outside my window
There were days when the sun was so cruel
That all the tears turned to dust, and I just knew my eyes were
drying up forever.
I finished crying in the instant that you left.
And I can't remember where or when or how

And I banished every memory you and I had ever made.

I closed my eyes, to prepare myself for the chorus as the piano slowed and played softly. With my eyes closed, and feeling myself sway to the music, I saw Leon's face and I opened my eyes quickly and began singing the chorus.

But when you touch me like this
And you hold me like that
I just have to admit that it's all coming back to me
When I touch you like this,
And I hold you like that
It's so hard to believe but it's all coming to me

The rest of the song slowly built into a crescendo before falling again when the next verse came. I gave my all into my singing. I closed my eyes and poured all my emotions into it. My spare hand was placed on my stomach, occasionally waving in the air as I sang, and my I bounced on the ball of my foot with a bent knee in time with the beat. The bar had fallen quiet. When before people were singing along with the karaoke singer, they had all fallen deathly silent as they listened to me belt out the song. Even the bartenders had stopped serving and cleaning to listen.

I was reaching the end of the song.

If you forgive me all this
If I forgive you all that
We forgive and forget, and it's all coming back to me
When you see me like this,
And when I see you like that
Then we see just what we want to see
All coming back to me
The flesh and the fantasies all coming back to me
I can barely recall but it's all coming back to me now.

I came to the end of the song and the room was quiet. Sam was looking at me wide eyed and opened mouth, and somewhere to my left I could hear a couple of people crying. Suddenly, someone from the back of the room stood up and started clapping. Soon enough, the whole bar was clapping, whistling and stamping their feet at my performance. I was taken aback at the reaction. I knew that I could sing, but I didn't think I was that good, the drink must have distorted everyones ears. Celine Dion had been my favourite singer growing up and I would forever sing her songs. '*It's All Coming Back to Me Now*' was one of my favourite songs of hers, and I felt that it was somewhat fitting to my situation and how I felt.

I bowed my head before I took my leave from the stage. A couple of people patted my back as I made my way back to Sam. My throat was feeling like the Sahara after that one, and so I removed the straw and downed the entire contents of the glass.

Sam looked approvingly at me. "You looked like you needed that." His tone was soft but there was a hint of something else in his words.

I nodded as I picked up my second drink. "I did, my throat is drier than a nuns cunt now." I chugged half of the glass whilst Sam roared with laughter, bringing tears to his eyes. As he regained her composure, he pressed the knuckles of his index fingers into his eyes to stem the flow before flicking the few small droplets from his eyes.

"I didn't mean that you needed a drink. I was on about the song you sang. You put your all into it and you could tell you was letting out your hurt and pain." Now calmed down, his eyes tinged lightly with sadness. He knew that I was still hurting, and I had given him and the entire bar an insight into just how tormented I was. But he was right, I felt better for it. It was the equivalent of screaming into a pillow to let out pent up frustration and anger.

I placed my hand on his arm and gave him a smile. I didn't want or need Sam to be sad for me. My problems were mine and he was so far doing a brilliant job in keeping me afloat. He placed his hand on top of mine and returned my smile.

Wanting to lighten the mood from my depressing song choice, I picked up the request paper and wrote mine and Sam's name on it. We were going up to duet and he had no choice or say in the matter.

He pulled his brows together in suspicion and looked over to see what I was writing. I thought he was going to protest, but I was delightfully surprised when he started getting excited at the idea of us singing "Islands in the Stream" together.

* * *

It was now one in the morning and me Sam and I were drunkenly stumbling up the steps of my apartment, the lighting from the streetlights only just providing us adequate visibility. I had told Sam to stay in my spare room tonight, I couldn't let him go home in the state I knew he was in - we barely even made it to the taxi. I was about to step onto the final step when my ankle gave way and I nearly fell over. Sam somehow managed to catch me before I fell. We burst out laughing before I became very hyperaware of his hand placement and just how close his face was to mine. He had a hand gripping my waist, whilst the other was holding onto my forearm. Our lips were so close I could feel his warm breath breathing against my parted lips.

I looked down at his lips and licked my own. I was so tempted and I moved closer slightly. We were millimetres from pressing our lips together when something snapped in me. I pulled back and shook my head with a giggle.

"No Sam, I can't. We're friends and it would complicate things more than they already are." My words were quite slurred. I was somehow drunker since leaving the bar. Sam still kept hold of me but helped me complete the steps and held me upright. He looked disappointed and forlorn at my pulling away. But that could be due to the fact that I was seeing two of him.

"It's OK, I understand. It's a shame. I do really like you Ava, but I know your heart belongs to someone else." He spoke with sadness pouring from his words whilst poking where my heart was, missing entirely and just poking boob instead. He hadn't realised he'd misplaced his finger and I found it too funny to care. I was grateful that he was so understanding about me and my situation, and despite his feelings towards me, he respected me and mine - even when not of sound mind. But I was more grateful that he was equally as shitfaced as I was.

I nodded, but it proved to be a mistake as my whole head began to spin and I felt like I was on a boat. I grabbed his hand and moved as fast as I could to my door, dragging him with me once the spinning subsided. I struggled getting the key in the door; it just kept sliding past the damn slot. Sam had been laughing at me the entire time with his running commentary of "how hard is it? Just put it in the hole" swiftly followed by my very childish response of "that's what she said" before he took the key from me and miraculously managed to get the key in the lock first try. I pointed to where the spare bedroom was and ran as fast as I could to my bathroom, my injured foot either miraculously healed in the last few minutes or completely numb. My stomach felt like someone was ruthlessly churning butter in it and I was beginning to feel a wave of motion sickness wash over me.

I just made it to the toilet bowl as I violently regurgitated the contents of my stomach. A few minutes of gagging and spewing later, I fumbled for the handle and flushed the toilet before letting my arm drop heavily. All of my energy had been zapped from me and I couldn't move. My legs were numb, and my head wouldn't stop spinning.

I placed and arm on the ring of the toilet seat and laid my head on it. As soon as I closed my eyes, I was instantly taken over by the darkness, with the final, universal lie of "I'm never drinking again" being whispered from my lips in a drunken slur.

38

Chapter 37

"Well done today Pops, that was a good work out. Your stamina's really improved, keep it up." I wiped the tiny droplets of sweat that were congregating on my forehead with the back of my hand as I complimented Poppy, my newest recruit. She was a pretty, young thing. Her features were delicate and soft, giving her a very innocent demeanour. She had beautiful brown eyes that were slightly almond shaped, and her pale skin was decorated with fine freckles randomly splattered all over. Her hair was a naturally curly, flaming red that spiraled to below her shoulder blades.

She was bent over, leaning on her bent knees with her head tucked into her chest as she tried to catch her breath. She was unable to reply through lack of oxygen, so she gave me a thumbs up. A few more weeks and the work out we had done will be a walk in the park for her. It was remarkable how quickly her body was adapting, and I was proud of the progress she was making.

Once she had regained her composure, I ran over her fitness plan with her for her to do on the days that I wasn't with her, and assured her that if there were any questions she had then she shouldn't hesitate to give me a call or message. She seemed happy with the plan I had designed for her and she took it with a big excited grin on her face. Every week I made little adjustments to make her workouts a little harder and she loved the challenge. She loved to push herself beyond her limits, and that was both good and dangerous – I knew that all too well. I've had to reel her in a couple of times already before she injured herself. The plan I had created for her was tailored not only to her needs but also to her lifestyle. Routine and structure were important to Poppy, and whist it took her a week or so to get used to the change, she was loving the new routine and breakdown in her day. Together, we went through what her work times are and anything she did with her personal life so that we could schedule in her fitness, otherwise she wouldn't be able to juggle everything and make any sacrifices. It detailed times on when to start and finish and how long each set should take, followed by length of rest in between.

I gathered my belongings and said my goodbyes, then started heading to my own apartment. I was now done for the day and that meant that I could relax with ice cream and a new Netflix series. The early July sun was blistering hot today, and I could feel my shoulders tingle as they began to burn under the damaging UV rays. Thankfully, it wasn't much of a walk back to my place.

I wasn't able run or jog at the moment after spraining my ankle from my night out with Sam, which was a shame because this weather had me longing to take my batons to the nearest park and twirl off the dust. I hadn't thought I'd done that much damage to it when it gave way on me on my steps, but the x-ray I ended up having the next day suggested otherwise. It was a week and a half later and my ankle was feeling so much more better and stronger, and so I had started to use it a little bit more, with the support of some bandages. I'd had to take some days off to allow for some of the swelling to go down, and even when I was back on my feet, I was only able to use my arms and verbally direct my clients. It was frustrating because all I wanted to do was to move my foot.

I had woken up the next day with my head rested on the toilet with the hangover from hell. It was easily in my top three of worst hangovers ever. I'd tried to stand up, but I collapsed as soon as I was upright with Bambi legs and I had to yell for Sam to come pick me up off the bathroom floor. I laughed at the memory of him skidding to the door, almost slipping over as he sprinted to me with panic written all over his face.

Once the fog had cleared from my brain, I was able to recall the events of the night before and was horrified that I had almost kissed Sam. But it seemed either Sam didn't remember, or he was being thoughtful enough not to mention it, because he hadn't said a word and had been acting indifferently with me. Either way, I was grateful that things were good with us, and I relieved that I had stopped myself from kissing him. Because that would've only been just another mess that I would have on my plate, and I already had a mountain stacked on my apparently indestructible plate.

I'd spent the time I was recovering thinking about Leon and deciding what I wanted to do. I came to the conclusion that I hadn't put enough distance between us, but I couldn't do that until my foot was back to being fully functional. I was seeing him more and more recently and it was only making it harder to think about it all. My body craved his touch and it was feeling neglected of it. Whenever I was around him, I could feel my body hum incessantly in reaction of being close to him and it was distracting me and clouding my judgement. My body and heart wanted him, needed him even, but my mind wasn't made up yet, and thus I was at constant war with myself.

With a sigh, I opened the door to my apartment and stepped in. Once I had taken a shower to get rid of the gross feeling of sticky sweat, I tossed on some grey loose jersey shorts and a white vest top, giving the girls some freedom as I remained bra-less. I walked into the kitchen and started to pick at some fruit and made myself a coffee. As I waited for the kettle to boil, I was popping some plump raspberries in my mouth whilst thinking about what I could do to add some distance between me and Leon, when I heard the faint tinkle of my phone as it rang from the living room.

Picking it up, I was surprised to see that it was my mum calling me. I'd not spoken to her since our argument, and I had to admit, I was missing her greatly. For some time I'd been thinking about reaching out to her and apologising for lashing out, but just like her, I was as stubborn as a mule. Taking a preparatory deep breath, I answered the call as I walked back over to the kitchen island. With my phone trapped between my ear and shoulder, I jumped up onto the counter and let my short, stumpy legs dangle in the air.

"Hey, Ava sweetheart." Her voice was edged with hesitation, as she was unsure as to how I would react, or if I would even talk to her. The sound of her voice hit me full force and I felt tears spring to my eyes. Her light, kind voice a sound I'd missed hearing. I'd missed telling her about my day and gossiping with her like teenagers.

"Hey, mama." My reply was choked out as I let the tears overwhelm me and a sob escaped from my mouth. I could hear my mum on the other end crying and that only made me cry harder. I felt bad for making her cry, and I wished that I'd just sucked it up, swallowed my pride and called her.

We did nothing but cry down the phone for a few moments until our tears ran dry and we had got ourselves together.

"I'm sorry for shouting at you mama. I know you was only trying to do what you thought was best for me." I was the first to speak, and my voice was still a little raw from crying so much.

"No baby, I'm the one who should be sorry. It was wrong of me to assume that you would be better off finding out on your own. I should've realised that leaving it would only make it worse for you in the long run." During our period of stubborn silence, I took the opportunity to think. Whilst her not telling me gave me more time to fall deeper for Leon and therefore made the heartbreak worse, it gave me time to learn about him from a clean slate and to have the happiest few months that I'd ever experienced. A thought that once made, was placed in the little box I had created of all things that were 'for' giving Leon and other chance, ready for me to unpack when my brain wasn't so overwhelmed.

We'd both calmed down now, no longer sniveling or crying and we spent the next half an hour catching up. I had told her about Felicity turning up on my doorstep with a bun in the oven and how I put her in her place. Then I told her about Wyatt and how he asked for me back, but I told him in a roundabout way to fuck off. She was proud of me, and she made sure to tell me just that. She had never liked either of them. Mum was very much kept in the dark with mine and Wyatt's relationship, I never really told her of the bad times, only the good. I supposed she noticed my omissions and knew that things were not as rosy as I thought I had led her to believe. She used to always warn me that they weren't good news, and every time she was here or me and

Wyatt was visiting her, she would always say something felt off, and every time I'd ignore her, refusing to acknowledge the faint agreement that was deep-seated in my subconscious. I wished I had listened to her sooner; apparently the phrase "mama knows best" holds some truth to it and hindsight truly is a wonderful thing.

With a very deep sigh, I prepared myself to explain the whole Leon situation, since I didn't get the chance to when I last spoke to her.

I could tell that was still pissed about Leon being with Stacey (welcome to the club) but she kept her opinion to herself. I could just feel her fury radiate through the speakerphone when I said to her "so, obviously you're aware of what happened with that plastic bitch Stacey" and she offered me a displeased "Uh huh". She let me ramble, getting the remainder of the story out: how I discovered who Leon was and the events that followed. She didn't offer any advice because it would only be biased. Instead, she gave me something to think about.

"You need to decide if Leon is worthy of your heart. He's broken it twice now; can you really trust that he won't do it a third time?" She made a very valid point, and it was definitely something for me to mull over.

She asked me what I was going to do. I know she knew how I felt about Leon, and she didn't want to force her thoughts and opinions on me. I had to think this through for myself, because whatever I chose, there was no going back.

"I need more distance from him. It's been a month and I'm still no closer to deciding. He's being so patient waiting for me, that I'm scared if I leave it any longer then it'll be too late if I decide I want to make a go of things again." I hadn't spoken these thoughts out loud to anyone, and it scared me hearing them out loud. I felt a little jealous at the thought of him with another woman, touching her in the way he had touched me. Making her feel as euphoric as he had made me feel. I shook my head to clear away the distracting thoughts and memories that were starting to traitorously infiltrate my mind.

"If it's space you need, why don't you come stay with me for some time? Until you've made your mind up? The spare rooms all made up and can be yours for however long you need. Plus, you and Kelvin can finally catch up." She sounded excited as she asked me. It had been a while since I'd been back to my hometown. I didn't like going there because of the memories, but now that I was a different person, it might be a good idea. It would be one more painful memory to put to bed, one more step to complete to help me fully heal.

I agreed to stay at my mums for a little while and she was elated that her baby was coming home. I know she now had Kelvin, but I also know she missed me and missed being needed by her baby. I'd joked a couple of times before about her having another child, since she was still within age, but she said the age gap between me and my non-existent sibling would be too big. I wasn't bothered though, I've always wanted a sibling, I'd had such a lonely childhood and I always thought perhaps having a brother or sister would have made my teenage years that little bit easier. Someone who looked up to their big sister, their role model. It was safe to say that it had crossed my mind a few times that maybe having a brother or sister would have made me rethink my choice to bid adieu to the world all those years ago, not that I'd ever told my mum that. Fuck me, that would be a guilt trip I would never forgive myself for putting her on.

I had been on the phone to my mum for nearing two hours and

351

I could hear Kelvin enter her house. I used that as my excuse to end the call so that I could unwind before getting started on packing for my trip back home.

"It was really good to talk to you mama, I'm sorry I didn't call you sooner." We'd had such a good chat and I felt so much better for talking things through with my mum. No matter how I had felt about the situation, she'd been my rock for so many years and I knew she couldn't help but try to shelter me from the exact thing that had nearly been the cause of my demise.

"Like mother like daughter baby. It should have been me calling you sooner. You're my baby girl, I should be the one making sure you're okay."

"I love you."

"I love you too, I'll see you tomorrow afternoon."

I hung up and switched the TV on. I'd long since moved from the kitchen island to the sofa; my butt had started to go numb from being sat on the hard surface for so long. Netflix had just loaded up when there was a bang as my front door smashed into the wall as it was forcefully slammed open. I stood up, fearing for the worst about who would just enter my house unannounced.

I cautiously moved towards the door and peered around the corner. My eyes widened in worry when I saw who was stood there, looking as if they'd just seen a ghost.

Chapter 38

Fi's slender frame was at my wide-open door, holding the door handle and frame for dear life as if they were the only things keeping her standing. She was a sight for sore eyes. She was sweating profusely, and her skin had drained of colour, except for the tint of pink in her cheeks from her sprinting to my apartment. Her eyes were vacant as she freaked out internally and her hair was jutting up all over the place. The door handle rattled under her trembling death grip as she struggled to breathe, panic squeezing her lungs.

All of a sudden, her knees buckled from underneath her and she collapsed to the ground. Luckily, I'd made it to her before she hit the floor; her legs were shaking like crazy, barely keeping her on her feet, that I was able to see her drop before she actually had.

"Fucking hell Fi, what's wrong?" She was frozen on the spot, still not moving as I was keeping her up in my arms. She was absolutely scared stiff. Tears silently flowed down her cheeks as she turned her head to look at me.

"A... I... I'm pregnant." The words shakily tumbled out of her mouth.

I stared at her with my eyes popped out. Well, that was not on my bingo card for this year. I looked down at her and let my eyes wander her body. I had noticed changes in her lately, but I hadn't thought that pregnancy would have been a candidate in the reasons as to why. She had put on a little more weight on recently, but I had just assumed that it was because she had stopped exercising with me recently and was comfortable in her relationship with Everett. It made a lot of the sense though; how off she'd been, the occasional snapping at me, not wanting to meet up at 'The Hub'.

I set her on her knees, still in the open doorway and kneeled in front of her. I cradled her head in my hand and pulled it to my chest, stroking her back with my other. As her head made contact with my cushiony chest, the sobs that had been begging and fighting to escape exploded out of her orifices.

"Oh babe." I spoke sadly as the sound of her crying her heart out almost made my heart stop. Her tears had already soaked my vest top, and I was beginning to regret my decision of not wearing a bra, as my nipples protruded at the sudden contact of the cold wetness.

"I'm scared, Ava. What... What if he doesn't want me? What if he doesn't want the baby? We've not been together long... This is all too fast." Her voice was quivering as she spoke through her tears. I hugged her tighter to my chest and kissed the top of her sweat-soaked head. They hadn't been together for long at all; only around five months, and so I could completely understand her worry. But I also knew that Everett loved her with his entire being. Anyone with eyes could see how much he adored her. He would never leave her, and he most certainly wouldn't leave her stranded with his baby. And even if he did, I wouldn't let him get very far.

Once her crying had quietened down to a few sniffs and some uneven breaths, I pulled away from her and stroked her hair that was clinging to her wet face like spaghetti on a wall out of her face.

"Come on, let's get you inside before Leon sees us and tells Everett." It was coming up to Leon's home time, so he could walk up those steps any minute. She gave me a small solemn nod and we stood up. She took my proffered hand to help her up and to keep her steady. I kept hold of her as we slowly walked towards the sofa with her legs jellified. My mind was going a mile a minute. I'd asked her over and over if she was OK and had just taken her word for it that she was fine. How could I mistake her changes as anything else but pregnancy symptoms?

I handed her a box of tissues and headed to the kitchen to make us some juice; deciding against coffee since I knew too much caffeine was a no-no in the pregnancy rule book. I could hear her soft blows into her tissue, and I felt my heart go out to her. Parenthood was a very scary concept. It's literally life changing, so I can only imagine what she must be feeling right now, even more so when it's unplanned. We both dreamed of being parents but dreaming and reality are two very different things. And now that it was happening for Fi, she must be scared out of her wits.

I carefully carried our cups to the living room, taking my time so as not to spill the contents onto the floor. I sat down next to Fi once the cups were safely on the coffee table and turned to face her, putting a hand on her leg. She looked at me with teary eyes and her lips trembled.

"When did you find out?" I asked softly. I passed her another tissue which she started playing with in her hands, anything to

355

keep them busy.

"Literally half an hour ago. I came here straight from A&E. I've had this pain in my stomach for a few days, and today was the worst, so I got it looked at thinking maybe it was appendicitis or some stupid infection. I haven't told Everett... not yet anyway. I'm only eight weeks and two days, due February eleventh." She rummaged in her bag and pulled out her scan picture. I picked it up and my heart exploded as I looked at the black and white image. It didn't look like a little ball of cells like I expected it to. It looked a little like I was looking at an old TV with no signal, except in the middle of the mass of fuzzy white, was a black circle that was shielding a white silhouette. I could make out the head and the nubby forming of the rest of its tiny body.

I know Fi was scared right now, but I couldn't stop the love pour from me as I looked at the picture of the new life that was growing inside of my best friend. The life that was no bigger than a raspberry. I placed the print-out on the coffee table and took my hands in hers. I looked at her earnestly, bracing myself for the big question I had to ask her.

"What do you want to do?" I asked slowly. It was a difficult question to ask and was equally as difficult for her to even consider. She snapped her head up and I was shocked that she was looking ludicrously at me. It seemed that she had already come to a decision. Difficult question to answer be damned.

"I can't get rid of it, Ava. It's a part of me, and it deserves a chance at life. Who am I to take that away from it?" She placed a hand delicately on her stomach and gazed down. Despite her fear, she had a loving look on her face as she gently stroked her belly, devoid of a visible bump. I placed a hand on top of hers and smiled lightly at her.

"With or without Everett, you're going to be a brilliant mum and you know I'm always going to be here for you." Returning a slightly sad smile, she twisted her hands so that they were now both cocooned in mine in her lap.

"But what about you? This must be hard for you since... you know..." She flicked her eyes downward as she said the last part. Even now she was thinking about someone else aside from herself. It didn't matter that she could get pregnant and I most likely couldn't. As long as she was happy, it didn't bother me. Sure, it would be a little bittersweet, but her good news and my love for this child would never be overshadowed by any jealousy I may feel. Plus, I'd have a little niece of nephew to spoil.

I shook my head at her selflessness. "This isn't about me Ffion. This is about you and your little one. You shouldn't feel bad about having a baby just because there's a big possibility that I can't. My issue doesn't take away my happiness and love for you and your little pickle." The worry vanished from her face and a relieved look replaced it. For as long as I had known Fi, she'd had an unhealthy obsession with pickles, and so one drunken glass painting girls night, we resolved that in the event of Fi falling pregnant, the child will be known as 'pickle'.

I gave her hands a reassuring squeeze and we moved on to making a plan on how she was going to tell Everett. We decided to do it tomorrow which meant we had to get our shit together and work fast. We browsed Amazon and started placing orders with next day delivery. Now that we had talked it out, she was feeling a bit better about her situation and was beginning to get excited.

I assured her that Everett would be over the moon at the news. But then that led to her freaking out about her having to move out and maybe moving in with him. "So, would that mean I would move in with him, or he moves in with me, or would we look for somewhere else?" As she reeled off her worries without taking a breath, I squished her cheeks with my small hands, making her lips pout like a fish.

"Fi. Stop it. First things first, you need to tell Everett. Then and only then can you worry about what comes next. Once he knows, you can figure everything out together." She awkwardly nodded her head as I still had hold of her face. I let go and let out a laugh as she scowled at me whilst rubbing her rosy cheeks.

I wouldn't ever admit it or show her, but there secretly was an itty bitty amount of jealousy creeping in about her being with-child the more we spoke about it. I knew I could have children one way or another, but Fi now had the chance to experience what I ached to experience for myself, an experience that had been robbed of me. My jealous thoughts had me traitorously thinking about Leon. I pictured little mini hims running around, their beautiful brown locks blowing softly in the summer breeze as they ran freely. Why was I thinking about babies with Leon? Hypothetical children with him should be the last thing on my mind right now, especially when our future was on very uncertain and shaky grounds at this moment in time.

With that on my mind, I told Fi about staying with my mum, that I would be leaving tomorrow for some time. I wasn't too sure how long I would be gone, and I was feeling bad that I wasn't going to be here for some of her pregnancy. I wanted to be there for her when she needed me or when Everett couldn't be there, but I had my own life and problems to sort out, and they took precedence in my life. Fi would still be pregnant when I got back, so there was plenty of time for me to enjoy being her helper.

She understood why I needed to go away for a while, and she was completely supportive. She agreed that some time away would help me not only decide on Leon, but also would help me find some peace with the past. She promised she would update me every day with how she was and any baby news that she might have.

I picked up the scan picture again and grazed my fingers over the top. I felt butterflies in my stomach as happiness pooled warmly in there. I instructed Fi to stand and I held the picture up against her invisible bump. She looked more bloated than anything, but I knew in a matter of weeks her mid-section would round out into a smooth curve.

"That's your baby in there, Fi. I'm so happy for you, you know." A huge smile was plastered on her face and her hands once again found their way onto where soon enough her pouch would become a prominent bump.

We spent some time browsing for some baby bits, just to add more fuel to our increasing fire of exhilaration, before Fi decided it was time for her to take her leave. Looking like she was about to burst with excitement, I walked Fi to the door, and opened it as the gentlewoman that I am. As Fi started down the steps, Leon walked up his own, briefcase in hand. He was late home from work and I was now telling myself off internally at my questioning on the possible whys.

As usual, my heart rate sky-rocketed and my skin tingled as his eyes scoured my body. His gaze stopped at my breasts, taking in my curves and the nipple bars that were visible against the tight material. He licked his lips and rolled his bottom lip under his top teeth, slowly releasing it to its full form. His eyes flicked to mine. Burning desire flickered intensely in them and I felt a little wetness between my legs as my body reacted to his shameless ogling. He quickly realised what he had been doing as he snapped out of his trance and picked up the pace in his walk and hurried into his apartment, fighting with himself to meet my eye.

I closed the door once Fi was off the steps and lightly banged my forehead a couple of times on the back of it. Stupid. Intrusive. Thoughts. I both loved and hated how just being under his burning scrutiny had me reacting like I was starved of sexual attention. Which when I think about it, I actually was. No matter how hard I fought, my body just reacted in whatever way it wanted to whenever I saw him. It was a good thing I was going away tomorrow; I wasn't sure I would be able to hold out any longer.

40

Chapter 39

Leon's POV:

I was laying stark bollock naked on the bed with my head up against the headboard, bathing in the warm rays that blared in through the windows, blanketing me in its warmth. I closed my eyes, enjoying the blissful comfort and found myself wondering how long this peace and serenity would last.

Whilst basking in the ambiance of the suns delicious rays as it ravaged my skin, my mind traveled – unsurprisingly – to thoughts of Ava. She pleasantly haunted my thoughts on a regular basis, and I was not disappointed with the image I had in my head right now.

She looked sexy in anything that she wore, even more so when she wore nothing, but seeing those tantalising nipple bars through her tight top yesterday had put me in a trance. I remembered what it was like to have them in my mouth, making her moan that sexy, melodic moan of hers, as my tongue and teeth performed a barrage of attacks on them. I could tell that she had got aroused at my undressing her with my eyes, as her nipples slowly started to harden against the material, trying to escape their confines.

I groaned as the memory had me rock hard. I wrapped my hand around myself, continuing my thoughts about her. Her breasts were perfectly perky and curved and had been pushed up slightly as she folded her arms under them. The cut of her vest top was low, exposing the soft, tanned skin of the top of her boobs. A small trickle of sweat excruciatingly slowly trailed down from the base of her neck and down the crack of her pushed together cleavage, as the afternoon heat warmed her skin. Her legs squeezed together as she tried to stop the throbbing of her core as she secretly enjoyed my eyes trained on her body. How I wished to spread those exquisite legs of hers and bury myself between them.

I picked up my speed as my memory changed to the many times we had been in bed naked together. *Fuck* I missed having her next to me. I missed the feel of her smooth skin on mine as I held her close to me. I missed feeling her shiver as my gentle, teasing touch made her weak. I missed wrapping her hair tight around my hand as I pounded into her from the back. I missed hearing her sweet sensual moans and her screaming my name in sheer ecstasy as I made her come.

I could feel myself reach my climax as I started to pulsate in my hand. I imagined Ava screeching my name as I brought her pleasure, only to call out to her as my warm liquid squirted onto my stomach before slowly drizzling down to my hand. Once my high had passed, I headed to the bathroom and had a warm shower, cleaning my mess up in the process. How Ava had showers as hot as the sun was beyond me, but I would always put up with the heat if it meant being in there with her. I craved to touch her constantly and when I wasn't touching her, my whole body ached from withdrawal.

I felt a little dirty masturbating to images of Ava, but if I couldn't act in the way I wanted to with her, then my hand was the only option. I had stuck to my promise and hadn't touched or looked at another female since Ava found out about Stacey. And as sexually frustrated and depraved as I was, it was worth it if it meant the chance of having her be mine again.

When I wasn't preventing myself from getting blue balls, I would think of Ava in non-sexual ways. She was the definition of perfection to me, but it wasn't just because of her body. Her laugh was light and always filled the room. Her smile was infectious and could cure anyone's sadness just by witnessing its kindness. Her eyes were like the gate to her secret garden where her most precious memories and inner most thoughts hid. Like a mood ring, they projected all of her emotions and changed colour accordingly to her mood. I could get lost looking into those beautiful orbs of hers.

She'd changed recently and it only made her all the more attractive. She was outspoken, ballsy and she emanated confidence. She had always been headstrong and assertive, but she'd reached a new level. I hadn't spent any time with her, but every time I had seen her, she seemed lighter. As a therapist, I could see what it was that was causing her to change and feel freer. She was confronting her past head on and dealing with them in a healthy way, rather than by burying her emotions and hurting and abusing herself. Pride swelled within me with how she was coping and of the incredible woman she had become. Once she had faced all her demons and conquered them, she would be indestructible.

I stepped out of the shower and dried myself off before tying a towel lowly on my hips. My morning release and shower had relaxed me greatly, taking away a bit of my tension. I still had no clue where Ava's head was at with me, and I prayed every day that she chose to give me another chance. Little things she did had given me hope, like letting me touch her when she was on the verge of a panic attack as she hesitated in contacting that wank stain ex of hers, or her small smile when we crossed paths. But I didn't get my hopes up too high, because there was still the possibility of her turning me away forever.

My phone dinged sharply on my bedside table and I picked it up. Seeing I had a text from Ev, I unlocked my device and opened his message.

E: Ava's going back to her hometown this afternoon for a while, not too sure how long for.

My heart sank to my feet. That meant that she was putting a big distance between us because she still hadn't come to a conclusion. It was easy to wait for her because I was still able to see her from time to time, but with her gone, I'll miss her an indescribable amount. I won't be able to stop the torrent of thoughts that I knew would hit me every day as I wondered how she was, if she was with anyone else or what she was thinking with regards to us. But that was the price I had to pay for my actions. I had it easy in comparison to her; I just had to wait. She on the other hand, was dealing with her memories, her feelings and her thoughts. She was the one who had the burden of making the decision. Yes, I had a job to do with regards to not giving her a reason to turn me down and instead show her every reason why she should take me back, but she had a more difficult job.

Before I could reply to Ev, a text from Ffion came through.

F: I need you to be at mine for twelve p.m., no questions asked. Ava will be here but she's OK with you being here too, since it was her suggestion to ask you.

I frowned in confusion at Ffion's text. Her text was rather cryptic and ominous, and I felt my stomach knot as I pondered on why she was inviting me to go to hers, it wasn't something that she usually did, if ever. The knot only tightened when I re-read the part of her message about Ava suggesting I was invited. She was somewhat comfortable about being around my presence. I hoped that meant good news for me.

I checked the time and shat my pants as I realised that I only had half an hour to get dressed and get to Ffion's. I quickly replied to Ffion, telling her I'll be there and rushed a reply to Ev saying that I'd speak to him about it later. I hurriedly got dressed in record time and headed to Ffion's.

* * *

I arrived at Ffion's flat with five minutes to spare. I assumed that Ev was yet to arrive; there was no way I'd be invited here without him having to be here too. Ava and Ffion were both buzzing like ten-year-olds hyped up on E numbers. Ava was adorable when she was excited. She really did look like a kid in a sweet shop. Her eyes twinkled with excitement and her stunning, full smile took up her entire face.

The girls were positioned behind the breakfast bar. I cocked my head and the mysterious object that was in front of them, that had a plain white cloth over it. I walked over and pinched the cloth between my finger and thumb and lifted it slightly, trying to sneak a peek. I felt a sharp sting on the back of my hand, causing me to drop the cotton fabric, as Ava's hand slapped mine.

"Not yet." She scolded. I was surprised she had touched me, and I think she was too, as she hid her hand behind her back, her cheeks turned pink with a blush. Her acting on impulse and without thinking had me smirking at the thought of her being somewhat normal around me, and a memory of her slapping me inappropriately zapped through my mind. I was getting hard just thinking about her briefly. I sat down at the breakfast bar on the opposite side to them and casually adjusted myself.

"Hey bab... what are you guys doing here?" Ev's voice had started off really happy and breezy and finished in a questioning manner. He didn't know that me and Ava were going to be here. The girls looked at each other, their smiles somehow getting bigger, and they squealed like excitable schoolgirls.

"I've got something for you under here." Ffion pointed to the object in the middle of us with a look glinting in her eye. Ev looked at the mysterious shape and then back to Ffion with a wonderous look on his face. He cautiously gripped the cover and slowly unveiled a basket with items thoughtfully placed inside. With the cloth now off, it only took a second for me to register what was going on, and I quickly turned my head to Ev with a grin on my face. My heart swelled with happiness that my best mate was going to be a dad. He, however, was struggling to process what Ffion was trying to tell him.

His shaking hand reached forward and picked up a white stick with a blue cap, his eyes glued to the plastic device as he inspected the message in the tiny window that showed a plus and a minus sign. Carefully placing it down, he then picked up a tiny white baby sleep-suit which had the words "*Baby Thomas*" and a few hearts printed in gold in the center. There was a small chalk board with Ava's elegant handwriting spelling out "*Making an Entrance into the World, February eleventh*" and just in front of that was a scan picture.

Ev wordlessly held the scan picture in his hands. I looked up to his face and saw a couple of droplets drop from his eyes. They glistened in the light as they raced each other to the ground. He looked up to Ffion, who was also crying.

"Are you serious? I'm going to be a dad?" His voice was quiet and uncertain. He wasn't too sure if this was real or not. Ffion nodded her head letting out a little laugh out of her mouth.

"We're having a baby." Ev hurried to her side and picked her up, spinning her around in her compact kitchen.

"Holy fuck Fi! This is the best thing to ever happen to me, to us. I love you so much Fi, I promise I'll do everything I can to give you and our little one the best life ever." They both had happy tears streaming down their cheeks whilst he blurted out his feelings and I could see the relief spread through Ffion. She must've been worried about how he would take the news. It was obviously none of my business, but I didn't know if they'd had spoken about children yet. What I did know though, was that before Ffion, Ev never wanted them, and since her he had mentioned to me how he pictured his life with Ffion, children included.

I turned my attention to Ava. She had a proud look on her face, as she watched the heart-warming interaction between Ffion and Ev. But her eyes held a different emotion, and I couldn't be sure, but it looked like a touch of sadness. Ev had placed Ffion carefully back on her feet and me and Ava both moved towards them both to congratulate them.

We had moved to the sofa and were discussing everything baby, but my mind was elsewhere. I couldn't stop the thoughts from penetrating my mind. Would me and Ava get to have a family of our own one day? Does she even want children? I'd never thought about having children of my own, I wasn't fussed about it. I knew what evil little pricks kids could be - I'd been one myself. But since meeting Ava, my whole perspective had changed. I wanted it all with Ava, and if I couldn't have it with her, then I didn't want it at all. I found myself picturing us in the future with a couple of kids of our own. A boy with his mothers' beautiful crystal eyes and my brown hair, and a little girl with her mother's gorgeous long blonde hair and my hazel honey eyes. My heart clenched at the thought that there was a possibility that this would remain just a dream.

Ava's sweet voice pulled me from my thoughts. I turned my attention to her. I never tired of hearing her voice. In a room full of a thousand voices, hers would be the only one I'd be able to hear. But what she was saying was tearing me in half.

"I should get going. My mum will be here in forty-five minutes to come get me. I don't know when I'll be back but when I am, I'll have a much better mindset." She said the last part looking at me, letting me know that when she returned, I'll have an answer. I just had to wait for her.

41

Chapter 40

Ava's POV:

I heaved the suitcase onto what was to be my bed for God knows how long, using both of my hands to grasp the handle and swing it up. I flopped down next to it and laid spreadeagled against the soft, yellow flowered bedding. I closed my eyes and breathed in the familiar scent of home. This wasn't my childhood home, but wherever we moved, mums comforting scent followed, and I was feeling very homey.

I missed being in my mums company. I suppose after it just being me and her against the world for so long, it was only natural. We'd been there for the other through our good and bad times, relying on no-one else – aside from the brief period of Kelvin. We'd been all the other needed. But now that I was grown up and I no longer lived with her, she was alone, and so it came the time for her to find someone. And lo and behold, Kelvin had come back on the scene. I was looking forward to seeing him again, but I had to wait until the evening when he would be joining us for dinner.

The drive here had been relaxed. The music was kept at a moderate level so as not interrupt our conversation, but loud enough to comfortably fill the silence as we simply enjoyed the atmosphere. The temperature had been rather mild. We had the air con on, since mum didn't like having the windows down. She said it was something to do with the sound compressing on her eardrums, and she had a fear of losing her hearing.

With Fi's approval, I informed her of Fi's unexpected news. To say that my mum was ecstatic was putting it mildly. She was so beyond buzzed, that she had almost veered off the road and I had to grab for the steering wheel to get us back into the center of our lane. After I told her of this, the rest of the journey to my hometown was us talking about Fi and her baby. Mum decided she was going to have a boy, whereas I was hoping for a girl.

I rolled my head to the side and stared at my suitcase, deliberating whether or not I should unpack it. I had no idea how long I'd be here for; it could be for a week, a month or even longer. I groaned and scrunched my eyes shut. I didn't want to be away for too long, but I needed to stay until I had come to a clear conclusion. How had I not been able to come to a decision after a month? Was I even being fair to Leon, making him wait so long for me? What if I decided I wanted him, but he no longer wanted me? My head was starting to hurt.

My body constantly cried out for his touch. It desperately begged me to let him have his way with me, to have his hands over every inch of my body. Yesterday was a testament to that; I was weak just by having his hungry eyes audaciously devour me. I had to squeeze my legs to try stop my hidden heartbeat that treacherously pulsated like a persistent whisper; it had been so long since I had been touched by him and I was not in control of my bodily functions. It baffled me how it was possible that he had that effect on me just by using his intensely burning look.

While my body was busy crying, its two control centers were arguing over what they wanted. Neither could admit defeat. My heart wanted Leon. It wanted me to take him for all he is now and for who had become. His past self wasn't who he was anymore, that much was obvious. But my head was hurting. He had hurt me big time in the past. Many people wouldn't be able to see past it and my brain was trying its best not to. He had caused me incomprehensible amount of suffering, and although he wasn't the only one, he was the main partaker. Even though he told me why he had done it, I couldn't help but hate that he had let Victoria of all people manipulate him to be the person he became for two years.

Thinking back to those years, it became apparent that although he was the ringleader of the group of his cronies as I used to call them, the real mastermind was Victoria. He refrained from physically hurting, and when he had, it was only ever in front of Victoria. She controlled him and made him into a monster. Even when Victoria would go too far, he had intervened. As I thought about this little bit of information, I remembered the dream I had that Leon brought me out of when we were on our romantic weekend away together. It was his voice that stopped Victoria from squeezing her hands tighter around my neck. How did I not recognise his voice then? Sure, his voice was way deeper now. But surely, I should have been able to have put two and two together?

Before I could get anymore tangled up in my web of thoughts, I was pulled out of them by the announcement of dinner. I had been so engrossed in my head, that I hadn't even heard the door go as Kelvin entered. I flew down the stairs with excitement bubbling up in my stomach. He was stood in the doorway between the kitchen and living room, leaning on the one arm that was rested along the door frame. His head turned to look over his shoulder and a huge grin spread along his handsome face. I ran towards him and leaped into his arms like I used to when I was a kid. My legs wrapped loosely around his waist and my arms were tight around his neck. I buried my head in the crook of his neck as tears started to trickle down my cheeks. Kelvin circled his arms around me, modestly holding me by my back. I felt a rumble in his chest as he let out a chuckle.

"I've missed you too, little legs." I hadn't needed to say anything for him to know that I truly had missed him; my actions sufficed enough. He was the closest thing I'd ever had to a father figure, and in the short time he was in my life, I desperately wished that he was my biological dad. He'd loved me as if I was his own child, and to be able to love someone else's child was a difficult thing to do. It showed what type of man you were if you were able to love your partners child as if they were yours.

I felt another pair of arms wrap around me and a chin rest on my arm. I pulled away from Kelvins shoulder and looked at my mum who had come over to join in on our emotional reunion. Kelvin removed the arm nearest to mum and I took an arm away from around Kelvins neck and we pulled her closer into our embrace. We stayed this way, all of us silently crying in joy at being together again, until the oven timer went off and mum started panicking in case the food would burn.

Over dinner, Kelvin and I got caught up with each other and I found that he had been given a promotion at his law firm and was now a partner. I told him about my career as a personal trainer and he beamed at me proudly. We didn't talk about my past, there was a time and place, and this was neither. He knew how bad it had been for me. The two years he was with my mum were the same two years of my torment, and so he bared witness to the effects that had on me. I looked over at mum occasionally and found that she was smiling lovingly at the both of us, enjoying our interaction. This was happiest I had ever seen her, and I had Kelvin to thank for that.

As I washed the plates and cutlery up, Kelvin sidled over to my side and began drying up. Mum stayed in the living room deciding on what board game we would play tonight. We washed and dried up together in comfortable silence, although there was a little bit of a weird feel to it. Kelvin looked like he wanted to ask me something, but he was trying to figure out how to say it.

"Go on, just ask me whatever you want to ask." I said in jest as I rolled my eyes. He looked to the direction of where my mum was, making sure that she wasn't within earshot. He turned back to me with hesitation and worry in his eyes. In his hands, the tea towel was being violently rung out.

"Well... I love your mum, more than anything. I'd do anything for her. You know that, right?" I nodded my head slowly at him, my brows fixed together as I looked at him questioningly, hands frozen in the soapy warm water, not knowing where this was going to go.

"I don't know how to say this, so I'm just going to say it. I want... I want to ask your mum to marry me, but I want your blessing first." He wasn't meeting my gaze, but he had a small, embarrassed smile on his lips and his cheeks had turned a light shade of red. I was screaming on the inside with excitement, as I felt a smile take over my face. I shook my hands free of the suds and walked over to Kelvin and gave him a hug crossing my wrists to avoid getting his shirt wet.

"My mum being your wife would make her the happiest

373

woman in the world. Who would I be to deny her that? You have always put us first, and I can see how much you both love each other. You both deserve a happily ever after, and I'm glad that you have finally found it and that you found each other again. So yes, Kelvin. You have my blessing to ask my mums hand in marriage." I kept my voice low so that mum couldn't hear, but I spoke sincerely to him. I felt a wet droplet splash silently on my naked shoulder and I pulled away and looked up at Kelvin.

"You know, when I was with your mum back then, I was considering adopting you." I smiled warmly at him. I had no idea that he had ever considered taking on such a role and it warmed me to think that he was prepared for such a challenge. I put a supportive hand on his shoulder and his eyes found mine, no longer caring about where I placed my wet hands.

"We don't need a piece of paper to state that you're my parent. I've always seen you as my dad and being your stepdaughter is just as official." Tears silently spilled from his eyes as he pulled me back in for an embrace. This meant just as much to him as it did me. I melted into his chest as I let him cry out his happy tears.

I was finally going to have a complete family. I was going to have a dad.

* * *

Leon's POV:

It was half two in the morning and I was tossing and turning restlessly in my bed. I couldn't sleep and I couldn't get comfortable. I knew why. It was because Ava wasn't near, and my brain wouldn't shut up thinking about her. Flopping onto my back with my arms out at my sides, I stared up at the dark void that was my pitch-black ceiling. The entire room was enveloped in the dark of the night, with only a faint light that subtly shone through the window into my room.

I knew that Ava needed to be away from me. I understood why. But knowing that she wasn't on the other side of the wall to me tugged at my heartstrings. If I thought I missed her when she was just next door to me, it had nothing on how tremendously I missed her right now. I selfishly hoped she wasn't gone for too long. But she could and would take as much time as she needed to settle the war between her head and her heart.

It wasn't that I couldn't wait for her, I could and I would until the end of time if I needed to. I needed her like an alcoholic needs booze. I felt my chest tighten as I thought about the possibility of not having her by my side ever again. About never being able to stroke her golden locks down her elegant back to soothe her of her worries, the possibility that I would never taste her sweet plump lips again. There was a chance that I would never have her wrapped up in my arms again. There was a chance that she would break my heart beyond repair.

I worried about how she was. I hoped she would look after herself while she was gone. I hoped she would be safe and not get into any kind of trouble. I hoped she wouldn't find someone else.

My heart squeezed as I became more breathless. It was starting to hurt to breathe, only to be made worse by the reminder that I can't live without her. She was the air that I breathed, and I was nothing without her; she literally gave my life meaning and purpose. If it wasn't for her, I wouldn't be doing what I do now, helping young people to deal with the demons that lurked in the shadows of their consciousness.

Desperate to get some oxygen into my lungs, I quickly put on some boxers and stood out onto the balcony, closing my eyes as I tilted my head up to the unknown wilderness that was the eternal night sky. Placing a hand above my heart, I imagined that I was listening to Ava's heartbeat, just like she had with me a number of times when I had to help her control her panic attacks.

I'd never had a panic attack, and the fact I was experiencing exactly what Ava goes through, put a lot of things into perspective for me. I felt the pain, anxiety and fear that she felt because of me. I was figuratively wearing her shoes right now and even though it added to the guilt I felt over what I had done to her, it increased my love and respect for her. I had said it many times before, but she was so remarkably strong. She had been dealt a shit hand at life, part of which was thanks to me, but she persevered and battled through it all, rolling with the punches and came out on top. She had the tenacity, will power and strength of an entire army all crammed into her small body. I couldn't help but be in awe of her.

My breathing had finally started to return back to normal, and once the elastic band around my chest disappeared, I returned back to my bed. I picked my phone up and pressed the button at the side, making the screen light up. I squinted slightly, the bright light blinding me before my eyes adjusted to the white light. I hadn't changed the lock screen of my phone. I couldn't bring myself to. It was the closest thing I could get to looking at her beautiful face. It was a selfie we'd taken when we had our weekend away. I was giving her a piggyback along the beach by the shore. The sun had been in our faces and Ava had placed her hands over my eyes, completely blocking my vision and she scrunched her own eyes closed, preventing the sun from shining into her dazzling eyes. Her mouth was set in an open smile as she giggled at our silliness and I had stuck my tongue out at her covering my eyes. Her long glossy hair framed her face wildly as the wind blew it about the place. She was perfect. In every single way.

Not thinking before acting, I called Ava. It rang for a while and just as I was about to give up, she answered.

"Leon? Do you know what time it is? This isn't exactly giving me space." Her sleepy voice a stern, quiet whisper, no doubt trying not to wake her mum. I thought about every time I ever woke up next to her, watching her sleep and hearing her breathy, tired "good morning baby." She was adorable when she'd just woken up. It was an interaction I missed having with her.

"I know, I'm sorry. Look, I just really need to get this off my chest. Can you just listen while I talk? Please? And then I won't bother you for the rest of the time you're away." I pleaded with her. She had gone quiet on the other end, and I thought she had fallen asleep when all of a sudden she spoke, her voice more awake and alert than before.

"Fine, I'll listen."

I took a deep breath and laid everything out on the table, with the hopes that maybe, just maybe, it would help sway her decision.

"I love you Ava, more than you could ever know. I know I fucked up big time with Stacey, and I know I hurt you in the past. I hate myself every day for the pain I've caused you and I wish that I could go back in time and rewrite history. I wish I never pushed you away. You deserve the world and beyond and

I hope you let me give that to you. I once told you I wanted to be the man to live up to the expectation of giving you all that you deserve, and I meant it then as much as I do now." I took a deep breath before continuing with my speech. My voice was starting to shake as I fought the tears from over-spilling. I couldn't let myself break down to her.

"There's no one in this world I want more than you Ava. I want to build a life and a family with you. You have my heart, my soul, my body; you control my very being. I promise you this now, I will live every day trying to prove to you that I am deserving of your love and trust. I will fight for you and prove just how sorry I am for what I did to you." My chest was feeling lighter, and my head was feeling clearer. It felt good to tell her how I felt. Perhaps I should have done it sooner.

"Leon... I-" She started but I wasn't going to let her finish, I didn't want a reply from her. I just wanted her to listen and think on what I said. I wanted her to know how I was feeling and where I stood with us.

"I won't interfere or try to contact you from now, I just needed you to know how I felt. Please make sure you take care of yourself Ava, I don't know what I'd do if anything happened to you." I could hear her crying down the phone quietly as she continued to listen to my rant.

"I'll be here when you get back, waiting for you. No matter how long it takes."

I hung up the phone and let the sobs that I had been holding back take over my body until I eventually cried myself to sleep.

Chapter 41

Leon's POV:

The past two weeks had been nothing short of tortuous. Ava still hadn't come home, and she wasn't showing any signs of being back any time soon and I was missing her something fierce. I had kept my promise of not contacting her after our call, or rather, my bleeding my heart out to her. I didn't know how she felt about the call, but I hoped against hope that it at least put across my love for her, and at most helped aid her in coming back to me. Calling her so late in the night did make me feel a bit shitty, knowing that I had woken her up, but it was the only way that I could silence the thoughts that rampaged wildly in my mind. I hadn't had a proper conversation with her about the situation since the day after it all came out, and I needed her to know how I felt.

Fi had kept me updated on Ava's welfare as usual. I could put up with the ache of missing her, just as long as I knew she was safe and well. Even though I truly believed she wouldn't harm herself again, I knew all too well how bad her panic attacks and nightmares could be once they were triggered, and I could only imagine how triggering being back in our hometown would be for her. She was in good hands at her mums, I knew that, but I was prideful of my ability at being able to calm her in a way I hadn't seen anyone else be able to, and I desperately wished I could be there for her when she needed to be comforted and calmed.

I found solace in the welcoming embrace of night and from the moment I woke up, I looked forward to going back to bed. I kept thoughts of her out of my mind during the day to enable me to focus entirely on my work and patients, and rewarded myself by seeing her in the sacred sanctuary of sleep. I was able to traverse the plane of my subconscious without any restraints, free of the shackles of worry that I would hurt Ava or that she was hurting, free to fashion a world where Ava and I blissfully shared a peaceful life together composed of boundless love and contentment. But as is the case with all dreams, you eventually get yanked out of the safety net that cradles sleep with no choice but to face reality; and that was the hardest part about dreaming of her.

Ev suggested loosening up a bit, and so here I was, stood in a club with him. I felt bad for taking him away from Ffion now that she was pregnant with his child, but he insisted that she was cool with him being out with me. She was starting to pop, and I knew Ev wanted to be with her as much as possible. He wanted to witness everything there was to see and feel with this pregnancy and I couldn't blame him. I'm sure I would be the same.

The club was spacious, and despite the amount of people that were here, there was still enough space to comfortably move and dance without hitting anyone. The area was dimly lit by lights embedded into the wall, and the odd classic metal chandelier that was decorated with fancy curls, were dotted about on the ceiling. The warm lighting brought about a relaxed and almost intimate ambiance about the place, allowing for those self-conscious about themselves to blend in and camouflage their insecurities. There were square pillars spaced out in the middle of the bar and attached around each was a narrow, dark wooden table and some square stools. Along the edges, more in the shadows of the quaintly modern establishment, were some private booths around the edges comprised of black leather two-seater sofas that barely rose from the ground. In the middle near the back, was a stage used for bands or any special acts that was softly illuminated by a lilac light that shadowed the lettering, spelling out the bars name.

I observed the rowdy crowd as me and Ev sat up one of the pillar tables, taking in the different types of people that were here as the music blared obtrusively. A few people were making easy prey of those who were intoxicated enough not to push away their advances. In the middle of the dance-floor, a group of young men formed a circle, and each one was having a turn at showing off their moves in the middle, whilst their mates boisterously hyped them up. Females highly populated the dance floor as they danced with their friends or the guy of their choosing for the night.

I was thinking about how Ava was so free when she danced. Like the graceful flickering flame of a candle, she swayed and moved perfectly in sync with the music as the rhythm took control of her body. I thought back to the night at the bar when we all were together, and she was grinding up against me. She had been teasing me all night and I had loved it. I lived for the thrill of the chase when it came to her, and conquering her gave me an unparalleled sense of exhilarating triumph. As I watched people dance together in an alluring way made me wish Ava was here with us, dancing like that with me. I missed holding her pinched waist in my hands as I held her close to me. I missed the way she made my heart race by looking up at me seductively through her long, fluttery lashes. I missed watching her lick the top of her lip with the very tip of her tongue, or when she tucked her bottom lip under her teeth. She knew it drove me wild. She knew exactly how to heat my skin with just the simplest movements or looks. I obviously missed her in non-sexual ways, but right now, jealousy burned through my veins at these couples. It should be me and Ava like that right now.

"Leon?" I heard Ev shout my name loudly in my ear, breaking me out of my thoughts. I faced him with a slight annoyed look on my face. The music was loud but not so much that he needed to bellow in my ear. He chuckled at my reaction and continued to speak.

"I said, you really miss her, don't you?" I had been so lost inside the jungle that was my mind, I hadn't heard him. Ev looked down to my wrist, and I dragged my eyes down to see what he was looking at. I'd been absentmindedly playing with the hairband still attached to my wrist as I thought about her. I never took it off. It was a small piece of her and just having it on my person brought me some semblance of comfort.

I let out a defeated sigh and felt my shoulders slack. I just wanted her home. With me, where she belonged.

"Mate, I feel like I'm drowning in an ocean of misery right now. I wake up every day feeling exactly the same as I did the day before. I'm just waiting for the day when I don't have to miss her anymore." He looked at me sadly and placed his warm hand on my shoulder.

"You did this to yourself, brother." His voice was low and honest. Our relationship was very similar to that of Ffion and Ava's. We never held back with our words and told the other exactly how it was. There was no sugar coating anything, and it was one of things I loved about our friendship.

Ev removed his hand, and he took a swig of his beer, lubricating his throat in preparation for what he was about to say.

"I know you're hurting right now but imagine how she must be feeling. She's torn between her head and her heart; she's literally battling with herself. The damage you caused her is irreversible. The memories of what you and the others did to her and made her feel will stay with her forever, even if she does forgive you. She may find it easier to forgive you for Stacey, but the past is much harder to face."

I tipped my head up and looked up to the high ceiling that was decorated with posh, perforated designs. Ev's words weighed heavily on my mind. They were harsh, but true, and hit me like I'd been doused in ice cold water. I was beginning to feel like this whole thing was a lost cause; that I had no chance of being with her again. I'd convinced myself that I'd lost her for good, that she would never forgive me. Yet, I couldn't stop hoping that I would be proven wrong, that she would find it in her heart to forgive me for my past, heinous acts towards her.

The whole point of coming out with Ev tonight was to have my mind off Ava, so that I could relax and be me for a while. With my head back in its natural position, I ran my hand slowly through my hair.

"Talk to me about something else, anything that isn't Ava." I told Ev. It wasn't fair of me to ruin our night out with me and the dilemma that I had put myself in. I looked towards Ev and he had his finger on his lips, deep in thought, his face plastered with apprehension.

"OK, but we're going to need another drink because what I am going to tell you is quite mega." With a resolute nod, Ev stood up and headed to the bar to get our next round in. I didn't know how to feel about this. I had no clue what he could want to tell me, but I was intrigued. I rifled through my memories and any logical thoughts about what major news Ev would tell me and came up trumps. There was nary a secret that we didn't divulge to the other. Well, except Stacey and whatever happened between him and Ffion. I still couldn't wrap my head around why he hadn't told me yet, and the only conclusion I could draw was that he'd done something that he was ashamed of. But then, why wouldn't Ffion tell Ava? Unless she had and had sworn Ava to secrecy, forbidding her from even telling me. I brushed my hand down my face in a single swipe. The whole situation was a fucking enigma.

As I poured the last drop of the bitter amber liquid into my mouth, I caught a girl from a couple of tables over eyeing me up. She was unhealthily skinny and had dark, dead straight shoulder length hair that stopped at her shoulders with matching dark eyes. She was watching me intently; her eyes never left me and her mouth curved into a smile when she noticed I was looking at her. I turned my top lip up in disgust and redirected my sight away from her to see where Ev was. My interest in her, or any other woman for that matter, was non-existent. Everything I could give was reserved solely for Ava.

Clapping eyes on Ev, I watched as he waded his way through the crowds, being careful not to spill a precious drop of our drinks. Just as he reached me, I flicked my eyes briefly back to the girl to see if she was still looking at me and I found that she was. Except now, she was blatantly pointing me out to her friends. I rolled my eyes and shook my head as I looked away. Shameless behaviour like that was a turn off for me. But the fact that she wasn't my beautiful blonde goddess was an even bigger one.

As I took a deep swig of my new drink, enjoying the soft feel of the foam in my mouth, Ev questioned me.

"You look like you've just stepped in shit. Who are you looking at?" I nodded my head in the direction of the girl as I swallowed my mouthful. Ev looked into the direction I pointed him in and saw that skinny britches was still openly staring at me. She wasn't even trying to hide it. Ev let out a little amused chuckle.

"Ah, I see. You've got yourself an admirer." He nudged my arm tauntingly. He knew I wouldn't go for her; I was serious about my promise to Ava.

"Yeah, well she can fuck off looking at me before I give her something to look at. Why can't she admire you?" I let out an annoyed huff. Crazy to think that once upon a time, I'd bathe in the attention, not really caring where it came from. But it was a totally different story now. Now, I didn't care for it. Unless it was Ava's attention, then I didn't want it.

"Women are such majestic and complex creatures, but they all share the same gift; the weird ability to sense everything. And I'm giving off dad vibes." He was laughing heartily, and it made me smile. It felt good to genuinely smile, it had been a while since I had felt the unfamiliar feeling on my face. Once his laughter died down, Ev guzzled almost half of his pint. He took a preparatory sigh and hugged his cold glass with both hands. Whatever he was about to disclose was bigger than I could have predicted.

"So... that thing with me and Fi..." My ears perked up and I turned to face him, giving him my full attention. He had listened intently and without judgment when I told him about my situation, and now it was my turn to repay the favour. He wasn't looking at me though. Instead, he was staring into his pint glass with an unreadable look on his face, pondering how to go about his news.

Raising his head, he looked into my eyes with anger simmering in them. But just as his chocolate eyes reached mine, his gaze swiftly lifted to behind me. I frowned and turned to see what he was looking at. There, stood with a fraction of space between us was Miss Stare-A-Lot with her hands clasped in front of her and a brash look on her thin face. She was in a tight red leather dress that only highlighted her scrawniness. There was nothing to her, she was literally skin and bones. The therapist in me felt sorry for the state she had got herself into, but the human me didn't care or want to know anything about the skeleton stood before me.

"Can I help you?" Annoyance at her sheer audacity to walk up to me and hover behind me like my shadow dripped from my lips, heightened by her interrupting mine and Ev's conversation.

She tucked her short, box-dyed black hair behind her ears, exposing more of her gaunt face. How no-one had brought to her attention that her pitch black hair made her look like Casper was beyond me. It was quite sad really, that her friends clearly aren't honest or opinionated about her questionable life choices. Her dark eyes briefly looked to the floor before they turned on me with pure dedication. "I was wondering if-"

I turned my back on her. I wasn't interested in her or in anything that she had to say. Give credit where credit is due, good on her for coming over and trying, but she had a ghost of a chance. My heart was already taken.

"I'm not interested." I kept my words blunt, making sure she knew I didn't want to know. Hearing her shuffle behind me, I thought she had gone away, only to have that thought corrected when I noticed Ev was trying to conceal his smile at my turning this girl down. He was doing as good a job at it as a pair of balls on a dildo. I opened my mouth to tell Ev to carry on with what it was he had to tell me, when the girls vexing pitchy voice tuned in from behind me, clearly incapable of taking a hint.

"It's just, I saw you look back at me earlier and thought-"

"Well, you know what thought thought." I looked over my shoulder, briefly catching her facial expression. She donned a frown of confusion: over-plucked, pencil-thin black eyebrows that even when in this expression, they looked like they were social distancing and red-painted lips pursed. My annoyance started to simmer at how dense she clearly was. I took a sharp breathe to keep myself from bubbling over and to preserve any sort of poise.

"You thought wrong. I didn't mean to give you the wrong impression, but I have no intention of doing whatever you want me to do." I was increasingly getting pissed off, and I could slightly hear it in my tone. Rudeness wasn't really a trait I dabbled in, but sometimes being nice gets you nowhere and this girl was seriously starting to get on my tits. I had swiveled in my chair to fully face her again and noticed that she had taken a step closer. She dropped her gaze slightly and was trying to look flirtatiously at me through her lashes.

"I can give you a good time, I'll make you feel a new world of good." Her hand found its way onto the top of my arm and she started to trace the length of my bicep with her Voldemort wand-like index finger, making my skin crawl under her bony touch. My body tensed under her unwanted touch, and I clenched my jaw as my anger started to ravage my body. I looked her deadpan

387

in the eyes, and tightly gripped her wrists, removing them from my shoulder.

"What part of 'no' don't you understand? Would you like me to say it in a different language? I. Am. Not. Interested." I snapped. It felt like I was talking to an insolent child. If Ava was here, she probably would've tackled the girl to the ground by now, and I honestly would have welcomed it. Her eyes flashed aggressively with anger that I had turned her down and she spun sharply on her heels and stormed off back to her group of friends. They'd been watching the whole interaction from where they were sat. Their eyes that once help hope had turned to disappointment that their friend hadn't been able to bag the eye candy from the next table over.

Once she was seated back down with a scowl on her face and her arms tightly folded across her chest as she sulked, I turned back to face Ev and he finally let out the laugh he had been holding in.

"Oh mate, she was a persistent one." I rolled my eyes at him. They were the worst type of girls. The needy, desperate ones who wouldn't leave you alone until you either gave them what they wanted, or you physically forced them away from you.

"Just tell me about Ffion." I wanted to just forget about the ordeal. What Ev had to say was more important. I didn't know what had happened between them and the look he had on his face right now told me that this was serious shit. I was ashamed to say that I thought a woman had got between them. With Ev's history, it wouldn't be surprising if that had turned out to be the case.

"I will, but I want to know what thought thought?" He dismissed my instruction with a wave of his hand, no doubt wanting to prolong telling me.

"Thought thought that he'd farted but he'd shit himself. Now, Ffion. Tell me."

His smile dropped from his face, his short burst of laughter cut off instantly and the angry flare had returned in his chestnut orbs. His face set in a stony, straight expression. That was warning enough for me to know that this was indeed some serious shit. I braced myself for whatever was about to come out of his mouth.

"Fi had a stalker."

43

Chapter 42

Spending two weeks away from home was doing me wonders. With the distance I had put between us, I was beginning to feel like I could breathe again. The cloudiness in my brain surrounding Leon and our situation was beginning to disperse. I was beginning to make sound judgements and decisions on a number of things, and gradually the stress was lifting off my shoulders. Everything I had done thus far was helping to make my decision easier and more definitive.

I'd spent my time walking around the town, reminding myself of what once was. At the start I'd had a couple of nightmares. Being back home put me on high alert of running into specific people - or more so a certain individual - and so my anxiety levels were through the roof. Thankfully, mum had been able to break me out of the chains that bound me to my nightmare of the given night, but I didn't fail to notice that she wasn't able to soothe me as quickly as Leon could; a thought that no matter how hard I tried, I just couldn't shake it.

The first place I visited was my old school. It felt like a good, natural place to start since it was the breeding ground for all that happened to me, making it the hardest to deal with. Standing outside of the grounds, I leaned against the wall where I had told Leon how I felt about him. The day before the worst two years of my life started and the course of my life had forever been altered. With my eyes closed, I felt myself being pulled into a time warp as my brain flung the memory at me.

He had been coolly leaned up against the brick wall, the top of his back flush against the orange brickwork and one knee bent, placing his foot on the back of the wall as he waited for his friends to evacuate the building. His hands were submerged deep in his pockets and he was listening to music through his earphones. There was a little that Leon and I had in common, and music was one of them. Whilst we both loved music and listened to a wide range of genres, there was a few differences between us with regards to the music world: Leon knew how to play an instrument and took private singing lessons, whereas my singing lessons were either shower performances or choir practice.

He bobbed his head along to the beat of the music and I remember smiling at the motion. I'd had the biggest crush on him for as long as I could remember. He was my first love, and I had mustered up enough courage and had chosen that day to make it known. At the thought of what I was about to do, I had become inundated with nerves and anxiety. In an attempt to calm myself, I had begun to play with the bottom edge of my skirt, my hands growing clammy.

Noticing my movement out of the corner of his eye, Leon pulled his headphones out and flashed a big, full welcomingly smile at me. He always did that when he saw me, and sometimes it felt like I was the only person he showed his true smile to.

His greeting was warm and he patiently waited and listened

as I stuttered out the secret that I had kept to myself for the past year and a half. Once the words had finally fell out of my mouth, his eyes lit up with joy and he opened his mouth to say something, but the slime ball queen herself had interfered, appearing out of the blue as if she had been lurking in the shadows, listening in on what was supposed to have been a private moment. I never knew what he wanted to tell me back then and up until the bullying, I had always been curious as to what he would have said to me. But after his recent disclosure of telling me that my feelings had been reciprocated, I could hazard a guess at what he was going to say.

But then that day happened, and both of our lives where turned upside down. Since being in high school, I had watched as Leon felt the need to constantly prove himself and keep up a persona that most definitely wasn't him. I never understood why he wanted to be popular. He was studious and smart and was destined for greatness, and it was disappointing watching it spiral away down a drain. Leon hadn't always been a bully. He had been one of the nicest kids in the school. He was funny, charismatic, and compassionate – not to mention he was extremely good looking too. He looked out for his peers and always offered a helping hand when it was needed. It's what made him so likeable. He was well-known in the school throughout. He spoke to and got along with everyone, regardless of social status. But then one day, he just, gave up. His new lifestyle with Victoria and his new gang took precedence and everything else became secondary and unimportant; being involved with a crowd as delinquent as the one he had joined, he soon fell to the bottom of the heap. With his new cruel and hostile persona, you would think that people wouldn't approach him anymore. This wasn't the case. As it turned out, people would go to him to sort out any problems that they had with other people with his newfound fear factor.

With my head leaned up against the scratchy brick surface, I let my mind become filled with memories that I had kept buried for ten years, the stories running through my mind like a flip book. There was being chased around the school by my tormentors, having to hide on the days when they were incessant on getting to me, and the times when I would be belittled in front of the whole class with name calling or snide jeers. Not forgetting the more physical side. The being pinned up against a wall, the bruising grabs, or Victoria's spiteful hands being on or around me. My mind was a never ending, inescapable torment.

At some point in the revival of my memories, I had begun to cry. I was caught off-guard by the sound of my sobs, as they brought me out of my reverie. There were some strange looks from people walking by, but I didn't care. They didn't need to know what hellish calamity I was remembering as I forced myself to face the past head on. With my reawakened memories, I had made my way back to my mums.

I'd spent a week sorting through my reawakened memories before coming to a conclusion about them and how I felt about it all. The second week was spent visiting the town and reacquainting myself with the familiar surroundings. My hometown was a beautiful, densely populated town. It had once been mostly an elderly demographic, but over the years, lots of new, younger faces had begun to invade the town.

I discovered that many people who I went to school with still lived here. It surprised me as many of the people I saw had been so ambitious and driven, that I thought they would have spread their wings and left the safety and predictability of their hometown. I suppose life never goes the way you plan it to. I saw a few of my old friends and they had greeted me as such. We briefly caught up on our lives and I could see the guilt that they had harbored for the past ten years settle in their faces. They had apologised for not stepping in with the bullying and I appreciated their kind words. Though it was a too little too late, it was humbling to know that they regretted their omission and knew how wrong it was. It was amazing how liberating it was to get closure on that part of my life - something I never thought I would be able to do.

Currently, I was stretched out on a sun lounger in my mums back garden, my body comfortably resting on the soft padding. The late July's sun was scorching as its pleasantly warm rays tickled my tanned skin, making me melt into a relaxed bliss. Perched up on my elbows, one hand holding the weight of my chin, the other holding my phone in front of me, I was on FaceTime to Fi.

I was missing her so much, and I really wished to be back home so that I could be there with her throughout this beautiful time of her life. She had balanced her phone against an object that was on her coffee table as she took a few steps further back, revealing her entire body. She lifted her top up so that it sat between the curve of the beginning of her bump, and under her breasts. She was now almost twelve weeks, and she was already showing.

"Oh, look at that cute little bump!" Her bump wasn't massive, far from it, but it was a visible gentle smooth curve. She was absolutely blooming. She had that pregnancy glow and it radiated through the screen. The grin she had on her face was one of pride as she looked down at her protruding belly, her hands stroking it delicately. This baby was so unbelievably loved already, and it was yet to make an appearance into the world. I took a screenshot of this moment. I was keeping all photos of this pregnancy with the plan of creating a scrapbook for Fi when the little pickle was born.

"I know," she rubbed her hand over her smooth skin, "I woke up a couple of days ago and it was just there. But look at this." Fi moved closer to her phone before picking it up and holding it lower, in line with her waistband.

"I'm growing a bloody snail trail!" She exclaimed. I let out a laugh as sure enough, there was the beginning of dark hair growing in a line from under her waistband, reaching towards her bellybutton.

"You could always shave it?" I offered.

"No thanks. Knowing my luck, it'll grow back thicker and darker and this is bad enough." Fi rolled her top back down over her exposed skin and plonked herself back down on the sofa. Her beautiful smile remained present as we continued to discuss the baby. Now that she had reached the safety of twelve-weeks, Fi and Everett had begun looking for baby bits and already have found an eight-piece pram they really love. They were going to visit the store tomorrow and have a look at it in person and give it a test drive.

"How is Ev dealing with the impending fatherhood?"

"He's actually been really good with me, coming to my appointments and making sure I'm eating properly. He did freak out at the scan though; hearing the heartbeat and actually seeing the baby himself just made it real for him. I'd never seen him so white and quiet bless him, but now he's wrapped his head around it, he's so excited. I thought I'd give him the night off, so I let him go out the other night." I let out a giggle at the thought that she had to "let" him go out. But it didn't surprise me in the least. Fi was the center of Everett's universe, even more so now they were expecting, and I knew he would be at her beck and call any time of the day.

"Oh bless him. Well, it was good of you to allow him to go out." I winked jokingly at her.

"Honestly, him and Leon came home absolutely trolleyed. They…" Her eyes went as wide as dinner plates as her brain caught up with her words. "Shit, sorry." We hadn't spoken about Leon since I'd been away, I'd asked for her not to bring it up. I needed to do this by myself, without anyone else's input, no bias or prejudices. Whatever I decided had to be *my* choice. Because of *my own* mind, thoughts and opinions.

I smiled softly at her. "Fi, it's fine don't worry about it. How um… how is he?" I hoped he was doing OK. I couldn't be selfish in this and just think about myself. I knew he was suffering too, albeit in a different way. No doubt he would be in his own personal hell; his own pit of torment at what he did. He'd appear strong and fine to everyone on the outside, but on the inside, he'd be battling with himself at the thought of losing me. Knowing that made my heart bleed. I loved him and I didn't want him to hurt. But just because I loved him doesn't mean it would be right to get back with him, especially when my mind was hung up on the past still.

"He misses you a lot. He calls or texts me every day for an update on you, asking if you're alright and are looking after yourself. Ev even caught him in a world of his own, playing with that hairband of yours he still has on his wrist." I felt myself grow warm inside. We weren't together and yet he was still checking in on me. I didn't mind that Fi had spoken to him and gave him a report on my well-being. I trusted her enough to know she wouldn't say anything other than that to him. He still cared and it felt like it was his way of trying to protect me from a distance.

"When they were out, some girl approached Leon, but he wasn't interested. He proper snapped at her too. Apparently, he had to be a bit forceful with her because she just wouldn't take the hint." My smile grew on my face without my giving it permission to. He was keeping to his word. He was waiting for me. He still wanted me. All sorts of scenarios played out in my mind at what Leon could have said or done.

In truth, I really was missing him too. The longer I was away from him, the more I missed him and the more I felt the withdrawal symptoms of his touch and presence. I missed waking up next to him, with his arms protectively circling me. I missed being cuddled up with him on the sofa as we watched some awful movie he had picked; he never had been good at choosing a decent one. I missed hearing his deep, infectious belly laugh that took up the entirety of his handsome, chiseled face, instantly filling the room. I had never felt so needed, wanted or special by anyone. But Leon had lit a flame that had long died out from inside of me, and I became alive again. While he once had made me the worst version of myself, he now brought out the best in me. The whole situation was contradictory and the more I thought about that, the more dizzy I felt from the whiplash.

"I think I'll be home soon. I haven't figured everything out yet, but my minds a lot more clearer than it was." Fi's eyes lit up with excitement as she let out a squeal and jiggled in her seat. I chuckled at her reaction. I loved when she would do this, she reminded me of a kid a Christmas and it was adorable.

Day by day, my anger towards him about the Stacey fiasco gradually ebbed away. Whilst I don't think that I had over-reacted, I did wish I had been stronger and not cried in front of him. But he needed to realise the severity of what he did. My brain had since cleared enough for me to look at the situation differently, from his point of view. We hadn't agreed to be exclusive at that point. We weren't even anything then, and that was mostly my fault for not wanting to put a label on us yet. But it still hurt that he had done it the day after our first time together and it made me question my ability at pleasuring him and that question hung over me like an ominous cloud, eating away at me for days.

As I processed what Leon told me had happened with my newfound open-minded brain, my anger towards Leon shifted fully onto Stacey. Not only had she gone out of her way to drive a wedge between me and Leon, but she had an inkling that Leon had a woman in his life, and yet she still had him do something she knew was immoral and would hurt not only Leon, but me too, no doubt me being her biggest target. I was very well aware of the fact that he had still gone along with the act, and although it was still bad, I somehow found comfort in the fact that he hadn't slept with her. He'd gotten rid of the problem to prevent anything like that from happening again, and while I had originally thought it was because he didn't trust himself around her, I instead thought it was due to protecting himself and his job. I could only imagine the uproar it would cause. His reputation he had worked so hard to build would be forever be tarnished for one mistake, and he didn't deserve that. Don't get me wrong, I was pissed that he had only transferred her rather than sack her, but he had a kind heart and it was one of the many things that I loved about him.

The past on the other hand was a difficult thing to get over and it would be the deciding factor on whether or not me and Leon would make another go of our relationship.

"I can't wait to see you A, me and bump miss you!" Fi spoke excitedly. I was about to tell her how much I missed them both too when her eyes averted to the top of her phone, reading a message notification at the top of her screen that made her face take on a sullen look, forcing me to stop what I was going to say.

"Fi. What's going on?" My tone was conservative and serious. I was baffled at how quickly her mood had changed. Looking back at me, Fi shifted uncomfortably in her seat and bit her lip, hesitant to tell me whatever was on her mind. She tucked her hair behind her ears and took a deep breath that came out with a slight shake to it. Her beautiful mossy eyes met mine through the screen, full of uneasiness.

"He came back A. He did it again." My eyebrows met in the middle as I dug into the depths of my brain, trying to think about who "he" was. I shook my head, annoyed at myself that I couldn't work out who she could be on about. My brain was on overload with all things Leon, that almost everything else was shoved into the furthest corner of my mind.

"Blake." Her one worded answer to my confused look was enough to instantly raise my blood pressure as my anger crashed down onto me like a tonne of bricks. I placed my phone down on the table next to me, my glass holding it upright and cracked my knuckles as if I was preparing myself for a fist fight. I was ready to spin Blakes jaw for whatever upset and hurt he had caused Fi.

"Tell me everything."

Chapter 43

I can't believe he'd come back again. His restraining order must have only just expired, because for a year, he had gone completely off the radar. Despite the terror he caused Fi, and it being his first offense, they let him off lightly, giving him a lenient punishment. The justice system really was fucked. Justice had not been served as they let him get away with just a slap on the wrist, and it enraged me still to this day – more so now that he'd emerged from the woodwork like the disgusting cockroach he is.

After Fi and Tyrone had split, she had been in a rough state. She'd discovered me from an advert I had hung on the notice-board in 'The Hub' and had given me a call. With my help, we began picking up the pieces and had rebuilt some of her confidence to a point where she started going on dates. One of these dates was with Blake.

After the date, he had invited her back to his, and she had told him that she just wasn't into him; there was no attraction to him. She was polite about it and was really apologetic, and he seemed to have understood. She hadn't realised that he had followed her home that night and from then on, it was only downhill from there.

I'd had no idea what was going on at the time. We weren't best friends then. Though we were friends, we was mostly client and personal trainer, and so her personal life was very much kept to herself. She had been her normal, peppy self around me. However, there was an instance where I had made a noise from behind her and she jumped ten foot into the air. That was the day she disclosed that she kept having the feeling that she was being watched. She would sometimes hear the odd floorboard creak in her flat in the middle of the night, as if there was someone walking around inside. She even said that she thought there were things being moved in her flat, but because it was something as trivial as the TV remote being moved from the arm of the sofa to the coffee table, she had put it down to her imagination.

The entire time she'd been telling me what was going on, she'd been physically shaking from fear with tears rolling down her cheeks. The poor girl was scared for her life. Her eyes glossed over, the film turning her beautiful orbs a dirty murky green, and her olive skin paled remarkably. I don't think I can recall a time ever seeing anyone as frightened as Fi was that day.

That night, I offered to stay at hers, just in case there really was something going on, but she was adamant that she would be fine. She seemed to have snapped out of her frightened demeanor and replaced it with a big fake smile. Her eyes gave her away though, as did her still trembling hands. So as a compromise, I made her promise to call me at any point of the day or night if she felt uneasy or scared. She seemed a little relieved that she'd finally told someone what was going on, and that I hadn't thought she was crazy. Her shoulders had dropped slightly, and the gloss had started to fade, the green of her eyes slowly resurfacing.

For a week, we texted back and forth with me checking in on her and making sure she felt safe. There were a handful of times when she had asked me to just come over to her place and sit with her for a bit, or to go for a walk to calm her down. However, come the second week of my knowing, I had a call at a stupid time in the morning. Fi could barely speak through petrification. All she had managed to get out was a shakily whispered "someone... here..." I reassured her that I was on my way and advised her to hide wherever possible.

I hadn't even bothered to get dressed. I remember jumping out of bed and chucking on some shoes before pelting it to Fi's flat in my pj's as fast as my little legs would go. Thankfully she didn't live too far from me then and I got there in ten minutes. Upon reaching her door, I noticed it was cracked open, meaning that there was in fact an intruder inside.

I'd called the police as I sprinted to Fi's. A bad feeling circulated in the pit of my stomach as anxiety swished and swirled like a washing machine as I thought about what I was going to find when I got to hers. I didn't know what I would walk in on, and the sooner proper help arrived, the better it would be for Fi.

It probably would've been wise to have waited for the police, but I just had to get to Fi; there was no way I was leaving her in danger. I slowly opened the door further, careful not to make a sound, and gingerly stepped inside. The building was eerily quiet. All of the lights were off, and her curtains were pulled shut, plunging the entire flat into bottomless darkness. I soundlessly made my way around the flat, checking every room for the intruder or for Fi. I hadn't come across anyone once I had checked the entire flat, leaving just her bedroom left to inspect. I'd just made it to her door, finding that it was slightly ajar, when I heard her piercing high-pitched scream, raising the hairs on my body straight stiff.

Wasting no time, I shoved the door open, flicking the light on as I ran inside her room. Fi was sat at the bottom of her wardrobe, which was acting as her hiding place, and looming over her was a slim man who I would later discover to be Blake. He was dressed head to toe in black and had light brown, wavy long hair that fell just below his ears. I gave him no time to react as flight or fight mode kicked in and I wrenched him away from Fi by the back of his top, flinging him down to the floor. Fi scrambled onto her bed and tucked herself into the corner of the wall, putting as big a distance between herself and Blake as possible, and pulled her duvet up so that just her fear-filled eyes were visible.

High on adrenaline, I made my way over to Blake, who had his back to me and trying to get back on his feet, but he had no such luck. I was so pumped, that I had found strength within me that I didn't know I had. I pushed him back down and he sprawled onto his stomach at the force of my foot on his back. With one hand pressing his head into the carpet fitted floor and another pulling one of his hands up his back, I pressed a knee into his back and restrained him. He hissed in pain underneath me as I pulled his arm further up his back. His free hand was slapping the floor next to me in an attempt to tap out.

"You crazy bitch, get the fuck off me!" He snarled through gritted teeth.

"The only crazy one here is you, you fucking creep." I dug my knee in harder and turned my head to Fi. Her silent tears dripped from her eyes, dampening the duvet underneath them. She was clutching the fabric for dear life, turning her knuckles paper white. Her knees were pulled tightly to her chest and it reminded me of the numerous times I had been in that very position at school; scared, defenceless and powerless.

"Are you OK Fi?" I spoke with concern, but my voice came out strong as the adrenaline pumped through my body. Her head twitched slightly in response, as the distant sound of sirens quickly made their way closer and closer to our location. Underneath me, the intruder wriggled and squirmed around, trying to break free of my vice-like grip but it was fruitless. He was no match for my temporary strength.

I looked back at Fi and saw her eyes soften slightly with relief, but the tears continued to pour. The sirens were deafening by now as a couple of police cars pulled up outside of Fi's place. Blake was still writhing underneath me, and it was beginning to piss me off.

"For the love of God, will you stop fucking moving? You aren't going anywhere." I snapped, applying a little more pressure to his body to prevent him from moving. I jerked my head towards the bedroom door as I heard heavy footsteps enter the building and an officer call out "Police!" to make us aware of their presence.

"In here!" I yelled, letting them know where we were. There was no way Fi would be able to call out, she was too terrified to speak still. Several footsteps pounded towards us as the officers hurried over. They took one look at the scene in front of them and they quickly took control of the situation.

Once a fighting Blake had been escorted out of the premises and into a police van, a female officer came and sat on the edge of Fi's bed. I was now sat with her, cuddling her into my shoulder with one arm around her, whilst holding her hand with my spare hand, as she found her voice, letting out loud sobs. The officer was so lovely and kind as she asked us both for a statement. She was incredibly patient with Fi, who by now had completely broken down as the realisation of what had just happened hit her like a tsunami.

From that day on, I worked hard with Fi to bring her confidence back up and to build her trust. She was petrified of going outside on her own and was even more scared of being in the flat on her own. She decided to move and so I helped in every way I could. She briefly lived with me once I'd kicked Felicity out for her infidelity, until she had found herself a new place. A year and a half later, she was the happiest I had ever seen her and she had met Everett, who turned out to be the best cure for her.

Back to the present day, after I had told her to tell me everything that had happened, she looked tentative to tell me. I was surprised that she hadn't told me beforehand and that she was only now telling me - especially because of how it was last time. The sun's rays were burning my skin by now, but for privacy of the conversation, I stayed outside; I didn't want mum to hear this.

My anger was still bubbling away under the surface of my skin, and I could feel a vein pulsate in my forehead at the thought of what Blake could have done this time. Playing with her fingers in her lap, Ffion looked down, unable to meet my eye as she began to tell me.

"Ev and I have spoken and decided that now it's over with, we can tell you and Leon what happened." I gave her an encouraging nod and she took a deep breath, building up her courage to relay the last couple of months to me.

"A little over two months ago, I started getting weird comments on some of my posts on Instagram from a profile that I don't follow. I had no idea who it was; the name was fake and the profile picture was just a standard shadow. I blocked the account and set my profile to private." I thought back and remembered seeing a comment with an account of that description on one of her pictures. The reply under one of her posts was something like *"Still as gorgeous as ever"*. While it seemed harmless, it was a little creepy coming from an unrecognisable account.

I shifted position leaning forward onto my knees, as Fi continued with her story.

"After that, whenever I was out on a run, I felt like I was being followed, but every time I looked over my shoulder, no one was there." The story was very similar to how Blake started stalking her the last time. The difference being they hadn't gone on a date and he had gone through her social media this time. I stayed silent, not wanting to interrupt her train of thought, just as she had done many a time for me with my current dilemma.

"After that, I thought it was best to tell Ev about Blake, and then I told him about what was now happening. I said that I wanted it to be kept between us for now, I didn't want to draw any more attention to the situation. Obviously, he wasn't very happy about it and he said about calling the police again. But I didn't want to because I wasn't sure if it was the same thing happening again."

I shook my head at her. I had stayed quiet so far, but I couldn't stay silent about her not going to the authorities about what had happened. Plus, I was disappointed she felt that she couldn't tell me what was going on.

"Fi, you should have listened to Everett and you should have come to me. What if you hadn't of been so lucky this time?" I knew it had been dealt with now, but the thought of something terrible happening to her was a disturbing image that sat on my mind, just as much as it had when I was the one to prevent it last time.

406

Fi let out a wistful sigh and brushed a hand through her wavy locks. "I know A, I know. But I'm OK, nothing bad happened."

Her ignorance and laissez-faire attitude towards this was infuriating. Did she seriously not realise the danger she was in? Everything she had just said should have rung alarm bells in her head – it was almost identical to the first time.

"That's not the point Fi. Something bad could have happened and me or Everett may not have been able to have got to you in time; not that it should ever even get to that point." My voice was snappy and raised a touch as I let my irritation known to Fi. Her previous experience should have been a lesson to her. She flicked her eyes down the floor again, she knew I wasn't impressed with her, and she was feeling sorry for herself.

"What was all that about back at your flat then, when you walked out on us?" I tried to control of the level in my voice. While I could be mad at her all I like, this was a serious subject, and what had happened couldn't be changed.

"Well, for days Ev had been getting messages and phone calls from a woman and I thought he was seeing someone behind my back. He would hide his phone from me so I couldn't see, but he wasn't quick enough. Whenever I questioned him, he would say it was no one and that I shouldn't worry about it." Both me and Leon had also thought it was a woman, and I had been ready to lose my shit at him that night for him making Fi react and feel the way she did.

"That night, I'd had enough of the secrecy and so I walked away from him. When he caught up with me, I gave him an ultimatum: tell me the truth or lose me." I felt my eyes stretch in surprise. I hadn't ever known Fi to be that forward with a guy, but good on her. Even with Tyrone she had let him walk all over her. She had grown into a strong woman who wasn't afraid to stand her ground in a relationship. I was proud of her for that, she'd come such a long way from the timid girl she once was.

"It turns out, the woman he had been in contact with was a private investigator who just so happened to be his cousin. He'd asked her to watch me and report anything suspicious. If it wasn't for him doing that, Blake wouldn't have been caught as soon as he was, and lord only knows what could've happened."

I let out a relieved breath. "Thank fuck for that. Honestly Fi, I was ready to raise hell with him that night." I was happy he wasn't being unfaithful; Fi deserved more respect than that. I'm glad Everett had taken matters into his own hands and protected Fi as best as he could – even if had meant going behind her back.

I looked into the screen and heard her lightly chuckle. "Oh, I know. Ev told me how you reacted once I left. I feel sorry for the boys, they've both been on the end of your wrath, and having seen it first-hand, I'm glad it hasn't been aimed at me; you're scary when you're all bent out of shape."

I laughed with her, feeling the anger leave my body. I wasn't mad at her. Disappointed? Yes, but never mad. I was mad that Blake was impertinent enough to come back and try it again, and I wished I had the opportunity to knock seven bells of shit out of him for the trauma he caused her, it was bad enough that I had to hold myself back when I caught him that first time. I wasn't a violent person, but I felt the need to protect Fi. She was like my little sister, and I always wanted to fight in her corner whenever she was in trouble. Perhaps it was because I never had anyone backing me when I needed it the most, that I felt this way.

Fi looked a lot lighter for telling me what she had been keeping for such a long time. She went on to tell me that Blake had a court date coming up in a few months, and until then he was to keep far away from Fi. There was a high possibility that he would end up in prison this time, and I hoped he would. He was a danger to society, and I didn't want any other female to feel scared to walk in the streets because of this sick man. It was about time justice was served and Fi could feel safe again.

"Anyway, Ev will be over soon, so I'll speak to you later." Fi rounded the conversation to an end. We had been talking for well over two hours and it was nice to hear her light voice – even if the conversation had taken a depressing route.

"Alright babes, loves ya."

"Loves ya too." She blew me a kiss through the phone, and I returned it before hanging up. That was one whirlwind of a conversation. I was a mishmash of emotions. I was in dismay that Fi hadn't told me what was going on, but at the same time, I was peeved with myself that I hadn't questioned the change in her behaviour back then. Whenever we ran together, she ran as close as possible next to me. Upon returning home, she would always let out a deep breath, which I now saw was her alleviating any feelings of stress and worry from being out in public. Furthermore, she had started locking her front door again whenever she was left alone. All of these little indicators were things I should have picked up on and questioned her about. It was one thing to be annoyed that Fi hadn't told me until now what had been happening, but I saw these small changes in her and I didn't ask her what was going on. And in my eyes, that made me a shit friend.

I ran my hands over my face as I let out an exasperated groan. The sun was unbearable now and my skin was so hot you could cook an egg on it. I pushed myself up off the sun lounger and made my way to the safety of the indoors, the cool air an instant relief.

I couldn't change what had happened to Fi, and I was happy she was safe, but I had even more reason to go home now. The sooner I figured out the last complication, the sooner I can get home and keep Fi and her baby safe.

Chapter 44

Ava's POV:

A little over a month had passed since I'd arrived at my mums, and though I had thoroughly enjoyed the time away, I was finally ready to go home. After much deliberation, I'd come to a decision. It hadn't been easy – I had a lot to consider. I spent my final couple of weeks taking my time to meticulously analyse my situation and to organise my thoughts. I wanted to be prepared when I came face to face with Leon.

After the chat I'd with Fi, I had asked her for complete isolation from her and everything else. She was only to contact me if something serious happened to her or the baby. I knew she was giving updates to Leon about how I was doing. I felt a little bad that I was putting a temporary stop to it, thrusting him further into the black hole of the unknown, but I needed a break from everyone. The home stretch was the most important part of this whole debacle and I needed to focus on that and nothing else. I'd been bombarded with drama after drama and it gave me no time or brain power to deal with my own. Despite the insatiable need to speak with Fi and check in on her daily, I knew the Blake situation was being dealt with and was under control. Plus, she had Everett for support, she didn't need me, not really. She'd come this far without me as it was, so I knew she would be fine.

Asides from our phone call, I hadn't spoken a word to mum and until today, Kelvin, about my situation. I knew they might try to sway my decision and I didn't want that. It wasn't their place. Yes, they were entitled to their own opinion, but when it came down to it, mine was all that mattered. They were understandably cautious about the possibility of me going back to Leon after what he did to me, more so because of the past, but they accepted that it was my choice if I so desired it. They could both see the difference in me since Leon had re-entered my life, and it had been a change for the better. As long as I was happy, they would support me whatever my decision.

I busied myself in my bedroom as I started to pack my suitcase. I felt a happy smile spread on my face as I thought about going home and finally having the stress lifted off my shoulders. It had been a long time coming, but I felt the lightest I had ever been. I had come to terms with my past and accepted it for what it was.

Coming back to where it had all started had absolutely been the right thing to do. It hadn't been a walk in the park, not by a long shot. I had to battle through panic attacks and nightmares for the first couple of weeks as I faced the worst part of my life. But it had all been worth it. I hadn't been able to heal, because I had spent ten years pretending that I wasn't hurt, pushing it all into the depths of my subconsciousness. Once I had ripped the band aid off and let it hit me all at once, I could begin the healing process. Once the past had been laid to rest, I could focus on Leon.

The thought of seeing Leon again made me feel both excited and nervous. For about two months now, all I had wanted was to see his full, beaming smile take over his face. I wanted to get lost in his eyes as they sparkled with love and happiness as he looked at me. I wanted to listen to his deep, harmonious voice as he sang along with me as I blasted my music through the apartment or in the car. I missed how simple things were with him. We could be ourselves around the other. There was no pretending to be someone we weren't and finding a person like that was hard to come by. I could let out my silly, childish side with him and he would join in, throwing caution to the wind.

Being away from him, from his loving touch and affective presence made my heart ache unbearably silently. You would think that by my constantly thinking of all the bad he had done to me, I wouldn't miss him. But it had the opposite effect – it only made me realise just how much I loved and missed his whole person; the good and the bad.

Waking up in the mornings without him had been hard, and I thought that they may get easier as time went on, but I was dearly mistaken. Every morning when I woke up, I'd imagine his deep sleepy "*Morning Sweetheart*" as I stirred from my slumber. He'd be looking down at me through sleep filled eyes with an adorable smile on his face that melted my insides. It was a scene I saw daily, and I wished to experience it in person again.

My hormones had been driving me crazy too. I missed his perfect nakedness overpowering me, dominating me in the ways only he had permission to. I ached for his warm, soft lips to devour me, exploring and rediscovering every inch of my skin. There were many times when I had been lost in thoughts of Leon when I would remember his skillful fingers coursing my body, making me shiver delightfully under his delicate, intimate touch.

My body tingled as I thought about him like this. The way we slotted together was like we were made for the other and I craved to be pieced together with him again. I'd fought with myself to not let my hormones control me. With my mind stronger than my body, I was able to think logically and realistically. It was all well and good missing Leon in sexual and non-sexual ways, and my whole being loved him with all it had to give. But it meant nothing if I was unable to forgive him for the past. As much as it would pain me, I wouldn't be able to be with him if I wasn't able to find peace and closure on what he did to me.

I hadn't just spent the last month thinking about forgiving Leon. I had to think about my future too. I'd spoken to Kelvin about him and mum and about their impending engagement. Their story made me realise just how two people sometimes needed to be apart for them to find their way back to one another. I'd always been a firm believer in everything happening for a reason, and me and Leon crossing paths again had a purpose. He was supposed to be in my life one way or another, and I truly wanted him in it. I tried picturing him being absent from my future, but it only made me feel daggers stab continuously at my heart as it pained me imagining him not by my side.

With my suitcase now packed, I heaved it off the bed, and made my way towards the stairs. Upon reaching the doorway, I half-turned, looking back into my temporary bedroom. The late afternoon sun had smothered the room with its vibrant orange light as its rays poured in through the windows. A content smile curved slightly on my face as I silently thanked the room for providing me the space I needed to get my thoughts in order. I turned away and made the descent down the steep stairs.

"You ready baby?" Mums voice was sad as she posed her question just as I reached the bottom of the stairs. She liked having me around, and as much as I enjoyed being here with her, I loved my independence too much. I placed my suitcase down by the front door and outstretched my arms, bending my fingers a couple of times as I beckoned her to come into my awaiting embrace. She shuffled into me and buried her head in the crook of my neck. Wrapping my arms tightly around her, I leaned my head against hers.

"I'll be back to visit soon mama." I spoke softly into her ear and flashed a wink over to Kelvin. He still had to propose to mum, but he was in the midst of planning it. He wanted me there when he did it, and so I would make a return when the time came. I pulled away from her and held her by her shoulders, looking at her with amusement.

"Anyway, you're taking me home! We've got two whole hours together still." Her eyes brightened and her beautiful smile crept onto her face. She really was radiant. I slung my arm around her shoulder, and we headed out to the car, with Kelvin following behind, pulling my suitcase with him.

I gave Kelvin a kiss on the cheek and a hug before I took my position in the front passenger seat. I pulled my sun visor down and swiped the little shutter across, exposing a small rectangular mirror. My crystal eyes were shimmering back at me, without a trace of uncertainty. I finally felt free. I had exorcised the demons of my past and now nothing could hold me back.

I brushed my nimble fingers through my now shortened hair with a relaxed smile on my face. I'd bit the bullet and had my hair chopped off to just below my shoulders to mark the end of an era. My head felt lighter at the absence of the extra weight and somehow, I now looked slightly older. Although I missed my long tresses, I welcomed my new change.

I loved this new me. I had been strong anyway, but I had

become even more so. Before, I'd just blocked out my past, locking it away safely in the deep caverns of my mind. But now, I had embraced it and let it consume me, before putting it to rest. My mental well-being was in prime condition for the first time in over a decade, and I was supremely proud of myself for being able to put myself through all of that mental torment and come out of it victorious, and all on my own too.

Mum slid into the driver's seat next to me, turning the engine on as she buckled up. "Are you sure you're ready sweetheart?" She turned to face me, a hand on the steering wheel, the other on the gearstick.

"As ready as I'll ever be." I smiled fully at her and she returned it, pride waving in her eyes. She pulled out of the driveway and headed in the direction of my home. I pulled my phone out of my bag and opened my photos. Even though I'd asked Fi not to contact me for a while, she had sent me only one message, and that was the picture that I couldn't stop looking at. It was a picture that had been taken by a professional photographer from the Ball before shit had hit the fan. Me and Leon were stood by the exquisite Victorian bar in each other's' arms. My small hands looked minuscule on his broad chest as I tipped my head back, laughing at something he said. He had his hands around my waist, hugging me close to him as he looked down affectionately at me with his warm amber eyes glistening in the light and a soft, adoring smile carved on his strong face. It was my favourite photo of us, and although that day came with some bad memories, it also reminded me of how we were together and of all of the good times we shared. Coming out of the app, I went into my messages and sent a message to the people waiting for me at home. Filled with satisfaction and excitement, I put my phone away and turned the radio up, singing at the top of my lungs with mum to "*Domino*" by Jessie J.

* * *

Leon's POV:

The park had become my favourite place to wind down – I could see why Ava loved coming here. It was remarkably picturesque in the summer. The trees rustled therapeutically in the slight breeze that gently blew, bringing the temperature down to a moderate, comfortable climate. Despite the thickness of the greenery, the sunlight still managed to pierce through the branches, creating little spotlights amongst the blanket of shadows cast by the luscious leaves.

My arms stretched along the length of the back of the bench I was seated at and I dropped my head back and closed my eyes, soaking in the rays. My other senses awakened as I focused on my surroundings, further calming my mind. Straining my hearing, I could hear the melodic singsong of birds as they sung their song to the world, impervious to the fact that only they could understand their language. My nostrils flared as it welcomed the delightful smell of fresh grass and sun cream that permeated the air. To my left, I could hear the happy, infectious giggles of children as they ran amock in their paradise of freedom, releasing all of their pent-up energy. To my right, I could hear the soft splashing sound of water as ducks dove under the cooling surface of the pristine, pacific pond.

I opened my eyes and glanced up at the unobstructed sky through the protective purple tint of my glasses. The last five weeks without Ava had been trying. For the first two, I had been thrown into a pit of depression and despair, and I had felt sorry for myself. When I wasn't burying myself in work, I was in bed dreaming about Ava and what could have been if things had been different. I had completely surrendered myself to the possibility that it was it for us, she wouldn't come back for me.

But my night out with Ev had been the kick up the backside I needed to get my shit together. I couldn't mope around. I didn't want her to come home and find me a miserable, pathetic mess. I wanted her to come home to a new and improved Leon. One she would be proud to have by her side. She deserved someone who could make her otherworldly happy, someone who she could put all her trust into without fear of being hurt, and someone who would give their all to give her the life she so absolutely deserved. And I desperately wanted to be that someone. And so, the remaining three weeks were spent working on myself.

Despite working on climbing out of my depressed hole, my heart still felt like it had a hand squeezing it as I missed her. Whether I was in a momentary lapse of sadness or fighting my way to greatness, she was always at the forefront of my mind. It didn't matter that she physically wasn't here; in my mind, she was my biggest supporter, encouraging me to persist, to keep building myself into a better man. To be the deserving man for her.

It was a true testament to my willpower and dedication to change for the better when Ffion told me that Ava no longer wanted contact from her. At first, I felt crushed that I had lost my only connection to Ava, to the only way that I could know she was OK. But after a few days of feeling disgruntled and downhearted, I decided to use this to my advantage. This was another chance to prove that I could give her the space she needed. That I didn't need to check on her every day. That I could trust that she could look after herself and not do something drastic.

My phone dinged in my pocket, pulling me out of my thoughts. I rooted around my person for my device, before I found it in the inside pocket of my blazer. I sat bolt upright, and my heart started to pound in my chest, fighting its way out of the confines of my ribcage.

A: I'm coming home.

I didn't know how to feel. Despite the summer heat, I was frozen, starring at the ambiguous words that were printed on the screen. There was no hint as to what she was feeling, no hint as to what her decision was. I had no choice but to wait until the time came when I saw her again. The anticipation was too much to bear, and the deathly tight grip of the imaginary hand had found its way back around my heart. I hadn't had a panic attack since my phone call with Ava all those weeks ago, and I couldn't understand why one was coming on now. But what I did know, was that I wasn't about to have it out here in public.

I briskly made my way back to my office, trying to control my increasingly ragged breath as I kept my head low, preventing anyone from seeing what was going on in my mind. The second I reached my floor in the building, I picked up the pace and stormed past a confused Ffion. I slammed the door behind me and made my way to my desk. With my hands gripping the edge of the cool, metal surface, I screwed my eyes shut and took deep breaths and exhaled slowly.

Breathing in through my nose and out of my mouth wasn't working. I needed Ava to calm me just like I had with her so many times. I took the position of having a hand on my heart and envisioned Ava again, pretending that it was her hand, just like I had that time on my balcony. I thought about the soothing vanilla scent of her hair as I buried my nose in it. I thought about the feel of her soft, smooth skin under my huge hands. I thought about getting lost in those beautiful, crystal clear orbs of hers. Gradually, my breathing was starting to regulate, but I wasn't quite there yet. I'd been so busy focusing on my breathing, I hadn't heard Ffion enter my office. Nor had I been able to sense her presence as she stood next to me. She placed a hand on my shoulder, making me aware that she was here with me.

"Leon, what's wrong?" Her voice was full of concern. I was embarrassed that she was seeing me in this weak state, but more so, I felt bad that she was dealing with me. She didn't need this added stress, not while she was in the condition she was in. I couldn't look her in the face and so I turned my head, my eyes focusing on the gentle curve of her ever-growing belly.

"She's... coming... home." I spoke through my breaths, struggling to get my words out. I could feel the excitement radiate off Ffion, but it quickly died out and was replaced with sympathy and consolation. She knew what this meant.

I should have been excited at the knowledge that my girl was coming home, but that wasn't all I was feeling. I was scared. Scared to be rejected by her. Scared she had decided I wasn't worthy of redemption or forgiveness. The love I held for her was immeasurable and I don't think my heart could take her walking away from me forever.

She had made her decision. My fate had been decided.

46

Chapter 45

The second my front door shut behind me, I closed my eyes as I was instantly greeted by the pleasant, sweet smell of home as it wrapped around me in a welcoming embrace. Deflating my lungs as I expelled the wasteful air from my body, I popped my eyes open and took in my apartment. It looked exactly the way I had left it. Fi had done a good job in watching over it for me; she'd even replaced my lilies that decorated my entrance way. I smiled at her thoughtfulness and walked further in. My blinds were pulled up, allowing the afternoon sun to flood in, coating the entire space in a mellow orange light. All of my windows were cracked open slightly, granting the cool summer breeze access to sweep through the area, bringing with it the plethora of summer scents.

I left my suitcase in the living room and hurried to the one household item I had missed the most. I leaped onto my bed, landing on my back in a starfish, bobbing gently as the springs underneath me bounced under my weight. The way I felt about being back home must be what it's like for a tortoise when it retracts into its shell; safe in the sanctuary of its cocoon, protected from the troubles of the world on the outside. There was nothing like your own bed.

With my eyes gently pressed shut, blocking out the bright light that beamed through the window, I focused on the familiar sounds that had serenaded me numerous times. The soft wind outside was teasingly blowing through the leaves of the trees, making them gently ripple under its taunting touch. The distant clock was still tick-tocking periodically, tempting me to gracefully slip into a peaceful sleep. I grazed my fingers over the cool silky fabric underneath me and felt myself sink further into the irresistibly inviting cloud that I was seemingly floating on. A satisfied moan rumbled in the back of my throat as I gave into the familiar comfort. It felt good being back home. I hadn't realised just how much I'd missed being here. But then, the only thing I had consciously been missing was Leon. Sure, I had been missing Fi and even Everett and Sam. But my mind had been mostly jam-packed with Leon.

Once again, my mind had fallen onto its recent favourite topic. Whilst I was away, I had thought about what was stopping me from going back to Leon. The only obstacle I could come up with was the past, and the more I thought about it, the more I realised that that was all it was. The past. It had happened. It was done. There was no going back and re-writing it. I could forgive, but that doesn't mean that I can forget, because that would mean not being who I am now.

Every hardship I had endured had paved the way of my destiny. Leon had inadvertently changed the course of my life, putting the Butterfly Effect into practice and had made me the person I am today, from his actions both then and now.

When it came down to it, it was about perspective, and I had chosen to look at my situation in a different light. Where

I once buried it, fearful of speaking or thinking about it, I chose to embrace my past. I shouldn't be scared to talk about it. I shouldn't be scared to revisit it and think of all that had happened. What I should be, was proud. I had overcome all of that and came out the other end a survivor, a fighter. It could have thrown me fully off the deep end, into a bottomless, woeful pit of despondency. But I'd used it to my advantage.

I didn't want to live my life in constant fear and trepidation, I didn't want it to control me and my life. My future was in my hands, and I wanted to make the best out of it with use of my past and experience as my motivator. I have helped so many women to get back onto their feet and evolve into incredibly strong and confident individuals, and it's all thanks to my past.

Leon had completely changed his life and had worked hard not just *for* me, but *because of* me. The pair of us had affected the others life unknowingly. We both wanted to be better people, to help others from feeling the same pain I had felt, and that held a dear, special place in my heart. He'd had no idea that we would ever meet again, and yet he still devoted his life to helping to change the lives of others. I couldn't ignore the effort he had made for the last ten years in trying to somewhat remedy the evil he had created.

I had met someone who understood my story in a way no other person could. Granted, he was one of the main antagonists in it, but because he had lived it alongside me, he knew how detrimental his actions and words had been and so he wanted to protect me; he didn't want to see me suffer that same pain again.

I arched my pelvis up, creating a perfectly curved bridge with my midsection and reached under me to the back pocket of my jeans. Feeling the rectangular shape, I inserted the tips of my thumb and finger in the soft slit of fabric and slid my phone out. Simultaneously, I brought the device in front of my face as I stretched my legs out towards the end of the bed, plopping my backside back down, resuming my relaxed position.

My notifications showed that Fi and Everett had messaged me back, but there was nothing from Leon. I wasn't too sure what to make of his lack of reply. I'd told him that I was coming home. Surely, he'd be bouncing off the walls at my return? Had he stopped missing me? Had he stopped fighting for us? I really had put him through hell the past two months, and although it was justifiable, I could only imagine how it must have affected him. I'd been gone for some time and had taken my time coming to a decision, that I wouldn't be surprised if he had grown bored of waiting and had given up all hope of me taking him back. I mean, I have every reason not to and I would be well within my rights to call it quits. But I didn't want to. I needed him in my life, even if it meant as a friend. He kept me grounded and focused, and I had learnt what its truly like to love and be loved. When it's the right person, everything just falls effortlessly into place. My eyes had been opened and the world was a much brighter place with him by my side.

In school, he had been my hardest hello and my favourite goodbye. But now the narrative was switched. I loved seeing him and having him close to me, and I hated when he wasn't around. These past two months of not being around him, not hearing his penetrative deep voice and not seeing his perfect, handsome face made me feel like a summer in drought, yearning for just a drop of refreshing, revitalising water.

I was going to wait until tomorrow, but I had been away from him for too long and knowing he was so much closer to me made it even harder to resist seeing him. I found his name in my messages list and sent out a text to him.

A: Come over after work? We need to talk.

I was about to lock my phone when three little dots flashed on the screen, twinkling individually as they informed me that he was typing back. I watched and waited, impatience building up in my body as they disappeared and reappeared a few times as he typed and deleted his message before starting afresh. A minute or so later, my phone made a bloop sound as the grey, stumpy oval popped up suddenly underneath my blue one.

L: Sure, see you soon.

It was such a simple reply, but it was confirmation that I would be seeing him sooner than I had anticipated. Just like I knew he wouldn't be able to read my thoughts or feelings through my messages, I couldn't decipher what was going through his mind from his reply. I hoped he would be happy to see me. I hoped he had kept to his promise and had waited for me.

I moved into a sitting up position with my legs over the edge of my bed, elbows pressed onto my knees and my forehead being supported by my suddenly clammy hands. A swarm of butterflies fluttered in a disorderly fashion in my stomach as the realisation that Leon would be here in just a couple of hours hit me full force. I couldn't make out if I was nervous or excited about it, but whatever it was made me feel the need to go for a run. I needed to clear my head of thoughts about how much I had missed him and get in a stronger mind-set for the talk I needed to have with Leon.

With a slap on my thighs, I heaved myself up and headed towards my wardrobe, flinging the doors open. I puffed my cheeks out as I browsed the selection of clothing in front of me, letting the air escape through the tiny hole of my slightly parted lips. I settled on some loose black running shorts and a tight-fitting sports bra, with a light and flowy tank top layered over top.

After a quick warm up and stretch, I securely strapped my phone to my bicep and inserted my earphones snuggly in the crevices on either side of my face. Deafened by the rhythmic beats pounding through my skull, I headed out.

With my feet thumping the ground in a constant, steady momentum, I could feel my whole body working as my limbs started to warm and my heart pounded rapidly in my chest as it worked to pump fresh oxygen around my being. I had neglected my fitness slightly whilst I was away, and it was invigorating to feel the ground under my feet again and the gradual burn in my calves.

I was focused solely on the music that blared in my ears as I took in the familiar landscape around me; the thoughts of Leon were shoved temporarily out of my mind. I lived in such a beautiful town and being away from it made me realise how much I took that for granted. The sky was void of any clouds, with only the occasional aeroplane painting white bleeding streaks along the multicoloured canvas. I usually took my runs in the morning, and so I never got the opportunity to appreciate the beauty of the late day scenery of where I resided. The distant city buildings stood tall and proud against the backdrop, providing the perfect hiding place for the sun, allowing only its never-ending rays to claw up the backs of the concrete jungle in a desperate attempt to remain visible as the immortal lightbulb took its leave for the day.

My route took me past 'The Hub', and whilst my veins were crying out for the succulent taste of caffeine to rip its way through my system, there was a chance I would see Sam. As much as I wanted to see him, I wanted the first person to see me since returning home to be Leon. Everyone else came second to him at this moment in time.

Beads of sweat had transpired along my hairline, and a few had begun to roll down my face. A thin film of wetness coated my body, glistening in the slowly fading light as the heat added to my perspiration levels. My lungs were starting to scream out at me at the starvation of oxygen and I could feel my breathing become more laboured, but I powered on, enjoying the rush of endorphins that flooded my body.

Soon enough, I had made it back home, with an hour to spare before Leon would come over for our long-awaited discussion. My first port of call was the kitchen. I filled a clean glass up with cool water, my fingers sliding slightly on the glass as condensation set in, but soon adjusting and regaining their grip. I downed the lot before filling it up for a second time with a numbness that flashed instantly in my head at the sudden introduction of a cool substance against my internal warmness. I added a couple of ice cubes and took my second drink slower, relishing in the feeling of the cold liquid streaming down to my stomach, quenching my parched state. Once the glass was completely drained, I poured the almost molten ice cubes into my mouth, holding them between my molars and crunched down, feeling the solid melt further into a gradually warming pool in my mouth.

Satisfied that I was adequately satiated, I leisurely moved to the bathroom. I turned the shower on for the first time in over a month and waited as the pipes groaned at the wake-up call, spluttering out water in a chaotic way before calming down to its normal flow. Whilst I waited for the water to be at its coldest temperature, I stripped out of my sticky gym clothes. A chill began to consume the enclosed room, indicating that the water was ice cold. I gingerly pointed my toe into the water, flinching at the sudden impact of the freezing water making contact with my skin. With a deep breath to brace myself, I submerged myself completely under the Arctic-like waterfall as the paralyzing water violently dispersed from the shower head. The bathroom was silent, with only the sound of water echoing through the room as it drummed on me, before silently cascading its way in rivers down my naked physique, and my chattering teeth.

As much as I loved the hellish heat of water when I showered, it was a nice change to have a cold shower. The heat when I ran had been slightly unbearable as my body had grown unaccustomed to physical activity in the heat through my slacking in exercising. My limbs were delightfully numb as the icy water deeply penetrated my muscles, relieving them of the ache I had acquired from my run. For the first time in days, I was alone in my head. It was an empty space as I just lived for the moment, enjoying the simple, basic human need of taking a shower.

When my legs had grown too numb to barely keep me up, I cut off the water supply and exited the shower booth before wrapping a towel around me. I glanced in the mirror as I walked out, only to do a double take. I stared at the reflection in front of me. I look refreshed, awake and almost not like me. Before this, I had been happy and felt like "myself", but after this charade, I was the most "me" I had ever been. I was free and felt like I truly was the epitome of happy; the final thing I needed to complete that was to tell Leon of my decision. It was the final burden that weighed on my chest, and I wasn't too sure how he'd take it. I hoped he understood my choice.

Now in the depths of my wardrobe, I pulled out a matching loungewear set that consisted of some jersey shorts and a cropped hoody. With some clean underwear and bralette on, I clothed myself in the chosen items and walked to the living room, tying the drawstring of the shorts as I did so. My eyes fell on my suitcase that was still by the door and I cursed under my breath to myself. I really couldn't be bothered to go through it and sort it all out, and so I dragged it into my bedroom and left it on the floor at the foot of the bed. I'll deal with that later.

I returned to the living room and seated myself down on my plush sofa, turning the TV on as I sunk into the soft cushion. I aimlessly flicked through the channels, but my mind couldn't focus. It was edging closer and closer to the time when Leon would be here, and my nerves were slowly creeping back. My knees were bouncing wildly as I stared at the wide screen, chewing away at the insides of my cheeks as I kept checking the time. I didn't know why I was so nervous to see him again. There was something about him being near me that made my body jolt awake and respond to him, and I couldn't stop myself from reacting in the way it did whenever his eyes fell on me.

I was ripped out of my own head when a loud knock came from the outside of my front door. Leon was here. I pressed the red button at the top of the elongated remote, turning the TV off - there was to be no distractions during our talk. In an attempt to calm and prepare myself, I took a deep breath as I pulled myself up and slowly made my way towards the front door. I wrapped my nimble fingers around the metal curve of the handle for a few seconds, rattling the metal object in my grip as my hand started to tremble. This was it. The time was nigh.

With a resolute nod as I let out a quick, forceful blow of air out of my pursed lips, I turned the door handle down and cautiously opened the door wide, unveiling an uncharacteristically anxious Leon.

Chapter 46

<u>Leon's POV:</u>

I had no idea what to think about Ava's text earlier. It was a simple question, asking me to go over so that we could talk. So why had my brain made it so complicated that I struggled to get out a decent response? I'd come across blunt and a little rude, when in reality I was optimistic at seeing her. Once my panic had subsided with the help of Fi, I remembered what I had spent two months doing. I hadn't worked hard to change for her just for it to fall flat. It was time to show her that I was a man worthy of her forgiveness and a second chance.

I gave Ffion a lift home after work, and I used the journey as an opportunity to ask her for some advice. She knew Ava better than anyone, and although she didn't know what her decision was, I thought she might be able to help me prepare for whatever I was going to be hit with.

"So... How do you think this will go?" I gave her a quick side glance as I asked, taking my eyes off the road for only a split second. I knew what to expect from Ffion, it would be an honest yet ruthless reply, and while I wanted to hear her opinion, I was scared a little to hear it.

She didn't miss a beat in replying to my question. "Look, you've just got to suck it up and be a man about it. It's going to hurt you big time if she says she doesn't want to be with you, but you fucked up. It's her decision and you need to respect whatever that may be." My heart had started to crumble when Ffion had said that. Her and Ev were almost the same person. They were both brutal with their responses and while it was hard to hear, sometimes it was necessary.

Fi had shifted in the passenger seat, resting her elbow on the window ridge, smushing her cheek up as she rested on her palm whilst stroking her growing belly in rhythmic circles with her other hand. It was still light outside and the sun shone in her meadow-green eyes, glistening as she was deep in thought.

"That being said, none of us know what's going on in that pretty little head of hers. She might just surprise us all and take you back, and if that's the case, then you need to take things slow with her. You can't just jump straight back in where you left off. Things aren't the same now, and neither one of you are the same as you were before." This was very true. Things couldn't go back to the way they were. Although I'd thought we had been a great match and our relationship had been perfect, there were changes that now had to be made for it to truly flourish. We had to adapt to one another again as both of us had developed into improved versions of ourselves. In all honesty, I was slightly worried that Ava had changed so drastically that she wouldn't want me anymore.

Once Ffion was dropped off, I was left with just my own thoughts. I didn't really know what I would say to Ava. I had no clue where any of this was heading, except it was going to be one of two ways. Either way, I knew for certain that it'll end in tears.

The rest of the short drive home was spent with me trying to remain calm but preparing for the worst. At least then maybe I wouldn't be as crushed when she told me there was no future for us. Normally, I enjoyed the views that flashed by as I drove home from work, but not even they could silence my resounding musings that rallied around inside my head.

By the time I found myself outside her door, I was a nervous wreck, my optimism slowly fading away. My hands were shaking uncontrollably, and my heart was on the brink of collapsing through exhaustion as it pounded furiously in my chest. I knocked a little too loudly on her door as I lost control of my hands. Whilst waiting for her to come to the door, I fought the urge to bite my nails and instead loosened my tie from around my neck with trembling, clammy hands.

My eyes were drawn to the elegant silver door handle, as the metal rattled slightly under an illusory hand. After a few seconds, the shaking stopped and the handle was turned down, revealing someone who looked like Ava, but at the same time didn't. The gorgeous woman that stood in front of me had blonde hair that only just completely fell over her curved breasts, and she had an air of confidence and determination about her. Her shoulders were set naturally, free of any stress or tension, and the frown that had resided on her perfect small face for days had disappeared. Her features were mesmerizing as always, her eyes were a sparkling ice blue, framed by thick, fluttery eyelashes. Her full, rouge lips were set in a half, almost uncertain smile. Despite her aura, her eyes, as usual, were a window into her mind and gave away her true feelings. She was as anxious and nervous about this as I was.

She pulled the door wider and held her arm out to the side, silently inviting me in as neither one of us said a word. I stepped in and I heard her bare feet softly slap the floor as she followed me into her apartment. Her apartment was unchanged and looked like she had never left. The kitchen sparkled in what remained of the suns light and there was not a speck of dust in sight. I knew this was down to Ffion and her daily visits to make sure the house was in pristine condition, ready for whenever Ava would return home.

I sunk into her sofa and instantly felt slightly calmer. Her homely scent wafted gently into my nose, infiltrating my senses. I hadn't smelt her in a while, and just a whiff was enough to slightly calm my racing heart. I hadn't felt this at ease since she had put some distance between us, and it only confirmed what I had thought before. She was my home. She was my comfort and if I lose her now, I don't know what I'll do.

She sat herself down lightly next to me, and I turned my body to face her. She was looking down at her petite hands that were rubbing together in her bouncing lap. A blonde waterfall cascaded down the sides of her face in a curtain, partially hiding her face from me. She was biting her lower lip as she was deep in thought, thinking about where to go from here. A leaden silence hung in the air, growing thicker with each passing moment. Neither one of us knew what to say, let alone where to start. I shuffled in my seat, moving into a leaning position, resting my forearms on my thighs and clasping my hands together, before clearing my throat to start the dreaded conversation. But before I could even get a word out, she held up her dainty index finger, shutting me down instantly. A soft sigh blew out from her pouting lips, before her crystalline orbs rose up, meeting my own. They swirled with resolve as confidence slowly began to build inside them. It was a good, sexy look on Ava, but it made me feel uneasy. Was she building confidence in turning me down?

"I'm sorry Leon. I'm sorry for making you wait this long." She sounded sad and genuinely apologetic for making me wait for her, and her eyes had found their way back into her lap momentarily.

I shook my head with a slight frown on my face. "You have nothing to apologise for. I'm the one at fault for everything; it should be me apologising, not you." My voice was strong as I spoke to her. As far as I was concerned, she had no reason to apologise; she had every right to take all the time in the world to get her mind straight. I was the only person who had anything to be sorry about. Her eyes snapped back up to mine and she looked shocked for a second, before she nodded singularly in agreement.

"Besides, I told you I would wait for you for as long as it took, and I meant that with all of my heart." My voice was lowered, taking on a sombre tone. Our eyes never left the other, and I tried my hardest to convey how sincere I was. Her eyes started to shimmer as they slowly began to fill with warm liquid. In an attempt to prevent the tears from spilling onto her supple skin, she tilted her head up to the ceiling and closed her eyes. Her lashes fluttered lightly on her cheeks as she tried to control her emotions.

"You really hurt me, Leon." Her voice was wobbling slightly as she recounted the pain I had caused her, and it pulled on my heartstrings. I already wasn't liking the way this was going but I couldn't break just yet. I remained silent, allowing for her to let everything out. This was her time to lay everything out on the table.

"I spent years forgetting about you so that I could live a normal life without the constant reminder of what you did to me. How could someone I loved, and supposedly loved me, hurt me like that?" My heart stopped at her use of the past tense 'loved'. I knew she was talking about our feelings for each other in the past, but it felt like she was talking about now. Had she stopped loving me? Thinking back, I don't think I had ever stopped loving her. Every woman that had ever made a pit stop in my life never had me feeling the way she made me feel. I have never imagined a future with anyone besides her. In fact, the thought of settling down with someone had repulsed me. Until Ava.

She slowly brought her head down and turned it towards me, meeting my sorrowful gaze. Sadness swirled in her eyes as she recalled the past, with her lashes damp from the tears she had tried to stop from spilling. She had been strong for so long and now that she had the opportunity to vocalise her bottled up thoughts, to get everything out into the open, all of her pent-up emotions had broken the dam she had built in her mind and gushed urgently out of her.

"You know, I used to wish that I could hurt you the way you hurt me. Just so that maybe you could understand and see what those horrific two years of torment was like for me. But I could never do that to you. That was the difference between us back then." Despite the sadness in her eyes, her voice was slowly getting more stable. She was beginning to regain control of her emotions. She slid herself into the corner of the sofa and leaned against the arm of the furniture, crossing her legs as she fully faced me.

She could dish out whatever punishment she saw fit for me, because Lord knows I deserved it. I had crushed her heart and soul and it had taken her nine years to piece it back together, just for me to come back into her life and pick at the cracks that remained. I could only imagine what long term damage I had caused, and I knew that no matter how hard she worked to "get over" it, it would stay with her forever, and being with me would only be a constant reminder of her harrowing teen years.

"I truly am sorry Ava. I hate myself every day for what I did to you, both then and now and if I could go back and change it, I would in a heartbeat." My eyes never left hers. I wanted her to know how serious I was being, that every word that would come out of my mouth would be the truth, the whole truth, and nothing but the truth. She closed her eyes and took a deep, preparatory sigh.

"But you can't. What's done is done and there's no going back from that. I'm physically scarred from that time of my life, and I will probably always be mentally scarred too." She was abnormally composed. Her sadness had dissipated and had been replaced with her newfound confidence and courage. It was admirable, but my heart was gradually making its way out of my arsehole. This was not going the way I had hoped. My hands resumed their quivering state as I dipped my head down, staring into endless nothingness. There was a growing sting in the back of my eyes as I fought to hold back my tears.

"Then there's Stacey. You went behind my back without a second thought about how I would feel if and when I would find out. I felt like I wasn't good enough for you, that I meant jack shit to you. You had literally just given me a key to your house. That very same day. How would you feel if the shoe was on the other foot?" My head fell deeper towards my chest in shame. She was right. In the heat of the moment, I had completely forgotten about her. I had been disgusted with myself as soon as what happened was over, but now I was revolted by my behaviour and deeply ashamed of myself. I had long put that lifestyle behind me, and yet I had reverted momentarily back to my old ways. I should've had better control of myself, and it made me sick that I had given in and touched Stacey so intimately. Ava was the center of my universe and I had gone and done that the day after I had finally become one with her.

The tears I had tried so hard to hold back had broken the barriers of my lids and plummeted straight down into my lap. My heart squeezed in my chest and a pain ripped through me like a wildfire, spreading across the entirety of my chest. One of my hands had found its way to my chest as I gripped my shirt, trying to reach into myself to stop my heart from cramping, while the other had a tight grip on my thigh.

I felt the cushions underneath me inflate briefly as a weight moved closer to me. Ava's delicate hands wrapped around my one that was holding on for dear life at my chest and she tenderly pulled my hand away from me, forcing me to lose my grip on my shirt. I blurrily looked up to her, my tears disfiguring my vision with my brows magnetised together in confusion. Her expression had changed. Her eyes were warm and was paired with a soft smile.

"Call me foolish, but I forgive you."

* * *

Ava's POV:

He was breaking in front of me, and it tore my heart seeing him like this. Whether or not he had it coming, I loved him and I couldn't deny my feelings any longer. It pained me seeing him like this, and yet I couldn't help feeling that seeing him cry was an honour. He was man enough to let out how he was feeling, and I felt privileged that he trusted me to see this vulnerable side to him.

His tears meant that he really did care about me. He had barely said a word while I had divulged a segment of my feelings to him, and I appreciated that he let me get it out. I tried so hard to keep it together, to stay strong, but the sincerity in his reminder that he would wait for me and the honesty that radiated out of his eyes was like a jackhammer to my emotional barrier.

His hands wrapped in mine, I caressed my thumb over his somewhat dry hands. He wasn't expecting me to forgive him and if I was being completely honest, at the start of this all I had no intention of it. But rash decisions are not best made on emotion alone.

The days remaining light trickled in through my windows, gradually disappearing as time went on. But the light that had faintly saturated the room shone in his glistening, swimming eyes. His beautiful amber orbs were looking back and forth between my own, checking to see the truth behind my words.

Everyone is capable of being toxic. But there were two types of toxic people: those that knew exactly what they were doing and didn't give a second thought to those they hurt. And those who realise what they're doing, take accountability for their actions and make the necessary changes to better themselves. And Leon had taken the latter route.

"I am who I am today because of you. I'm a better person for going through all the shit you put me through. Granted it wasn't in the nicest way, and although it will stay with me forever, I can still find it in my heart to forgive you. I can see the changed man you've become because of me, and I respect you deeply for it. Someone who wasn't regretful or remorseful of their actions wouldn't do that, and to me, it proves just how truly sorry you are." His sniffs were becoming more regular, but the tears were beginning to falter their dripping from his eyes.

"I'm prepared to give things another shot with you, but we can't jump feet first into it. You broke my trust once, and while I'd like to think you wouldn't do it again, you need to prove that I can trust you wholeheartedly." His eyes had stopped wandering about my face and had paused at my own once again. His hands were no longer shaking under mine and his shoulders relaxed, the tension melting away from him. The dark shadow that had glazed over his eyes disappeared, and was replaced with a light of hope, as they rounded out in surprise before resuming their natural stance.

"Ava. I swear to you that I will spend the rest of my life fighting for you and proving to you just how worthy I am of your love and trust. I won't ever hurt you again, I couldn't. I love you too much and my heart wouldn't be able to take you leaving again." Despite the tears that had now slowed down to a snails-pace, his voice was strong and clear. He meant everything that had just come out of his delicious mouth. I took a hand and placed it on the side of his face, attempting to wipe some of the tears away, only to spread them along his face even more. His eyes were rimmed red and had begun to get a little puffy, and his face was slowly becoming more tear stained as the wetness dried naturally.

"I love you too Leon, more than I ever thought possible. Just don't let me regret this second chance I'm giving you." My voice was stern and soft, indicating to Leon that this was it. This was the last crack of the whip and if he fucked up again, there's no going back.

His thick hand had made its way onto my cheek, mirroring the hold I had on him. He had a growing grin on his face, his eyes beaming with sheer happiness. With a gentle shake of his head, his deep voice whispered into my ears as he spoke earnestly and lowly, his head inching slowly closer to mine. "You're always at the forefront of my mind. I always get lost thinking about your smile..." Our lips met for the first time in a long time and the spark that I had so deeply missed and craved zapped life back into me. The kiss lasted only a few seconds when he pulled away, with barely a breath apart between our lips.

"... the way your eyes look at me with adoration..." He pulled away a little further from me as he watched his hand on my face move from my skin, leaving a cold air where his hand was, to tuck my falling hair behind my ear. With my hair secured in the small crevice of my ear, he replaced his hand back to my face, reigniting the warmth underneath it and leaned his forehead against mine, staring deeply into my eyes. Love and happiness emanated from his pale honey eyes, pulling me in and trapping me in their sticky grip.

"It's you baby. It's always been you. You complete me in a way nobody else can and I promise you this now, I will never hurt you; I won't ever give you a reason to regret this. To regret us." I felt it in my very core the truthfulness behind his words, and my smile took over my face as a tear of joy appeared unannounced and rolled down my face. We both stared at each other, smiling like love-struck idiots, tears gently trickling down our cheeks.

When we first originally got together, I was excited to see where things would take us. But now, it felt different. It felt better. It felt *right*. We fully understood one another in a way that nobody else ever could and had a connection that wasn't faked or forced. I hand on heart had never felt so completely drawn to anyone in my life and my love for him ran deep in my veins. There was no doubt in my mind that I had made the right choice. I wanted and needed him in my life. Like the sun, he lit up my life in such an astronomical way and had helped me breathe new life. Before our reintroduction, I thought I had conquered it all, that I had moved on from the past. But he had taught me that I hadn't, and although it wasn't in the most fitting way, if he hadn't of come back into my life, I wouldn't have been given the opportunity to overcome the past and finally be free from my haunting curse.

With Leon back in my life, my happiness was complete. I could move forward with my life, free of any doubts and fears. It was time for me to really start living my best life, and with Leon by my side, it really would be the best life I could ever ask for.

Chapter 47

Autumn was fully setting in. The temperature had dropped and there was a chilly air circulating that had replaced the summer heat and the leaves of the trees

were gradually turning into a beautiful kaleidoscope of shades of yellow, orange, red and brown. They were yet to fall from the trees' numerous limbs, but it wouldn't be much longer before the branches would be completely naked.

I pulled the zip of my coat further up, covering my chin, and buried my hands deep in my pockets as the chill found its way through the openings of my outerwear. Taking a long, deep breath through my nose, I felt my lungs expand to welcome the cool air. My favourite scent of summer had been wiped away by the earthy autumnal scents of wet grass and pine cones, mixed with takeout coffee as people walked around and sipped from their plainly decorated cardboard cups in an attempt to warm themselves.

It had been two months since I had told Leon I wanted to give things another go with him, and so far they were going really well. He'd respected my wish of taking things slow, and so far, we'd only gone as far as groping. In all honesty, there was a number of times when I had wanted things to go further, but I was somehow able to control myself. Although, I would occasionally test Leon to see what he would do. He didn't disappoint and remained level-headed when things were heated, putting a stop to anything progressing. His resilience proved to both himself and me that he was a changed man and that my wishes were always being put first, and I appreciated his strong resolve.

While I slowly made my way home from a clients' house after a rather intense workout, I cast my mind over the past couple of months. Fi and Everett were incredibly supportive of my decision, and they were over the moon that me and Leon were back together. Though, I think it's more relief that neither of them had to deal with Leon's moping anymore and that his smile and jovial personality had returned. Fi had told me about the panic attacks he'd been having, and while I felt bad that I had been the cause behind them, I couldn't help feeling a little smug. He'd peered through the window of my world and could now somewhat understand how it had felt like for me because of him. Thankfully, I'd found peace with the past and no longer had panic attacks, and since our reconciliation, Leon hadn't had any more either.

I was proud of how far the pair of us had come, both as a couple and individually. Things were different than the last time and it made our connection deeper and stronger. Over the period of me being away, we'd both become different people, and so we now had to learn to love and accept the new aspects of our personalities. He'd always put me first and had held me in such high regard, but his reverence and commitment towards me and us this time around was second to none. He showed me just how much he loved me every day. Whether it was cooking dinner for me, sending me a sweet text to let me know he was thinking about me, or even just rubbing my feet after a long day, there was never a moment where I felt unloved, unappreciated or unwanted.

Soon enough, I was rounding a familiar corner and began walking through the park. This was my usual route for my daily walks and runs, and it was a destination that I never tired of visiting. The trees were a patchwork blanket of red and gold, with the odd green leaf dotted here and there. Some of the crispy leaves danced in the air as they performed the waltz before settling on the damp ground. The sky was turning peach with thin white clouds stretching across the ethereal celestial dome, as the sun was setting earlier and earlier with each passing day. Occasionally, a flock of birds traversed the plains above, forming an array of shifting shapes as they migrated to warmer countries.

The vast area was calm and blissful. There weren't many people around as it was getting darker earlier and the night cold had started settling in. But despite this, there were still the odd few people enjoying the mid-late afternoon. I found myself smiling as I watched a couple of young children run and jump into a mass of leaves, with a few strays being ejected into the air at the force before floating gracefully back down to the ground. Their sweet, contagious and free-spirited laughs rang throughout the park as they were submerged in the leafy pile. In a few years, that could be mine and Fi's children. If by some miracle I have one by then that is.

I found an unoccupied bench and positioned myself down, stretching my legs out and crossing them at the ankles, and let my mind continue to wander. With my thoughts having skimmed over Fi, I delved deeper into the topic and thought about how well her pregnancy was progressing. At twenty-two weeks and six days, she was absolutely glowing. She had been blessed with not suffering from sickness, although she had been hit with waves of nausea for some time, but that had seemed to settle down recently. Her bump was rather prominent by now, and there was no hiding it. She was forever caressing it and talking absolute nonsense to it. I always found myself smiling at the sweet interaction between mother and unborn child, and when we were chilling at either one's home, I found I was talking to her stomach too.

I'll never forget when I first felt her baby move. Fi's face had contorted slightly as she winced in discomfort. When she realised what was going on, her face lit up like a Christmas tree and she grabbed my hand and pressed it against her bump. It took some time, but eventually, underneath my palm, I felt her roundness do a little Mexican wave as the baby made themselves comfortable inside of Fi. My eyes never left her midsection as I removed my hand and tried to see if her skin bulged with every movement. It was a beautiful moment for me, and my heart had swelled with love. I couldn't help jealousy creep in ever so slightly though, as I thought about myself possibly never having to experience the feeling for myself. I had shook my head vigorously to rid such impure and selfish thoughts, and continued to bask in Fi's happiness.

She'd had her twenty-week scan a couple of weeks ago, but her and Everett had decided to keep everyone in suspense and not find out the gender; wanting to wait until the baby was born. I was still certain she was having a girl, but it seemed that I was the only one who thought as much. Fi wanted a girl, but she was convinced it was going to be a boy.

She had lifted her top up the other day to show me the update on her dark snail trail of hair that led from her belly button to under the waistband of her joggers. The old wives' tale of having a hairy belly symbolising a boy was one that she firmly believed in, and Lord knows she had come across some crazy ones; some that were for the gender, and some about pregnancy in general. The most ludicrous one states that a mother cannot have a bath whilst pregnant as she'll drown the baby. Now, I never took Fi as naive, but she took her superstitions seriously, and since finding out she was pregnant, she has refused a bath through fear of drowning her baby. I'd had to explain to her that there's liquid surrounding the baby anyway and they don't breathe while in utero, so there's no way they can drown. Safe to say she still refuses to have a bath, instead showering, "just to be on the safe side." I on the other hand, wasn't superstitious. There was no way on Gods' green earth, things like craving savoury over sweet, or the bump sitting high or low could aid in determining the gender of a foetus. The whole thing was a farce.

Fi's housing worry had been answered when Everett had suggested moving in together. Fi had been all for moving into Everett's place with him as it would be much less hassle for him and his house was significantly bigger than her modestly small flat, but he had put his foot down and said no. He wanted to get a new place that they could own together to start their new life with their little bundle of joy. I understood it, and I think it meant a lot to Fi that he wanted a complete fresh start with her. They had been to a number of viewings but were yet to find the family home of their dreams, and Fi was getting more worried and frustrated as the days went on that they weren't going to find anywhere before the baby was born.

I couldn't wait for Fi to have her baby. I was excited to spoil them how I would no doubt spoil my own. I often found myself daydreaming about looking after her little one, which then led to me wondering about my own future. It was too soon to say for sure if I would have kids with Leon – if at all it was possible - but I couldn't imagine it with anyone else. I was yet to tell him that I may not be able to conceive. I was petrified to tell him. I didn't want him to leave me because I couldn't give him a family of his own, should he desire one with me. I knew it would be best to tell him sooner rather than later, while the relationship was still fresh and new because it would hurt less if he chose to leave. But we'd just gotten back together, and I didn't want to be without him again. I knew he loved me, and I hoped that he would stick by me regardless, but the possibility of it being a deal breaker for him scared me shitless. The future wasn't something we'd really discussed yet. Even when we were first together it was never something that was brought up, and so I had no clue if a family was even in his life plan. There's really only one way to find out, I suppose, but I wasn't ready to have that discussion yet. Even just thinking about it made my stomach turn and tie a million invisible knots. I was excited to be with him for as long as possible. I knew that I needed and wanted him to be around forever, but I was anxious and worried about losing him to something as major as this.

Closing my eyes, I slouched further down the bench and tilted my head back until I felt the bench become a pillow underneath me, and took a long deep sigh, letting my mind still for a moment. The breeze was crispy as it brushed over my face, tousling my hair as it blew. It had picked up in the last few minutes, and where it once caressed everything it touched, it was now a gust, impatiently ripping the leaves from the trees in an attempt to make them bare.

My brows furrowed together in confusion as I flinched at the sudden feel of a droplet of water smashing soundlessly on my cheek. I opened my eyes one at a time, and found myself eyeing a dark, angry sky of grey clouds that hid the tranquil candy floss atmosphere that was there not too long ago, and were threatening to unleash a violent downpour of water. I looked around and watched in amusement as the people around me quickly dispersed, eager to get out of the impending rainfall that would be bestowed upon us very shortly.

I quickly made the decision to follow suit, but before I had even made it out of the park, the gentle droplets that had started to fall had soon turned into a shield of bullets that both surrounded me and drummed down on me forcefully. I was regretting not wearing a coat with a hood, as the rain wasted no time in dampening my hair before trickling down my face and into my eyes. Picking up the pace with my head tucked into my chest, I started to sprint to try get out of this heavy rain as quickly as possible, only to bump into a hard object.

Chapter 48

49

Ffion's POV:

Buzz... Buzz... Buzz...

Would someone please kill that bee already?

The buzzing sound stopped, and I felt a soft, sleepy smile creep onto my face at the disappearance of the annoying sound and thanked whoever answered my silent wish, only for the curve on my lips to drop when it started up again.

Reluctantly, I opened my eyes only to discover that it wasn't a bee that had rudely awoken me from my daily nap, but instead, it was Ava incessantly calling me. I rubbed the sleep from my eyes and pushed myself up slightly with my elbows, leaning my head against the headboard of my bed.

With a groan, I reached over to my bedside table and grabbed my phone, only to be rewarded with a strong kick from the baby for interrupting its slumber. I looked at the screen as it lit up, showing that I had already missed three phone calls from her. Clearly it was important, but my sleep fogged brain was debating whether or not I should answer. Annoyance slowly rose inside me. She knew 4 p.m. was my naptime, so why would she disturb me? With a short, quick huff, I pressed the green phone icon on the screen and answered her call.

"About fucking time!" Her pissed off voice rang through the phone so loud that I had to hold the phone away from my ear. If anyone had any reason to be mad, it was me. After all, she had disturbed my sleep.

"Well, I apologise but I'm trying to grow a baby here. What's going on? It best be life or death because the baby is going nuts." I could feel the life I was growing wriggling around inside of me, seemingly telling me off for not going back to sleep. I placed my free hand on my mound and slowly stroked it in an attempt to calm the baby.

"You will never guess who I literally just ran into." I couldn't place her tone, but it was a mix of disgust and shock. She had already gone through so much the past few months, and I was sure she had come face to face with everyone from her past... everyone except Victoria. But why would she be in these ends? I closed my eyes as I silently prayed that no-one else had made an appearance that could jeopardise Ava's long-overdue happiness.

"Hit me with it."

"None other than Tyrone." Instantly, my breath got caught in my throat as my mind turned blank and my eyes pinged open. Tyrone? What the fuck was he doing back? My mind flashed images of my past with Ty and my heart rate picked up at the memories. My mind settled on the last memory I had of us. The one where I found him in bed with another girl, and he spent the entire night gaslighting me into believing that I had made it up and was just seeing the things I wanted to see, that it had never even happened.

"Fi? Are you still there?" I had no idea how long I'd been in a world of my own for, but by the time I came back to my senses, Ava was yelling down the phone to me, bringing me back to the present.

"Er, yeah I'm still here. You saw Ty? Where? What did he say?" I tried to keep my voice steady. I didn't want her to know that I was freaking out on the inside. Ty being here was too close for my liking.

"Come and open your door and I'll tell you." My eyebrows furrowed as I awkwardly swung my legs over the side of my bed and sort of rolled myself into a sitting up position before pushing myself up. I was out of breath just from the struggle of getting onto my feet, so I took a few seconds to get my breathing under control.

On the other end of the phone, I could hear the soft downpour of rain and Ava's jagged breathing from where she had no doubt been running. Waddling slightly, I made my way through my tiny flat to the front door, where once opened, I found a drenched and very unimpressed Ava. I ushered her in and instructed her to go for a shower whilst I pulled out some dry, warm clothes for her to put on.

Twenty minutes later, a now dry Ava walked into the living room after having a quick shower, sporting some tapered grey joggers and a matching hoodie. Her blonde hair had been dried with a hairdryer and was pulled up into a messy bun. Her natural beauty never ceased to astound me. It didn't matter what she wore, she always looked beautiful.

She had barely parked her backside down next to me on my sofa when I started quizzing her.

"So... you saw Ty. Did he say what he wanted and why he was back? Did he ask about me?" My hands were clasped in my lap as I leaned forward slightly, my mouth running a mile a minute

451

without a breath. After all that he did to me, I shouldn't even be this interested in his sudden reappearance, he was a prick of the highest order, but my mouth blurted out the words before I could even think about saying them. I watched A's face twitch as she went through a number of emotions ranging from amusement to curiosity.

She shook her head as she settled on a neutral expression, giving away nothing. Looking me in my eyes, her blue orbs were the only feature showing how she was feeling as they danced with anger and revulsion.

"I was running home to get out of the rain...

* * *

Ava's POV:

The wind was knocked out of me and my face was pressed against a hard surface that was covered by some sort of material. I stumbled back to put some space between myself and the wall I had crashed into and began to stutter out an embarrassed apology. My eyes coursed up to meet the face of my obstructer and discovered an arrogantly handsome face looking down at me. Recognition clicked in his rich chocolate eyes and a cocky smirk grew on full lips that were framed by a thin, dark beard. I felt confusion begin to set on my face as I speed-ran through my memories to see how I knew this guy.

"Ava?" A deep throaty voice rippled through my eardrums, sending a traitorous, delicious shiver down my spine. A hand- some face matched with a sexy voice was a recipe for disaster and was a sure sign that however this guy recognised me, it wouldn't be without some sort of drama. With this in mind, I wasn't going to let him fool me with any niceties. I settled into my resting bitch face and crossed my arms, the rain drizzling down the back of my neck before being soaked up by the clothing underneath my coat.

"That depends on who's asking." My voice was cold and unbothered, hopefully showing him that I was uninterested. Mirroring my stance, he folded his arms across his chest and raised a singular brow. His eyes ran up and down my body, hungrily taking me in.

"Still as feisty as ever I see. I like that in a woman." A pink tongue poked slightly out of his perfectly lined lips and slowly traced the top lip as he took a step closer to me, which in turn forced me to take a step back. I didn't want to be any closer than needed to be to this guy – I was getting bad vibes.

"Come on now, I know we only met a couple of times but surely you remember this handsome face?" Arrogance radiated off him like a suffocating heatwave as I took in his face properly. I had never met anyone as cocky as the man that stood before me. Well, no one except for...

"Tyrone."

"In the flesh sweet cheeks." He smoothly waved his hands from his chest in a downwards motion as he spoke; shooting me a wink that was paired with a cheesy grin surfacing onto his flawless face. I rolled my eyes at the comment and motion. This guy seriously thought he was God's gift. Though he was incredibly good looking, he was an arsehole with a hideous personality.

"No surprise that you've not changed a bit; forever still an obnoxious, egotistical piece of shit." I spoke calmly, almost patronising, with my hands now on my waist. The last thing I wanted was to converse with this absolute waste of space. I respected and valued Fi enough not to entertain her ex, especially after what he did to her. He wasn't worth losing our friendship over.

It was still raining, but it was gradually easing up. I was resembling a drowned rat and was anxious to get out of these wet clothes before I caught a cold. Quickly glancing around me, I found that I was under the small canopy of the local florist. There weren't many people about now as everyone had scattered to find shelter from the rain, leaving only the odd straggler who hadn't been so lucky and had been caught in the sudden downpour.

"Seriously? It's been what, two years and this is how you greet me?"

"What did you expect after what you did to Fi?" I was stunned slightly at the audacity this man had to complain about my lack of polite greeting. He was deluded if he thought I was going to be nice to him after what he put Fi through. I was rewarded with a bored eye roll from Tyrone.

"I didn't do shit to Fi and everyone knows it. That little bitch was just an attention seeking liar." He scoffed, his top lip curling upwards slightly in disgust. I felt anger bubble inside of me. Fi was one of the most virtuous, down to earth people I'd ever met. The entire time I've known her, not once had she ever lied to me. I remember as if it was yesterday when she told me her story with Ty. The fear in her eyes rolled in thick and fast like a hurricane as tears formed and rolled viciously down her face, so I knew for a fact that she wasn't lying. I felt my palms tingle as I desperately fought the urge to wipe the sneer off his face, and instead closed my hands into tight fists. He knew he'd gotten to me, but I wasn't going to give him the satisfaction of giving him a reaction.

"What are you doing back here Ty? Because it certainly isn't to see Fi."

Shrugging his thick shoulders nonchalantly, his lips curled on one side into a smirk as he dug his hands deep into the front pockets of his jeans.

"I'm a free man, Ava. If I want to come back here, then I will. I have no interest in Ffion, although I did hear that she's pregnant. I can't say I'm surprised. That little slut probably opened her legs to the first guy that showed her just an ounce of attention." He started to laugh at his own disgusting comment, but it was cut short by the satisfying sound of my hand making contact with his face, my body losing its battle of wills. His own giant hand flew up to his face which was now tainted red with the imprint of my hand.

"How fucking *dare* you speak about her like that. She did nothing but be loyal and love you, only for you to fuck her up emotionally with your abusive, brainwashing ways. Everything was always her fault when in actual fact it was you that was the problem." Heat was radiating off my now stinging hand. Angry tears were beginning to build in the back of my eyes, and my throat was going tight from my trying to hold them back.

An old couple who were in the street had stopped to watch the scene unfold before them, tucking themselves under the nearest shelter that they could find to protect themselves from the persistent downpour. I could see the shock on Tyrone's face slowly wear off as the thick vein in the center of his forehead started to protrude.

"I see that she managed to feed you her lies just like she..."

"Will you quit with the "woe-is-me" act? Because no-one

is buying it and they never have. It's about time you pulled your head out of your arse and started realising that your shit does stink." I cut him off, my increasingly raised voice full of loathing. Once again, he was playing the victim when he was far from innocent. I wasn't going to stand here and let him drag Fi's name through the mud when she wasn't present to defend herself.

"You put her through absolute hell, and yet she managed to come out stronger than ever. So don't you think even for a second that you broke her, because you made her the person she is now." My finger was now pressed into his chest, jabbing him harder with every word until I had him up against the wall of the florists. His dark eyes flicked back and forth between mine, anticipating my next move. A few more people had stopped to look at the exchange between us, which made Tyrone noticeably uncomfortable and his gaze kept shifting past my shoulder.

"Not got a come back Ty now that we've got ourselves an audience? What happened to Billy big bollocks?" After a final push into his chest with my finger, I took a step back and slowly dragged my eyes up and down his body, with my lip curled up in utter revulsion. He was looking slightly terrified, which only increased my inner sense of pride. With a final shake of my head and a disapproving scoff, I turned my back to Tyrone and strutted off into the rain and headed in the direction of Fi's house with my head held high.

* * *

Ffion's POV:

"And that brings us to now." She was looking at me with sadness in her eyes. I shouldn't care that Ty had said those things about me, that he didn't even show any interest in my well-being, but I couldn't help feeling like my heart had been ripped from my chest. But, at the same time, love and appreciation swelled within me for A. She'd stood up for me and fought in my corner when I wasn't there to do it myself. And if I was being realistic, even if I had been there, I would've folded like a house of cards.

Looking down into my hands that were squeezing the life out of the other, I was a mish-mash of emotions. I was furious at the words he used against me, wary as to why he was back, but more importantly, absolutely mortified and sickened that he tried to flip the narrative and make out like I was the delusional, compulsive liar.

"I'm sorry Fi, I know it wasn't nice to hear him say those things about you." Her voice full of sorrow, she shuffled closer to me and took my hands in hers. Tears dripped down my face, splashing on A's fair hands that encased my own.

"Why do I still care A? I don't love him and I don't miss him, but why does it bother me that he's here? Why do I want to know if he's thought about me or come back for me?" I couldn't understand why I was feeling the way that I was. Pregnancy hormones were raging through me so they weren't helping how I was feeling, but I felt betrayed by myself for feeling so vulnerable.

"Because he refuses to take accountability for what he did you, and instead paints you out as the bad guy. You did nothing wrong Fi, so don't for a second think that you did. And he was your first love; they're difficult to get out of your head." Her thumb was gently rubbing over the top of my hand, comforting me as I slowly hiccupped my way to calming down.

"Fuck him," she said with a wave of her hand, "You've come such a long way since him, you should be proud of yourself." I *was* proud of myself. Although I hadn't fully gotten over the abuse, I had become stronger and knew that if ever I was in that situation again, I'd be strong enough to fight, to talk to someone about it and walk away sooner.

I smiled weakly at A and pulled my hands from hers to wipe away the tears that had started to dry on my face, my breath stuttering as I gained control of myself. With a deep breath I placed my hands on my bump and looked down.

"You're right, and now I have someone else to focus on and to make proud too. If things didn't happen how they did, I probably wouldn't be in this position." As if backing me up, the life inside of me pressed against my hands. The pressure was stronger than ever before, and wanting to share this moment with her, I took Ava's hand and pressed it against where the movement was and watched as her eyes widened in amazement at the feeling of her niece or nephew pressing against her palm.

"Thank you, Ava, for all that you've done for me. You've brought the best out in me and if it weren't for you boosting my confidence, I wouldn't have had the guts to even speak to Ev, and here I am carrying his child. I couldn't have asked for a better best friend to have by my side. I truly am lucky." Taking her hand away from my protruding abdomen, she scooted even closer and pulled me into a strong and affectionate embrace.

"No need to thank me Fi, I'll always be by your side no matter what. You've been my rock and I wouldn't be where I am without your support and guidance. What kind of best friend would I be if I didn't return the favour?" I could hear the honesty in her voice as she spoke softly in my ear.

"I love you, A." I squeezed her tighter, indicating just how much truth lays within those words, and felt her tighten her hold on me.

"I love you too, Fi."

I really had been blessed with the best and I honestly couldn't imagine my life without her in it. She truly had saved me from the brink of utter despair. I was at my worst when she met me, a recluse, always hiding in the shadows of my depression and hopelessness. I had no friends, my confidence and self-esteem was non-existent, and it was having a knock on effect on my abilities at work and in my life all over in general. Light, love and colour had been brought back into my world because of her. I met Ev and am now having his baby because I had the confidence to walk up to him and speak to him when I saw him at work. I'm able to voice my opinions and thoughts and be brazen about it, because she taught me that it was okay to have a voice; to speak up for what I believe in. After so long of not being able to tell people what was truly on my mind, I felt liberated that she'd helped me find myself and my voice again.

I hand on heart can honestly say that I don't know where I would be without her.

50

Chapter 49

Ava's POV:

The October air was chilly as we walked through the city on our way home. Our arms were crossed behind us with Leon having a hand on my waist, holding me close to him, whilst I had my hand buried deep in his back pocket. Neither one of us talking as we simply enjoyed being in the others company, basking in the still autumn night. The sun had long ago set, and now the sky was pitch black with the moon gently lighting the world around us and lamp posts guiding us through the streets like aeroplane runways. The stars were stammeringly beautiful tonight; the silver minuscule diamonds were scattered across the dark eternal void like bejewelled grains of sand as they pulsated in silence.

We'd spent our evening in the arcades, reliving our childhoods. The arcades were dark, only illuminated by the fluorescent lights of the machines that were dotted around the spacious area. All around us the constant sounds of the games circulated as we made our way from machine to machine, attempting to entice us to play. We mostly stuck to the slot machines, although after a lot of begging I managed to get Leon onto a dance machine, where I was surprised to learn that the man's got some moves. I'd forgotten how competitive he was, and there were a few near wins on his part, but he was never a sore loser. Instead, he would pull me in for a kiss on the head by gently holding my cheeks with his soft giant hands and congratulate me.

Our first date since getting back together had gone without a hitch so far, with our last date being the Summer Ball, and we all know how that went down. But rather than being worried about there being another disaster, I decided to put the past behind me and instead focused on the now. I fully trusted Leon and knew that he wouldn't hurt me again, but I couldn't help the occasional feeling of vulnerability creep in. I'd taken a leap of faith in him and in us, but my overthinking brain would sometimes stray and wander into the dangerous zones of what ifs and maybes. What if he got bored of me? What if I wasn't enough for him anymore? Maybe he'd rather be with someone who can give him what I can't? It was a never-ending dialogue and I'd have to fight internally with myself to shut my brain off from thinking such pessimistic thoughts.

"Ava, baby?" Leon's voice echoed in my ears as it brought me out of my thoughts. I blinked and turned my head up to look at him and found him looking down at me with amusement in his eyes. I'd spaced out and got completely lost in my thoughts. He let out a small laugh and lightly shook his head.

"I said, are you coming into mine?" The faint light around us caught in his eyes, highlighting their beautiful honey hue, as he looked down at me. He really did have the most unique eyes I'd ever seen, and I felt lucky that they were only for me.

We'd just approached the pillar of the wall that separated our houses from one another when I stopped us from walking any further by standing in front of him with my arms now wrapped around his neck. A playful smile befell my face as I thought about what was to come. "Don't ask silly questions babe, you know I am."

Our heads moved towards the other, and just as our lips were about to touch, I turned away and dashed for the front door, letting out a devilish giggle. Leon was hot on my heels and just as I reached the top step, he swept me off my feet, inciting a squeal to escape my lips, and fireman carried me into his home. The warmth of his house quickly engulfed us and the sensation that I had lost in my fingers and toes soon returned.

I wasted no time in making a move on Leon. As soon as the door was closed and I was back on my feet, I grabbed his hand and pulled him to the room I wanted to be in. I figured that if I wanted things to go further, then I had to take charge, I had to take the lead, otherwise he might stop us from going to the next level and I didn't want that anymore. I both wanted and needed him to satisfy me in the way I so desperately craved.

I'd taken him into his office, and once we'd entered the room, I was all over him like a rash. Pulling him in closer to me by the waistband of his jeans, I tucked my fingers underneath the fabric, making contact with his warm skin. A hungry desire burned between us as our lips crashed together and our tongues intertwined. It wasn't enough to sate my craving, but I had to be patient and pace myself.

With my hands flush against his broad chest, I walked him gently backwards until his legs were touching his chair that was coincidentally already facing the way I needed it to be and pulled away from his lips. I looked him in the eyes and could see bewilderment in them as he wondered what was happening.

With a smirk and a wink, I pushed him a little forcefully so that he fell into the chair. I trapped him with one hand on the arm of the chair, and the index finger of my free hand under his chin, tilting it up to look at me as I loomed over him slightly.

"I want you to fuck me and fuck me good." Need and desperation flooded my quiet, breathy voice, and I was rewarded with a deep groan from Leon.

"Oh baby, I'll do whatever you want me to do to you." He made a move to grab me by my waist, but I slapped his hand away and shook my head.

"Ah, ah, ah. You don't get to touch me until I say you can." He resigned himself into the seat with each arm on the arms of the chair, and an excited look flashed in his eyes. Tonight was the night we would become one again, and it had been a long time coming.

I took a step away from Leon so that I was still within touching distance, just to tease him more and make him itch with temptation while he wasn't allowed to touch me.

"Take your clothes off." I kept my voice strong, yet lowered, and kept my hands on my hips. I watched as he started taking his top half off, exposing his beautifully crafted torso, before he began on his bottom half, tossing his clothing behind him onto the floor. He was already sporting a semi and I could feel a buzz coming from deep within me. It brought me so much pleasure knowing that I could do this to him, that I could get him hard without even touching him, that it turned me on even more.

I dragged my eyes over his naked body, and I could feel my heart pound in my chest, making my pulse quicken. He was gorgeous and it was taking everything I had in me not to cave and give in. Instead, I gave a singular satisfied nod and began my own little tease.

* * *

Leon's POV:

I'd never seen her so in control like this before. Sure, I'd seen her handle people when they've done her wrong, but when it came to sex, she liked to let me take the lead; she was happy for me to do whatever I liked to her. On occasion she'd be the dominant one, but this was different. She was different. Seeing her so strong and commanding was such a huge turn on, and I was fighting with myself to stop from touching her and taking over. She'd started to slowly strip for me, revealing her delicious body part by part. Her cheeks were flushed pink out of shyness, but she never once took her eyes away from mine.

The moonlight was the only light source in the room as it cast a spotlight through the open blinds on her petite frame. She really was beautiful and sitting here only being able to observe her, gave me the opportunity to fully appreciate her looks. Her body perfectly toned, the light bounced off her fake tanned skin, giving her a healthy glow. Her now short hair glistened as she shook it loose from the ponytail it had been in, tumbling over her shoulders. Her bare body was now only clothed in a matching lingerie set. Its red and black lace hugged the curves of her breasts perfectly, with matching panties whose narrow back was snuggly tucked between her perky round cheeks. All I wanted to do was rip the minimal fabric off her luscious body and devour every inch of her.

She gradually moved towards me, before dropping to her knees and pulling me closer to the edge of the seat so that she was face to face with my cock. Taking it in her hand, it looked giant in her small fist with her nimble fingers wrapped around the shaft. I could feel my dick twinge in her hand as she looked me dead in the eyes and she enveloped me with her warm, wet mouth.

I don't know how but she'd somehow gotten so much better at sucking me off. She'd always been good, but this was next level. As her head bobbed up and down, her hand kept a comfortable grip as it followed her mouth in twists, while her spare hand delicately caressed my balls. Her little moans vibrated against me, adding to the pleasure I was feeling. I couldn't contain the moans that escaped my own mouth, and they only seemed to spur her on even more. She alternated her pace and suction and wrapped her tongue around me as she went like I was her own personal lollipop.

There were a few times when I wanted to grab her hair or the back of her head and ram myself down her, but she had requested for me not to touch her, despite it being all that I wanted to do. So instead, I resorted to gripping the chair. I had glanced at her a few times and she seemed to fully be enjoying herself with her eyes closed whilst she slurped and gagged, occasionally pausing at my tip and sucking with her tongue gently caressing the smooth head.

"Fuck baby, if you keep going like that, you're going to make me cum." She was sucking the soul out of me to say the least, and I was so close to blowing my load right into the back of her throat. With a final slurp, she let me go and opened her eyes. She used her thumb to wipe the spit from the corners of her mouth.

"You make that sound like a bad thing." She'd never swallowed me, let alone had even the slightest taste, and the fact that she was suggesting she wouldn't mind was driving me wild.

"Listen. If you really wanted me to fill that pretty little mouth

465

of yours, I wouldn't stop you." She sat herself on my lap facing me and held my chin in her hand as she forced me to look at her.

"Mmm, but I'd much rather have you fill me up elsewhere." She spoke softly with a sensual undertone. Before I could respond, she turned my head away and took to kissing along the side of my neck, starting at my shoulder and gradually making her way up, sucking and gently biting as she did so. Once she reached my ear, she took my lobe into her mouth and sucked before pulling it tenderly with her teeth. Uncontrollable moans escaped my lips as she tortured me with her delicate, purposeful touch. She was grinding into me and moaning softly into my ear as she did so – and that was the tip of the iceberg for me. I couldn't restrain myself anymore.

I held her waist and pushed her down, making my stiffness dig into her even more and a gasp escaped those full juicy lips of hers. I was achingly hard now and I needed to be inside of her. The suspense was killing me.

"Baby, you haven't told me off for touching you without your permission." I whispered into her ear. I had been expecting some sort of repercussion for placing my hands on her and was surprised when there wasn't one. But I was even more taken aback by her response.

"I'm past caring. Can you just fuck me already? Please?" There was urgency in her plea, and I was more than happy and ready to oblige to her request. I stood up and held her by her butt as I moved her onto the edge of the desk, pushing anything that was in the way onto the floor in one fell sweep.

With her positioned, I unhooked her bra with one hand and threw it onto the floor before moving her underwear to the side and began teasing her folds with my fingers before feeling her entrance that was practically dripping already for me. I slid a

466

single finger in, but she was already ready for a second. She was so turned on and all I wanted to do was satisfy her every need.

As I pumped away inside her, I delicately circled my thumb over her clit, applying perfect pressure, making her buck as the sensitive sensation sent a volt up her spine. Her moans were like music to my ears. They weren't forced, nor were they fake. They were unhinged and full of pure pleasure. Each movement I made, no matter how minuscule or gentle it was, made her entire body shake and vibrate. It was empowering knowing that I made her body react in this way.

Wanting to make her wait for me even more, I bent down and began to tease and taunt her with my tongue. With my fingers still inside her, I flickered my tongue over her swollen clit, taking it into my mouth and sucking it every now and then. Her entire body twitched in reaction to the pleasure overload that swept through her body. Taking my fingers out, I fucked her with my tongue, savouring the taste of her as I lapped her up.

"Baby... I..." She grabbed a handful of my hair with one hand and the edge of the desk with the other, squeezed her eyes shut and threw her head back. She lost her voice as a wave of euphoria flooded her body and she became undone onto my fingers, and a small squeak came from her as she came to the end of her high.

"Can you handle anymore baby girl?" A challenge; I wasn't finished with her yet. She'd relaxed under my touch after such an intense orgasm. She opened her eyes sharply and began an attack on my lips that was full of intention and need. I felt her lift her hips off the desk as she took her underwear off single-handedly, whilst her other was hooked around my neck, enabling her to keep her balance. Once the thin fabric was strewn somewhere on the floor, she took my throbbing dick in her hand and guided it inside herself. Her eyes rolled to the back of her head and a delightful "ohhh" came from her as the first stroke slid inside of her, stretching her to accommodate my girth.

I started off slow, enabling her to get re-used to my size. But it wasn't long before I could sense the impatience emanating from her for me to speed up. I placed a hand around her throat and gripped tight, just enough to send the right amount of blood to her head, and with my spare one braced myself on the desk as I picked up the pace.

"You feel so fucking good." Her warmth tightly enclosed around me as I pounded into her, her moans gradually getting louder with every thrust as I buried myself deeper and deeper inside of her. The desk beneath her shook with each penetration, slamming against the wall it was up against.

I opened my eyes briefly to look at her. I always thought she looked good when we were having sex, but in this position, in this lighting, she looked breath-taking. A thin line of sweat slowly trailed down between her cleavage, heading south towards her tiny belly button. Her boobs bounced and jiggled with every movement and her nipples were erect, enticing me to play with them. Her luscious lips alternated between making a perfect 'O' shape and being tucked underneath her top teeth. I got a handful of her hair in my hand and pulled with a little force.

"Oh, baby... " Her voice was raspy as she tried to catch her breath. I removed my hand from around her neck and gripped her chin as I pressed my lips against hers. She was struggling to keep her moans at bay as we kissed, and as she came towards her second high, she couldn't multitask and paused mid-kiss with her sweet vocals of enjoyment becoming barely audible. Our lips only a whisper away, I tried to keep the rhythm so that she could come, but it was proving to be difficult when my own orgasm was mere seconds away.

"Come for me, Ava." I whispered my demand in her ear, feeling her tremble as my hot breath blew down her neck. Her delicate hand had moved around to the front of my neck with a light hold with her nails digging into my skin, and her legs tightening around me as a wave of ecstasy hit her full force, just a split second before I exploded inside of her.

Once we'd both stilled and our breaths were more regulated, I pulled out and took a moment to look at her face. She was glowing, she was happy and that brought me great peace. I took her cheek in my hand and stroked it with my thumb. She looked up at me, her eyes glistening like a lake at night-time in the moonlight and it melted my heart.

"You are so fucking beautiful, you know?" I spoke honestly and softly, looking into her eyes as I did so. Naked or clothed, with or without makeup, bed hair or hair done all nice, she always looked amazing to me. There was nothing and no one that could deter me from her, that could take my eyes off her or turn my head. She was it for me, and I felt incredibly lucky everyday that she gave me another chance, that she let me in after I had broken her heart and soul in more than one way. I'd been desperately trying to fix the damage I'd caused; to glue her back together. I knew it would take a while, but it was worth it. She was worth it.

"Leon..." Her eyes were glossed with tears as they balanced on her lower lash line, threatening to spill onto her rosy cheeks. I told her all the time how attracted to her I was, and sometimes I felt like she didn't believe me. It was my own fault that there was some doubt in her mind. I knew she knew I was being honest but that doesn't mean that doubt doesn't reside in her mind. Yes, she'd chosen me and given me a second chance, but I hadn't failed to notice how she looks a little longer at her body in the mirror, how she scrutinises the smallest thing that she doesn't like about herself, or how she hovers over females' pictures on Instagram and questions herself in comparison to them, and it kills me every time I see her do it. I had put that insecurity and doubt there, and I would do whatever I could to get rid of it. She was way better than that and she deserved more. So much so, that I questioned myself with regards to her being with me. Someone who had ruined her not once, but twice. She'd taken me back and I was going to earn my place in her life.

"I don't want to keep bringing it up, but I know I've hurt you in the past and I know you're still suffering because of it, no matter how well you think you're hiding it. But I want you to know that it's always going to be you. I love you Ava, you're the only one that has or has ever had my heart. You've trusted me with yours and I will protect it and cherish it forever."

Burying her head in my chest, I felt tiny water droplets drip from her ocean eyes before trickling down my chest. She clamped her legs around me, along with her arms as she tightly embraced me. I cradled her head in my hand and stroked her hair whilst my other hand was holding her close by the base of her back. Her shoulders shook lightly as she silently cried in my arms.

Once she had calmed down enough, she looked up at me with her chin resting on my chest. Her lashes were still damp from tears and her cheeks were saturated with wetness. There wasn't a hint of sadness in her eyes, rather, there was relief and happiness gleaming from them.

"I love you too, Leon." She loosened her hold on me and shifted so that there was a small distance between us, and were face to face.

"Don't think for a second that I haven't noticed your efforts in trying to prove how much you love me, because I have picked up on it and I appreciate your constant reassurance. But you can't blame me for my doubts." She had every right to have doubts and to feel the way that she did, I just didn't like that she had them.

I shook my head and took her hands in mine. "I don't blame you for it, not in the slightest. I hate myself because I've caused this, I made this happen and all I want to do is prove myself to you and make you trust me fully again. But like I've already said, I'm prepared to do anything and everything that I can, no matter how long it takes. I can see such an amazing future with you, and I'll go the distance to make it happen."

A look crossed her face for a brief second at the mention of our future, a look I can't quite put my finger on. This wasn't the first time she'd gone a little funny when speaking about the future and I wondered what had her so scared and frightened. Either way, I wasn't going to let that worry take over her life. Whatever it was, I'm sure she'll tell me all in due time, on her terms.

I took her jaw in my hand and tilted it up to look at me. "Stop it. Whatever it is you're thinking about, stop it. I know there's something you're not telling me, and as much as I'd like you to tell me what it is, I'm happy to wait because I know that you will when you're ready. No matter what it is, we will deal with it together, OK?"

Her eyes widened in surprise. She didn't realise I'd long picked up on the correlation, but her eyes returned to normal and she seemed relieved that I knew there was something going on. I don't ever want her to feel pressured into telling me anything, especially if it was about her past and it was affecting her future.

Her hands cupped my cheeks as a small smile spread on her face.

"I'm so lucky to have you, you know?"

"No, I –" She cut me off with her lips against mine, kissing me passionately like it was the last time she'd ever get to.

I wanted to tell her just how wrong she was, because she had no idea that I was the one who was lucky in this relationship, and it was something I will never take for granted.

51

Chapter 50

Ava's POV:

After a couple of months, a lot of planning and side stepping, the day had finally arrived and so far, it was all going without any hiccups, and we were all excited to see the final result.

Leon and I had arrived in the afternoon to get the place prepped and ready. We had everything set up within a few hours and I was bursting with pride and excitement at our handy work and what was to come.

The sun had almost set just as we were coming to the end of our setting up, signaling that it was soon time for the surprise. A cotton candy sky with long white clouds like a scarf hugging the landscape, was shedding its orange coat, teasingly revealing its darker under layer that would blanket the entire sky in an instant. It was the perfect setting.

I pulled my phone out of my pocket to check the time for the millionth time today. We had half an hour until they would arrive, and I felt restless just waiting for them. There was nothing else to do aside from waiting for them to show, and so I decided to take a walk around the site, ensuring all tasks had been done.

"Calm down babe. You've got nothing to worry about; they'll be here soon, and it'll all go perfectly to plan." I'd finished my tour and found Leon underneath a tree that had a golden umbrella that occasionally dropped leaves. His black woolen trench coat was taunt on his bicep as it was bent above his head on the trunk, holding him up as he leaned against it.

He walked over to me and stopped my pacing by pulling me into him so that my back was to his chest, wrapping his arms around my waist and kissing the top of my head. I was grateful to have been able to have him by my side these past few weeks. Planning this had been incredibly stressful, and he'd somehow been able to deal with my moody and snappy behaviour and remarks. If he wanted to be with me for the rest of time, then this had really been a true test to see if he would be able to deal with my occasional outbursts, and he'd passed with flying colours.

"I know. It's just... we've worked so hard for so long and I just want this to be perfect for them. What if none of this goes to plan and it's all been for nothing?" It was hard work being a perfectionist. I'd planned everything down to the last detail, and if it went tits up in any way, shape or form, I'd have a full-blown meltdown.

With a chuckle that made his shoulders shake, thus sending a vibration down my spine, I felt the reverberations of Leon's voice as he spoke to the top of my head.

"You're such a worry head. Now, stop worrying. It's game time."

Sure enough, a car drove through the gates and came rolling towards us, its headlights guiding its way up the driveway. My nerves converted to excitement as I turned away, taking Leons' big, warm hand and pulling him with me. It was time to get into position.

* * *

<u>Julia's POV:</u>

Blind folded and being chauffeured in a car by some stranger was not how I envisioned my Friday night going, yet here I was. Kelvin hadn't explained what was going on or where we were going. The only instruction was to trust him and to ask no questions as he placed a dark silky fabric over my eyes before guiding me to the car.

The entire journey had been in silence after my futile efforts at trying to get Kelvin to tell me where we were going, with only the sounds of Kelvin restlessly moving around next to me while Smooth Radio droned quietly in the background.

After what felt like a lifetime, the car turned onto a gravelly, bumpy road, driving slowly as it jostled us about before coming to a complete stop a couple of minutes later.

The door next to me opened and I was helped out of the car. An arm looped through mine and I was carefully escorted a short distance, taking slow deliberate steps so as not to fall flat on my face. The autumn wind gently blew the stray strands of my hair out of my face as we walked, and by the time we had reached our final stop, my face was almost numb.

The arm let go of me and the presence was now positioned behind me. Feeling the cool sheath gently being pulled away from my eyes, I squeezed my eyes shut, waiting for my next instruction.

"You can open your eyes now." Kelvin's voice was smooth and buttery in my ear, a hand each on the tops of my arms. After giving myself a countdown to prepare for whatever could be in front of me, my eyes fluttered open, and a gasp escaped my lips at the beautiful sight before me.

October was my favourite month, and what I saw encompassed everything that I loved about it: the foliage boasting a beautiful array of technicolour, the fresh, crisp air blowing through my hair, and even though they were candles and fairy lights, the comforting and warming flames of fire in a dimly lit surrounding. It was a magical time of year, where the transition from summer to autumn had been completed and the cooler temperatures were setting in.

We were at a maze that was spaciously walled by the trees of the forest it was situated in. The multicoloured natural hundreds and thousands of the world had been sprinkled all over the floor from their trees, crunching under each footstep as I made my way towards the entrance.

Even though it was still relatively early, it had turned dark quickly, making the fairy lights that decorated the hedge of the maze shine prominently as if they were stars themselves that had fallen from above. A tall lantern with fake leaves wound around the base was placed either side of the entrance, with a pumpkin each on its inside, with a flickering candle in its center, enabling the carving of "*Enter*" on one and a silly face on the other to be seen.

A table was situated to the side before the maze and decorated with a thin wood log slice that had plastic candles with a small, dainty glass vase that held a small selection of white, beautifully arranged flowers. To the left, behind the table décor was a small black easel with white, elegant writing that read:

"Julia, welcome to the maze. Find your way around to the center where all of your questions will be answered".

"What is all this?" Despite my itching need and curiosity to go in and explore, I tore my eyes away from the beautiful layout as I spun around to face Kelvin, who was wearing an incredibly proud smile on his handsome face.

"Go in and you'll soon find out. I'll follow a little after you." He planted a delicate kiss on my forehead and turned me back around by my shoulders. With my intrigue beginning to pique, I did as I was told and started my journey through the maze.

The inside of the maze was lit up with fairy lights, just as the outside was, with small orange and white pumpkins decorating the footpath, leading me the way into the middle. After the first corner, the maze had become a literal walk down memory lane, displaying pictures of me, Kelvin and the odd one with Ava. I was like a kid in a candy store, my eyes completely agog at the beauty before me.

One of the pictures I came across was of the three of us standing under a log flume, in the process of getting drenched by a tsunami of water as the log came swooshing down. The memory of that day brought a smile to my face. Ava was twelve years old and had put up a fight about going because going to the theme park with your mum and her partner wasn't "cool". But once we got there and she'd been on a couple of rides, she let loose, and she really started to enjoy herself.

At the end of the day, Ava had fallen asleep in the car. Kelvin had carried her into the house like a babe in arms and took her to her bedroom where he gently placed her in bed and snuggly tucked her in. He hadn't known I'd followed him to her room and had stood leaned against the door frame as I watched him lightly tuck hair that had fallen onto her face behind her ear. I placed my hand on my chest as I remembered the feeling of love and contentment that filled me in that moment.

From the get-go, he'd been a brilliant father figure to Ava, and I truly couldn't fault him. It had broken Ava's heart, just as much as it did mine when we split. She always said, "I don't need a dad when I've got you" but having someone like Kelvin in her life truly did make her realise what she had been missing out on.

My feet carried me forward, and as I rounded the final corner, I could hear the soft playing of "I Swear" by All-4-One. I entered the center of the maze and continued to walk into the middle under an arch of autumnal leaves and chunkier fairy lights intertwined around them. My hand clamped to my mouth, I took in what was in front of me. There were tall posts with thin white fabric draped down with bronze, white and light pink balloons along one side before arching to the top corner of the other side. Stood to the emptier side of the makeshift wall stood Ava and Leon, holding hands and both wearing beaming smiles.

"Is someone going to tell me what's going on?" I was overwhelmed at all of this, and I couldn't make sense on what was happening. But my confusion and impatience for answers seemed to amuse Ava and Leon as they let out an amused laugh.

"Turn around." Ava's voice was soft but full of happiness. Her eyes had turned glossy, like she was about to cry and somehow her smile had grown even wider.

I turned around and my heart dropped to my feet when I found Kelvin bent in front of me on one knee with a silver ring which had the most beautiful gem on the top, gleaming in the lights.

"Julia. Since the first moment I laid eyes on you, I knew that you were the one for me, and us finding our way back to one another just proves that we were destined to be together forever." He'd started off strong, but halfway through, his voice had started to crack and wobble as tears began to well up in his eyes, his gaze never leaving mine. My own eyes were streaming with the salty liquid and my hands had moved to holding my cheeks.

"There's not a day that goes by when I'm not in awe of your strength, beauty and integrity. You've made me a better man..." His eyes flicked to behind me, finding their way to Ava, "...and you've also made me a father to an incredible young lady who I'm incredibly proud of." I could hear Ava sniff loudly behind me, making it even more difficult for me to control myself.

"I want to grow old with you, until we're both in our wheelchairs and you're still falling asleep straight after choosing what film we watch. I love you so much Julia, will you marry me?" The cry I had been holding in broke free through my throat, and completely lost for words, all I could do was vigorously nod my head until I finally found my voice.

"Yes! Of course, yes!" A smile spread across my face and Kelvin was now looking incredibly relieved as he brushed the tears off his cheeks with his free hands.

He stood up as he slid the ring onto my shaky finger. Once it was securely in place, Kelvin's hand cupped my chin as he tilted my head upwards and he bent down, sealing the deal with a loving, passionate kiss.

"Get in here you two." Kelvin had pulled away from my lips and pulled me in for an embrace with one arm, whilst holding the other out as he invited Ava and Leon to join us.

Surrounded by my family, the people I loved the most, this

moment couldn't have been anymore perfect.

Chapter 51

Leon's POV:

To celebrate Julia and Kelvin's engagement, Ava had organised a meal at a local restaurant whose outside appearance was rather deceiving. The exterior looked shabby and worn down, whilst the interior looked modern. Upon entering, the rich aroma of all kinds of food flooded our noses, and the low hum of happy chatter amongst the customers could be heard.

The restaurant had high ceilings with semi-flush lights that stretched out like spider legs. The interior was of white bricked walls with thin rectangular mirrors every few metres that didn't quite reach the ceiling or floor. The tables were round glass, being held up by a golden metal pole. The glass was protected by a white tablecloth that was laid over the top and velvet red chairs tucked under. Ava truly did know all the best kept secret treasures of our hometown.

I'd been incredibly apprehensive about coming face to face with Ava's mum – today was the first time since she practically walked in on us when she'd come to visit Ava all those months ago. We had spoken on Facetime since Ava had decided to give me a final chance; one I would not take for granted. She'd given me a right bollocking, and I was grateful that it was over the phone, because that woman truly did scare me; I could only imagine the damage she'd cause had it been in person – even if it was justified.

On the way to the meal, Julia had made a comment on the sly, threatening to cut off my prized jewels and shove them so far down my throat, I'd be spitting pubes for the next month if I dared stray or mistreat Ava again. But aside from that, she'd been a dream. I wasn't expecting to be welcomed with open arms, not by a long shot, but she'd given me the benefit of the doubt and I appreciated it greatly, even if I was unsure as to whether or not I deserved it.

Kelvin was a real stand up guy, and I could see why Ava respected him so much. He was so upbeat and chatty, and despite knowing who I was and what I did, he treated me as if it was water under the bridge. I made his soon-to-be daughter happy and that was all that mattered to him. He had kind, wise eyes that crinkled in the corners whenever he smiled or laughed. I'd not had the chance to speak to him on the phone whenever Ava had been on the phone to her mum as he was a Partner for a top law firm, and so had been working long hours, making this my first time meeting him.

My first impressions of him had all been positive. I wasn't expecting to be welcomed into the group hug at the engagement site, but it was kind of him to include me. He was polite and well mannered and seemed to have the time of day for everyone he came into contact with. Whenever anyone spoke, regardless of who you were or what you had to say, he listened to you and made you feel as if what you had to say was important and held great value. He was a man that wore his heart on his sleeve and was always there if you needed him, but he most certainly wouldn't take anyones bullshit.

As we were coming to the end of the main course, Ava and her parents were chatting about some local gossip that I really didn't care for, and so I found myself zoning out, getting lost in my thoughts. As I observed her and her family being so happy and the way they interacted with one another, I could feel jealousy start to creep in as it made me think of my own estranged family.

I hadn't seen my family since I left for college. Following in Jax, my older brothers' footsteps, I moved out as soon as I could to escape my crazy and dysfunctional family. Dad was a workaholic who spent as little time at home as possible to avoid the person he loathed the most. As a child, I never understood why he stayed with mum when he quite clearly didn't give a rat's arse about her. But as I got older, I realised it was so that he could protect his sons in his own way, even if he was absent for the majority of our lives. He just wanted to keep an eye on us. I suppose it was better than nothing, but I wish he would've gotten us out of that hell hole.

Mum was a paranoid schizophrenic who very rarely took her meds because "there's nothing wrong" with her. She was a nightmare when she was off her meds, always thinking someone was watching her, or that me and Jax were someone other than her sons who were out to hurt her. The number of times we were on the receiving end of her fear and state of confusion was off the charts. No matter what we did, no matter how much we pleaded and tried to convince her that we weren't out to hurt her, it still wasn't enough to quell the demons in her mind. To this day, I have no idea how our schools never reported our family to Social Services - we were constantly covered in dark bruises and cuts.

Having shared the same unfortunate life and only having one another, you'd think that me and Jax would have a close relationship. Unfortunately though, that wasn't the case. Jax decided to distance himself from me from the get-go, especially when he moved out. Having one less person to worry or care about made his life easier. In the beginning, despite never really talking or playing with me, he did all that he could to keep me safe, taking the brunt of our mum's confusion and anger by either hiding me, or standing between me and our mum. However, as I got older, the protective brother I knew and loved turned into a faint and distant presence and soon it was my turn to fully be at the hands of our mum.

During my training to be a therapist, I'd learnt that the reason behind the way I treated Ava was partly because of my poor home life. I was scared and alone and I didn't know who to turn to or what to do, and so to fill that empty void, I got in with the wrong crowd and took it out on someone else. It truly is a wonder how all that I did went unnoticed to the adults in power. I was a prick in school until I turned my life around; you would've thought my outrageous cries for help wouldn't have gone unheard.

Not wanting to let old, resurfaced memories ruin such a wonderful time, I did my best to block them out of my mind and looked around the table. I felt lucky to finally be included in a family – even if it was one I had almost broken. I wasn't officially a part of her family, but it felt like a slight insight into what could be. Sure, things were a little shaky right now with her mum being uncertain of me and my only being in Ava's life for a short time, but they were still including me, and it felt good.

I watched Kelvin and Julia and how they interacted with one another. They were holding hands on top of the table, with

Kelvin lovingly stroking the back of Julia's hand with his thumb. Julia laid her head on Kelvin's shoulder, earning her a sweet kiss on the head from him that made her smile like a Cheshire cat. They really were a picture-perfect couple who were clear as day head over heels in love with one another.

Turning to look at Ava, I scanned her from top to bottom. Every time I looked at her, it was like seeing her for the first time, and I would never tire of the sight of her and her beauty. She was wearing a deep V-neck, burgundy satin wrap dress, exposing her beautiful, tanned cleavage. Her hair was pinned up in a fancy bun with stray strands of hair framing her face in cute curls. She was a true sorceress when it came to hair styling. Whenever I watch her work her magic, I'm constantly astounded by her talent at creating such intricate looks. Her toned, bronzed legs were crossed with one over the knee of the other, shining in the lights, enticing me to touch her. I placed my hand on her smooth, soft skin, and gently stroked my hand up to where the skirt of her dress gaped, unable to control the rise that was happening in my pants.

Ava's facial expression didn't give away that anything was happening under the table out of her parents' vision, but she shifted her position so that her feet were flat on the floor, her legs spread apart slightly, inviting me to travel further up. However, I was in a teasing mood, and wanting to make her wait, I didn't move my hand. Frustrated at my lack of progression, she tried to subtly move my hand towards her warm core, but instead, I took her hand and placed it on my growing bulge. Still engaging in the conversation with her parents, she quickly rolled her bottom lip into her mouth before letting it bounce back out as her fingers started to stroke me through my trousers.

As she tickled me through the fabric, I began to picture

bending her over the table and just burying my dick inside of her, one hand wrapped in her hair pulling her head back to meet my lips, enabling me to be as deep as possible, the other held her by her waist, all the while pounding away as I made her scream in pure ecstasy.

"Leon?" Julia's soft voice yanked me out of fantasy. Seriously? Again? How does this woman know how to unintentionally interrupt such an intimate moment?

"I'm sorry, what did you say?" I kept my tone polite despite being annoyed that she had broken my dick tingling thoughts. Plus, I didn't want her to have any idea that I was too busy thinking about fucking her daughter senseless. She smiled as she tutted at me, rolling her eyes with the shake of her head.

"You men are all the same – only hear the things you want to. I said, are you wanting dessert?"

"Oh! No, I'm good thank you." I absolutely did want dessert, but not the kind she had in mind. I was craving something much, much sweeter. While Julia and Kelvin were talking to our waitress and ordering their desserts, I leaned over and once again found the delicate skin at the bottom of Ava's dress and delicately traced random patterns as I whispered into her ear and placed my own order.

"Meet me in the bathroom." I nipped the lobe of her ear with my teeth and was rewarded with a barely audible moan from her before I stood up and excused myself from the table.

The restaurant was one of the only ones in the area where there were unisex toilets. It was in a bid to promote equality and to be inclusive, but to me it was an open invitation to abuse the trust the establishment put in me as a customer. Let's be real, I'd be stupid not to take advantage of such an opportunity.

Hot on my heels, Ava stormed in and wordlessly stalked over

to me. Purpose fueled her power walk, making it almost a run, and an insatiable hunger burned in her eyes. Upon reaching me, her lips were instantly magnetised to mine and they began to desperately devour my own. I picked her up with a low grunt, cushioning her perky cheeks with my hands as she securely wrapped her legs around me, our lips never parting.

I kicked a stall open and locked the door behind me, all the while supporting her, and leaned her up against the door. If I had it my way, I'd be fucking her on the bathroom sinks, in clear view of anyone who walked in, but I knew Ava wouldn't feel as comfortable with that, and so the cubicle it was. Her lips parted slightly, and her smooth tongue urgently prodded mine, desperate for a taste of me. As our tongues tangled, I slid a hand up the back of her thigh and under the riding fabric of her dress until I once again came to the soft curve of one of her perfect cheeks, giving it a squeeze before slapping it, eliciting a delightful gasp that forced her to temporarily pause our kiss.

"I'm so fucking horny for you right now." She spoke quietly with a voice full of lust and desperation. Sliding my fingers a few inches from her backside round to her front - where I was pleasantly surprised to find that she wasn't wearing underwear - her body told me just how true those words were as I felt her on my fingertips. She was wet. So, so wet. It was all I needed to hear and feel to be at my optimum, raging hard-on.

"I want to rip your clothes off and fuck you senseless while everyone around us hears so that they wish they were us." I growled in her ear. I sucked on my fingers, tasting her delicious wetness and making them slick to the knuckle, before I glided two fingers into her, making her head tilt back against the toilet door and a melodic sound slip from her moist lips.

As I gently stroked away inside her, gradually building towards her high, her hand found my hair and she grabbed a fistful as she pushed her chest out and arched her back slightly, losing herself to the pleasure I was providing her. My thumb gently massaged her swollen clit as I added a third finger making her suck in her breath at the slight pressure of me stretching her. As much as I loved finger fucking her, my dick was aching to be inside her moist pussy.

"Just put your dick in me and fuck me already." She whined as she seemingly read my mind, begging me to satisfy her in the way only I could. I pulled my fingers from her momentarily to unbutton my trousers, which resulted in Ava protesting at the loss of my fingers. I resolved this problem quickly by replacing my fingers with my throbbing cock, coating myself with her wetness. I watched her face as her eyes rolled into the back of her head at the introduction of my cock inside of her.

As I pumped away inside her, I kept one hand on her backside to help support her as she tightened her legs around me, and my other hand was flat against the door. Although the door was locked, it still rattled under her with each thrust, making anyone who walked in well aware of what was going on. The thought of being caught fucking in a public place brought me such a thrill, and I couldn't help but smile at the thought of people catching and listening to us.

Ava was trying her hardest to suppress her moans of pleasure as she bit down on her plump bottom lip, and it was only getting harder for her as she got closer to finishing. Her hand came to her mouth in an attempt to stifle her moans, but I wasn't having that at all. I *wanted* to hear her moan. I *wanted* her to be loud.

"Don't cover your mouth. I want everyone to hear how good I make you feel. Now, scream for me baby girl." I took her hand away from her mouth, interlocking my fingers with hers as I pinned it up above her head, whilst her other hand was gripping my shoulder for dear life.

"Ohhh, fuck baby... you feel so good." Her warmth and wetness were unmatched to any I'd felt before, and it was something I don't think I'd ever get used to. My words of encouragement enabled her to find her voice as her moans started to get louder, turning me on even more. I pushed myself as deep as I could inside of her until I could feel her twinge and start to tighten around me.

"Shit...Like that, keep going like that... I'm so close." She sucked her lips in as she focused on how I was making her feel. I kept my rhythm, making sure I was hitting her in her sweet spot over and over again just as she'd asked.

"That's it, come for me Ava." Her nails dug into my shoulder through my shirt, her legs started to spasm around me, and her mouth fell open, letting out a little squeak as she peaked. Still moving inside of her, Ava's hand moved from my shoulder to my jaw, holding it firmly in place as she looked me square in the eyes with a mischievous smile on her face.

"Fill me up baby." That was it. The final straw. I let out a groan as my lips found her neck and I gently began to suck her soft skin as my cock tensed, spasming as I released my load into her. She squeezed me tight, the heels of her feet pushed against my arse cheeks, pulling me into her as deep as possible whilst I emptied myself into her.

Her legs loosened their grip on me, and still attached to her, I turned and placed her on the toilet seat, before pulling myself out of her. She closed her eyes with a soft, fulfilled smile spread on her face. Fuck, she was radiant post sex.

After cleaning up, we left the bathroom as if nothing had happened, but I didn't fail to miss the mix of looks from other customers positioned near the area: Men were jealous they didn't have the balls to have sex somewhere so public. Women were jealous they weren't being railed to high heavens as Ava had been. Then there were those who were either completely disgusted or were impressed at our brazenness. I couldn't help the smug smile that was plastered on my face. I pulled Ava closer to me with my hand low on her waist and basked in the atmosphere as we made our way back to our table.

Julia and Kelvin were too into their desserts and conversation to have noticed how long we were gone for and they seemed none the wiser about our cheeky quickie.

They finished up their desserts whilst talking to us about a few ideas they already had for the wedding. Julia and Kelvin both had small families, and so the wedding would only be an intimate one, which in my opinion, was the best way to have it; being surrounded by the people who mattered the most.

"So Ava..." Julia was done eating and she delicately dabbed the sides of her mouth with her napkin as she deliberated how to get out what she wanted to say. She reached across the table and took Avas hand in hers and inhaled a breath.

"Would you... do me the honour of walking me down the aisle?" To my left, I heard Ava let out a little happy squeal, her spare hand joining her other in her mums and squeezed.

"What a daft question, of course I will!" Ava's grandparents were sadly no longer with us. I remember the conversation me and Ava had about them. As she told me of her memories with them, she fluctuated between smiling at the fond times and tearing up at the pain of them no longer being here. She had such an amazingly close relationship with them, and it broke her heart when they had passed away whilst she was at college. It reminded me just how much trauma she'd endured, and yet her strength preceded her and proved just how resilient she was. I placed my hand on Ava's shoulder and squeezed it proudly; I just knew she'd look extravagant arm in arm with her mum as she walked her towards her forever after.

By the time we were ready to leave, the restaurant had started to empty out as the time slowly crept towards closing time. As we walked through the restaurant towards the door, it was noticeably more quiet with the lack of people that were in the building as the hubbub of chatter and voices that once surrounded us became but a murmur.

We'd driven here in separate cars as Kelvin had secretly booked a little night away for him and Julia, and they were going to their hotel straight from the restaurant. And so, after saying our goodbyes, we went our separate ways.

Ava's delightful laughter filled the car as we drove home, being silly as we sang and danced to the charts as they played through the radio. Her laugh was a sound that filled me with serotonin. It was infectious, and seeing her happy just instantly lifted my mood.

I pulled up to a set of traffic lights and took a moment to watch her lose herself to the music, holding an invisible microphone. It was in that moment, seeing her completely oblivious to how beautiful and perfect she was and lost in her happiness that I decided I wanted to forever be surrounded by her light, love and laughter.

I was going to marry this girl. My girl. Whatever it took.

53

Chapter 52

If there was one thing in this life that I hated more than anything, it was my weekly food shop. All I wanted to do was to be in and out, get what I need and go. However, the public have other ideas and seem to know that I am on a mission and do all they can to prevent me from completing it. Regardless of what day or time I go shopping, everyone and their mother seemed to be out, but today, just to piss me off that little bit more, they'd all brought their bloody nans too.

All morning I'd been on edge. I'd woken up with a strong sense of foreboding that was just casually lingering in the pit of my stomach. I felt like my stomach was vehemently churning butter and I couldn't put my finger on what it could be, or why I felt this way, but it didn't help with my impatience as I shopped.

To help keep me cool and grounded, I had my headphones in and was playing some upbeat music. Miming the lyrics, I bobbed my head and tapped the fingers of my hand that wasn't holding the basket on the side of my leg; browsing the aisles in my hunt for the items that were on my list, whilst attempting to ignore the growing annoyance at the slow walkers, abrupt halters and people clogging up the aisles, all of which being fuel to my growing hate-fire.

After arriving at the fresh meat section, I welcomed the cool air that encompassed me as I opened the fridge door and picked up a packet of diced chicken. As I read the protein contents on the flip side of the container, the music that was blaring in my ears was abruptly cut off by the default ringtone of my phone. Slightly annoyed at the interruption, I pulled my phone out of my back pocket and looked to see who the caller was, only to find "No Caller Id" to be displayed on the screen. I didn't usually take calls with No Caller Id, however the funny feeling in my stomach had turned, knotting into even more of a tangled mess than it already was, and thus I found myself answering the call.

"Hello?" I hadn't bought chicken from here before, but looking at the protein content, I may start having to.

"Hello. Am I speaking to Miss Brooks?" A soft, unfamiliar feminine voice drifted through the buds that were snuggled securely in my ears. I turned the packet of chicken over to check the best before end date. Only a few days left.

"You are. Who's this?" I quizzed bluntly as I dropped the chicken into my basket before moving on to the next section.

"I'm so sorry to bother you, but I'm calling from St. Francis Hospital. I have you down as the next of kin for Ffion Carter." Ffion. Hospital. Those two words were enough to make me be completely engaged and have my full attention on the purpose of this phone call. A red warning light came on in my brain, singing its alarm call as panic began to infiltrate my entire being and made me stop dead in my tracks.

"Ffion's in the hospital? Is she OK? Is the baby OK?" My questions were short and sharp, and with my voice raised in worry, I earned a few looks from nearby shoppers.

493

"Unfortunately, I can't give you the full details over the phone due to confidentiality, but she's been in a car accident this morning and is in a serious condition. If you could come down so we can discuss options moving forward..." A few people a short distance from me had stopped to observe me as I remained frozen on the spot, but my face was embossed with growing panic. Nosey bastards who clearly have nothing better to do than listen in on other peoples dramas and issues.

"I'll be there as soon as possible." I didn't want to hear talks about 'options moving forward'; it suggested that Ffion and the baby really weren't in a good condition, and it didn't bear thinking about. I hung up the call, my music exploding back into my ears, and abandoned my shopping basket before sprinting out of the supermarket, not missing my audience following me with their heads in my peripheral as I ran past them. How I didn't knock some poor old soul to the floor as I zig-zagged between the customers is beyond me.

The only person I wanted to talk to and see during this moment was Leon, and so I decided to give him a call. I both wanted and needed him with me for support; hospitals weren't my favourite place to be; I didn't want to walk the white corridors on my own. Once outside the supermarket, I waved down a taxi and jumped in, giving the taxi driver the address to Leon's place of work.

After clicking in my seatbelt, I found Leon in my call log and pressed the green phone and listened to the beeps of his phone number.

"Please pick up..." I willed, as I waited for him to answer, my knees bobbing up and down like a set of pistons; left, right, left, right, gradually picking up speed with each passing moment. However, I was disappointed when the call went straight to voicemail. The entire ten minute journey to his place of work, I chain called him, only to either be sent to voicemail or left his phone to just ring. I was growing incredibly annoyed with him for not answering. I appreciated that he was working and maybe had a patient with him, but surely my chain calls were a sign that I was calling for something urgent? My annoyance must have been aggressively radiating off me, alongside my cursing at Leon's clear inability of being able to pick up his phone, as the taxi driver kept glancing into his interior mirror at me with eyebrows almost touching as he frowned and his lips forming a thin, tight line.

By the time I was standing outside Leon's building, I was a bag of worry for Ffion and my frustration at not being able to get a hold of Leon only made me feel worse. I was desperate to be by Ffions side, to know what was going on and if she was going to be OK.

I stomped my way up to Leon's office, where I found him angrily pacing the office hallway where Ffions desk was, empty of her presence, phone to his ear for a few seconds before pressing a button and putting his phone to his ear again. Just seeing the way he held himself instantly set my own annoyance at him aside; he had something important going on which was clearly why he hadn't answered me. Hearing my footsteps, Leon looked to me with relief, only to be instantly replaced with confusion at seeing it was me and not the person he had been expecting.

"Ava, what are y-…" He'd started to walk to meet me, tucking his phone securely in his pocket.

"Can you cancel your appointments for the rest of the day? Fi's been in a car accident and it's not looking good. We need to get up there like, now." I cut him off and held my hand up to stop him continuing on. There was no time for unnecessary talk.

"Jesus fucking Christ! That would explain why she's not here and I can't get a hold of her or Ev. Let me get my coat and I'll take us." He started to briskly walk towards his office, only to pause at his office door, and turning his head to look at me with a panic that matched my own flaring in his eyes as a realisation hit him.

"Ava, was there any mention of Ev?" Desperation and dread saturated his voice. I turned my bottom lip up and half shook my head as I recalled my phone call, before completing a full shake.

"No, there was nothing about him. I thought he would've been in contact with you to tell you what had happened?"

"He brings Ffion to work everyday. If she was in a car accident, then chances are, so was he." *Fuck.* It had slipped my mind that Everett had started to take Ffion to work as she became more heavily pregnant. Leon disappeared to grab his coat from his office and grasping my hand as he went past, power-walked out of the building towards the car. It wasn't just Ffion we now both worried about.

* * *

We arrived at the hospital and Leon hadn't even turned the engine off when I was already getting out of the car. There was no time for piss-balling around, I had to get to Fi and Everett; assuming he too was in the building. Leon had caught up with me as I finished asking the lady at the front desk what ward Fi was on.

496

Following the directions given to us, we soon arrived at the ward and I informed the nurse who was on the ward reception that I was Fi's next of kin and was here to see her. She pointed down the hallway, turning her hand to direct us to the right to where we would find Fi's room.

We walked down the corridor hand in hand as Leon tried to help me control my shaking hands. I didn't like hospitals at the best of times; it brought back too many bad memories. I tried to focus on Fi and how I needed to keep a clear head so I could fully take in what the doctor had to say and be there the best I can for her. Leon, sensing my uneasiness, leaned down to my ear and whispered "breathe baby, breathe" whilst stroking the back of my hand with his smooth thumb. With a few deep breaths, I started to feel the wave of panic slowly start to diminish until it was but a calm ripple in the breeze. The usual lightheadedness I had prepared myself for had been reigned in; I had to be strong for Fi, her well-being far out-weighed my fear of hospitals, and so for her, I had to be courageous. As we walked, I resisted the urge to look at the patients in the open wards, imagining there were blinkers blocking my side vision, and concentrated on getting to Fi. I wasn't here for them, I was here for Fi.

As instructed, we took the corridor down the second right turning, and pinpointed Fi's room by finding Everett sitting outside it with his head in his hands and his elbows resting on his knees.

"Everett!" I called out to him as we walked up to him. Upon hearing us, he looked over to our direction and slowly stood. Even from a distance he was a sight for sore eyes; a rich, dark purple bruise was beginning to form over his right eye and the edge of his jaw where the airbag had blown up into his face and fresh tears streamed down his face, missing the silver path that

497

had been created by dried old tears.

By the time we got to him, he'd just managed to straighten himself up. I carefully pulled him into a hug, being wary of hurting him any further, but despite my efforts he still sucked in a sharp breath at my slight squeeze, making me hastily pull away to prevent further pain. Leon placed a comforting hand on his best friend's shoulder, before taking a seat next to him.

I could only imagine the embarrassment of having Leon hold his hand with one of his own hand, and resting his other on his back as he helped Everett slowly lower himself back into his chair, and so not wanting him to add to his embarrassment, I lifted my eyes and found myself looking at my own reflection in Fi's window. I wasn't too sure if I was relieved or disappointed to find that the blinds on the inside had been completely pulled down. Unable to tear my eyes away from the white plastic slats that blocked me from seeing her, I thought about what awaited me when I eventually went in to see her. As much as I was itching to be in there with her, I was also scared to see her in whatever condition she was in.

"Are you alright? What happened mate?" Leons voice broke through my thoughts and I took the seat on the other side of Everett. There hadn't been a time where I was required to console Everett, let alone in the absence of Fi, so I was unsure how to show my sympathy. I settled on taking his warm hand in mine and stared down at where we had joined together, focusing on what he was telling us.

"I was driving her to work... He came out of nowhere... The light was green... I'm *sure* it was green." He stuttered through his cries as he tried to recount to us what had happened. I gave his hand a small squeeze and stroked his arm with my free hand to reassure him to tell us in his own time, at his own pace.

"Take your time, brother." Leon spoke lowly, his voice full of patience and compassion. I flickered my eyes past Everett, who was staring at the floor, to Leon who met my gaze and gave me a tight smile. We both knew this wasn't going to be good. Did they go through a green light? Was Everett at fault for the accident? Everett wouldn't do anything to put his future in danger, I knew that. But you just never know. I needed to hear the full story before I jumped to conclusions, but I couldn't help my mind coming up with scenarios with the little snippets he had just told us. Seeming to read my thoughts through my eyes, Leon subtly shook his head, telling me to stop thinking, and just listen.

After a moment, he took a deep breath as he leaned back in his chair, his head against the wall behind us, tilted up to the ceiling with his eyes zoned on a spot of the brilliantly white tiles above our heads.

"I was driving her to work and we were talking about baby names. God, you should've seen her. She was so happy and chatty, rolling name after name off her tongue. You know, every night in bed, all she does is look up baby names." Talking about the baby brought a small smile to Everett's face as he recalled the memory, but it quickly faded as he carried on with the story.

"We were at the intersection on Stephen's Street and the lights we were approaching had turned green, so I went. I didn't see it until it was too late. A drunk driver drove through their red light and hit us on Fi's side, so she took the brunt of the impact." Not once had he looked down or at me and Leon. Instead, his head stayed against the wall, but his eyes were screwed shut like he was trying to stop the vision of what happened from entering his mind.

"I tried to swerve out of the way, but it was pointless. If only

I'd have seen him coming, then maybe... maybe we wouldn't be in this position." His voice broke and wobbled as he struggled to keep his emotions at bay and his face gave up control, scrunching up as his emotions began to push their way out. It was a side to Everett that I had never seen before: vulnerable, broken and emotionally exposed.

Feeling more comfortable with this form of intimacy with Everett, I moved to crouch in front of him, keeping his hands cocooned in mine as I stroked the smooth top of his hand with my thumb in a soothing wiper motion.

"Everett. Everett, look at me." Doing as instructed, he lowered his head and looked down at me. His eyes were swimming with sadness and guilt and it made my heart clench in my chest.

"This was not your fault, so stop blaming yourself. He was drunk and ran a red light; there was nothing you could've done to stop that, and unless you can see into the future, you most certainly wouldn't have seen him coming." A warm tear splashed on my hand and a cry finally managed to escape from Everett with my reassurance. I stood up and cradled his head into my stomach, holding him there as he let out his sobs. Leon shuffled to get as close to Everett as he could and wrapped the pair of us in his arms in a group hug. We stayed this way for a few minutes until Everett's cries had just become sniffles and stuttery breathing.

"Oh, I'm sorry. I'll give you guys some space, I can come back." A deep, yet apologetic male voice came from behind us, making us all jump and turn in the direction of the sound. Before us stood a doctor in black tapered trousers, and a light blue shirt that was tucked into his waistband and rolled up at the sleeves, exposing his tanned forearms that were cradling a clipboard.

I looked down at Everett who shook his head to the doctor. I may be next of kin, but Everett was Fi's partner. I would only speak with the doctor if Everett was ready for it.

"No, it's fine. You can stay." He sniffed and buried his head into his palms as I stepped away from him, wiping his tears from his face, but only succeeding in smudging them all over his face. The doctor had a sympathetic look on his face as he watched Everett wipe the evidence of his vulnerableness from his face. Reaching behind him into his back pocket, he retrieved a small packet of tissues and held it out to Everett, inviting him to take one. A small grateful smile tugged on the corner of Everetts lips as he took a tissue and began to dab at his face before he took a deep breath through his nose and prepared himself for what the doctor was about to disclose to us.

"I'm sorry I wasn't able to tell you anything about Ffion, but I can only disclose information with the next of kin present; hospital policy." Everett nodded his head and told the doctor that he understood before the doctor turned his attention to me.

"You must be Ava, Ffion's next of kin. I'm Dr. Tate and will be overseeing Ffion's care." He offered his hand to me. It was warm and steady in mine - a surgeon's hand - as I took it in a gentle handshake.

"How is she? Is she going to be OK? The lady who called me said about discussing options moving forward?" Questions spluttered out of me like a backed up tap. To slow me down, the doctor held his hand up before glancing down at his clipboard, making sure that what he was about to say was correct, whilst holding a solemn facial expression.

"We've had to put Ffion into a medically induced coma due to swelling on the brain. The extent of the damage once she wakes... I'm afraid we can't say for sure at this moment in time. There's a forty-sixty chance she'll be fine, or she could be a victim of brain damage to some degree. This means she could gradually regain her consciousness and be able to move and speak normally. Or, she could go into a vegetative state where though she is awake, she won't show any signs of being aware of herself or her surroundings." Time froze around me as I wordlessly stumbled back into my chair, my eyes wide in disbelief whilst the news began to sink in. The "options moving forward" would be discussing care for Fi, should it come to it. Why was it that bad things always happen to good people? Her nor Everett deserved to be in this situation, and yet here they were. My strong walls began to crack as my emotions finally caught up with me and a couple of tears I was fighting to hold back betrayed me and slipped down my face. But I couldn't cry. Not yet. I'd have a proper cry about this when I wasn't in the presence of Everett or Fi – they both needed me.

Dr. Tate wasn't finished reeling off his list of Fi's injuries. Looking back down his clipboard, he dragged his finger over the piece of paper until he came to the list of her injuries. I couldn't focus on much else of what was said: severe bruising caused by her seatbelt, a lisfranc fracture from having her foot crushed, and your standard cuts and scratches. None of these were life threatening he assured – just the swelling on her brain.

It was Everett who asked the question that I had been too into my head to think about asking, much to my shame, but the second he asked it, something clicked in my brain and my mind seemed to shift and focus on the doctor fully again. The fact that he'd asked showed that he truly hadn't been told even a whisper about Fi and her situation. Surely when it came to his child they could have told him?

"We had to perform an emergency c-section to give the baby

any chance of life. The trauma Ffion endured caused some internal bleeding, which led to the baby's heartbeat to drop drastically and without immediate attention, we would've lost her." We were all silent as we processed what Dr. Tate had just disclosed.

"We... Our baby's a girl?" Everett, the first of us to speak of the bombshell that Dr Tate just unknowingly dropped on us, choked on his words as he got them out. Dr. Tate looked between us with confusion sketched all over his face, until the realisation of what he had accidentally just done finally hit.

"You didn't know." Not a question, a statement. His fingers drummed in a wave on the back of his clipboard as his lips formed a thin, apologetic line. He'd put his foot in it without realising, and his face said he knew how big of a revelation it was to us, but more so to Everett. But the new daddy had fresh tears pouring out of him, although now they were a mix of joy from the sudden birth of his daughter and sadness at what brought about the early birth.

"A girl. Wow. Fi always said she wanted a girl." A soft, adoring smile broke through the sadness, and a small laugh with a shake of his head as he followed up with, "she won the bet..." and then his face crinkled up again and the anguish struck him as he finished with, "...if she ever wakes up to call it in." My heart truly did break for him. His love for Fi was made abundantly clear in this moment as he felt every segment of his heart shatter individually. Everett placed an elbow on his knee and pressed his forehead against his palm.

"Come on mate, let's not think the worst. This is Ffion! She's a fighter, she'll get through this - especially with us by her side and your daughter waiting to meet her." Leon's strong voice, now a soft wave of compassion as he spoke to his chosen brother. After a pat on his shoulder, he pulled Everett into him and hugged his head to his own shoulder.

"It's going to be fine, I'm sure of it." With a sad, half-hearted nod, and a couple of taps on Leon's knee, Everett pulled himself away from Leon's and took a tissue that Dr. Tate was once again offering.

"Are we allowed to see Fi now?" I took my eyes away from the short display of brotherly affection and support and focused them on Dr. Tate who was tucking the packet of tissues away back into his back pocket.

"Of course, but just a forewarning that what you're going to see will be upsetting." Dr. Tate held a serious gaze before walking the few short steps to Fi's room, and held the door open for us, allowing us to file in one after the other, before closing the door behind us on his way out.

It goes without saying that no amount of preparing or guessing the state Fi was in could have prepared any of us for the reality of what we were now looking at.

Chapter 53

<u>Ava's POV:</u>

Just over a week later and Fi was still in her coma. Only a few days ago they had started to reduce the drugs that were coursing through her body keeping her asleep. She could wake any moment, any day, either as the Fi we all know and love, or a complete shell of herself. I couldn't imagine a world without Fi's bright and bubbly personality, and it hurt to even think about it, but we had to face the reality that the worst could indeed happen.

None of us could have even comprehended what we walked in to on that very first day - it was quite the shock to the system. Her face was splotched with dark bruising with a stitched gash on her forehead, her foot was in a cast and slightly elevated in a sling that hung from the ceiling. Cuts hatched haphazardly on the visible parts of her body, as if someone who couldn't see had taken to cross-stitching along her once flawless tanned skin. Any other bodily injuries were hidden from view as she was neatly tucked into the white sheets, her arms placed outside the fabric beside her body.

The thing that really tore my heart out of my chest was seeing the amount of tubes coming out of her from basically every orifice possible; she was completely comatose and looked like a science experiment in progress. A nasogastric feeding tube was taped to her nose to prevent it from moving, a breathing tube that was attached to a mechanical ventilation system was down her throat, and a tube coming out of her head to drain the fluid that had built up around her swollen brain. An IV had been inserted in one hand, whilst on the other a clip resided on her finger to monitor her heart rate. Anything that was for waste was discreetly hidden from view by the covers.

Before visiting Fi, I paid a visit to her and Everett's little girl for the first time today. Born at twenty-seven weeks, Dr. Tate had informed us that she was at risk of complications and medical problems but that she had a ninety-percent chance of survival. With the odds in her favour, she was doing amazingly. The nurse in the NICU explained to me that although she was now outside of the womb, she still developed as she would if she was still inside Fi. She could respond to sound, she could open her eyes - although she wouldn't be able to focus or move them - and she can practise her suckling skills. She was the smallest thing I had ever seen.

She was laid in the center of her incubator cot, a tiny cushion around her head giving her support, almost a mirror image of her mum. She had tubes in her nose and throat, feeding her and breathing for her, heart monitor patches stuck to her chest and an IV drip in her hand - like mother, like daughter. Around her ankle that was so thin I could wrap a finger around it, was her identity bracelet, with the name Baby Carter on it.

I placed my hand on the glass, the closest I would get to touching her for a long while, as a tidal wave of memories pelted me full force. Memories of looking at her baby scans. Memories of the numerous FaceTime calls with Fi to discuss the impact that such a small being had in Fi's life. I stared in the incubator at the small life, and was taken back to Fi telling me she was pregnant. How scared she had been, yet determined to carry and have the little human despite that fear. From the look in her eyes that had shone through when I asked if getting rid of it was an option, I knew she already loved her unborn child, and that that love would only grow with each passing day. And yet, regardless of knowing how scared she was, I still left her. A tear dripped down my cheek, at my selfishness. If Fi didn't make it out of this, my guilt at the loss of time and not being there in person for her would consume me for life.

I spent a good couple of hours with her, just listening to the beeps of the machines before I headed to Fi's room in the ICU.

She was still laid on her bed, slightly raised, with her arms out of the blankets by her side, just as she had been for the past eight days. Looking through the open door, I leaned against the doorframe and observed Everett who was perched on the edge of a chair next to her, holding the hand that had her IV in, being careful not to knock it out of place, softly caressing the skin around it and placing occasional delicate kisses on her hand. The bruising around his eye and jaw had turned into a galaxy of blue, green and yellow. He'd been with Fi morning and night, only leaving to shower and eat. The staff had been so understanding and wonderful and had provided him with a pillow and blanket so that he could sleep on the sofa at the bottom of Fi's room. The bags under his eyes - which were only visible from under one eye - were puffy and getting darker by the day. It was all well and good for him getting some shut-eye here, but he needed a proper sleep. He'd say no, just as he had done every time I told him to, but he could do with going home and getting the sleep he clearly needs.

I quickly took in her room. The collection of flowers had grown by the day, adding colour to the plain, characterless room. Helium balloons with the message "*Get Well Soon*" floated in the corners, their white winding ribbon attached to weights to prevent them from being lost forever. I smiled at the thought that if she was awake, she'd have sucked all of the helium out of those balloons by now, not being able to resist the temptation.

"How's she doing?" Everett turned his head to look at me, giving me a weak welcoming smile, before his gaze was back on Fi.

"Not too bad. No change really, but her eyelids have been moving a lot more today, so hopefully it's not long until she wakes up." It sounded like encouraging progress, but there was no use in getting our hopes up. She'd wake up when she was ready to.

"That's really good news Ev. How about you though? How are you holding up?" I just reached Fi's bed, the side where Everett was, and gently perched myself on the edge, after feeling for any tubes to avoid sitting on. He dragged tired eyes slowly to look into my own.

"Barely if I'm being honest. I just want to take my girls home and live the life we're supposed to be living. Why did this have to happen to us?" He was working his way through the five stages of grief, although it seemed that rather than going through them one by one, he was experiencing them in one tumultuous blow, all at the same time.

"I know. It's not fair that this has happened to you both. But all we can do is weather the storm and pray for the rainbow on the other side." I had no other comforting things to say to him.

Truth be told, I just didn't know what to say anymore, we'd heard it all.

"You look like you could do with a decent sleep in your own bed. Why don't you go home for a couple hours, I'll stay with Fi until you're back." Everett sharply turned his head to me with an upturned upper lip as if I'd just asked him to take a shit on the floor.

"I am not leaving Fi for that long. What if she wakes up? I want to be here when she does. So no. I am not going home to sleep." This week, I'd learned something new about Everett; he became a complete sassy-pants without proper sleep. Whilst it was quite amusing, his stubbornness was bloody aggravating.

"Well, at least go and get something to eat or take a walk outside. You need a break Ev. I'm here now so if anything changes, I'll call you straight away." As much as it entertained me to witness this side of Everett, I knew better than to rattle his cage while he was in this mood. He sat quietly for a moment, watching Fi for any kind of movement while he contemplated his option.

"Fine. I suppose some air would do me some good. But you promise to let me know if anything happens?" He looked even more drained as relief settled in his features at having some time to himself.

I reached over as I gave his upper arm a slight, reassuring squeeze. "You have my word Everett." He heaved himself up, heavy from tiredness, and gave my shoulder a squeeze as he walked past. Once he'd left the room, leaving the door open, I positioned myself to face Fi, remaining perched on her bed.

Dr Tate had told us to talk to Fi when we visited. Apparently, she could hear us, she just couldn't respond. Though I wasn't sure if that genuinely was how it worked - how could someone who's asleep hear you? - it helped ease my mind by somewhat believing that maybe, just maybe, she could hear me. Due to this half-hearted belief, I began keeping a journal about everything that had gone on, just in case she hadn't heard and I could fill her in when she woke up.

"Hey Fi, how you doing?" I scoffed at my idiocy, "What a dumb question. You obviously aren't doing alright or else you wouldn't be here and I wouldn't be talking to myself." If she heard me and remembered, there was no doubt in mind that she'd tease me for it. I smiled at the thought.

"I met your little bubba today. She is the smallest, most precious thing I've ever seen. You know that app you obsessively go on, the one that tells you what size the baby is in gestation? Well, I had a look and apparently she's the length of an eggplant and weighs the same as a litre bottle of drink. How mad is that?" At this point I was just rambling; I always did whenever I had one of our one-sided chats, and just like every single time I went on and on and on, I had no idea where I was going. I just let my mouth run.

"She really is beautiful, Fi. She's got your square nose and she has the thinnest eyebrows that they look almost invisible." As I smiled through the thoughts and descriptions of Fi and Everetts baby, I felt the muscles in my face drop and an unsuspecting tear plummeted into my lap as I thought about how Fi couldn't see these things for herself.

"You need to wake up Fi. You need to meet your baby, your beautiful little angel." My plea forced its way through my dry, constricting throat as I tried to keep from crying, like hearing me beg for her to wake up would make any difference. I dropped my gaze to her hand that was lifelessly laid in mine, unable to look at her despite her closed eyes with the truth I was about to offload. What better time to open my heart up about something I had kept from her than now when there's a chance she won't hear or remember it.

"I'm so happy for you, you know? But I can't help feeling jealous at how blessed and lucky you are to have created something so pure. To experience something so magical. To not having to worry about telling such life changing news to the person that you love that would jeopardise your future with them. I know I need to tell Leon, but how do I even do that? Where do I start? I'm so scared to tell him Fi, because what if he walks away from me?"

"What could you possibly say to make me walk away from you?" Leon's voice came from the doorway, making me jump so hard that I had to check Fi's hand to make sure that I didn't knock or dislodge her cannula. I turned to look at him and found him standing in Fi's room, one hand in his pocket whilst the other held a cardboard cup holder holding two takeaway cups. He walked over to the table at the end of Fi's bed and placed the cup holder down onto it, before making his way over towards me and sat himself down on Everetts seat.

Normally, he would tell me that I didn't have to tell him anything if I wasn't ready to or if I didn't want to. But for the first time ever, he patiently waited for me to open up to him about the thing that I have been hiding from him since he came back into my life. There was no avoiding or hiding this any longer. But how do you tell someone something this life altering? Especially when it's someone whose life it will affect. Telling Wyatt hadn't been this hard. But then looking back, I don't think I minded the risk of losing him. My gaze dropped to my hands, both no longer holding Fi's hand, but instead were interlaced with each other.

"Whatever it is, no matter how big it is, you can tell me." His warm hand was placed on my thigh, giving it a squeeze of reassurance. The tears were pricking at my eyes, my lips trembling as my fear threatened to overwhelm me.

"You'll leave me, Leon. You won't want me anymore." How could he want to be with me if I couldn't give him the one thing that he has said he wants with me? I had grown to accept my fate, but I wouldn't ever forgive myself if I went a lifetime preventing Leon from the life he wants and deserves.

"No, I won't. Whatever it is, we'll deal with it together." He'd shuffled himself and the chair closer, closing the gap between us. His face showed no emotion, not letting on how he was feeling about what could come out of my mouth. He deserved to know. It had been far too long keeping it from him and better now than never. Right?

I took a deep sigh to compose myself, then started to finally uncover and disclose my secret.

* * *

Leon's POV:

She hadn't heard me come in. She was sitting on Ffion's bed, holding her hibernating hand. Her beautiful hair, a blonde, sleek sheet down her back with the side bangs tucked behind her ear. As the winter drew nearer and the sun was making less of an appearance in the day, Ava's hair had grown darker, as if the sun and season dictated her hair colour.

I hadn't meant to eavesdrop on her one-sided conversation to Ffion, but after bumping into Ev, I knew she was here and thought it would be funny to make her jump. She was easy to scare and I loved catching her off-guard. Instead, I had heard the tail end of her talk, where she said I would walk away from her with whatever she was scared to tell me.

I had known for a while that there was something that she had kept from me, but because it wasn't my story to tell, and so I'd waited for her to tell me on her terms. Even though I had put her on the spot and there was no way for her to get out of it this time, I was glad that she finally opened up to me. However, I couldn't stop my heart from skipping when I heard her truth. I was not prepared for what came out of her full lips that darkened with each tear that crawled down her pale skin.

It had taken a little coaxing, and where I usually never pushed her for information or to talk, I couldn't let it go now. She started by telling me how she was messing around with someone in college. Nothing serious, just a little fun to satisfy each others' needs. She then went on to tell me how she had miscarried whilst not even realising she was pregnant. Her pregnancy had been an ectopic one, and so her pregnancy was doomed from the start anyway. She'd been rushed into hospital because she was bleeding heavily, and there she discovered her condition. She'd needed surgery to fix the damage the ectopic pregnancy had caused to her fallopian tube, which meant that the scarring would mean her chances of conceiving were slim. If she did manage to conceive again, her pregnancy would be high-risk and would need to be monitored regularly.

I sat in silence as I processed this new information. I'd told her a few times that I wanted a family of my own. The more

I remembered the times of telling her this, the more the guilt crept in. She knew that she may not be able to make that happen for me - for us. The more I thought, the more I saw the signs of what she was thinking. The way her face would crinkle for a split second, or her eyes would go distant at the mention of having children. How could I be so blind?

"Are you going to say anything?" Her voice, quiet and unusually timid, broke through my thoughts. She was looking down at me with tears holding on for dear life on her lashes, her cheeks flustered and her lips now a deep red.

"See, I told you..." Her voice had cracked again, her insecurity walls being rebuilt as she started to pull her hands out of mine. I held on tighter and pulled them back towards me. I was not going to let her recoil back into herself.

"It's just... it's a lot to take in Ava. I can understand why you felt like you couldn't tell me and I can only imagine how hard it's been for you to have gone through this on your own. But it's not the end of the world. There's ways around this, there's options for us to explore." A small sniff and a drop of a tear came from Ava.

"But..." I stood up, placed my hands on the side of Ava's wet face and tilted it up so she was looking at me, my thumb softly stroking her warm skin, spreading her tears like wipers across her rosy cheeks as I cut her off.

"No buts. This doesn't change the way that I feel about you." I didn't have the answers right now, I didn't know what the right thing to do was, and I didn't really know how I felt. But what I did know was that I loved Ava more than anything and I would not let this come between us. Where there's a will, there's a way and we would have a family one way or another. A cloud of anxiety began to dissolve in her eyes as relief flooded into them.

I pulled her into a hug, and cradled her head into my chest, her tears soaking my t-shirt.

"I love you Ava. We'll work this out together." She turned her head up at me, her chin resting on my chest. I gave her a squeeze and a kiss on the forehead, her eyes closing at the affection.

"About... time..." A dry, croaked whisper came from the bed, a voice that didn't belong to either one of us and one that we hadn't heard in over a week. Ava ripped away from me and stood up by her friend's bed, leaning down to give her friend's head a hug. Ffion's eyes were half open with a slanted, small smile on her lips.

I took that as my cue to leave them both to it. I gave Fi's foot a gentle squeeze on my way out of her room. I called Ev's phone, and while I waited for him to pick up, I called for the doctor who was behind the reception that Ffion had woken. The ring ended and Ev's panicked voice sounded from the other end. No hello, just a desperate "What's happened?" came from the other end.

"She's awake, Ev. She's awake and talking."

Chapter 54

<u>Ffion's POV:</u>

An empty, black void had been blanketing me for God knows how many days. Or minutes. Or even hours. It's so dark here - wherever *here* is. I had no idea what was going on or where I was, just that I was isolated and locked away on my own. It was scary not knowing anything, smothered in complete darkness. Occasionally, I could hear people talking or sometimes crying. I didn't recognise everyone but I have heard Ev, A and Leon's voices. Hearing them brings me a little comfort; it makes me feel less alone, although it upsets me hearing the people I love in some sort of anguish.

Whenever A spoke to me, she'd tell me about her day, and the latest celeb gossip she knew I'd love hearing about. Leon would talk about Ev and how Ev has been feeling. It hurt me to hear it, and this pain was made even worse by not being able to see him or move to comfort him. The evidence of Leon's statements were backed up by Ev's cries. That was what I heard the most. I haven't seen or heard him cry in a while. I couldn't see it, but

I feel like I felt him hold and kiss my hand whenever he was around. Why couldn't I squeeze his hand back?

Right now, it's just me and A. Ev walked out not too long ago after A told him to take a break. How long had he been with me? She was now going on about meeting my baby and saying how small she is, but I don't remember having her. Ev had spoken about our baby too and he'd also said we had a little girl. Honestly, if I could, I would have cried. I'd always wanted a girl, and I couldn't wait to hold her in my arms. But she wasn't ready to come out, I was only twenty-seven weeks pregnant. Would she even survive?

Sometimes, I thought I was dreaming when I heard people talking. It was frustrating not being able to see who was speaking to me, if it was real. I sifted through my memories to try to see if I could remember anything else. It was getting slightly easier to remember things. My head had become clearer with each passing moment, as piece by piece the jigsaw was slowly becoming complete. I vaguely remember the car crash. It was the only thing that I could see that wasn't total darkness as it played like a movie in my head. I'd been in the car with Ev, and someone ran a red light and hit us on my side. I don't remember much else after that, aside from bright white lights flashing over my head as I was being transported somewhere. I remember the muffled talk of people around me. I didn't know what they said, but I do remember the term 'emergency surgery' being used. Maybe that was about removing my baby from me. But then that would suggest that my unborn child had been in some sort of danger, and the thought of that was unbearable.

It was horrible being in the dark on my own, with utter uncertainty as to where I was and even worse that I couldn't ask anyone where I was or what was going on. It was difficult to make out if I was just out of it and waiting to wake up, or if I was stuck in my own eternal hell loop; trapped in bottomless emptiness. Occasionally I'd get a whiff of white musk and I knew that Ev was nearby. It was comforting to smell something so homely, although I should be mad. I'd banned him from using my favourite perfume. That stuff was too expensive for him to go squirt happy with. But if it consoled him during my absence, then how could I possibly be mad at him? It was actually quite sweet and endearing. Maybe I'll let him use it on the odd occasion if I am able to find my way back to him.

A's voice swirled wistfully around in the blackness. She was rather happy a second ago as she spoke about my baby - my sweet, beautiful child - but she had quickly turned sad as she started talking about her lack of being able to conceive. Why hadn't she told me before that she was jealous of me? I'm not a complete heartless bitch, or at least I didn't think I was. I understood why she would feel that way. It would be my worst nightmare too if I was unfortunate enough to be in her position, but she should know that she can tell me anything. She was the first person I wanted to tell my news to. She was the first person I *went* to. I hadn't thought about how she'd feel until I'd actually told her. Her poker face was second to none, but I knew her well enough to notice the slight drop in her smile, the single twitch in her eyebrow that was almost invisible to the naked eye. Perhaps I shouldn't have told her so soon. Perhaps I should've given myself time to digest the news myself so I could think about the other people in my life who this would affect. Was it bad of me to have shared my pregnancy journey with her and to do it so shamelessly enthusiastically? No. I shouldn't let someone else's misfortune dwindle my happiness and impede my future and choices.

Her voice began to quiver, making the swirls vibrate like a rippling water surface before a tsunami. She knew she needed to tell Leon. She'd said this plenty of times to me previously. But she also knew the risk that came with it. She was frightened that he was going to walk away from her, to go find someone who could give him what she potentially couldn't. However, I highly doubt this would be a deal breaker for Leon when it came to her, and I had endlessly tried my best to encourage her to open up to him. He loved her more than anything, and to prove that, he would go to the ends of the Earth for her. After everything that they'd encountered together and despite their tragic past, they'd overcome their differences; had conquered their demons that had skulked surreptitiously in the shadows for so many years. A love like that was unbreakable, untouchable, and she was a fool for not seeing it.

At some point, Leon had come into the room. He'd caught her off-guard by approaching and entering the room as silent as an assassin. And so, like a fly on the wall, it was all I could do as I listened to her letting out the next biggest secret that she had kept from him with her quivering voice filled with sorrow and fear. He was quiet, letting her speak and get it all out into the open uninterrupted. He was good at that. He was a good listener. I suppose it was an attribute he needed, else he'd be pretty shit at his job. I'm glad that he wasn't letting this slide, just as I knew that he had done many times before. This secret had been kept for far too long and it was about time she told him. Out of nowhere, the strange blacked out world that I had been inhabiting started to have some light break through it, and I felt like my eyes were opening; the light from the outside blinding me after them being closed for too long. I caught glimpses of Leon holding Ava's hand as she struggled to meet his gaze, instead focusing on where the pair of them were joined, before my eyes fluttered shut.

Once she finished telling him, he hadn't said a word. I couldn't say I could blame him. Something that monumental is quite speech rendering and takes some time to sink in. But I also knew what A was like and that she'd take his silence in a bad way. He spoke to her in a calming manner. He wasn't angry at her for keeping this from him, and he kept any feelings of sadness that he may be feeling at bay. His tone remained steady, yet quiet. This was a private matter between the pair of them, and apparently me. He stayed strong and composed and I knew without a shadow of a doubt that he would do anything to make their future family happen for them, one way or another.

I willed my eyes to open and was surprised when they slowly opened, now more adjusted to the lights that flooded into my retinas. Leon held Ava in a loving embrace, telling her he loved her. She turned to look up at him, her eyes pooled with relief and infatuation and her chin lightly resting on his chest. It warmed me seeing them like this. It wasn't uncommon for them to be affectionate around people, letting their love for one another flourish and fill the room.

Suddenly, I felt Ava hugging my head and Leon shouting out for a doctor. Out of nowhere, I had surprised both myself and my visitors by speaking for the first time in a while. Still somewhat out of it, I raised a weak, single hand to hold A's head as she cuddled my own and breathed in her sweet vanilla scent. I was back. No more darkness. No more loneliness. But there was a feeling of emptiness. There was something missing. A hollowness occupied my stomach and panic quickly overwhelmed me. My baby... where was my baby?

Feeling me tense underneath her, Ava pulled away and cupped

my face in her hand. "Your baby's fine Fi. She's in NICU and she's thriving under the best care possible. Oh Fi, she's absolutely perfect." A soft smile fell upon Ava's lips as she informed me of my daughter. So I had been hearing things right. I had a baby girl. Before I could ask to see my little angel, I was interrupted by some commotion going on outside in my ward.

"Fi!... Fi!... Get out of my way!" I heard Ev's voice and the pounding of his feet before I saw him as he hurtled his way through the hospital corridors, before bursting into my room. He swam his way past Leon, Ava, the doctor and nurses who had started to congregate into my room. Upon reaching my bed, he dropped himself down next to me, before cradling my face in his hands, his forehead pressed against mine.

"I'm so glad that you're okay. I was so scared Fi." His tears dropped onto my cheek, the cold wetness a pleasant welcome in this stuffy room. I'd missed him more than I could've ever imagined possible. Being able to hear his voice every day, yet not be able to see or hold him had been complete torture. My hands shakily moved up to stroke his rosy cheeks, my thumb grazing his skin as I swiped away his tears.

"I'm here baby. Everything's OK now. I'm not going any-where, I promise." I didn't know what I was expecting to sound like after having not used my voice in so long, but I wasn't expecting to sound like someone who smokes sixty cigarettes a day. But it didn't matter. Nothing mattered when I was here. Alive. Being able to see, speak and feel again.

"Don't ever do that to me again, Ffion. I... I don't know what I'd do if I ever lost you." He couldn't meet my eyes, the guilt of our accident eating away at him. I had heard him multiple times apologise for the accident, one that wasn't his fault.

"Well, don't get us into another car accident then." Ava

snorted a laugh in the background and I could almost hear Leon rolling his eyes as he smirked. To some it would be too early to joke about being in this sort of predicament, however jokes were a fabulous coping mechanism for me, and if I didn't laugh about it, well I'd simply cry instead. Ev just gave me a light smile and a soft chuckle before pulling away to kiss my palm and then nestled my hands in his.

"I'll do my best not to." Returning the smile, I then looked around to the rest of the room. The doctor and a nurse were checking the monitors that surrounded my bed and comparing them with the notes that were kept at the end of my bed. For the first time, I noticed the flowers that brought life to the bland hospital room I was being kept in. It touched me that so many people cared about me.

"Now then. Where's my baby girl?" I addressed no-one in particular, the void in my stomach reminding me that there was someone missing from this reunion. Someone who everyone had met. Everyone except me. Was it wrong to feel left out? To feel jealous that everyone had met my baby before I had? And yet, I also felt excited that though she arrived insanely early, it meant that I get to meet my baby sooner and have more time to love and be with her.

"Your daughter is currently in NICU, as I'm sure your friends have already told you. She's doing very well, but she won't be able to come out of her incubation pod until at least thirty-five weeks. I'm sorry, but we can't let you see her just yet." A doctor in a white long coat that covered blue scrubs was positioned at the foot of my bed. He snapped my notes shut before tucking them under his arm. He spoke in a sharp, no-nonsense manner, and though I could hear him speak, I couldn't see his lips move due to them being buried somewhere in the depth of the dark jungle of hair that resided on his face. As I zeroed in on his beard, I came to the unequivocal conclusion that there was enough hair there to carpet my lounge. I felt my heart shatter at his pithy response, and Ev squeezed my hand as he jumped up off the bed to challenge the offspring of King Kong. How come everyone else was able to see her apart from me? Her own mother? Alas, the doctor continued to speak, preventing anyone from getting a word in edge-ways.

"When patients come out of their coma, they experience what's known as Post-Traumatic Amnesia, or PTA for short. This means that you may be disorientated, emotional and have little to no-memory, alongside having erratic or bizarre behaviour. Memory takes the longest to recover after a coma, and it is completely normal to experience this. So until we can rule this out and are happy that your conscious state is stable, you're prohibited from seeing her."

"But I *can* remember. I remember the accident. I remember the names of Ev, Ava and Leon. I remember I was pregnant before the accident." Confusion swirled and clouded my mind at what the doctor had said to me. I'd never heard of this PTA before, but I wasn't suffering from it. Nope. Not a chance.

"When was your due date for the birth of your child?" Trying to prove his point, the doctor started putting my memory to the test. Something as important as that I would surely remember, and yet while the date should've been on the tip of my tongue, it wasn't, and the harder I tried to think what the due date was, the thicker the fuzz in my brain became.

"What was the name of your first school?" Leon's voice trailed from the back of the room, chipping in on the spontaneous quiz. Something no person ever forgets and yet... *blank.* Both hands over my eyes, pressing into my face until I saw white, I tried to squeeze the information out of my brain.

"What was the name we decided on if we were having a girl?" Ev looked back down at me, the worry already seeping back into his eyes as he too began testing me. But again, I didn't know the answer, nor could I find it in the depths of my mind. A sudden burst of frustration lashed out of me as I banged my fists beside me on the bed and tears sprang to my eyes.

"I... I don't know. I don't know the answer to either of those questions." The anger fizzled away inside of me as defeat and despair replaced it just as quickly as it appeared. All the why's and how's circled my mind as I dive bombed straight into a pool of self-pity and depression.

"Since when did you start feeling sorry for yourself? Come on, it's going to be OK! Your memory will be back before you know it and you'll be able to hold your little angel in no time. Everything will be fine. I promise." Little Miss Optimism piped up from next to Leon. I laid my head back against my pillow, my mind a jumble of despair and doubt.

Ava made her way the short distance over to me and placed her hand on top of mine that were still balled up in tight, white knuckled fists. Her hand was warm against my cold one. It seemed that whilst I was in my coma, my blood had stopped pumping.

"We'll get through this together. All of us." Her tone was soft and kind, and although I knew it wasn't intentional, it came across as condescending. I slipped my hand from under hers, closed my eyes and turned my head away from the group.

"Could you all leave me be, please? I'd like to be alone." Ev tried to protest but Ava steered him away from me with a gentle "come on", and walked him towards the door, grabbing Leon by the arm on their way out, the doctors joining the conga line and exiting my room. Although I'd been on my own and in my own head for however long, all that I wanted at this moment in time was to be on my own. I needed to collect and organise my thoughts without everyone here to confuse me even more.

But first, in the privacy of my own room, I needed to grieve the pregnancy that was cut short as the emptiness I was feeling within began to grow deeper, and mope over the fact that I'm medically grounded from seeing my own daughter until my brain decides to work.

Chapter 55

Once Fi had settled, Leon and I left the hospital, with Everett staying behind with Fi. The drive home from the hospital had been peaceful. The roads were devoid of any vehicles as ours traveled the lonely journey back home. Streetlights and the beams from our headlights guided our way as the day slunk away, the sun dipping behind the buildings and the black of the night bleeding down the sky away from the sinking pinks and oranges like ink running down paper. The radio singing its tunes at a beautifully low volume and the gentle hum of the engine were the only sounds infiltrating the tranquil atmosphere.

It was pitch black by the time we arrived home, the clouds had quickly become pregnant with rain and the darkness was increasing the speed of which my tiredness was overcoming me. I'd barely slept all week and now that I knew Fi was awake, it was catching up to me faster than a junkie on their way to get their next fix and I found myself looking forward to blissful sleep to carry me away into the night as I fought to keep my eyes open.

The cushions of Leons plush sofa bounced underneath me as I plonked myself down next to him with a sigh. My body felt heavy with the stress of the week that had just been consumed by endless worry and lack of sleep. I laid my legs atop of Leons and rested my head against his shoulder as he wrapped an arm around me, pulling me in closer. Being next to him was my happy place, where I felt the most relaxed. And whilst I felt some of the stress slowly melt away from me, there was still residue of it left over.

Fi was awake. Fi was OK. But it seemed that at the moment it was only obstacle after obstacle, and now we had to work to get Fi's memory back. Never in my life had I heard of this PTA and it seemed like the Dr was only making it up, until I did some research on the way home and discovered that it was in fact real, and was incredibly common for those who had just woken from a coma. The health website stated that it could take minutes, hours, even weeks or months in worst case scenarios. There was a glimmer of hope as the article stated it would eventually pass and she'll remember again. Once we were outside of her room, the doctor had said that in Fi's case, her memory is likely to be returned sooner rather than later due to how stable she was out of her coma, meaning that the head injury she sustained hadn't been too severe, and therefore we shouldn't be too worried about it. To say we all felt relieved would be putting it mildly.

"She'll be okay, you know." Leons voice was quiet and reassuring as he stroked the hair from my face, sensing me getting lost in my own head as I mentally recapped today's events. I nodded in agreement as I snuggled in closer to him with a sigh. I knew she would be. Of course she would be. There wasn't really any reason to be concerned anymore and knowing how stubborn Fi is, there was no way she'd go longer than the end of the week to get her memories back – especially now her little one was in the world waiting to meet her.

We sat in silence with Leon stroking my hair, occasionally giving me a peck on my head and I began to let the bottomless chasm of sleep begin to wave over me. It was comforting being in his big arms. I felt safe and calm with my ear pressed against his chest, the rhythmic drumming of his heart a lullaby aiding me to sleep.

"Thank you for telling me by the way," Leons voice quiet above my head, slightly stirring me from my dazed, confused state. "About your conceiving situation." Now fully awake and immediately no longer confused, my eyes magically cured of tiredness as they now focused on the dark silhouettes of Leons lounge furniture. In my joy at Fi waking up, I'd somehow forgotten my own important news that I'd finally divulged. Too scared to move, I sat still as I quietly listened to what he had to say next.

"I know it must've been difficult for you to tell me, and I appreciate that you did. But it doesn't change how I feel about you. I love you and if it means spending a life childless, or you warm to the idea of adoption, then so be it. As long as I've got you, my life is complete." I began to sniff as tears began to well in my eyes; a silent partner in the act of crying. Spending my life with him was something that I wanted, and as much as I also wanted a child, there was a strong likelihood it wouldn't happen. And if children were something Leon was desperate for, then I wouldn't blame him for taking this as an opportunity to walk away. But with him saying he wanted to stay with me and go through life like this, the last thing I'd ever want was for him to feel chained to me because he had made a promise to stay by me, regardless if he changes his mind down the line.

Shifting my position so I was sat a little way from him, I was still unable to meet his gaze as I told him, "Leon, it's unfair of me to ask that of you." Because it was. I couldn't and wouldn't expect him to put his life on hold for me whilst we waited and hoped for a positive pregnancy test that may never come. It wasn't fair to ask him to go through the same heartache that I do and would continue to go through with every inevitable negative test result.

"Baby," I stubbornly kept my head down, "Baby, look at me." My chin gently pinched between his thumb and index finger, he gently raised my head up, encouraging me to do as I'm told, my water-filled eyes the last to meet his soft gaze.

"You falling pregnant isn't impossible. It's just a low probability, which means there's always still a chance you can fall pregnant. So if you really want our own kid, no matter how long it takes we'll do our best to make it happen. And if it doesn't, then we'll become dog parents until I convince you to get a cat." A gross, choked laugh came out of me whilst my crying quietly continued through Leon's speech at the thought of us being animal parents. He was very much a cat man - a fact that I'd only recently learned one morning when we were in bed, tangled up after an incredible morning sex session - whereas I was a dog woman. He then spent the rest of the day trying to convince me in the future to get a cat with him, even going as far as to saying we can have a farm of dogs and one outdoor cat. In the end, he had said it didn't matter if we got a cat; whatever made me happy.

"But you're not asking anything of me. I'm telling you I want to be with you no matter what. With or without a baby. My happiness lies with you and enjoying what we have; and that is each other." He was right. Absolutely right. All that mattered was that we had each other; anything else was a bonus. I grabbed the hem of my top, feeling the cold that was slowly creeping in from the outside against my exposed skin, and covered my face to soak up the wetness that clung to my skin as I nodded. I felt Leon let go of me and move away from me, assumingly to grab me a tissue, but instead heard a little click. When I removed the fabric from my face I discovered he hadn't got me a tissue, but was down on one knee with the most beautiful, oval-cut diamond ring displayed in a velvet red box.

"Will you marry me?"

* * *

Leons POV:

I hadn't intended to do it this soon. I wanted it to be perfect for her, have it all planned out. But fuck it. I've done it now. No going back. She hadn't looked at me yet, her eyes just fixed on the ring unblinking; the ring that her mum helped me pick when we'd gone to visit them.

Her parents had been over the moon when I asked them for their blessing; and we'd very nearly been caught out by Ava. We'd gone for a walk along the river of our hometown that wound itself through the vast green wilderness of the countryside, nothing but clear blue skies with the odd tuft of cloud that slowly sailed across the opening above us. Ava was a way ahead of us, as she usually was, like an excited toddler on an outing. She stood up on a ledge with steps that descended down to the river bank, gazing out to the peaceful watercourse before us, the midday sun a gold medal beaming down on her as the breeze from the water caressed her blonde hair in wisps about her head. With her back to us, I asked if they would allow me to make an honest woman of their daughter. Julia had said yes instantly and gave me a tight embrace, happy tears sliding down her face, and Kelvin had placed his hand on my shoulder and said he was honoured to have been asked and that of course I had his blessing. It was then that Ava decided to turn and see how far back we were. Luckily we jumped away from each other just in time and Ava was none-the-wiser.

That evening, we'd taken a stroll through the town center and came across an extravagant jewellers. Its fascia was glossy white with warm yellow lights projecting down from the hidden ledge to the brand name that had been carved into the paneling. The inside was all white and gold, with clear display cases creating a "U" shaped walkway. Ava, ever the magpie when it came to jewellery, dragged us into the store to peruse their shiny and expensive wares. Between us, Julia and I took pictures on the sly of any rings that caught our attention and reconvened later in the evening once Ava was asleep to decide on the ring.

Finally, Ava's eyes found mine with shock plastered all over her face. She wasn't saying anything to me and the longer she went without speaking the more I could feel the sweat trickle down my back in nervous anticipation. Her eyes blinked back down at the glistening jewel that was snugly cushioned in the red velvet box in my hands before she was looking back at me.

"Are... are you sure?" Her voice was quiet and catching as she fought herself from releasing her emotions prematurely. I carefully removed the gold ring from the box and grasped it in my right hand between my thumb and index finger. In the background, the rain had started to pour, the droplets pitter-pattering on the windows before slowly rolling down the glass.

531

The only light in the room was the lamp set at a low brightness, the dim illumination hitting the oval gem at all the right points. The unintentional perfect set-up.

"Sweetheart, I have never been more sure of anything in my life. You are the strongest, most inspiring and determined person I have ever met and everyday you make me want to be a better man. I want to be by your side through the good and the bad. Whatever life throws at us, I want to be battling through it with you." Her lip started to wobble as she tried her hardest to fight the emotions threatening to our from her, a couple of stray tears that were too strong for her to keep in escaped and dropped heavily onto her lap. She gave a little sniff and wiped at her face with the sleeves of her top gripped over her hands in her fist.

"I love you, Ava and I want to spend the rest of my life with you and only ever you. So..." I freed her left hand out of the fist, the fabric sliding back up her wrist and hovered the ring at the tip of her ring finger. "Will you marry me?" A final glance back at the ring now shaking in my trembling fingers before she looked at me dead in the eyes with pure happiness shimmering through the teardrops that flooded her lash line and a toothy beautiful smile spread across her flushed face.

"I would love nothing more."

57

Epilogue

As I sat on my own at the white-clothed head table, I looked around the dim, yet romantically lit barn at all of our nearest and dearest who had come to celebrate our big day with us and felt my heart swell with happiness. A few people were seated, deep in conversation, whilst others were on the dance-floor, dancing to Whitney Houston. Leon was at the bar, engaging in a grossly animated conversation with his brother Jax.

Shortly after our engagement, I'd encouraged Leon to get back into contact with his brother, and ever since, the pair had been inseparable. Jax was the spitting image of Leon, aside from having blonde hair and a softer nose. Both owned those beautiful, rare, whiskey coloured eyes, the gold a halo around their dark pupils. Both tall - Jax maybe an inch taller - and equally well built. Watching the brotherly bond grow and form made my heart happy. They both finally had some closure and understanding of each other and their past, and though he never told me himself, I think Leon was finally able to heal from that part of his life and be at peace with it.

In reconnecting with his brother, Leon discovered he had two nephews and a niece, all whom he absolutely adored. Over the past year and half, it's been such an honour to watch their bond form and flourish. Leon was incredible with them. They insisted on dragging him in all of their games and shenanigans. They loved running around the park with their Nerf guns, tag teaming against Leon as they chased him and jumped on him full of giggles when he dramatically died when he finally got hit with the foam bullets. They stayed over every Friday and enjoyed baking with us, the late nights, takeaways and movies with all five of us cuddled up on the sofa. The three children were now currently running around the venue, high off the amount of sugar and E numbers their dad had allowed them to consume "just this once", not knowing that this is how they usually spend their Saturday daytime's with their favourite aunt and uncle.

Tilly ran past me, bringing with her a swoosh of warm air that was refueled by her brothers, Harrison and Brody, a short distance behind her. Her brunette, braided hair in a plait was gradually becoming loose; frays of hair slipping the braid and framing her little heart shaped face, swinging like a pendulum across her back with the movements of her body. I chuckled at her girlish squeal as she looked back and saw how close to her they were, Harrison teasing "we're gonna get you!" I watched them until I lost sight of them in the crowd on the dance-floor.

As I observed the room, I took some time in appreciating our hard work with the decor. It hadn't taken us long to decide on a venue. I'd always loved the thought of a summer barn wedding and Leon had been more than happy to turn the thought into reality. After endless visits to different wedding barns, we had found this one and instantly fell in love with it. It was rustic both inside and out, with wooden beams arching from side to side above us. We'd wrapped fairy lights around the top of the beams and tied bouquets of blush pink and white roses on alternating beams. Up by the top table, white silks draped from either side before being tied to the wooden post by the brick walls, and in the center of the building was a lowly hung chandelier with candles providing its lighting.

We had six tables seating ten people per table, three per side with a walkway down the center leading to the dance-floor, keeping our wedding an intimate celebration. Neither of us had many family, and so our guest lists largely consisted of our friends.

My bridal party had been composed of my little bestie Clover who had been the bravest three year old I had ever met as she was the first to walk down the aisle, solo, grabbing as many flowers in her small hand as she could from her little wicker basket and launching them above her as she made her way to Leon who held her hand until her mummy joined her, her excited little feet having her in a near run in excitement. Fi was my maid of honour, and hand in hand with the best man Everett, they followed behind their daughter, who, whilst patiently waiting with Uncle 'Eon', was beaming at them with love and pride at what a big girl she had just been. With one either side linking their arm with mine, my mum and Kelvin proudly walked me down the aisle, each giving me a kiss on the cheek before they gave me away to Leon, who to my delight had cried whilst watching me slowly make my way to him.

The ceremony was beautiful. Achingly long, but neither me nor Leon were able to take our eyes off of each other, both with huge, uncontrollable grins plastered on our faces, eagerly awaiting for the "Mr and Mrs Myers" announcement. Everyone else became invisible, fading away into the background as we listened to our officiant read her script whilst we gripped hands

- the only form of intimacy we could give each other until we could have our first kiss as newly weds.

It had taken two long years of planning, and as I looked out at our guests and reflected on the day so far, it hit me just how perfect and magical today had been; and the night wasn't over yet.

The music changed, and '*Cotton Eyed Joe*' started playing. I was itching to get back up and dance with everyone, but I was taking a much needed break. I clocked mum and Fi who were furiously waving at me in an effort to entice me onto the dance-floor, but the best I could do was pump my fists in time to the beat from where I was sitting.

"Why don't you go up and dance with them? I know you want to." Sam shouted in my ear, taking a seat in Leon's chair and placing his drink down on the table. The music was, in my opinion, unnecessarily loud and so everyone was literally having to shout to have a conversation. I just knew that I would be waking up tomorrow morning with little to no voice, something which I'm sure Leon would relish.

I shifted my seat so I was facing Sam. Over the last couple of years, we'd formed a really good friendship, with Leons approval. I'd taken Leon to The Hub where he finally met Sam. Recognition had flared in his eyes as he realised Sam was the guy who was putting his number in my phone outside my apartment when we were taking our break. Leon had been understanding about that time with Sam when I explained that nothing happened, and never would have. Sam was more like a brother to me. Leon took the time to get to know Sam, knowing how important his friendship was to me, going as far as to inviting him to join him and Everett when they were having guys night, and the three of them very quickly became an absolute nightmare together. The children at this wedding where much more tame in comparison to how feral the three grown men were when together. To this day, I'm still waiting to have my coffee table replaced. One night, they'd come back to mine, absolutely bladdered, bottles of beers in their hands and thought sword fighting with my batons on top of said coffee table was the most fun they'd had all night.

"Nah, I need a break. There's enough sweat pouring off me to fill a paddling pool." As if to emphasise my point, I dabbed at my forehead with a clean serviette, careful not to ruin my makeup. Sam chuckled, the sound barely audible as it was consumed by the violin section of the song. Sam was flying solo at our wedding; poor soul had not been having much luck on the dating scene lately.

"Cor, that's an image going into the wank bank for later." He joked with a wink before swiftly changing the subject after I playfully smacked him on the arm.

"So, how does it feel being Mrs Myers?" He'd shuffled the chair closer so we could hear each other better. His cologne scent wafted up my nose, so strong I wondered if he'd poured the entire contents of the bottle over himself.

"A relief now the stress of the planning and build up is out of the way," I looked over to Leon who was watching our exchange and gave him a wave and a smile, one he responded back to by blowing me a kiss, before I turned back to Sam. "But honestly, I couldn't be happier. I've married my best friend, my soul mate. It just seems crazy with everything we've gone through, how far we've come." Sam nodded his head in understanding. He still didn't know about our past, but knew it was some serious shit.

"That's my chance has well and truly gone then." He joked, giving a cheeky side smile with a raised eyebrow. I gently shoved him, a laugh coming from me. It hadn't been a secret that Sam once had a little crush on me, one that he did grow out of once he realised that the only man for me was Leon and his chances with me was next to zero.

"That ship has long sailed my friend," I patted his hand that was resting on his lap. "But there's plenty of girls out there for you Sam. You're just looking in all the wrong places." Sam rolled his lip up as he scrunched his nose in disagreement.

"I don't think so. Maybe I'm just destined to be forever alone." Ever the drama queen. I rolled my eyes at him as I felt a strong hand squeeze my shoulder. I looked up and found my husband standing by my side, his eyes twinkling with a cocktail of happiness and booze.

"I hope you're not trying to steal my wife from me Sam. I know where you work, don't forget." He said to Sam jokingly, a small smile on his lips. God he was handsome, even more so in a suit and I don't think there will ever not be a time when hearing Leon call me his wife will make me go a little feral on the inside. There was something about him claiming me that had my insides go funny.

"Would I ever?" He gasped, putting a hand over his heart and feigned offense. Leon patted him on the back before pulling a chair round to join us.

"I was just about to tell Sam about one of my clients that hasn't stopped looking at him." I nodded over to where Reina, sure enough, was glancing our way before quickly turning away when Sam looked over. Even from here, I could see red starting to spread up her neck and onto her cheeks, as she untucked her hair from behind her ear in an attempt to cover her face. She was a pretty girl. Hair a beautiful, brilliant shade of shiny red with natural, oscillating waves flowing down the length of her back to her waist, paired with forest green eyes. Her skin was a pale canvas with light brown freckles splattered haphazardly over her otherwise flawless skin. She too was here on her own, taking a brazen step at building her confidence in being in situations that would usually scare the shit out of her. She only knew a few people here who had been part of one of my group classes they were in together. It had taken some convincing to get her to come as she feared being here on her own without knowing many people, and I was beyond proud of her that she had made it.

"Well, what are you waiting for? Go introduce yourself!" Leon encouraged, squeezing his shoulder in that approving way men do. We didn't miss how intently Sam had been staring at her, his eyes slowly gliding over her. As if he suddenly had sweaty hands, he rubbed them up and down his navy suit trousers, took a large mouthful of his beer for some extra courage before standing up, eyes still zoned on Reina as he said a quick "see you later" before making his way over to her. On arrival, he gently placed his hand on her shoulder blade to get her attention, swapped his glass into the opposite hand and offered his hand as he introduced himself. He looked over at us, knowing we were watching to see how successful this would go when he grinned at us, giving us a thumbs up.

After returning the motion, I looked out through the open barn doors, which was useless even being open. It was only bringing in more hot air. But the scenery that the doors opened too was truly beautiful.

"Fancy coming for a walk with me? We haven't been to the dock yet and it would be such a beautiful photo-op." Leon followed my gaze, before looking back at me with a cheeky look in his eyes.

539

"Is my gorgeous wife hinting that actually, she really wants to consummate the wedding?" My eyes flashed with temptation. It wouldn't be a bad idea, but today of all days I had to be practical. There was no way I was going to get my dress dirty. I paid too much for it to just get dirtied up and to potentially lose it to the lake beyond.

"As much as I would love to have you fuck my brains out baby, I want to be able to enjoy you and relish in every single moment." My eyes flickered down to his lips as I spoke, lingering as I watched him roll his plump lower lip under his top teeth. We'd made sure to schedule in time for us to have our first time as husband and wife because we knew we would be too desperate to wait and would have been more than willing to be absent from the entirety of the reception so we could make love over and over, thoroughly, wildly, sloppily. Any and every way possible.

But he didn't know that I had to squeeze in this photo-op on the jetty, and time was of the essence if we wanted to stick to our already tightly packed schedule. Ignoring the throbbing between my legs, I stood up and made my way around Leon, before holding my hand out to him as I nodded my head in the direction of the invitingly open barn doors. He took my hand and side by side, we made our exit.

The photographer, on cue followed at a distance behind us as we walked along the cobblestone winding pathway, the loose stones crunching under our feet. Changing into flats had been a very good idea, it would've absolutely been my luck to break an ankle from walking on these stones in heels. Trees guarded the pathway either side, standing proudly to attention with their lusciously dark green leaves gently waving in the soft breeze that caressed my bare skin, but not offering much respite from the heat radiating off the sun.

We arrived at the jetty, and found the sun had taken its seat just above the horizon, flourishing its romantic hands upwards in red, orange and pink, the sentiment mimicked across the surface of the lake as if it too was reaching an offering towards us. Occasionally the lake would ripple, the vibration spreading as wide as possible, as fish came to the surface to get a taste of the oxygen-rich air. A cabin was stationed to the left of the edge of the lake, it lights on but blocked out by red, white and green plaid curtains, the shadows of its occupants infrequently appearing against the thin material.

The photographer instructed us how to stand and position ourselves, using the lake and the sunset as our back drop. We'd had shots taken facing her, looking out to the great beyond, and now we were facing each other, hand in hand. I gazed up into his eyes as he looked down at me, as instructed. Once I heard the camera capture a couple of shots, the photographer sending encouraging words out towards us, I took my hands out of Leons hand and wiped them on my dress, the sweat starting to become uncomfortable, and turned back to face the lake.

"It really is beautiful out here, don't you think?" We'd been out here long enough that the sun had had enough of posing for the camera and was starting to slowly slink away.

"It really is." He nodded towards the cabin. "Imagine having this on your doorstep. How peaceful it must be." I hummed my agreement. It must be nice to be so out of the way, no one to bother you. But at the same time, how lonely and isolated it would get after a while.

"I just can't believe we're married now. After everything, I don't think our fourteen-year-old selves would've ever pictured that we'd be here." I shook my head as if I myself couldn't believe it, and in all honesty, it was quite the miracle that we are where we are now.

"Maybe controversial, but honestly? In a way, I'm glad things happened the way they did."

"Oh yeah? Why's that?" I turned to face Leon, curiosity riddling my features.

"Well, we wouldn't be standing here married if that were the case. Our experiences helped us map out our lives, helped make us the people we are now. Granted, they weren't always the nicest or best of things for either of us to go through, but we grew stronger because of them. The only differing factor that helped us come together again, was destiny."

"You think we were destined to be together?" Leon took my cheeks into my hands before planting a soft, lingering kiss on my forehead - the clicking of the camera going off - before resting his own forehead on mine.

"Absolutely." There was nothing but pure conviction in his voice. It was nice to think that we were made to be together, that our souls were destined for one another.

"Destiny, fate; it all works in mysterious ways doesn't it?"

"It does indeed." Leon nodded against my head, the snapping of the camera never silencing as we held our position.

"But while we're on the topic..." I pulled away from Leon, a puzzled look crossing his face as his recently shaped brows came together, creating shallow lines to appear on his tanned forehead. I reached into the pocket of my dress - something I'd been incredibly overjoyed at discovering and was therefore the deciding factor that this was *the* dress -, pulled out my hidden secret, unraveled it and held it out for Leon to see.

"Is that..." He gently took the object from my hands with a hand whose tremble matched my own.

"Yep." I couldn't say anything else, there was a cry clawing its way up my throat preventing me to say anything more than that one, singular confirmation.

"We're pregnant?" A sob escaped Leon's mouth, the words coming out fast, the emotion forcing them to tumble out. All I could do was nod as tears started to escape my eyes, a silly, insuppressible smile spread wide across my face. Leon crouched down, the news shaking him to the core, making it difficult to stand. I crouched in front of him and held his hands still clutching the edges of my scan picture.

"We're only ten weeks. I found out last week. I was having a follow-up with my gynecologist to talk about our third round of IVF, and one of the tests flagged that I was pregnant." Despite the happy tears that were now trailing slowly down my face, no doubt washing my make-up away with it, my voice was stable and composed enough to coherently relay the information to Leon, who was currently staring at the scan and shaking his head in disbelief.

"I just... I can't believe we're having a baby." He stood up before bringing the scan closer to his face. "What does '*A*' and '*B*' mean?" I stood to meet him.

"Twins." His head shot up, his eyes swimming wildly with joy as he looked between each of my eyes and silver, erratic lines marred his face as fresh tears trickled down the winding routes before splashing on the wooden deck beneath us.

Leons wet, salty lips were pressed hard against mine, like he was desperate to pass his love into me before pulling away and placing a hand on my tummy, the scan picture being tucked safely away in his suit jacket pocket. Nothing and no one is this moment mattered. It was just me, Leon and our little unborn babies on this joyous day of love, family and union. A day that never in my wildest dreams could I have seen coming.

543

"I love you, Ava Myers." He placed a warm hand tenderly on the side of my face.

"I love you and our miracle babies. You have made me the happiest man in the world." His thumb grazed back and forth on my midsection as he pressed his lips back against mine, but this time with such a lovingly soft touch.

Finally, against all odds, our lives were complete.

Printed in Great Britain
by Amazon

56179852R10304